CHECK MATE

McCann was doing a periodic check of the airspace behind the tail when he said, "Looks like he's blown his cool, Axel. He's heading down like he means it."

They were flying between two mountain peaks at five hundred feet, which for them was a high altitude. The Eagle had gone skyward for better missile acquisition, but the target Tornado, darting across and between the peaks, was making life impossible. The Eagle decided to come down for another try.

Hohendorf was now baiting the trap.

McCann studied the threat display. "I've got him at twelve miles, and going through three-zero." He meant three thousand feet. "Still heading down. This guy's after blood."

"Arming the Kraits," Hohendorf said. "Keep an eye on him."

"He's still there, and closing. He wants to make sure."

"A man who likes a precise kill. Good."

"For him? Or for us?"

"For us, of course."

Books by Julian Jay Savarin

MacAllister's Run
Pale Flyer
Trophy
Target Down!
Wolf Run
Windshear
Naja
The Quiraing List
Villiger
Water Hole
The Queensland File

Published by
HarperPaperbacks

MacAllister's Run

JULIAN JAY SAVARIN

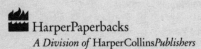

HarperPaperbacks
A Division of HarperCollins*Publishers*

HarperPaperbacks   *A Division of* HarperCollins*Publishers*
10 East 53rd Street, New York, N.Y. 10022

Cover illustration by Edwin Herder

First printing: March 1995

Printed in the United States of America

HarperPaperbacks and colophon are trademarks of HarperCollins*Publishers*

❖ 10 9 8 7 6 5 4 3 2 1

for Rhiannon

MACALLISTER'S RUN

OPENING SHOTS

She lay in the snow, warm within the hide she had carefully constructed, virtually invisible in her winter combat gear. Even her Dragunov SVD rifle, a sniper's dream, had become part of the whitened landscape. She had carefully wrapped it in white fabric so that its now subtly mottled appearance blended neatly with its surroundings. Her quarry, another sniper, had no idea she was there.

It seemed to her she had been in Bosnia for years, carrying out the systematic elimination of snipers who chose to target members of the United Nations forces, or one of the aid agencies. The past months had certainly seemed like years: years of shifting from area to area; of passing herself off as Serb, Croat, or Muslim, depending on where she'd found herself at any given time; of wondering whether the time would come—if she remained too long—when her guard would slip just sufficiently to enable a suspicious militiaman to unmask her. So far, her luck and skills had served her well. She had killed a hundred snipers by now, fifteen of whom had been women, and one, she'd later discovered, a boy barely in his teens. All she'd seen had been the snout of the rifle, aimed down a slope at a soft-skinned UN truck. He'd already killed the driver, and had been lining up on the person in the passenger seat.

She'd had no choice. Days later, in a village, she'd seen a woman weeping by yet another fresh grave. Graves were the growth crop of Bosnia. The boy had been the woman's son.

Now she waited for the sniper up ahead to make a move. She knew exactly where her quarry was, though she did not shift in her hide to check. There was little need. The expected UN convoy would not arrive at the precarious bend in the pockmarked road for some time yet. It was with good reason that the bend had been dubbed sniper alley. She was in place to change all that; she had been there for three days, waiting.

At last she heard the faint sounds of laboring engines as the distant convoy came into earshot. The sounds were not yet loud enough to drown out the barely perceptible noise of the muted scurryings of animal life on the snow-clad wooded slope where she lay hidden. But suddenly the scurryings stopped. She knew it meant that the sniper up ahead, though some distance away and on the opposite slope, was now on the move. The animals knew.

She smiled grimly. Even though whoever it was up there had no awareness of her presence, a survival instinct was causing the change of position; or perhaps the sniper was about to take up the actual position for the shoot.

She had moved forward very slightly, careful not to shift the Dragunov, to take a look. A swiftly moving shape was running in a crouch across her line of sight, from left to right. It was a small shape. A woman, perhaps?

That was careless, she thought. Whoever it was clearly believed he or she was alone in the area. She watched closely, now using the Dragunov's sight as she traversed the rifle with infinite slowness, keeping it zeroed in on the flitting target.

The figure stopped between a pair of trees that grew close together and began to move backward into a bank of snow that had piled up against them. It was swiftly done, clearly not for the first time.

She could not see the sniper's face; his head was wrapped in white to aid camouflage, with just a darkened space showing where the eyes were. The rearward burrowing had stopped, and if she had not already pinpointed his position, the sniper would have seemed to have disappeared completely.

The sounds of the engines had grown louder. She had listened to those characteristic noises so often she could tell which were the scout cars, the armored personnel carriers, and the trucks—and how many of each there were. Today it was a small convoy, using a back route to try and bypass the more lethal ambush areas. Whoever was leading the convoy had clearly not used this route before. There was a lot of starting and stopping. Then the first of the scout cars was coming through. She knew it would be allowed to pass. The sniper was after the trucks. That would keep the entire convoy bogged down until the sniper's comrades turned up in their own good time to loot. It was good economic use of manpower.

She kept her attention firmly fixed on the sniper, ignoring everything else.

The first of the trucks, looking like a fat white goose, whined toward the bend, swaying slightly.

She watched as the snout of the sniper's rifle began to track its first target. She was ready, and had the Dragunov's sight squarely fixed upon the dark space that marked the sniper's eyes. The noise of all the trucks and the scout cars and the APCs would drown out the sound of her fire.

She squeezed the trigger. The Dragunov barked and seemed to vibrate along its entire length with the recoil.

Almost immediately she saw a sudden red bloom in the sights. The sniper's rifle lowered itself, unfired and with a strange slowness, into the snow.

She remained where she was as the convoy struggled past, its personnel probably wondering why they had not yet come under any fire. She waited until the cacophony at last faded into the stillness of the mountains.

This was her hundred-and-first kill, and she was going to break her own rule and do something she'd never done before. She was going to take a close look at the person she had killed. It was both dangerous and foolish, she knew. The smart thing was to leave the area swiftly, as she'd always done. It was the professional way. It had kept her alive. But something was driving her to look.

With the rifle dismantled and secured in a pack, she began to remove traces of her presence. When she'd finished, she carefully made her way down the slope toward the road, obliterating her footprints as she progressed by haphazardly taking quantities of snow with gloved hands and dropping them over the prints. In a short while, the resettling snow had covered the evidence of her passage. It was slower going, but safer.

She crossed the road swiftly and made her way up the opposite slope toward the dead sniper, taking the same care with her footprints. At last she arrived at her destination. She stared at the body for a long time. The Dragunov had made a mess, and the head seemed to be held together only by its camouflage wrappings.

She felt a strange emotion as she reached in to widen the burrow and check the body. She felt her worst fears being confirmed as it was soon clear to her that she had just killed someone who had been little more than a child. She felt the heat of tears in her eyes as deep within her a powerful rage simmered. She cursed the self-serving politicians who had brought this nasty war upon their own people, and wondered why the outside world allowed such creatures to get away with it.

She buried the body gently in the snowbank, then drove the rifle, muzzle down, into the snow next to it. It was a marker as well as a salute. Then she made her way from there, feeling a despoliation of the spirit.

Three days and seventy-five kilometers later, she entered a small town. It was a place she had used once before, and the local militia commander knew her as a Russian "volunteer" whose movements were secret. There were many other Russian volunteers, and he had lumped her with the genuine ones. It also helped that he hoped to get her into bed—or anywhere convenient to his purposes.

The town, like so many others, was a living shell of its former self—a shattered, abused hulk, ravaged by the insanities of a brutal and pointless war. Yet amongst this landscape of destruction, incredibly, a café stood virtually intact in a small square. It was, inevitably, the center of everything, serving in a range of functions from the commander's headquarters to a social gathering point. Its continued survival was one of the many mysteries of the conflict.

She entered the café wearily and found a corner table that was unoccupied. She sat down, her back to the cozy enclave of the adjoining walls. There were soldiers and militiamen about, laughing with some local girls. No one took much notice of her.

A serving girl she had not seen before, who was not much older than the sniper she'd killed, came up with a smile.

"A coffee," she said in Russian-accented regional dialect. "Or whatever is passing for it."

The girl's smile widened. "We've got the real stuff today."

"Oh?"

"French. Some of the boys got a convoy yesterday."

"I see. Well, I'd better have some of that before it's all gone."

"Of course. Anything to eat?"

"I'll take whatever you're offering."

"I'll see what I can do. Oh, by the way . . . " The girl's voice lowered conspiratorily. " . . . the commander is coming in today. He'll be pleased to see you."

"Then I'll be happy to see him," she lied and smiled, hiding her true feelings.

The girl went away with her order.

She was two minutes into her meal when her luck ran out.

"Ah, Nadia!" a familiar voice called cheerfully. "See whom I've got with me. A new friend from the motherland."

She looked up and saw a man with the commander who was looking at her neutrally. Her blood felt as if it had congealed.

The last time she'd seen the newcomer he had been a captain in the old KGB. Now here he was, dressed like an ordinary UN soldier, with the rank of major.

The two men came up to her table and sat down unasked.

"Nadia," the commander began in introduction, "a compatriot, Major Rinovsky of the UN. The major is here to ensure fair play, now that we are supposed to be moving our heavy weapons." He grinned, as if "fair play" were something that existed in mythology. "We always call her Nadia," he went on to the major. "One of our best helpers. A very good shot."

"I have no doubt," the major said in the Russian of a well-educated man. His eyes bored into her. "When were you last at home, Comrade?" he asked, using the old form of address as if nothing had changed in Russia.

"It seems like years," she replied, using the same level of the language. She remained remarkably calm, she thought, all things considered. "But really just a few months."

"Still . . . your friends must be missing you."

The words were delivered without apparent hidden meaning, but she knew better. There was a sly edge to the remark. As soon as he could, he would be doing some checking. She remembered him as being extremely ambitious. In the current climate back home, ambition was a most valuable commodity.

"I'm certain they are. But they know I'm okay."

"Obviously. I can see that . . . though you seem weary."

The local commander, who could follow Russian well but spoke it haltingly, said, "Nadia is always out, sometimes for days. Those who have seen her work say she is very dedicated. With the world against us, we need dedicated friends like yourself and Nadia."

"Of course," the major said. He glanced at his watch. "Nice to have met you, Comrade Nadia, but I must be going." He made a grimace of displeasure. "I have to liaise with some British troops, fifty kilometers from here. Their commander will no doubt talk to me slowly in his Sandhurst English, as if I am some peasant from the backwoods of Russia." He gave a passable imitation of what he meant, in perfect English, and they all laughed.

As he left with the commander, she knew she could not trust him for a second. It was time for those who had sent her in to pull her out.

Her life was now in extreme jeopardy.

I

**The Moray coast in the Grampians,
Scotland, the same day**

It was the kind of weather that would have made
even ducks hold a conference before deciding to take to
the air. The cloud base seemed to be at ground level, but
at November One, the birds always flew. Out on the wet
runway, a pair of barely visible Super Tornado ASVs—
Air Superiority Variants—were lined up for takeoff. Their
all-gray paintwork seemed to match the day, and only the
sudden flaring of their afterburners as they started their
takeoff run marked their positions precisely.

That paint was something very special. Made up of
intelligent crystals that could be electrically excited into
changing into various colors, the ASVs could blend into
their surroundings like chameleons. It was thus inevitable
that the November crews would call their magic kit the
Chameleon. The system could be programmed by the

backseater, or be left to its own devices, working via the various aircraft sensors. Most crews, however, preferred the hands-on programming. No one wanted to be caught crossing a green background while looking like something from a snowfield.

The ASVs hurtled along the runway, streaming spray, to leap almost vertically into the murk, which seemed to swallow them instantly. The weather was so dense, even the glow of the afterburners dimmed visibly and quickly disappeared as the aircraft climbed. There was a muffled quality to their engine roar, which soon faded.

In the officers' mess, Elmer Lee McCann, U.S. Air Force, peered out at the inclement weather.

"Jesus," he muttered. "You guys in Europe really know how to have crappy weather. Who're the poor jokers they've just sent up?"

"Don't you ever read the rosters, McCann?" someone asked patiently. "They're put up for people like you to read . . . if you can read."

"Ha–ha," McCann said without looking around. "That was a joke, right? So who is it?"

His informer sighed. "A fellow colonial, McCann. One of yours. Chuck Morton, with one of the deputy bosses on his wing to hold his hand."

"Which one?"

"Helm."

"He's got *Dieter Helm* up there with him? Shit. Poor bastard."

"Oh, I don't know. Our German deputy boss may be a hard man, but he's fair."

"You're kidding. He hates Americans."

"Only you, Elmer Lee. Only you. Getting up people's nostrils is your party piece."

"You're only saying that because you wish you had me as your backseater."

"Lord preserve me," came the retort in mock horror. "No! *Anything* but that. Selby is welcome to you. Forever."

He was in one of the mess anterooms with a couple of

the crews from Zero-Two squadron, the second of the November flying units that was now virtually operational. They knew all about McCann, and were unsuccessfully trying to read some newspapers.

McCann, irrepressible as ever, took the friendly insult with good grace. "Hey, what do you guys want of me?" No one answered him as he stared balefully out at the weather. "Goddamn. I want to *do* something."

"You could always stop breathing," someone else suggested hopefully. "Now that would be original."

McCann was still not offended. "You guys would miss me. Besides, you'd have to attend a full-blown military funeral."

"That's a point. Gawd. A parade! All right, Elmer Lee. Keep breathing."

"Thanks, guys. I'd do the same for you. I'd better check to see who's in the TV room."

"Oh, good!" they said together.

He grinned at them as he went out.

In the TV room, Axel, Baron von Hohendorf, formerly of Germany's *Marineflieger*, and Hank Stockmann III, U.S. Marines, were watching the news from Bosnia. Like McCann, they were veterans of the November program and, as the founding members of Zero-One squadron, had been blooded in battle. Hohendorf, also like McCann, had been in combat three times, while Stockmann had experienced his first with the November unit only recently. As backseater to Nico Bagni—prized from the AMI, the Italian Air Force—he'd flown the recce mission for a strike on a clandestine radar site in the Sahara. The mission had been spectacularly successful, but he and Bagni had been shot down. Fortunately, they had ejected without injury.

Hohendorf, one of the unit's top pilots, had flown the strike mission. He was now staring angrily at the television screen as the news camera panned across a grisly scene. Someone in the mountains of Bosnia had thought it a good idea to lob a mortar into a food queue. There were dismembered bodies everywhere, and the blood on the ground seemed to glisten especially for the camera. The rear wheel of a child's bicycle, lying forlornly on its side, spun accusingly.

"Why don't we *do* something about this?" he demanded tensely. "We have the firepower! This is the kind of thing we are supposed to prevent. That is what the November program is meant to do. How can we stand by and watch this day after day and do nothing?"

Stockmann was surprised by the vehemence of Hohendorf's words. Everyone knew Hohendorf's reputation for being totally unemotional. There were those who only half-jokingly suggested that if you were to slit his veins, ice cubes would tumble out. There was someone, however, who knew the side he normally was successful at keeping hidden from his colleagues: that of a very passionate man.

"No point busting a gut, Axel," Stockmann now said. "We've all heard the politicians."

"Don't make me nauseous, Hank. I have lost count of the number of times they have talked about 'one more step for peace' while they run around searching for a worthless answer, doing their best to ignore the only real option they've got. There is just one way peace is going to come to that region, and if we take too long about it, we shall all be in a war . . . in Western Europe, too, and quite possibly throughout the world. Many, many more lives will be lost. I am very serious about this. These people are fools because they cannot see it. We should have stopped this terrible madness two years ago. Now . . . " Hohendorf ended with a shrug that displayed both his sense of frustration and his resignation.

"They did shoot down those four aircraft. . . . "

Hohendorf was skepticism personified. "And you believe that will change anything?"

Stockmann, despite having spent the time with the

November program, still looked the typical U.S. Marine, complete with brutal haircut. He gave Hohendorf a sober stare.

"Hey, I'm with you, buddy . . . but there's not a damn thing we can do until those guys in Washington, London, and the rest, make some kind of decision."

Hohendorf pointed at the screen, where the camera was lingering obscenely over the body of a child. "And meanwhile, this sickness goes on."

"I guess."

Hohendorf stood up suddenly. "I don't think I want to see any more of this." He made for the door just as McCann barged in.

"Yo, Axel . . . , " he began, voice fading uncertainly as Hohendorf practically brushed past.

"Captain," Hohendorf said politely, and walked on.

McCann stared after him in surprise before entering the room. "'Captain'?" he said loudly, mainly to himself. "What's happened to Elmer Lee? Or even McCann, if he wants to be formal? Talk to me, Hank B. the Third. What's up with the Red?"

"Don't say it, Elmer Lee."

"He's our very own Baron. . . . "

"You must be suicidal, McCann. You just happen to like living dangerously, don't you? First you wash out of pilot school back in the States after nearly killing your instructor during a landing and totaling an expensive F-15 Eagle. Then when the air force, which should have known better, puts you in a backseat, you call your pilot, a *major*, an asshole during air combat training!"

"The guy was an asshole," McCann said unrepentantly. "We lost that goddamned fight because of him."

"Yeah, well, brand-new second lieutenants don't go calling majors assholes even when they're right and the major is wrong." Stockmann was emphasizing each point by hooking the thumb of one hand to the fingers of the other as he enumerated. "Then you wind up here . . . "

" . . . where I'm the hottest backseater around . . . "

Stockmann sighed. "Such modesty. Then you wind up here and fall for the woman belonging to the hardest man in the British Air Force. . . . "

"Yeah," McCann interrupted again, gleefully, "but he's been in the States on detachment. Not due back for a while."

"I hear he got promoted," Stockmann countered, with a degree of malice. "Squadron Leader. That makes him equivalent to a major. He outranks you now. You've got a thing with majors, McCann."

"I can handle it."

"He'll handle *you* when he gets back. You been taking her to bed, McCann?"

"A gentleman does not divulge," McCann began with dignity.

Stockmann's huge teeth were bared in a grin that looked as if it wanted to take a bite of something. "A gentleman . . . "

"Leave my love life alone. Let's get back to Axel. What's eating him?"

Stockmann pointed at the TV. "What planet are you on?"

McCann glanced at the carnage on the screen. A reporter with a tormented expression was describing what had occurred. McCann seemed unmoved.

"Yeah? Well? It's on every day."

"Don't you feel anything?"

"Sure. I'd like to go out there and give those guys some of what they've been dishing out. But I can't. So why lose sleep?"

Stockmann stared at him. "Elmer Lee, you're either the biggest innocent that ever walked and nothing touches you, or the most pragmatic person alive . . . or a fool."

"Hey. I like pragmatic."

Stockmann closed his eyes wearily.

Chuck Morton felt like the new boy at school. A major in the U.S. Air Force, he had made it to the November program as a reward for discovering the experimental stealth-radar site that had been clandestinely constructed beneath the Saharan sands. To be more precise, it had been MacAllister, his female U.S. Marine assistant and a sergeant, who had discovered it. That had led to the successful strike.

Grounded after he had run out of fuel in an F-16 Falcon—despite having successfully landed the aircraft dead-stick, thus saving the taxpayer a great deal of money—he had been further punished by being posted to a redundant unit deep within the bowels of the Pentagon. Then Mac had discovered the site and success had brought its reward. Now he was flying with arguably the most elite unit in the world.

Wonderful Mac, he thought warmly, wondering as he'd done so many times before where she was now. She'd sent him just the one card, which he still kept, carrying it on missions in a pocket of his flying gear.

He did a complete visual check of his immediate environs as his mind teased him with the memory of how he had fallen in love with her. He had never dared say so, and she had gone without knowing. An air force major falling for a marine sergeant. Joke.

He looked about him once more. There was nothing to see. He was flying deep within the grayness. There was no sky and no ground, just the all-enveloping gray. He was trusting his displays and instruments, trusting the aircraft's sensors to tell him what was going on. He had to. This was no time to begin doubting your airplane. That was the certain route to disaster. He'd known of guys who'd begun to lose faith in their instruments and had ended up flying into rock faces, believing they were in open sky, flying the right side up.

It was all so different from the F-16. Where the smaller aircraft was a nimble electric hot-rod, the Super Tornado F.3S ASV was another kind of beast altogether. For a start, its twin engines developed enormous power that far outstripped his old single-engine mount. The ASV was also a bird of many colors and capabilities. Longer, sleeker, with bigger wings than the original Tornado, it had all manner of modifications that made it a ship that was far removed from the aircraft of its genesis.

Morton was still getting to know it. Its phenomenal acceleration still held him in thrall, and on previous occasions he'd had to remain highly alert so as not to let the aircraft run away with him. He had also discovered that at November One flying was done very differently. He'd had to "unlearn" his old style of flying and be inducted into the November way. As a result, he'd discovered more holes in his flying abilities than he'd thought possible. As he'd always considered himself something of a hotshot, it had been a mortifying experience.

"Fight's on!" a hard voice suddenly barked in his helmet.

Jesus! he thought. *Helm!*

He rolled the ASV onto its back, slammed the throttles into combat burner, then hauled firmly on the stick. The aircraft, invisible in the murk to an onlooker, reversed its original course to first plunge earthward before again rearing skyward, the twin tongues of its afterburners scorching the moist air into billows of steam.

"Take it easy, Chuck," another voice said calmly. His backseater, Carlo Carlizzi, was also a major, from the Italian Air Force, and one of the instructor backseaters. "Don't let him panic you. Although I'm an instructor, while I'm flying with you I'm on your side. I want to nail him as much as you do. So we work together. Okay with you?" Carlizzi spoke English with a strong Italian accent, heavily laced with New York.

"Okay with me."

"Right. Let's get his ass."

"This will not be a missile engagement," Helm's voice came on again to say. "The helmet sight will *not* be used. This will be a turning fight, and we are simulating guns only. Remember the lessons of the simulator, Major. This aircraft will help you willingly. Learn to use it to fight. And remember also, hard deck is zero altitude, which in this case means the cold sea below you. If you foul up, you'll be fish food. You may like underwater swimming, but I'm certain Major Carlizzi does not under these circumstances, and we at November One don't like losing our ASVs. So watch it, and watch your six, Major. I'll be on your tail if you don't. The next time you hear from me, it will be a gun lock. And Carlo, you're not going to get my ass."

"Shit," Carlizzi said to Morton. "I was broadcasting."

Morton had the distinct suspicion the broadcast had been deliberate, and it occurred to him that whatever Carlizzi said, the instructors worked together. Instructors always did.

Morton kept up a continuous search of the unremitting grayness. Somewhere out there Helm, after his long speech, was waiting to pounce—a shark hunting prey.

He listened to the aircraft's noises, muted hummimgs of electronics and machinery. The roar it made outside was so subdued it was hard to believe the engines were working. Only his instruments and displays confirmed they were, and doing so perfectly. All the power he needed was there at his fingertips.

He was not connected directly to the ASV's control surfaces. Its multiple redundant fly-by-wire system interpreted his commands and instructed its computers to carry them out, while simultaneuosly making continuous infinitesimal adjustments that brought razor-sharp responses from the aircraft. It was a dream to fly, and he fervently hoped he would make it through to become a permament member of the November team. It would be hard to return to more normal jets, even beauties like the Eagle and the Falcon, if he didn't succeed.

"Wake up, Major! I'm on your six!"

Christ. Where had he come from?

Chagrined, Morton flung the ASV into a tight, corkscrewing right-hand turn before rolling left suddenly, reversing, rolling upright, and heading once more for the upper reaches. In the constant grayness, it was as if he were trapped within a gigantic ball of soiled cotton wool.

"Knock it off, knock it off!" came Helm's voice once more, signifying an end to the current engagement. "Not a bad evasion," he continued. "Pity you would have already been dead."

Shit, shit, *shit*, Morton thought. The bastard didn't have to sound so smug.

"Let's try that again. Fight's on!"

"Carlo?" Morton began to his backseater between grunts as he reefed the ASV into a body-punishing turn, determined not to be caught this time. "You asleep, or what?"

"He fooled me, too," Carlizzi explained mildly.

Oh, yeah, Morton thought grimly. Sure. And hens have teeth.

Bosnia

She had removed the white outer layer of her combat gear and now sat in the camouflage outfit that had become the normal everyday style of the ravaged country. For some time she had been aware of the pointed scrutiny of a young militiaman, scarcely older than the boy she had killed only three days ago. The militiaman's interest, however, had little to do with the ongoing war. It was far more basic.

Forget it, boy, she thought. I am more than a match for you. Find yourself one of those flirty little girls.

But he kept smiling at her whenever he managed to catch her eye. Finally she decided to put an end to it. She looked at him directly, letting him see the coldness in her eyes. He paled visibly and hurriedly turned to his friends, whispering something to them. One by one the other young men with him stopped clumsily groping the girls to favor her with hesitant glances.

She could imagine what he'd said. That one's a cold bitch. There'd been fear in their eyes, too. It mattered little to her. It was a reputation that had served her well. But the claustrophobic nature of this conflict meant that

eventually people became known wherever they oper-
ated, and the presence of the Russian major made it a
matter of urgent priority that she be pulled out.

She'd once witnessed an incident where a sniper,
believing he'd be safe in a place he'd never been seen
before, had been caught by soldiers of the opposing side.
Someone who had once been his friend had recognized
him. He'd been taken into a shell-devastated building and
beaten to death by his vengeful friend, whose sister he
had killed months before simply because she had been a
convenient target. The friend's comrades had stood by
and watched, and while not participating, had ensured he
could not have escaped. Other people had watched, too.
Humanity at its most savage.

She could still hear the screams. . . .

"I would like to be like you," someone said.

She looked into the eager face of the girl who had
served her. "Why?"

The girl smiled shyly, displaying more than a hint of
hero worship. "You make even the men fear you. I saw
that soldier looking at you and what you did. That is
good for a woman, especially in this war. I want to be
strong like you."

No, child, she thought. You don't want to be like me.

"It is not an easy thing to be," she told the girl instead.

"I would not expect it to be easy. To many people, you
are a hero."

"Am I?"

"But of course. How can you not know that?"

"I don't think about it."

"Ahh." To the girl, this was even more profound. "Perhaps
you can talk to someone for me. I would like to fight."

"You are doing good service here, looking after us.
This is also important work."

"It is for children and old people," the girl said
vehemently.

"Do not dismiss the old ones. They were brave partisans long before you were born."

"I'm . . . I'm sorry. I didn't mean . . . "

"I know you didn't, but in the future, think before you speak."

"Yes."

The girl was now so downcast, she felt she had to soften the reprimand. "If you want to be a fighter," she added in a gentler voice, "you must learn to respect those who went before you."

The girl brightened. "I shall! And you will talk to someone for me?"

"I'll see what I can do," she lied.

"Oh, thank you, Nadia! Thank you."

She watched as the girl went away again, happy with the false promise.

If I were crazy enough to get you into a front line, she thought grimly, you'd be dead within a day.

She took a swallow of a second cup of coffee and wondered whether Chuck Morton still thought of her. Suddenly her features softened, and despite the cropped, dirty hair, she looked unexpectedly beautiful as she thought of him. The young militiaman, glancing surreptitiously at her, was astonished by the transformation and became confused.

Had Morton ever realized, she wondered, that she knew he was in love with her?

The Moray coast

Above the cold North Sea, still enveloped by the unending grayness, Morton was heading back to the November base. He had lost all three of the air-to-air engagements that had been practiced. Despite all his efforts, which he had considered superior, Helm had still unerringly found his six and gotten the first gun lock each time.

Morton felt humiliated. In his F-16 days, he'd been

known as a very aggressive hotshot who won most of his engagements. Helm's abilities had made him feel like a rookie on his first hop.

"We shall make a nice long approach," his tormentor's voice was now saying in his headphones, "with only the instrument landing system. There will be no use of any other sensors, and you will not communicate with the ground controllers."

As if I haven't got enough problems, Morton thought.

The practically blind approach was intended to simulate battle damage. The aircraft had supposedly lost all its primary navigation systems, save for the instrument landing system capability. Likewise, the airfield sustained damage and though there was degraded ILS capability, there would be no ground control. No one was going to talk him down. All that, plus a weather condition that took the cloud base right down to ground level.

Which is just great, he thought, convinced that Helm was about to wash him out of the November program for having performed so poorly. In the back, Carlizzi was suspiciously silent, he felt. Carlizzi, of course, would have all his own systems working normally as he assessed Morton's performance in the front seat.

Morton found the ILS beams there on the head-up display—the vertical and horizontal lines that would guide him in. These were repeated on the only multifunction display he was allowed to use for the purposes of the exercise. The central of the three MFDs showed the gently pulsing lines on a black background. That was all. Despite the fact that by the mere touch of a button he could call up the forward-looking infrared display that would give him a daylightlike view of his grayed-in world, he could not use it. If Helm had not already failed him, calling up the FLIR would ensure it.

Morton glanced at the tantalizing button but left it strictly alone.

Up on the HUD, the lines did not pulse but moved in response to his own maneuvering of the aircraft. At the moment, the vertical line was to the right. He banked the ASV gently right, bringing the line toward the center. The horizontal line was almost in the middle, indicating that his height for distance from the runway was reasonably good and that he was virtually on the glide path. He was aiming for a perfect cross, which would indicate that he was heading for a precise touchdown.

The automatically adjusting HUD gave the symbology the correct intensity for the conditions. There was a manual override, but Morton decided he had enough to do without messing about with the rotary button that controlled the multilevel brightness. The HUD was doing nicely all by itself.

Now he had the cross. He was on a perfect ride all the way to touchdown. In the confining cloud bank, the ASV hummed to itself as it headed home. Morton handled the controls firmly but lightly. His corrections were minute movements of the stick, while the control computers interpreted his demands with incessant, microscopic flutters of the control surfaces, keeping the aircraft in the required attitude.

He could have used the autothrottle mode, which would have given him any desired speed for any selected configuration of the wings. He was allowed that much. But he chose not to. He was going to fly this bird manually, all the way down to the best landing of his life. He would not give Helm the satisfaction of seeing him take the slightest possibility of an easy way out.

And then the ILS beams disappeared from the HUD.

Sweet Jesus, he thought, then glanced down at the MFD to check. The blank screen mocked him. No ILS.

Carlizzi, Morton thought venomously.

The instructor ASVs were special. They were the only aircraft that gave the backseater some real power. The instructors in the backseat could disable some of the pilot's systems to simulate battle damage or simply system failure. Legend had it that many navigators wanted to do at least one tour as instructors, so as to get their revenge on pilots.

Carlizzi had obviously been briefed to test his resolve as far as possible, Morton decided. Should Morton prove unable to handle the situation, Carlizzi would reactivate those systems he could control and authorize Morton to go back to full sensor integrity for the landing.

Morton stared through the HUD at the gloom and kept the aircraft on course. He was not going to play into their hands. He'd been warned that November instructors could be real sons of bitches at times, because the stakes were so high and competition for selection to the program so fierce. He'd also been warned that his part in the attack on the radar site would win him no favors. It had been just enough to get him into the training schedule.

Now he knew.

His standby instruments were operational. It was back to flying without fancy navigational aids. He gave no indication to Carlizzi of the dismay he was experiencing.

As if suspecting, Carlizzi, innocence itself, said, "You okay up there?"

"I'm okay."

"Just checking."

"Sit back and enjoy the ride."

"You're the pilot."

"You said it," Morton remarked, with just the merest touch of firmness.

He could almost see Carlizzi's smirk.

Morton kept steadily on course, maintaining the rate of descent he'd achieved prior to the ILS's vanishing act. He could see nothing beyond the aircraft. The standby instruments were his only guides. Even the ground proximity warning system had been turned off. The long approach, however, had been deliberately selected so that he would be clear of any high ground, and the chosen runway did not have any obstacle on approach to the threshold. At least he did not have those problems to worry about. Even so, it did not help to know that out there in the gray murk and a mile or two off his starboard wing, Helm would be following everything like a goddamned hawk stalking a rabbit.

Wisps of cloud whipped past the cockpit. The ASV continued its descent, twenty-five tons of aircraft in its current weight configuration, heading inexorably toward the hard ground.

Morton eased the throttles back and held engine power at eighty percent. He wondered what Mac was doing.

Hell, he thought. Why am I thinking of her now? I've got enough on my mind.

He pushed the thought away and concentrated on his landing.

Good Christ. There was just no land to be seen. His instruments told him he should be over land by now, judging by his rate of descent and the altitude on the standby altimeter. Distance to the runway should be less than three miles. The wheels were down, flaps in landing configuration. He was nearly there. He felt proud of himself. He had not once felt like reaching for the FLIR button, which would have displayed the runway in all its welcoming glory and made life very much easier.

Then he watched in further dismay as the power setting on the left engine rapidly counted down toward idle thrust of sixty percent. He immediately increased power on the right engine to compensate and maintain speed, and tentatively tried to see whether the left would respond. No go. He tried a relight. Still no go. He followed procedure and shut it down. No sensors, no ILS, and now, no left engine.

Carlizzi again, damn him!

There was not a peep from the back seat. Morton kept his own counsel.

The beauty of the ASV was that the aircraft remained stable, with very little trim change . . . as long as the fly-by-wire system continued to work. He hoped Helm and Carlizzi had not planned to include that little surprise in their package as well. No FBW was like trying to drive a big bus with bald tires on a sheet of ice, someone had told him. But he was spared that particular torment.

The Super Tornado continued it descent, seemingly

unbothered by the loss of an engine. It would be a long landing run, as the thrust reversers would not now be engaged.

Come on, Morton, he urged himself. You put down an F-16 dead-stick. You can hack this.

But that momentous day had been in diamond-bright California sunshine. This was European standard, A-1, down-to-the-ground murk.

Displaying once more his uncanny knack for knowing what was going on in his victim's mind, Carlizzi said, "Walk in the park, huh, Major? For a man who put down a silent F-16."

Speak for yourself, Morton thought. I'm busy." Out loud he said, "If you say so, Major."

Carlizzi did not respond, but Morton was certain the man in the backseat was grinning.

Then there it was. Almost at the moment of touch-down, the runway threshold lights emerged out of the unending gray, the central running sequence pointing the way home. He put the aircraft down gently and without drama. The landing run was not as long as he'd expected.

As he taxied off the runway and toward the aircraft shelter, Carlizzi busied himself with returning all the affected systems to on-line status. Morton ignited the shut-down engine, which restarted smoothly. They halted before the shelter, engines whistling at idle, and the ASV was turned. The ground crew attached the air-craft to a towing vehicle via a boom to its nosewheel strut. The ASV was then backed into the shelter, where Morton shut down both engines. Carlizzi let the inertial navigation system recognize it had returned to its start-ing point, then shut down the systems.

Morton climbed down from the aircraft using the lad-dered steps that one of the ground crew had propped against it. He could see Helm approaching him with pur-poseful strides.

The deputy boss carried his helmet beneath an arm,

blond hair plastered to his skull, the square planes of his face deeply marked by the indentations of his face mask.

"Good landing, Major," he greeted. "You did well. You found it easy, *ja*?" He gave Morton a brisk thump on a shoulder. "Tomorrow we must see if we can give you something that will test your skill." He walked away with a brief wave.

Morton heard Carlizzi descending the ladder behind him and turned. "He's got to be kidding."

Carlizzi grinned. "That was real praise, Major. You did good. He likes you. I have seen him reduce people almost to tears."

"I should be so lucky. I thought he was going to wash me out for sure," Morton went on. "Hell, I never got him once."

"I would have been surprised if you had. Don't lose sleep over it."

Morton frowned at Carlizzi. "So what was all that about up there—about knowing how to get him?"

"I couldn't have let you lose heart, could I?"

"Well, thank you, Carlo."

"Don't feel so bad. Nobody gets him so early."

"I hear Hohendorf, Selby, Bagni, and even Cottingham nailed him pretty damn quick."

"Ah, well . . . ," Carlizzi began diplomatically. "Look . . . anyone who even makes it here is pretty good to start with. That means you, too, Major. There are no passengers. Think about it."

"You trying to smooth my feelings, Carlo?"

"Perhaps. Let's get debriefed, put this gear away, then you can buy me a coffee in the mess."

"You in the backseat tomorrow?"

"But of course. You have me for the duration."

"Aren't I the lucky one."

Carlizzi grinned.

2

Washington, three days later

It was mid-afternoon on a Friday, and Major General
Abraham Bowmaker, U.S.AF, was feeling depressed. The
reasons for his depression were the same ones that had
afflicted him ever since Bosnia had erupted, putting an
end to the West's complacency. With the dissolution of
the old Soviet Union came the mistaken belief that peace
had suddenly been achieved and all was right with the
world. Bosnia, and all the other nasty flash points in the
former Eastern Bloc, had merely served to convince
him—and those who thought like him—that the problem
had merely mutated into something else.

The general hated what he saw as a politically motivated movement to cut back on the armed forces, a policy fueled by the unrealistic belief that they had become
unnecessary. He was quite happy to eliminate waste,
and God knew there was plenty of it. A whole fighter
wing could probably be equipped with the latest ships
using just some of the money saved. As far as he was

concerned, judiciously-pruned forces were far more effective, provided they were allowed the right equipment with which to get on with the job at hand. But on that particular Friday afternoon, the depression, always a lurking companion, was stronger than ever.

He had returned to his Pentagon office after having attended a meeting called by the Joint Chiefs. He'd hoped to hear of a firm decision to take hold of the Bosnian problem by the scruff of its neck and shake it until those blighted people were forced to stop killing each other. Instead, he'd listened to various staff officers patting themselves on the back because of the downing of the four ground-attack aircraft by NATO F-16's.

The general gave a snort of derision. Those Galebs, or Jastrebs, or whatever those half-assed aircraft were called, would have been no match for even a cannon-armed Second World War fighter aircraft like a Spitfire or a P-51D Mustang flown by a mildly competent jock, never mind an all-singing, all-dancing electric jet like the missile-toting Falcon. But here was everyone thinking that was all it would take to bring sense into the minds of the people killing each other over there.

Things were never that simple. He wished the decision makers would pay a little more attention to history. Perhaps they just might see the unending trail, littered as it was with the corpses of the wishful ideas that had perished before harsh reality. Perhaps it would prevent them from repeating the same strategic mistakes over and over.

Now *he* was guilty of wishful thinking, he thought wearily. If decision makers did in fact take note of history, there would be no corpses for them to look at.

He idly glanced through a pile of documents on his desk and sighed. Unfortunately, mistakes would continue to be made, and repeated; and soldiers and airmen and sailors would continue to die while attempting to pull other people's chestnuts out of the fire.

"We're always the ones who've got to go into harm's way," he muttered. Except that from the beginnings of warfare, the civilians tended to pay even more horribly.

The general paused suddenly, his depression forgotten. He was looking at a thin red folder. It had not been there when he'd gone to the meeting. Further, it had been slipped among the other documents already on the desk rather than having been left on top where he would have seen it immediately upon his return. Whoever had brought it had deliberately placed it in a half-hidden spot, as if to prevent anyone else who might have entered the office in his absence from noticing it.

Bowmaker stared at the folder and chose not to call the army lieutenant colonel who was his personal staff officer or the air force captain who was his ADC (*aide de camp*). He doubted whether they would know about it. The colonel, a woman who was exactingly meticulous, would certainly have drawn his attention to such a document, while the captain was little more than a bag carrier.

Slowly, after checking that the folder was not wired to some kind of explosive, Bowmaker opened it . . . and gave a sharp intake of breath. Inside the folder was a photograph of someone he had not seen in a while, but whom he would never forget. He found himself looking at the face of Mac, the young woman he'd first come to know as a sergeant in the U.S. Marines, only to later discover she was some kind of spook with the real rank of lieutenant colonel in two armies. She was wearing her sergeant's uniform in the photograph, and a simple message was attached: *Get her out. Use your November friends.*

Bowmaker stared at the message. Get her out of where? And who would know enough to mention his November connections?

He was now even more certain that his personal staff was completely unaware of the presence of the red folder. Yet someone had gotten by both his staff officer and his ADC to place it among the papers on his desk.

Another spook. Plenty of those around in the Pentagon.

Bowmaker studied the photograph of the woman he'd known as Mac. She must be in very serious danger for this to have come to him; perhaps they, whoever "they" were, had fouled up and were desperate. But what could he possibly do that whoever in her shadowy organization was responsible for her could not? Running spooks was not his province. "They" must have known that. He wouldn't know where to begin. And how could the November boys help?

Bowmaker began to wonder whether this was yet another elaborate scheme to undermine the fledgling NATO unit. Was someone trying to get them entangled in something so sticky it would terminally discredit them? There were many, both in the East and the West, who for their own particular reasons would like to see that happen. Sometimes your worst enemies were right on your doorstep. . . .

Bowmaker stood up and placed the folder in his own combination safe. Then he left the office, saying nothing to either his colonel or his ADC. There was someone he wanted to talk to.

He was making his way along one of the Pentagon's myriad corridors when a man in civilian clothes caught up with him, pausing only briefly without seeming to break stride.

"She's in Bosnia," the man said calmly as he passed, "and needs help. Treat yourself to a French dinner this evening. Tell *no one*." He mentioned an expensive restaurant. "Shred the folder," he added, and walked on.

As if without volition, Bowmaker felt his own footsteps slowing down until he had come to a complete halt. By then the man was gone.

Bosnia? What was Mac—he would always know her as Mac—doing in Bosnia? And could he even believe the unknown man in civilian clothes?

Thoughtfully, with all sorts of questions in his mind, Bowmaker returned to his office, having decided for the time being not to see the person he'd intended to. He shredded the folder in his personal shredder, then buzzed his staff officer on the intercom.

"Yes, General?" came the familiar businesslike voice.

"I may be going to Europe, Colonel. Prepare the paperwork, will you, please?"

"Any idea when, General?"

"I'll let you know tomor—oh, hell . . . it's Friday. Assume it's anytime between now and Monday, unless you hear different from me."

"Yes, General. Will you be flying a fast jet over? Or do you want me to alert your Saberliner crew?"

"Neither. Book me on a civilian flight, as *Mr.* Bowmaker."

The colonel was startled. "*Civilian*, sir?"

"You heard me, Colonel. Consider I'm saving the tax-payer money."

"Yes, sir." The colonel was sounding more and more puzzled. "Will you be traveling alone, sir?"

"I will."

"Without Captain Gaines, sir?"

"Last time I heard, Colonel, traveling alone meant without a companion."

"Is that wise, General?"

Bowmaker shut his eyes briefly. She was a very good staff officer, but sometimes . . . "Colonel . . . "

"Excuse my interruption, sir, but terrorists . . . "

"*Colonel!*"

"Sir?"

"Just do it."

"I'd like to put on record that I advised against the general's decision. . . . "

"Do it if you must, Colonel, and I'll sign it."

"I'm only thinking of you, sir."

"I know you are, Colonel," Bowmaker said in a milder voice, "and I thank you. But I'm not changing my mind."

"No, sir." The colonel sounded annoyed.

"And Colonel . . . "

"Sir?"

"As you know, my wife's visiting family in Arizona. No need to contact her. I'll do that myself." And not from here, Bowmaker thought.

"Yes, sir." The colonel was sounding less and less happy. "Anything else, sir?"

"What engagements do I have for the rest of the day?"

"You've had the meeting of the Joint Chiefs, so that leaves that reception this evening—"

"Cancel."

"But, sir! This was confirmed. The reception's by the defense minister of—"

"Cancel, Colonel."

But she was determined. "Sir, they want to buy F-16's—"

"If I remember," Bowmaker interrupted, "you were to accompany me."

"Yes, sir."

"Good. You will deputize for me. I have every faith in you. I'll have my beeper if you need me urgently. And I mean *urgently.*"

A long silence followed.

"Are you still there, Colonel?"

When she finally spoke, there was a strange quality to her voice. "Sir, you know how they think about women, especially those in—"

"Goddammit, Colonel, this is America. They want our F-16's, they'll have to learn to treat our women officers with respect. We respect their customs in their country. We take good care not to offend them when we send women over there. We don't like it, but we put up with it. They'll have to respect *our* customs when they're here. Go in and represent me, and give 'em hell. If it will make you feel better, take a male officer with you, but make sure you're the senior rank. Make my apologies in the gracious way I know you can. Reasons of national importance."

"Yes, sir." She hated the idea so much, only service discipline prevented her from protesting more bluntly. "There'll be questions. . . . "

"How long have you been with me, Colonel?"

"Six months, sir."

"Well, Colonel, refer all questioners to me. You're covered."

"But, sir, you won't be available."

"Exactly."

At eight o'clock that evening, Bowmaker, in civilian clothes and wondering whether he was perhaps taking too serious a risk, entered what was probably one of the most expensive French restaurants in Washington. He was ushered to a table that seemed isolated from the others by a surrounding area of vacant places, and which was already occupied by someone he was most surprised to see.

"I'll be damned," he said, as the maître d' moved away on silent feet.

"I sincerely hope not. Do sit down."

The man who had spoken looked as if he belonged in the financial center of London. Every inch the sartorially elegant banker clone, Charles Buntline beamed shamelessly at Bowmaker.

The general had once been told that Buntline was a highly educated, highly bred thug, who was very good at his job. His informant had been a Royal Air Force air vice-marshal, for whom he had plenty of respect.

When dealing with the military, Buntline's status was that of a one-star general; but to judge by his manner and despite being outranked by Bowmaker, it was as if he wore three stars to Bowmaker's two.

This was clearly the day for spooks, Bowmaker thought dryly.

"And what brings you to this side of the pond?" Bowmaker demanded as he sat down on the one other chair at the table. "Not enough to keep you happy in London?"

"I think you know why I'm here."

"I wasn't expecting to meet you."

"That was obvious by the look on your face. Let's just say your people and my people are working in concert."

"Not my people, Mr. . . . "

"Uh–uh. No need to say who we are. We already know."

"If you're so worried, why meet here? This is a very popular restaurant . . . for those who can afford it."

"Everyone comes here." Buntline spoke as if those who didn't hardly mattered. "Interesting conversations. With everyone trying to listen to what everyone else is saying, nothing worth listening to is said. Best place to be for our purposes. But before we start, let's order." He did not look at the leather-bound menu. "I do hope you like bouillabaisse. They do it most wonderfully here. I make a beeline for this place whenever I'm in Washington. Overdose on the stuff."

"I hate bouillabaisse," Bowmaker said with satisfaction. It was a lie. His wife, who was very good at French cooking, made the dish better than anyone else, as far as he was concerned. But Buntline's manner irritated him. It was a small victory, but it made him feel good.

Buntline was unperturbed. "Too bad. You'd have enjoyed it. Order whatever you'd like."

"I'll have the steak. They do serve steak?"

Buntline did not bat an eyelid. "Of course. Whatever takes your fancy, my dear chap."

Bowmaker had the distinct feeling that Buntline had seen through him, but he did not change his mind.

"I'm surprised your expense account covers this kind of place," he said, wanting to needle Buntline, "given your cutbacks."

"Pay my own way, old chap," Buntline said easily. "Her Majesty's government can't seem to afford my culinary tastes. At least that's what the accountants tell me. They watch too much of your TV. They appear to think that when I'm in your delightful country I should eat like those police officers who seem to be eternally at hot dog stands, squirting some ghastly concoction over sorry looking sausages. Awful people, accountants."

"I like hot dogs."

"Good for you."

Bowmaker decided Buntline would have an answer for everything, and left him with the last word.

After they had given their orders, Bowmaker said, "So what's going on?"

"You got the folder, or you would not be here. You'd have been suffering through that tedious reception instead, while trying to think of an excuse to leave early. How fortunate to be a man who can send colonels to be sacrificial offerings."

"How do you . . . " Bowmaker paused. "Of course you know."

"Yes. And your erstwhile hosts will take very badly the fact that you sent not only a relatively junior officer to deputize, but a *woman*. Dear me. Very bad form."

"We're in the States, not some benighted country. . . . "

"That benighted country wants to buy large numbers of F-16s."

"*If* the sale is approved."

Buntline shrugged. It mattered little to him whether the sale of the aircraft was approved or not.

"And what's the person in the folder doing in—" Bowmaker began to say, intent on returning to the purpose of the meeting.

But Buntline interrupted him. "That's not the issue. The important thing is to get her out. Fast."

"Why come to me? You know it's not my province. I would have thought between your firm and the firm over here, you had all the muscle and organization you needed."

"Ahh. Well, you see, it's rather a complex problem. Easier said than done. We need a diversion."

"You mean you guys dumped her out there, then fouled up. I don't think I like the way this conversation's going."

"You're the best option," Buntline said, smoothly going into steamroller mode in order to flatten any possible forthcoming objections. "You worked with her, and I know you think very highly of her. Somehow I don't think you could easily stand by and let her get caught out there. The media is full of explicit details of what they do to *civilian* women. In her shoes . . . "

"You're a cold bastard. You know that?"

Buntline was again unperturbed, but his eyes had grown hard. "Under the right circumstances, so are you," he countered. "As I've said, complex issues are involved. . . . "

"And you want me to get the November boys to run your diversion for you."

Buntline gave a deprecating smile. His eyes had returned to a semblance of bonhomie, but their true nature was merely hidden until the next time. "They do look upon you as their champion, especially after that last little job they did for you. It was, after all, your people who spotted that radar.

"Despite their successes so far," Buntline went on, as if discussing a sports team, "you and I both know their opponents have not left the field. They still need champions from whatever quarter they can find them. They've got the air vice-marshal, of course, and even I in my own small way feel a certain . . . solidarity. But a supporting voice from across the water does add a certain *cachet*, if you see what I mean."

"I can see exactly what you mean," Bowmaker said grimly. "I'm glad I ordered that steak."

Buntline smiled, knowing he had won.

In Bosnia, it was 0230 hours

She lay warm and secure in the snow hole, and though she was asleep, her senses were acutely tuned in to her surroundings, the steep slope of the mountain where she'd gone to ground. She could sense every rustle beyond her snow fortress, and could judge whether it was hostile or not.

She had left the small town on the same day that she had been introduced to the Russian major. She had not waited for the local commander's return, judging it to be more prudent to be gone by the time he would decide to pay her another visit. In the past days, she had also not visited any other community, choosing instead to remain in the mountains. She had sufficient supplies for the time being. But those basics would soon be gone, and she would then have to live entirely on what she could find or hunt until she was picked up.

She had already given the emergency signal, which she hoped had been picked up by those she expected to pull her out. It had been simple enough. With so many television crews crawling all over Bosnia, it had not been difficult to get fleetingly into the range of one of the cameras.

She had briefly joined a guerrilla group that had mistakenly believed her to be on their side. They had been posing for a Dutch TV crew, and had been more interested in displaying as much machismo as they could muster, firing their AKs into the air in the time-honored fashion of modern guerrilla armies everywhere. On her left arm had been a black ribbon, a common enough sight in the ravaged country. She'd gained the sympathy of the guerrillas by claiming her lover had been killed.

But she had tied the ribbon like a string tie, below the elbow. That had been the signal. Those watching for it would know she needed to get out quickly. There had been no need for her virtually unrecognizable face to be seen as well.

From now on, she would make her way to the various rendezvous points. At one of them, a helicopter should be waiting. If the aircraft was not there at the specified time, she was not to hang around awaiting its eventual arrival. Instead, she would immediately head for the next point, and so on, until the helicopter came. She would also have to ensure that she did not again come across the guerrilla band, which was made up of both Bosnians and other nationalities, some of whom had come from the former-Soviet republics. But word would be getting around. She'd have to be extremely careful.

The first helicopter pickup was in two days—if her signal had gotten through. The news tape might well have been edited, and her urgent signal relegated to someone's cutting room floor.

She listened in her sleep to the world outside her burrow. She was a hundred kilometers by foot from the local commander and the Russian major, and at least a hundred and fifty from the guerrilla band's last position. The first helicopter pickup point was only twenty away.

She was safe . . . for the time being.

Whitehall, London, 1000 hours the following morning

Wing Commander Christopher Tarquin Jason, MA, RAF, in civilian clothes, was in a foul mood. His legs were hurting, and he had no desire to see the minister who had summoned him. As he sat in the traditionally decorated reception area, with its heavy furniture and dark leather upholstery, he rubbed the legs gently, as if hoping to ease the pain. Resting against the deep armchair in which he sat was the cane he used to help him walk.

Not so long ago he was on crutches, and according to the medical officer, should still be. But Jason was also impatient with his enforced incapacitation. He wanted to walk properly again, and his convalescence, though rapid by any medical standard, was still too slow for his own liking.

That he was alive at all was in itself quite remarkable; for he had survived a deliberate attempt on his life. A small remote-controlled drone had brought down the aircraft he'd been flying in. He was occupying the backseat of a Hawk advanced jet trainer, which was being piloted at the time by one of the tiny number of female pilots cleared for fighter training; they had been on a routine low-level flight through the Grampian mountains. Flight Lieutenant Caroline Hamilton-Jones had previously been a fighter controller at November One, and had been selected for pilot training on Jason's personal recommendation. She'd made it this far through sheer skill and hard work.

She had carried out a perfect emergency landing on a grass airstrip that would have been a tight squeeze for even a light propeller-driven aircraft. Unfortunately, at the very end of the landing run the soft ground caused the Hawk to hit a ditch. As the landing gear collapsed, the rear ejection seat had fired, and though it had separated cleanly, there had not been sufficient height. Jason, already badly injured in the face, had landed heavily, breaking both legs. Months of convalescence had followed. The November project detractors, and those opposed to female jet-fighter pilots, had seized the opportunity to mount their attacks from both angles.

As a result, he'd found it extremely difficult to keep away from the program and the task of attempting to prove it was a worthwhile undertaking; that it was, in fact, the very necessary evolutionary route for a post-Soviet-era NATO to take. He had been responsible for creating and nurturing the program against powerful odds and vested interests. There had even been attempts to promote him—he was well qualified for higher rank—but he had resisted, knowing this would bring the risk of his being moved away from the project.

He had already returned to flying, after having been passed as fit by the barest whisker. On being told his legs still needed more time, he'd retorted that people without legs had flown fighters. He still had his, after all.

He rubbed the legs absentmindedly.

The minister's young secretary looked at him sympathetically. The scars on his face had healed, but some were still visible. "Would you like a cup of tea, Wing Commander?"

"Thank you, no."

"I'm sure he won't be much longer. He's been with the air vice-marshal now for a good half hour, and he does know you're here."

"I know he does," Jason said grimly.

The minister was practicing power play by letting him stew in the outer office. Jason had little time for such transparent games. He wanted to get the meeting over with and head back to the base.

"Sorry," the young secretary said apologetically.

"Not your fault."

Ten minutes later, the minister's voice was deliberately loud on the intercom. "Send the wing commander in, will you, Louise?"

"Wing Commander . . . "

Jason grabbed the cane and heaved himself up. "I heard."

She hurried from her desk to open the tall double doors for him. He nodded his thanks and went in.

"Ah, Wing Commander," the minister greeted. "Thank you for coming. I'm sorry to have to drag you all the way here from your base. On a Saturday, too. I'm sure you have better things to do with your weekend. How are the legs?"

Bloody hypocrite, Jason thought. "Bearing up, Minister," he replied civilly. He nodded at the air vice-marshal, who was standing to one side, distinctly unrelaxed. "Sir."

"Christopher," the senior RAF officer responded.

Air Vice-Marshal Robert Thurson, resplendent in uniform and himself a pilot, was Jason's firm supporter and protector from conniving politicians. Thurson was the person who had confided to Bowmaker on Buntline's thuggishness. A tall slim, man with the face of an aesthete, he had backed Jason from the time his subordinate had come to him with the idea of the November program. He was, however, not looking very happy—though he was very careful not to display his own contempt for the minister. It was clear the meeting had so far not gone very well at all.

The minister came forward solicitously. "Do sit down, Wing Commander."

"Thank you, Minister," Jason said gratefully, and sank slowly into another deep armchair.

"I shan't beat about the bush," the minister went on,

pacing slowly and not looking at Jason. "You'll have noted that the air vice-marshal and I have so far not seen eye to eye. The problem is, as you and everyone else are aware, that we have a substantial need for cuts in the armed services."

"Do we, Minister?" Jason asked mildly.

Thurson's eyebrows shot up, but he said nothing.

The minister was taken aback and briefly looked uncertain. "Of course we do. Savings must be made."

"By so denuding the armed forces that they cannot be expected to carry out their job properly? What's the point of having an armed force at all? It would be cheaper to abolish them completely."

The minister looked from Jason to Thurson and back again, as if he could not believe his ears. "You're on shaky ground, Wing Commander," he warned.

But Jason was past caring. His legs hurt, he'd been deliberately kept waiting, and here was yet another politician seemingly incapable of learning from history, trying to soften him up for some budgetary blow.

"Minister, I am very much aware that the big financial idea these days is to slash everything in sight. If it moves, slice away at it. The fact is, the national forces have already taken a beating. In the case of the Royal Air Force, I can foresee a time, if this trend is not halted, when we shall be back to the days when we sent young men into the air with so few hours they were easy targets for the opposition. A turkey shoot, to coin an American phrase. Where is the saving then? Even now they would be hard put to provide a proper defense of this country. . . . "

"Nonsense, man! Our armed forces are the envy of the world. Small, but extremely efficient."

Jason made no comment, feeling that to do so would put him in a position that even Thurson would be unable to defend. When people started bragging about how wonderfully their armed forces performed with less, it usually meant they knew they were well insulated from the consequences of their actions. No front line for them.

Stifling his true feelings, he chose reason and prudence instead.

"That may well be so, Minister, but there comes a time when we enter the domain of diminishing returns. I believe we've already reached it. I am assuming that you have ordered me here to tell me that the November program is now itself under the microscope in earnest."

"There are those who think it's an unaffordable luxury; that it is in fact a duplicate force, with highly expensive equipment. There are those who seem to think your unit is getting rather more than its fair share of the cream."

Thurson actually rose on the balls of his feet, as if about to start a race, poised to intervene should Jason, forgetting his own status in the pecking order, choose to rail at the minister's stupidity. It was as if the minister had totally forgotten the very dangerous and highly sensitive missions that the November crews had already successfully completed; missions that had definitively proved the crucial need for such units.

Thurson waited for Jason's outraged comments, but none came. Remarkably, Jason kept his peace.

Jason had in fact been hit by a spasm in one of his legs, and had decided not to waste his energy trying to counter the minister's crude attempt to prepare the ground for the really nasty news. He concentrated on overcoming the pain.

Mistaking this for acquiescence, the minister warmed to his theme.

"In some quarters," he continued, "it is being suggested that perhaps it would make financial sense to put out some of your servicing requirements to civilian contractors—"

"*No!*" Pain or no pain, Jason was having none of it.

It was the minister who looked outraged now. "No?" The word had been spoken softly, expressing Jason's sense of shock.

"No, Minister," Jason repeated. "The November units

are highly sensitive, with an extremely high security status. We cannot risk putting any of our work to outside tender. We cannot risk the potential damage to highly sensitive equipment and aircraft by contractors who do not possess the same exacting standards, and who would only be concerned with the profit margin. They would have to be, to give any substance to what is being suggested. Further, we would not have the disciplinary control to ensure that the work done is consistently to the required standard.

"We cannot risk the lives of our crews by exposing them to potential security threats. Such contractors would be open to infiltration, and thus the possibily of sabotage would be that much more real. My own recent experience has shown that despite even our current level of security at November One, it is still possible for a highly motivated professional to score a strike. Finally, I will not expose any of my crews—"

The minister's anger had been growing by the second. "*Your* crews, Wing Commander? Since when did you own the personnel of several nations?"

"With all due respect, Minister, as long as I am in command of the November program, these people are my responsibility and yes, are therefore *my* crews. I chose them very carefully after intensive selection procedures—from a great many eager candidates, I might add. It is my duty, my job, to ensure their safety at all times, within the parameters of the duties they are required to perform. You cannot ask me to stand by while people make politically expedient—"

"*Wing Commander!*" both the minister and Thurson said together.

The minister had turned an unhealthy shade of purple, while Thurson had decided it was time he reined Jason in.

But the damage had already been done. The minister had already decided he was not going to be spoken to like that by any wing commander, no matter what he commanded. A wing commander was, after all, only the equivalent of a lieutenant colonel. Since when did lieutenant colonels tell ministers what could and could not be done?

"For your information, Jason," the minister raged, deliberately omitting the rank, "your objections will have little effect. My colleagues in the other NATO and European Community countries will make their decisions and you will abide by them, or resign!"

"Gladly," Jason said with feeling. "If those decisions put my crews in unnecessary danger, either by giving them substandard equipment in the spurious belief that this will save money or placing them at risk because of poor security, I would rather resign."

"That can be arranged!" the minister snarled.

But Jason knew he was bluffing. If the minister already had full support from his opposite numbers, he would not have been working so hard to convince. He would have been smirking in triumph. He was that kind of person.

Jason opened his mouth to retort but was stopped by Thurson.

"I think you have said quite enough, Wing Commander," Thurson put in firmly. "The minister was merely outlining a possible scenario for future policy—"

"Don't fight my battles, Air Vice-Marshal," the minister said rudely. "I do not need you to explain my intentions to a wing commander." He paused, then turned suspiciously to Thurson. "Or are you attempting to get him off the hook?"

"No, Minister," Thurson replied evenly. "I was bringing him to his senses."

"Somebody needs to." The minister turned once more to Jason. "You're perhaps laboring under the illusion that you are indispensable. No one is."

Yourself included, Jason thought sourly. If only the legs would stop hurting. But the doc had said it was okay. They were healing nicely, despite the fact that Jason was pushing them too hard.

He did not make further comment, but simply shut his eyes briefly. The minister, still enraged, noted this. "Are you dismissing me, Wing Commander?"

"No, Minister. My legs have begun to hurt."

"Oh." The minister was not certain how to respond. "Oh," he said again. "Perhaps we ought to call a halt for the time being. I shall put down your conduct today to the fact that you are still convalescing, and will make no more of it. Thank you for coming."

Saving your face, Jason thought. "Thank you, Minister," he said.

"Very well. Unless the air vice-marshal has more he wishes to say . . . "

"I'll see the wing commander later, Minister," Thurson said quickly. "Perhaps you'd care to wait for me, Christopher."

"Sir." Jason stood up, making a production of it. "Minister." He hobbled out of the office.

As the double doors closed behind him, he said to Louise, the secretary, "I'd like that tea now, please, if it's still being offered."

She again hurried around solicitously. "Of course, Wing Commander." She reached forward to help him into the chair. "Bad in there, was it?"

"Not really," he said.

She might be nice to him, but that didn't mean he could trust her with the truth. She was, after all, still the minister's secretary.

In the office, the minister said, "You really must exercise some control over that man, Air Vice-Marshal. He does seem to think he's immune to censure—even more so since his . . . er . . . accident."

"I think not, Minister," Thurson remarked soothingly, like Jason hiding his true feelings. "But he is very concerned, and as an exemplary officer, I would expect him to be. Remember, Minister, the November units have carried out some very dangerous missions with absolute professionalism and success. Let us take the attack on the radar site as an example. Four aircraft—two for the attack itself and two for fighter cover—each with its own designated task, took out a very well defended target, destroyed four advanced fighters, and sank the only known submarine aircraft carrier. We lost one aircraft, but all the crews returned safely." He chose his words with care, knowing that the minister secretly took credit for the November units' successes and basked in their reflected glory.

"In pure military terms," Thurson continued, "the success achieved was well out of all proportion to the forces used. Under normal circumstances, a conventionally mounted attack would have entailed the deployment of at least two mixed squadrons, plus possibly ground forces. And as for that monster of a submarine, an entire fleet might have searched for it for months and found nothing. From what we now know, it could have lain silently, thousands of feet deep, for as long as it needed to. To imagine that thing loose within the depths of the world's oceans does not bear thinking about. I very strongly believe, Minister, the November units give more than their money's worth, if we must use such terms to measure their value."

The minister was not about to be shown up in the wrong. "That may be, but the fact is, cuts are needed."

This is like a bloody record, Thurson thought frustratedly.

"If I may demonstrate something, Minister. We all know how protracted the decision-making process on the future of the European Fighter Aircraft—perhaps I should now call it Eurofighter 2000—has become. The aircraft is desperately needed, but by all accounts, it seems that it may be very late being put into service. Wing Commander Jason has managed to show with the November program what can be done when freely cooperating international powers work for a common goal. Even those who now balk at the E-2000 program have given their support to the November units, because in the long run it makes both strategic and financial sense. Are you now saying that this support may be withdrawn?"

"I'm saying no such thing. I'm merely pointing out that savings need to be made, and as the wing commander has himself noted, his program is under the microscope."

"He is serious, Minister. He will resign."

The minister considered that. Although it would please him immensely to get what he saw as an unmanageable officer out of his hair, it would not reflect too well upon him if he was seen to be the cause of such a resignation. It could become messy. The minister hated to be involved in messy situations. He didn't mind it happening to others, however.

"Perhaps," he began only half-jokingly, "he should get himself involved with some little tart, then be seen by some tabloid. Security and all that. Who knows where that might lead?" Thurson made a supreme effort to control his distaste. "My daughter, Antonia, happens to have taken a bit of a shine to the wing commander," he informed the minister stiffly.

Caught out once more, the minister could only say, "Oh! Oh, I see. I didn't mean . . . "

"I know you didn't, Minister."

Later, in Thurson's own utilitarian office in Whitehall, the air vice-marshal said, "One of these days, Chris, you'll go too far, and I won't be able to stop your fall. I had to drag poor Antonia's name into it."

"I only spoke the truth, sir."

Thurson sighed. "When are you going to learn that politicians don't want to hear the truth. It spoils their day. They might have to grasp realities then. There's a spirit of meanness and of mean-mindedness abroad at the moment, Christopher. Around here, everything's up for sale.

"There are those who I believe would be very happy indeed to see us quartered in tents rather like those poor unfortunates in the post-Soviet army, all in the interest of saving money. Others talk of leasing the forces out to the highest bidder. Things have come to a pretty pass when the defense of our country depends upon a bean counter's balance sheet. You do realize, by the way, that you've totally ruined your chances of ever receiving a knighthood," Thurson added, only partially meaning it as a joke.

"I think I did that a long time ago, sir." Being given a knighthood mattered little to Jason. In his view, the honor had long since been demeaned by political favoritism and was well down the line of anything he particularly desired in life. For the moment, he was simply determined to build what would one day become the best coordinated rapid response and defensive units the world had ever seen. "Did you really use her name?" he went on. "And how is she, by the way?"

"Still wondering why you haven't been in touch, apart from the thank-you card you sent for the flowers she'd had delivered to you in the hospital."

She had sent him at least a bunch a week, and had visited him once.

"She keeps asking herself," the AVM continued, "why she's pining after you when she could have her pick of eager young men. . . . "

"You've just said it, sir. 'Eager *young* men.' I'm too old for her. I'm rapidly approaching forty. . . . "

"Don't weasel out of it, Christopher. You're nudging toward thirty-eight and certainly not too old. And in any case, shouldn't that be her decision?"

"She's a child, sir. Barely into her twenties. . . . "

"And you're a stubborn man, as I well know. And if you value your life, don't let her hear you call her a child. However, I'm not about to get involved. It's entirely up to you two. We have more serious matters to deal with."

"As McCann would say, tell me about it."

Thurson studied the barely perceptible twitches of pain on the mildly scarred face. He would always remember, the day not so long ago, it seemed, when he had first met the newly qualified pilot who had been assigned to him for weapons instruction, and who years later had himself become an instructor.

Of medium build with a receding sandy-colored hairline, Jason would be anonymous in any crowd. No one would easily be able to guess his profession. Closer inspection, however, would reveal the intensity of the dark eyes, set in regular features. They were eyes that demanded attention, and it would only be at that juncture, belatedly, that the casual observer would come to realize he or she was in the presence of someone who was far from ordinary. Today the eyes were clouded with pain.

"Look, Chris," Thurson began sympathetically. "Why don't you give yourself a rest for the weekend? Antonia's going to be at the town house. Spend the weekend with us."

"I'd love to, sir," Jason said. "Believe me. But I think I should go back to November One. For the present, I'd feel less worried up there. I don't trust the minister's intentions."

"Neither do I, Christopher," Thurson told him gravely. Neither do I."

3

November base

"Yo, Mark," McCann said. "I got something to show you when we're back down."

"Keep it to yourself," Selby retorted, voice made slightly alien by the grip of his mask. "Better still, show it to your lady love."

"I aim to. I aim to. She's going to love it!"

"I don't think I want to hear about your sexual deviations, McCann."

They were on a high transit to an air combat exercise at the North Sea ACMI range, and would be pitted against German Air Force MIG-29s, which had been inherited after unification. To add to the realism, neither side knew how many aircraft each was putting into the fight. Once the start time had been reached, it would be no-holds-barred from then on.

The Air Combat Maneuvering Instrumentation system, a highly accurate electronic arena created by the planting of mini-towers in the cold gray waters of the North

Sea, would precisely monitor the action. Every action taken by each aircraft would be monitored and relayed to display and debriefing systems on land, with a full simultaneous repeat to November One base.

"Oh, ho-ho-ho," McCann was saying. "Another joke. You wait till we get down. You'll be surprised."

"Nothing you do will be a surprise to me, you Kansas City Neanderthal. Just keep your eyes open for the Preschen boys."

"You got it."

The MIGs, originally sited at the former East German air force base of Preschen, had in their new all-German identity been moved to a newly refurbished home. To the November crews, and despite the fact that the Russian-built aircraft were now flown by NATO-trained pilots from West Germany, they would always be the "Preschen boys." Those pilots were known to fly their MIG's ferociously, and they took no prisoners. The coming fight would be as real as it could get without their blowing each other out of the sky.

"Oh, I'm as horny as . . . " McCann suddenly began to sing, mutilating a well-known song from a famous musical.

"McCann!"

"Yo."

"Don't sing."

"Hokay."

"And besides, it's not yet August. Too soon for Kansas corn. I've seen that movie."

"Hokay," McCann repeated.

Despite his apparently casual approach to the job at hand, McCann was in fact incessantly checking and operating his displays. Every now and then, at irregular intervals, he would very fleetingly "light up" the seemingly empty sky with his search radar. The system would infinitely quarter the flashed area, and if a target fell within its clutches, even for the briefest of instants, would calculate speed, heading, bearing, and altitude, then quietly and indetectably work out a selection of probable positions over a given period of time. Each suggested position would be given a priority, based upon the danger it posed. Given multiple targets, the system would prioritize those, too.

Another flash and the system would update, then continue with its predictions, giving McCann the changed priority order of the targets, if the current tactical situation required it. The system could handle up to fifteen different targets at different speeds, headings, and positions, simultaneously.

A scanned target, even if its warning systems were sensitive enough to register this ultra long distance search, would still not be able to identify the direction from which the hostile attention had come until too late. The ASV's recently upgraded search and attack radar had a reach of well over two hundred nautical miles at altitude, a new range extension of fifty miles.

On this day, six ASVs were going out to do battle. Hohendorf and his usual backseater, Wolfgang Flacht, were in the lead some five miles to starboard and at forty thousand feet to Selby and McCann's forty-five.

Five miles behind them and ten miles to starboard were Bagni and Stockmann, with Cottingham and a recently qualified backseater called Christiansen, from Denmark's air force, holding a similar formation. They were at thirty thousand and twenty thousand feet, respectively.

An additional five miles behind, the last pair were Morton and Carlizzi in the lead, with Helm and Jason positioned out on their starboard wing. They were almost down on the deck at two thousand and one thousand feet. Helm and Jason's aircraft was a dual-control version, and though Jason was acting as backseater for the exercise, he also intended to take part in the fight. The call sign for the mission was Viking, with Hohendorf and Flacht as Zero-One and the last aircraft as Zero-Six.

●　　●　　●

As Zero-Five, Morton was thinking it was bad enough having a deputy boss riding shotgun on his wing, but infinitely worse having the boss himself there as well. Listening as the sounds of his own breathing in his mask mingled with all the other sounds of the aircraft, he recalled his conversation with Carlizzi just prior to takeoff.

"What you must remember," Carlizzi had begun, "is to concentrate on the fight. So the deputy boss *and* the *capo di tutti capi* will be there," Carlizzi had continued with a kind of ghoulish humor as he'd made the gangland reference. "So what? They'll be on your wing. *You* are the leader. Forget about who they are. Up there, Helm will be your wingman. You lead, they follow, and watch out for your ass. And don't worry about the MIG's. Those four ships ahead of us will give them a bad day and clear the coast for you. So not to worry. You will be fine."

Easy for you to say, Morton now thought. Helm and Jason will be watching me like hawks. Jesus. I'm in at the deep end. If I screw up, that's it.

Failing to make it at November One, he'd already decided, would be followed almost immediately by his leaving the air force. If he didn't qualify, everything else would seem tame by comparison. There were lots of other outfits that could use a good air force pilot. Otherwise, he might as well fly a bus.

"Chuck?"

"Yeah."

"You remember what I said?"

"I remember."

"Okay."

"Anything yet, Wolfie?" In Viking Zero-One, Hohendorf was itching for the fight.

"Patience," Flacht said calmly. "I hear it's a virtue."

They tended to speak German to each other when things were relatively quiet; but once the first target was sighted, it would be a swift reversion to English, the language of combat.

"Don't get philosophical with me, Wolfie. They're out there. I can sense them."

"Of course they're out there. They're after our heads. It would be a good score for them if they get us."

Hohendorf was dismissive. "They won't." He switched briskly to English. "I'm activating helmet sight and slaving it to the HUD. Do you have a repeat?"

Flacht tapped at a button with a gloved hand and the central MFD changed mode to show the symbolism of the helmet sight superimposed upon the ASV's head-up display.

"I have it," Flacht confirmed in the same language. "They'll probably try a multipoint, multialtitude attack."

"They almost certainly will, and we'll be ready."

Hohendorf scanned the sky about him, helmeted head moving like something from a science fiction fantasy as he searched for a possible target; but the targeting arrow on the helmet sight remained stubbornly invisible.

"No bogies," he said.

"I could have told you that," Flacht commented dryly.

"Smart-ass backseaters," Hohendorf remarked, using the American term he had picked up from the early days of pilot training in the States. "That's what the gods give us."

Flacht grinned in his mask and said nothing.

It was a brilliant, cold day, with visibility literally limited only by eyeball range. Clouds were so scarce, the sight of a wispy tuft was an event in itself. A high, bright sun looked down upon it all.

"That sun will be good for spoofing any heaters," Hohendorf said, meaning infrared heat-seeking missiles.

Even the presence of the warm sun in the cloudless sky would be taken into account by the instrumentation pods on the various aircraft, and the sensors and computers of the ACMI range. A pilot firing a simulated IR missile at a target maneuvering into the sun to evade would find his shot being accurately monitored by the systems. If the target aircraft maneuvered succesfully, the system would register it as a miss.

Already, Hohendorf was planning his own evasive moves, assessing possibilities. With no thick, moist cloud cover to help degrade the IR signature, it would be down to hard maneuvering and defensive aids like flares and spoof IR jammers. For the radar-guided missiles, the ASV's other stealth features and its extremely powerful electronic countermeasure capabilities would all come into play. For close-in visual knife fights, the Chameleon would be used to confuse the opposing pilot. But most of all, it would come down to his own skill.

The MIG-29 pilots would not only be flying in the former Soviet style, which generations of NATO pilots had been taught to recognize, but as NATO pilots themselves would also be using their own NATO-trained skills— plus a few tricks not in the book.

Hohendorf actually knew one of the pilots in the MIG-29 wing and had flown against him at Decimomannu, in Sardinia, during his own time with the *Marineflieger*. The pilot was Luftwaffe. He had no idea whether the man would be out today, but he would recognize the style if he did come. As Flacht had not crewed with him during that period, he wondered whether his backseater knew of that particular pilot.

"Wolfie, did you ever come up against a Luftwaffe guy called Kempte at Deci? He was on F-4s then. He was also an F-104 man before that, and has done a tour with the Italians on F-104Ss."

"Phantoms and Starfighters," Flacht said. "I've heard of him, but never came up against him. But I know of a couple of MFG guys who've been caught by him. I hear he is bad news."

"He's a hard, tough bastard," Hohendorf confirmed. "Very bad news to get on your tail. But I know his style. He uses a combination of Phantom and Starfighter tactics. Now that he's with the MIG-29s, he will have added some new surprises to his repertoire, in addition to the MIGs. Last time I heard, he was a major; might even be a light colonel by now. He was going places."

"You think he's coming out to play today?"

"I don't know. But if he is, you'll know about it. He might even have the lead of the whole formation. When I warn you, don't lose sight of him whatever happens. Lose sight just once and we've given him the fight. He's that good."

"Better than you?" There was a teasing edge to Flacht's voice.

"We've had three meets. He's never got me yet."

"But did *you* get *him*?"

"No."

"Ah! So we have a needle today, if he comes. Will he recognize you?"

"I'll make certain he does."

"Ah!" Flacht repeated. "This sounds like fun."

Hohendorf put Kempte briefly out of his mind to think about Bosnia. Ever since the newscast, he'd given an idea that had been forming in his mind considerable attention. It was a crazy idea, perhaps, and potentially highly dangerous. It could also terminate his career, even if he did get through unscathed. But it had to be done, and he couldn't ask Wolfie.

McCann, he thought, was the person crazy enough to accompany him. He would ask McCann. Selby wouldn't like it, of course. In fact, Selby would be livid if he ever found out—which he eventually would. But by then it wouldn't matter.

Yes. McCann would be the person.

McCann looked about him at the clear sky and said, "Today is a good day to kill MIGs, and . . . Hey, I got something coming in on secure datalink. Ooh, shit."

"Don't keep it all to yourself. Patch it over."

"Coming up."

Selby stared as the message appeared onscreen.

MISSLE ENGAGEMENTS WILL BE LIMITED TO MAX RANGE OF
THIRTY NAUTICAL MILES. REPEAT. THREE ZERO NAUTICAL
MILES. ALL OTHER SENSORS AND AIDS MAY BE USED AS
APPROPRIATE. ENDS.

"Well, thank you!" McCann exploded. "Hell, they're
tying our hands behind our backs. We can't use our long-
range weapons. Shit! I bet that was Helm's idea. He
hates Americans and he's got three up here today . . .
Chuck Morton, Cottingham, and me. He must feel he's
got the whole damn U.S. of A in his outfit and he wants
us to lose."

"Difficult as this may be for you to comprehend,
McCann, this isn't a personal vendetta. By preventing us
from using long-range weapons, he's making sure we do
have a reasonable fight, otherwise those MIGs would be
dead meat at a hundred miles. This *is* supposed to be an
air-to-air tactics exercise."

But Selby had some sympathy for McCann's feelings.
The Tornado ASV when fully tooled up for battle was a
fearsome fighting machine. Its specially developed
lightweight armament gave it a payload of twelve high-
speed advanced missiles: the latest long-range Skyray B,
the medium-range Skyray, from which the B had been
developed, and the highly maneuverable short-range
Krait. Each missile was self-guiding after launch and
possessed multiple seekers that could ignore defensive
aids. For really close-in encounters, the ASV's highly
accurate internal 20mm six-barreled rotary cannon completed the armory. From its longest killing reach of more
than one hundred and thirty miles down to the gun,
there was no gap in its arena. Each weapon merged into
the other's range.

"Well, that message says nothing about the long-range
radar," McCann was saying defiantly, "so I'm sure as hell
going to use it. And don't try to stop me."

"I won't. Unless we're told differently, I concur. Anything out there yet?"

McCann studied his display. "Nope. Zilch. Clean as a baby's . . . "

"Thank you for the colorful report."

"Anytime."

Selby shook his head in slow resignation and turned on the helmet sighting system. Neither the targeting box nor the arrow, appeared. The vast, cold sky was seemingly empty.

Then a warning tone sounded briefly. They had entered the arena. Life was about to get hectic.

As soon as he'd heard the warning tone, Niccolo Bagni in Viking Zero-Three activated his helmet sight. Like Hohendorf's and Selby's, his targeting arrow remained conspicuously absent.

"They are not going to be easy to take, Hank," he now said to Stockmann. "Keep a good watch."

"I don't expect them to be, and I will, especially now that we've had our long arms neutralized. It could be tough, Nico."

"Just how I like it."

Stockmann made a sound that was clearly a chuckle. In the mask, it sounded like a deep belch.

Almost immediately, a second tone similar to the first gave an urgent warning. It meant that the opposing force had now also entered the area.

"Looks like the fight's on," Stockmann remarked softly, the tension of anticipation sharpening his voice. "No bogies yet. They must still be out of range. Nothing up here."

"They will be with us."

Bagni held the Tornado lightly, feeling the power of its energy through the stick and throttles. It was part of him, an extension that was sniffing out the invisible corners of the sky, hunting out the approaching MIGs.

He was alert, sharp, and ready.

• • •

In Zero-Four, Cottingham spoke to his Danish back-seater.

"Let's do some hot stuff out here today, Lars. I want me a couple of MIGs for lunch."

"I will do my best," Christiansen told him seriously.

It was not an apologetic remark. Christiansen was being precise. He would do his best, and considering he had beaten many hopefuls to become operational in the backseat of the ASV, his best would be considerable. Having been paired with him for some time now, Cottingham had great respect for his capabilities.

While not quite in a class with McCann, Flacht, or Stockmann, Christiansen had nevertheless become one of the top four backseaters. Cottingham was glad to have been the fortunate pilot to get him. Most importantly, they got on well together, both in the air and on the ground. They had already been nicknamed the Double-C, and an unofficial *CC* atop crossed American and Danish flags had mysteriously appeared on the left side of their cockpit. No one had as yet claimed responsibility for the artwork, and Jason seemed quite happy to leave it in place.

"I know you will," Cottingham now said as he turned on the helmet sighting system. "All right you turkeys out there," he went on to the sky at large, "Mama Cottingham's boy is ready for you."

"Mama Christiansen's, too."

"I stand corrected. And Mama Christiansen's."

In Zero-Six, both Jason and Helm had their helmet sights on. The dual-control ASV was no less formidable than its single-control counterparts. The major difference with two pilots aboard was the faithful duplication of the displays from its sensors and sighting systems, and the two helmet sights. Not only was the main HUD available on the backseater pilot's central display, but his helmet sight was just as capable. This meant that despite not having as good a forward view, the pilot in the back could still effectively track a target with his helmet and fire the selected weapon with the same ease as the man up front.

Configuration as a dual-pilot machine meant that the displays had additional pages that could be called up, so that limited backseater work could still be carried out. Having himself undergone a short backseater course, Jason was able to carry out that task competently. However, once close-quarter battle was joined, he'd be doing what all the professional backseaters would be engaged in: keeping his eyes glued to the fleeting opponent, and the front-seat pilot informed of its whereabouts. Under such conditions, rank gave way to the pilot in charge.

"How do you think Morton will cope, Dieter?" Jason now asked.

"He's a little worried about having us on his wing," Helm replied. "But he will hack it just fine, sir."

"Do you have confidence in him? Real confidence, I mean."

"I've made it tough for him," Helm admitted. "But that is because I believe he is too good for the November program to lose. He needs to forget he has once been grounded. The injustice he still feels about the way it was done now has to be put behind him. Otherwise it will be a permanent block. That is why I have been pushing him. To make him angry, and determined to prove to me he can beat me."

"And?"

"One day, he will do it."

"Praise indeed. Are you quite sure?"

"Yes. Today should show us some of the fire I believe he has. Those MIGs should make him work."

"Do I detect a scheme?"

"Perhaps I shall be a little slow to swipe at any that get on his tail."

"That's mean, Dieter." Jason did not sound at all disapproving.

"You said it. The mean deputy boss they all love to hate."

"Which is why you're my best weapon to turn these already aggressive warriors into tigers."

"Praise, sir?"

"That's all you're getting for today."

"Then for small mercies, I am thankful. Now let us make life a little more interesting for them."

Each knew the other was smiling.

"Hey!" McCann exclaimed, outraged. "What is this shit?"

"I hope you're going to tell me," Selby said.

"New datalink message. Patching to you."

"RADAR DEGRADATION," Selby read in consternation. "RADAR LIMIT FORTY, REPEAT, FOUR ZERO NAUTICAL MILES. ENDS."

"Radar degradation, my . . . my . . . " McCann was so annoyed he was temporarily at a loss for words. "Goddammit! Nobody messes with my radar. Nobody! We've got the best radar there is. It's that sadist Helm. He's loading the dice."

"He's simulating battle damage."

"What battle damage? Fight's not even on yet. And don't say a glitch in the radar. Since upgrading, we've never had a failure. Goddammit!" McCann repeated as he restricted the search radar to a mere forty miles. "He'll be cutting our balls off next."

"That's an exaggeration, Elmer Lee."

"Oh, yeah?" McCann fumed. He really hated it when anyone messed with his radar, deputy boss or no deputy boss. One of his joys was being able to tweak more out of the system than any other backseater, bar none. He could pick up returns from well beyond the "official" two hundred miles. Helm's directive had virtually blinded him, as far as sniffing out long-distance prey was concerned. "Bet you the bad guys will have all systems go."

"Perhaps not."

"The hell they won't."

●　　●　　●

"Well, Wolfie," Hohendorf began, "they're going to make us work today. We're blind beyond forty miles. If Kempte is here today, I wonder if he knows about this."

"I don't think so . . . but he'll start wondering when he doesn't get a light on his threat warner. At first he'll think it's because we are planning an ambush, then . . . "

"Then let us do that. Let's go in closer, much closer than forty miles, before we use radar. That will keep him guessing. He won't realize we can't go beyond the forty-mile range. But keep an eye on the deck. One of his tricks is to come in very low at high speed, then suddenly climb, straight for you. Or he'll make his climb unobserved, and the next thing you know he's above you, ready to pounce."

"I'll be ready."

Hohendorf was certain Flacht would be. Despite the imposed range limit, the capabilities of the search-and-attack radar would not be diminished. It would still be able to work its magic, sneakily updating the positions of simultaneous targets with the most fleeting of sweeps. He intended, therefore, to get as close in as possible before being detected by the opposing force. Flacht would choose the best moment for the initial sweep and would hopefully catch their opponents like startled moths in a sudden flash of light.

As luck would have it, and because his combat pair was at low altitude, Morton was the first into battle.

Carlizzi, making a fast sweep at the allowed range limit, had caught two of the MIGs in a head-on approach.

"We have two bogies!" he announced tensely. "Bearing zero-five-nine at forty and heading this way! Altitude two hundred feet and descending. They are moving very fast, and look mean. Instruct your wingman."

Morton felt a tightening in his gut. Their own course was in a northeasterly direction, and the first pair of the pretend hostiles was right on the nose, very low down.

From what Carlizzi had just said, they were obviously planning something nasty.

"Okay, Carlo," he said as calmly as he could. "Give Zero-Six a secure patch of the situation. I'll call the break."

"Patching over," Carlizzi confirmed as he sent a fleeting electronic burst across to Jason and Helm. The approaching MIGs, even if they had managed to catch the high-speed transmission, would not have been able to decode it. They would have been warned that something was happening, but would not know what.

"Zero-Six, break high," Morton called sharply. There was no need for anything further to be said.

"Roger," came the response.

Helm, having received the tactical information and understanding the meaning behind the call, would know precisely what to do.

Morton glanced upward and saw a flashing movement above his head. Helm was on his way. There was no tone on the threat indicators to warn that the approaching fighters had "painted" them with their radars. He held his course.

"He's gone," Morton said to Carlizzi. "Any change?"

Carlizzi risked another fast sweep, then watched as the computers presented him with possible tactical solutions.

"The bad boys are still giving us the head-on approach," he replied. "This is unusual. They must have caught our transmission. But they're still not using their radars—" Carlizzi paused suddenly.

"What? What! Talk to me, Carlo."

"They have *increased* speed, still on the same bearing. I have a suggestion."

"I'll take anything."

"Break right suddenly when I tell you. I want to check out a hunch."

"You got it."

"Break . . . *now!*"

Morton hauled the ASV into a punishingly tight turn to the right, not letting up until he was heading on a reciprocal course.

"Now break left and head one-eight-zero. I'll sweep as you break."

Morton complied.

"Well . . . well . . . well . . . " Carlizzi murmured as they settled on the new course. "The original guys have not changed course in response to our maneuvers. Two other guys were sneaking up, also very low down, and at high speed. They were going for a bracket. Your helmet should be getting excited soon. They're just coming within range."

As soon as Carlizzi had finished speaking, the targeting arrow on the helmet sight was suddenly pointing like an accusing finger, low down toward the sea.

"Got them!" Morton announced.

"Don't be too certain. I don't like the look of this."

Instinctively, Morton suddenly glanced upward, through the top of the canopy. The targeting arrow whipped from its previous area of interest to turn into a dot as it pointed straight up.

"Shit!" Morton exclaimed and rolled the aircraft hard left, continuing the roll another one hundred eighty degrees, then pulling hard, pivoting the ASV in the opposite direction.

"What . . . what was that for?" Carlizzi demanded, gasping as his body tried to cope with the sudden crushing G-forces.

"Someone up top. The bastard sneaked up on us. How the hell did he get up there? And where the hell's my wingman? He should have been tagging that guy."

Morton had just met the dreaded Kempte.

At twenty thousand feet, Jason, in the backseat of Zero-Six, studied the tactical situation. Morton had made the right decision in calling the break, and Zero-Six was now perfectly positioned to take the high MIG; but Helm was playing his own game.

In the front, Helm watched the repeated tactical display and decided to take his time about intervening. He wanted to see how Morton was going to react. Like Hohendorf, Helm knew all about Kempte. Unlike Hohendorf, Kempte had nailed him at Deci. He knew it was Kempte who had sneaked to altitude and was even now getting ready to take out his first victim of the day. Helm knew it was Kempte because he had specifically asked that Kempte lead the opposing force. Kempte, always eager to demonstrate his prowess with the MIG-29, would have accepted with alacrity.

It would, Helm now thought, be rather pleasing if the great Kempte were beaten or at least given a hard time by a rookie. It would make up in a small way for the defeat at Deci.

"Are we going to let him catch cold?" Jason now asked.

"If he has the instincts I believe him to possess, he should have spotted the high bogey by now. If not . . . ah!"

"Yes. I see it. He's spotted him. Good man."

Helm looked on approvingly as the green diamond on the MFD began to rapidly change course and altitude. The orange diamond was countering.

"Kempte's lost his surprise," Helm said, "but he's still going after Zero-Five."

"His friends don't seem to be joining in," Jason observed, watching as the other MIGs headed for the remaining ASVs. "They're clearly working to a plan. I do hope Hohendorf's awake."

Hohendorf was very much awake, with multiple problems of his own.

"Four bogeys," Flacht announced urgently. "Head-on. If you're interested, Six and Five have a tangle of five more to deal with."

"Oh, I'm certainly interested, Wolfie," Hohendorf said as the targeting arrow on the helmet sight decided to choose the target it had selected as top priority. "Kempte's with us."

"The one that went high?"

"The very same, and he's brought eight more of his friends to play. Six against nine. Well, Morton will have to cope. He's got Helm with him, and Three and Four are going in, so he's not too naked out there. It all depends on what Helm's got up his sleeve. We're going to the water. Give the signal to Zero-Two."

"Done."

In Zero-Two, McCann and Selby heard the prearranged tone.

"And it's time for fun," McCann said in a deliberately exaggerated drawl. "Down we go, Mark, baby. Chameleon on. Let's see those bozos try to find us above the water."

Selby rolled the Tornado onto its back and pulled into a steep dive, heading fast for the lower reaches. The still distant MIGs caught the maneuver and split in four directions.

"Look at them go!" McCann crowed. "You ain't seen nothing yet, suckers. There's just fighters and targets up here, and you're the targets."

"Elmer Lee."

"Yup."

"They can't hear you."

"They can feel the spirit of Nemesis bearing down upon them. Me."

"Us."

"What? Uh, yeah. That includes the pilot, I guess."

"Thanks," Selby said dryly.

"Anytime, baby."

They now appeared to be virtually skimming the surface of the water, and with the Chameleon active, a hostile pilot would have great difficulty spotting the speeding aircraft visually over the reflective surface of the North Sea. In the MIG-29, the pilot's single pair of eyes was having to cope with the tasks that were being handled by two pairs in the ASV. Formidable machine though the MIG was, meeting a hungry ASV was not the way to have a good day.

"We seem to have pulled a couple down with us," McCann said. "The other two have gone after Axel and Wolfie. Are you guys in for a surprise," he added to the images on the MFD.

"Talking to your pictures again, McCann?"

"You know how it is."

"Don't I just."

Selby hauled the Tornado into a sudden tight left-hand turn. They were now heading directly for the still high oncoming MIGs.

"Ahh *shit!*" McCann exclaimed. "You always do that. Warn a guy, will you? Goddammit!"

"Stop moaning, Elmer Lee. You've been with me long enough now."

"Yeah, and you're still trying to knock my brains out with those high-G turns when I'm not ready."

"Be prepared. Always. Were you never a scout?"

"Never!" McCann replied with feeling. "Thank God. Now if you're quite finished, the guy on the left's our meat."

A sudden warble came and went on their headphones, briefly interrupting further conversation.

"He's trying for a lock, poor deluded man." McCann said. "Sorry, buddy," he went on to the approaching MIG. "We're not at home to you."

Selby had selected the medium-range Skyray. The helmet sight gave him a firm lock. On the display, the targeted MIG went into a wild dance, but the lock remained solid, burning through its countermeasures.

"Sorry, buddy," McCann repeated. "You're hooked, but good." Though the other aircraft was still out of visual range, he could accurately visualize the maneuvers being performed by its pilot. The readouts were showing the constantly changing figures for the target's altitude, course, heading, bearing, and speed.

"Just watch out for his pal," Selby cautioned.

"I'm watching."

Selby squeezed the release. The simulated shot took flight electronically. The MIG pilot would be hearing the tone that would tell him he was cornered by an unshakable missile. In reality, unless he could break its lock, his sole option for survival would have been to eject. Under the circumstances, he wouldn't eject, since the aircraft was not in any real danger. The tone continued to hound him as he put his MIG through an impressive set of evasive maneuvers. He was, McCann reflected clinically, a good pilot. That MIG was dancing all over the place—but to no avail.

Then a simulated flaring on McCann's MFD denoted a "kill."

"Yeeeharr!" McCann gloated. "You are toast, my man."

"Now for his mate," Selby announced crisply, then hauled the ASV into another punishing turn before rocketing skyward.

Oblivious to the whirling sky about him, McCann kept his attention firmly on his displays, punctuated by periodic surveys of the world outside to check for the remaining MIG-29.

"What the . . . " he exclaimed. "He's off my screen."

"Impossible," Selby retorted. "He must be close." But he too was sounding puzzled.

"You got him on the helmet?" McCann asked.

"No."

"There you go. He's vanished."

"Impossible," Selby repeated with some asperity. "He's got to be there."

McCann, now searching the sky with constant head movements, thought he'd caught a flash of something. Hardly daring to believe it, he checked just to be sure.

It was the MIG.

Its pilot, displaying exceeding nerve now that his companion was to all purposes "dead" and out of the fight, had made a purely visual approach, killing all sensor sweeps to avoid alerting his intended prey. The MIG was keeping station directly beneath them, hiding like a shadow. The pilot must have followed Selby's exit maneuver faithfully, biding his time until the moment when he would slide back to their six and nail them with a guns shoot. It was a fantastic display of close-quarter flying.

"Okay, Mark," McCann said quietly, as if afraid the MIG pilot might hear. "When I give the word, roll one-eighty. You got that? *Roll*, not break. Then look through the canopy. There's a surprise waiting."

Selby's trust in McCann's capabilities in the backseat was total. He did not waste time questionong the strange command.

"All right," Selby said. "Call it."

"Okay . . . okay . . . " McCann murmured.

He could just see a sliver of the MIG's wingtip when it briefly shifted out of hiding from time to time as its pilot worked to maintain a perfect shadow position.

It was like being stalked by a damned shark, McCann thought. But this was one shark that was going to be unlucky.

"Hit it!" he yelled suddenly.

Selby's reaction was instantaneous. He flicked the ASV onto its back and looked through the canopy. And there, caught like some creature whose rock had suddenly been lifted, was the MIG. The targeting arrow was already pointing unerringly, but there was as yet no missile or gun targeting box since neither weapon had yet been brought to bear. Selby would have to position himself for the shot.

In a continuous fluid motion, the one hundred eighty degree roll had turned into a barrel roll that fractionally slowed him down, sliding him nicely behind the startled MIG as he armed the gun.

But the MIG pilot was no slouch. Despite his surprise at being discovered, he was already countering Selby's move and had flicked tightly into a turn to bring his nose to bear on the ASV.

"Jesus, Mark!" McCann cried. "He's turning into us. The guy's going to get away!"

"No, he's not," Selby said firmly, rolled level, hauled the stick back, and slammed the throttles into combat burner. "Just keep the Chameleon working." He switched weapons to the Krait.

"It's working."

The ASV leaped skyward, turning the MIG into a fast-receding dot. He cut the burners and snapped down the air brake switch on the edge of the inboard throttle. The panels on either side of the tail fin popped into the airstream, slowing the upward rush as if someone had dropped an anchor. He snapped the switch in the opposite direction and the air brakes came back in as he kicked the left rudder firmly, even as the wings began to spread forward, biting at the air for more lift. The Tornado was heading back down and the MIG, on its way up, was nicely boxed. Selby got the tone of a solid Krait lock.

The MIG pilot thought he could see something hurtling down toward him, but wasn't sure. Its form seemed insubstantial. He'd turned on his radar. Something was definitely there. He abandoned his climb and began to evade. It was too late. The solid tone of a missile launch with unbreakable lock assaulted his ears. He'd been suckered.

McCann watched gleefully as another flare greeted the simulated shot. "And that's two to us! Good stuff, Mark, ol' buddy. Good stuff."

"With a little help."

"Ooh, God!" McCann said theatrically. "Acknowledgment. Can I have that in writing? Please?"

"Shut it."

"Now that's more familiar. You had me worried back there."

"Let's go hunting."

"I like the sound of that, too."

The final tally of the day, showed a clean sweep for the Super Tornadoes. Selby and McCann did not score further. Morton did not score, but at least he escaped Kempte and no one else got him. The teams of Cottingham and Christiansen, and Bagni and Stockmann, got one MIG each. Jason and Helm got another, with Jason doing the flying. Hohendorf and Flacht got Kempte.

Those who saw the battle considered it one of the most spectacular they had ever witnessed. The fight went from fifty thousand feet down to almost sea level, where Hohendorf had dragged his opponent. Back at November base, the fighter controllers in the underground operations complex affectionately known as "the hole" were glued to their screens as the battle progressed.

For some glorious minutes, the noncombatant aircraft—MIGs and ASVs together—circled out of the way while they watched, either on their screens, through their helmet sighting systems, or visually, the furious contest that was taking place. In the end, Hohendorf dragged Kempte so low that the MIG pilot became pre-occupied with avoiding hitting the water. He made a mistake, and Hohendorf, waiting for just such an opening, nailed him.

"So who is this?" Kempte's voice, full of chagrin and respect, came at the end of the fight.

"Hals und beinbruch!" Hohendorf responded.

There was a stifled exclamation in German, then Kempte said in disbelief, "Hohendorf?"

And Hohendorf laughed.

4

Whitehall, London, the same day

At about the time the November crews, flushed with their success, were returning to base, Charles Buntline entered the minister's office suite. In the outer office, Louise gave him a genuinely welcoming smile.

"Nice to have you back, Mr. Buntline," she greeted. "Enjoy Washington?"

"Washington was . . . interesting."

"That covers many sins."

"Ah, Louise, my dear, I never sin."

Oddly enough Buntline's relationship with the minister's secretary bordered on fraternization. His normal attitude was that he never spoke to the hired help. Thus, his overt friendliness had a purpose the details of which were known only to himself. He'd informed the minister's office of his trip, but not its purpose.

"One day, Mr. Buntline, I might believe you. One day."

"You're a hard woman, Louise. See myself in, shall I?"

But the minister beat him to it.

"Good to see you, Charles," the minister said, appearing suddenly in the doorway to his office. "Do come in."

"Minister," Buntline said. The single word was at once a greeting and an acceptance of the invitation.

"And how was Washington?" the minister asked, indicating with the wave of a lanquid hand that Buntline should take a seat.

"As Washington always is," Buntline replied vaguely. "Boring embassy functions."

The minister fixed Buntline with a skeptical eye. "You never go to Washington simply to trudge the embassy circuit. However, I'm not certain I do want to know what you've been up to."

That's a surprise, Buntline thought with well-concealed distaste, knowing the minister's finely honed survival instinct for dodging anything that might pose the slightest risk to his career—or eliminating it, when all else failed.

"Rather glad you came in, Charles," the minister went on. "I had the air vice-marshal and that wing commander in here a few days ago, to inform them of budget-cut proposals."

Buntline was immediately interested. "Oh?"

"Wretched man."

"The air vice-marshal?"

"No. That impertinent, insolent wing commander."

Impertinent. Insolent. The minister had obviously been rubbed the wrong way by Jason, who must have had a field day.

"From your comments, Minister," Buntline began mildly, "I gather Wing Commander Jason was less than . . . cooperative?"

Reliving the incident in his mind brought color to the minister's cheeks. "The confounded man was totally insubordinate! Clearly forgot his place. Deliberately so, I might add."

Insubordinate. Forgot his place. The minister was

gathering a head of steam. Whatever Jason had said must have hit pretty hard—and must have been right on target. Buntline waited patiently for the rest.

"He was practically telling me to mind my own business!" the minister continued in outrage, taking shameless license with the facts. "He even threatened to resign."

Bull's-eye, Buntline thought with dry amusement.

He wished he'd been there to observe the fun. He also knew there was more to it, and that the minister was carefully glossing over his own role in the affair. He said nothing.

"The man's become a damned nuisance, Charles. He believes himself indispensable. When people start believing such things about themselves, it's time they move on . . . voluntarily or otherwise."

And here it comes, Buntline thought.

"Perhaps . . . " The minister hesitated briefly. "Perhaps if he were to . . . er . . . become embroiled with some young floozy . . . " He paused. "You know what I mean, Charles. All the rage these days. You read the newspapers. Reasons of security, and all that. You could arrange that rather neatly, I'd have thought." The minister paused once more, gauging Buntline's reaction. "If you see what I mean."

Buntline knew precisely what he meant. "You want me to arrange a smear," he said bluntly.

"Steady on, old man. I didn't mean . . . "

"Exactly what do you mean, Minister?" The edge that had suddenly come into Buntline's voice caused the minister's eyes to briefly widen. "We are talking love nests, convenient photographers, articles in suitably scandalized journals, videos, pillow talk about sensitive matters—that sort of thing?" Buntline decided not to mention the obvious hypocrisy of it all. The minister would not have gotten the point—or more correctly, would have chosen not to.

"Well . . . "

"There is a problem."

Not sure what Buntline was getting at, the minister said, "Problem?"

"To give such an exercise the right impact we need the wronged, faithful wife. Jason is not married."

The minister brightened. "Ah, well, you see . . . we may have something even better. Quite by accident, I have discovered that the air vice-marshal's daughter is . . . er, fond of Jason. I've seen her once or twice at functions. Pretty young thing . . . perhaps a bit young for Jason . . . which may be a good thing for our purposes. . . . "

"Are we going for the air vice-marshal as well?"

"I didn't say . . . "

"Good angle," Buntline said, plowing on. "Brings the air vice-marshal's decision making into question. Allowing his young daughter to become involved with a much older man—a man at the heart of the highly sensitive November program, a man who's the air vice-marshal's very own protégé. It has meat. Long-running series of articles."

"He did appear to support Jason's rudeness," the minister remarked defensively, justifying the unpleasant scheme to himself.

Buntline stood up suddenly. "Interesting concept."

"You're leaving? We haven't . . . "

"Not much more to say, Minister. I've got the drift."

"Then you'll . . . "

"It's an interesting concept," Buntline repeated enigmatically. He made for the door. "I'll be in touch. Thank you for letting me into your confidence. I'll show myself out."

He left the room, the minister staring after him, mouth working over words that would not come. He knew the minister would now be wondering if he'd view holding their conversation as a sort of Damoclean bargaining chip, potentially damning evidence against him to be called upon when appropriate.

He had been about to tell the minister about the operation he had planned with Bowmaker in Washington, but had thought better of it. He did not smile with satisfaction. There was little need.

"That was quick," Louise said as he entered the outer office.

"Some days," he told her, "it happens that way."

The Bosnian mountains, early evening

She rested against the trunk of a tree and considered her next move. She intended to keep traveling during the night and would go to ground during part of the day. The first rendezvous point had been a dud; the helicopter had not come. She had three days to make the second. From now on, she would have to eat whatever she could find on the run, being sure not to remain in any area where she had killed, trapped, or picked her food. All areas of habitation had to be avoided, as anyone she came across could be an enemy, or someone who would betray her.

She was certain that once the major had contacted Moscow, there would be pursuit. This was probably even now in progress; there had certainly been time enough. It was imperative that she stay ahead and try to avoid any combat. She might be able to take a few soldiers out, but could not prevail against anything bigger than a six- or perhaps ten-man patrol. In any case, being bogged down in a fight would cost valuable time and make her eventual rescue less and less likely.

The sound of a fast jet streaking high above cut through the twilight. A NATO aircraft? she wondered.

She had to keep moving.

In the small Bosnian town where she had last been, the Russian major was in serious conversation with the local commander. They were standing next to an armored personnel carrier. The APC, known more commonly in the West as a mechanized infantry combat vehicle, was a

modernized version of the BMP, and rather special. It
was air-portable, and was of the kind normally used by
airborne troops. It was fast, amphibious, and armed with
a turreted 73mm automatic gun with an individual load
of thirty rounds. It also carried antiaircraft missiles on
launch rails, plus two 7.62mm machine guns mounted on
each front corner of the hull. Within its armored body it
could accomodate six fully armored troopers in addition
to its commander and gunner.

It was the lead vehicle in a patrol of six, and was not
in the familiar United Nations white but in battle camouflage, with no national markings. There was also a large
group of infantry standing by. Their alert manner and
the way they held their weapons showed these were no
undisciplined militia. These were hardened troops. They
were not wearing the blue UN beret. Some wore the
mottled white combat gear of mountain specialists.

"She certainly fooled me," the militia commander was
saying in a savage voice, in his bad Russian. "I want her.
I will—"

"Do nothing," the major interrupted coldly. "My people in Moscow want her. This is out of your jurisdiction . . .
Comrade." The emphasis was deliberate. "A wise man
knows when not to interfere in areas that are outside his
interest."

"She *is* my interest! She has killed my people!"

"You are not certain."

"We have discovered snipers we thought were killed by
the other side," the militia commander protested hotly.
"But some time ago, one of my patrols spotted her in one
of the areas. They thought she was only killing the other
snipers, not ours as well. There is no one else who could
have done it. If it's a local person, we eventually find out.
Everyone knows someone who knows someone. And we
have sometimes taken our revenge. I have personally
killed an old friend who was a sniper for the other side.

"For many months we have heard of snipers being
killed with precision, and had thought that the other side

had brought in mercenaries; so we were glad when Nadia seemed to be helping us. We never thought she was killing our people as well. But there must be more of them. Even she cannot be in so many places at once. I want her," the commander repeated emphatically. "And I want to know who she is working for, and why." His demeanor suggested there would be no limits to what he would do to her in his efforts to gain the information.

The Russian major's eyes were lifeless. "This is a friendly warning, with your interests at heart. Keep out of it. She is a Russian national and will be dealt with by us."

"She is in my country!"

The major laughed softly as he glanced around at the ruins surrounding the relatively unscathed café.

"What country?" the major asked, eyes fastening once more on the commander. "You are destroying what used to be your country," he went on with a sudden snarl that vanished as he continued. "Don't push Slavic solidarity too far. We can help you, but we can also be less than helpful if you get in the way. Battalions that come to help can have . . . other uses."

"You would not dare!"

Again the major gave his soft laugh. "You believe the West would prevent it? I think a good long look at what has become of your 'country' should prove my point. The West will not risk a confrontation with us just to save your foolish necks. They may even leave you in the cesspool you have created. Take my advice, my friend . . . forget personal reasons. She is just one woman . . . "

The local commander indicated the line of APCs with a chin-jutting, aggressive jerk of his head. "That is why you have brought out a small army?"

There was still sufficient light to show the stillness in the cold eyes. The Russian gave another quick glance about him, taking in the militia commander's four macho-looking bodyguards, who stood a discreet distance away.

"I have enough men," the major said quietly, "to take on your ridiculous militia and still carry out my orders—

and those bodyguards would be of little use to you. Besides," he continued in his quietly dangerous voice, "it would not be a good idea to start killing Russians. You would not like the consequences. Do not interfere, and life will be relatively pleasant for you. Kill your fellow Bosnians, if you must. We are not like the West. A single dead Russian will be avenged. Ferociously."

The major turned abruptly and walked along the line of APCs, pausing to talk with the commander of each. Then he returned to the leading APC and held out a hand to the militiaman.

"Let us part as friends and comrades. I shall see you when we have got her."

The man hesitated, then took the hand, shook it, and suddenly gave the major a fraternal hug. The major did not look as if he enjoyed that very much, but suffered the familiarity with dignity.

"You are right," the local man said. "We are Slavic brothers and should save our fighting for our common enemies."

If the major thought this was sloganized rubbish, he gave no indication. He had a specific mission to carry out and was impatient to be off. With a brief nod, he turned to climb into the hatch of the leading vehicle. Soon the infantry started out and the armored convoy began to move. The specialist troops were also on their way, heading on foot for the mountains with unnerving silence. They had spoken to no one, except quietly among themselves.

The local commander watched them until they were out of sight, vanishing like malign spirits into the gathering darkness. Despite his desire for revenge upon her, he found himself thinking he would not like to be in Nadia's shoes when the major's troops eventually found her. Whatever the orders he had received from Moscow, and whoever from, it had been clear that finding Nadia was a matter of extreme priority. And while the major had not given any details, six heavily weaponed armored vehicles and so many troops for one woman meant Nadia must be very dangerous to the major's superiors. It was hard to tell what was going on in the East these days, and who was really in charge over there.

He did not like the way he had been spoken to by the Russian major, but he was also smart enough to know there was little he could have done about it.

He decided to go to the café. That young waitress who was always going on about wanting to fight was nicely plump despite the privations of war, and unspoiled. She would be very grateful to a commander who made her wish come true, now that there was no more Nadia to help her. A spell on one of the fronts and away from this relative haven would soon open her eyes.

The militiaman gave an ugly grin. It could even be suggested that she had talked too much to Nadia. A kindly commander might be inclined to overlook her possible involvement with an enemy . . . for the proper display of gratitude, naturally. She could never be a substitute for Nadia, whom he'd failed to bed, but she would do as consolation. In a way, it would be a kind of revenge. He knew Nadia had cared enough about the girl to try to keep her from going into battle. First he would enjoy her; then, if she liked the sound of guns so much, she would get all she wanted.

The commander's grin widened as he motioned imperiously for his bodyguards to follow him.

Before the war had transformed him into a patriot, the commander had been a bouncer at a seedy club in Sarajevo. He still looked as if he belonged there. His wrestler's body and gait, the cropped hair, and the mean eyes gave him an air of palpable menace. The fact that reality had forced him to back down to the Russian major, a man he privately looked upon as being comparatively effete, did nothing for his current sense of well-being. He was thus in no mood to be refused anything he demanded.

He entered the café, was pleased to see that the waitress was there, and went into the small room at the back that was always reserved for him. The room was furnished with a table and two chairs, plus a single bed pushed against a wall. It was all scrupulously clean, and against all odds, there was not a single bullet hole in any of the walls. Like the café itself, it seemed preserved, an oasis within the encircling, man-made ruins.

One of the bodyguards had entered with him. The others remained in the café proper and took up watchful positions in the relatively crowded place, unsmilingly studying the clientele. The looks on their faces showed they trusted no one, not even those wearing the uniforms of their own militia. They felt this way with good reason. They had previously shot and killed three people who had attempted to assassinate the commander. All had been in militia uniform.

The commander got the bodyguard who had accompanied him to summon the girl. She entered shyly, looking at once pleased and uncertain.

"So you would like to do some fighting?" he began immediately.

She brightened instantly. "Yes, Commandant! I want to do my share."

"You are doing good service here, waiting on the fighters."

"I would like to do more, Commandant."

He pretended to think about that. "Perhaps . . . " He paused deliberately.

She went right in. "You will help me? Oh, Commandant!"

"Not so fast. Not so fast. I only said perhaps."

She could not hide her disappointment. "I see. . . . "

"No, you do not." He looked at his bodyguard. "Leave us." The man hesitated.

"Go, I say! I shall be fine." The commander turned to her. "I am in safe company. I am quite safe with you . . . yes?"

"Oh. Oh, yes!"

He again turned to the bodyguard. "You see? Nothing to worry about."

The bodyguard left with seeming reluctance. The commander knew the man would be outside the door, both to act as protector and to ensure no one came looking for the girl until the commander was finished with her.

"And now, we are alone. Please. Sit down."

Her uncertainty returning, she did as he told her.

"So you wish to go to one of the fronts."

She nodded.

"I suppose you also wish to be like Nadia?"

Again, she nodded. "But she says I should not be."

"With good reason," the commander said, his voice suddenly harsh. "What would you say if I told you that the woman you admire so much is a *traitor?*"

Her eyes widened in sudden alarm.

"Yes," he went on in the harsh voice. "The woman with whom you have spent so much time has been unmasked as a traitor and a spy. Those Russian troops and armored cars are now hunting for her. And what have you to say for yourself?" he finished in a demanding voice that had suddenly quieted. His eye bored chillingly into her.

"Commandant! I . . . I . . . did not know! I . . . " She had begun to leave her chair.

"*Sit down!* You will leave when I order you to!"

She sat down again quickly, her eyes filled with fear. A slight tremor went through her. She was now watching him, waiting like a trapped deer for the hunter's pleasure.

The commander let her wait, knowing her fear would do most of the work for him. When she seemed near to collapse with the anxiety of not knowing what action he intended to take, he spoke to her softly.

"I am not an unkind man. It is clear to me that you are the innocent party. However," he continued as her eyes began to look hopeful, "not everyone will be as kind. My bodyguards, for instance. They hate traitors, as you know by their reputation. Of course, I command them and therefore you are now under my protection. Now . . . how grateful are you for this?"

It took her a short while to interpret the meaning of

his words, but only because she did not want to believe it. The frightened deer was back. She was fully aware of the one thing that made women vulnerable in war, no matter how tough they were.

"Do you understand me?" the commander demanded.

She nodded slowly. "I . . . I understand, Commandant."

"Good," he said. "Good." He ignored the sudden moistening of her eyes, the disillusionment he could see within them.

Outside the little room a short while later, the bodyguard inclined his head slightly as he thought he heard the short, high-pitched cry of a woman. This was followed by a low, rhythmic grunting that obviously came from the commander, who was being very energetic in his endeavors. The bodyguard smiled to himself, fully aware of what was happening. There was no other sound from the woman.

The bodyguard gave a sour grin, searched for and caught the eyes of the other guards. His expression told them everything. One by one, they grinned knowingly. When the commander was eventually finished with her, be it days or weeks, she'd be passed on to them. It was his normal practice.

The bodyguard outside the door listened to the subdued sounds of the rape and felt an excitement grow within him. He was usually first after the commander. He hoped the commander would tire of her quickly. Though she would be well used by then, he would still enjoy his turn. She was the sort of woman who would always look fresh, unless very badly treated. He hoped that the commander would be a little less rough with this one. Many had looked like hags by the time the ex-bouncer had finished with them; often not even the ordinary fighters had wanted to touch them then.

Before long the eavesdropping bodyguard heard the low grunts become a groan, followed by a long, drawn-out straining sigh. Then came the sounds of soft weeping.

The bodyguard couldn't have cared less for the weeping and violated girl.

As for the customers in the café, if any of them under-stood what was going on in the little room, none showed overt interest. They knew better.

The café staff, who must have been aware, carried on as if nothing unusual had taken place. In a war in which atrocities were commonplace, this was nothing. They knew it had been only a matter of time before the commander would go for the girl. They kept their thoughts to themselves. They had their own worries, and in any case, none would dare go up against the commander.

The Pentagon, Washington, the same day

At about the time that the local commander was intro-ducing the young waitress to his version of reality, it was midday in Bowmaker's office. After his unexpected dinner with Buntline a few days earlier, he had post-poned his trip across the Atlantic. He would still be going to the November base, but there had been some things to arrange before making the flight over. What Buntline and his unknown colleagues had proposed was risky in the extreme, and Bowmaker wanted to ensure he had his own back covered.

He wasn't about to allow himself to become anyone's scapegoat if things went wrong—and there was every chance that they could and probably would, if he was not very careful. They had gotten Mac in, but now couldn't get her out. At least not without a big dose of unwelcome attention. She had to be rescued under the cover of a NATO strike, which would allow the November boys to do their stuff.

Easier said than done. Such strikes thus far carried out by NATO aircraft had received undivided world attention. Trying to mount a clandestine November operation in that theater would be about as easy as . . .

" . . . putting a block of ice in an oven to prevent it

from melting," he finished the thought aloud. "We can't rig a strike just to provide the cover."

A reason had to be found to get the aircraft over there at the right time, and in the right place.

Bowmaker touched the office intercom button. "Colonel."

"Sir?"

"Europe's on again."

"Yes, sir," she said. "How will you be traveling?"

"Colonel . . . "

"Sir?"

"You sound pissed at me. Am I still not forgiven for the embassy reception?"

"As I said before, sir, I did as the general ordered."

"But you still think it was a lousy break."

"Well, sir . . . it wasn't what I'd have called a fun evening."

"Diplomatically put, Colonel." Bowmaker was grinning at the machine. "I'll be using my jet," he went on. "Alert the crew."

"Yes, sir. When will you be leaving?"

"Tomorrow. And Colonel . . . "

"Sir?"

"You're in charge while I'm away."

"But, sir! Brigadier General Wilkinson's your deputy . . . "

Wilkinson was not strictly Bowmaker's deputy, having his own unit to command, but he usually took the helm when Bowmaker was away.

"The Brigadier General's handling a little business for me. You're in charge. You did well at the embassy. You can mind the store till I get back. I have every confidence in you."

"Yes, sir," she said uncertainly.

Bosnia, just after midnight

The commander was finally satisfied. He came out of the little room, reeking of sex as he strutted into the dark of the café. He reveled in the smell of it. Behind him, there were no sounds to be heard from the abused young woman. He grinned to himself in the gloom as he shut the door on her.

There were no customers, no staff, and no lights showing. The four bodyguards were the only other people in there, ghostly shapes made visible by a flickering glow that had permeated its way through cracks in the building, from beyond the hills. Every so often, the distant *crump* of landing shells came to them. The flickering glow was itself punctuated by intermittent arcs of tracer, shooting stars on their way to a killing.

The commander went to a shattered window and looked out.

"Ahh," he began expansively. "*Son et lumière.* I like that." He turned to them. "Didn't think I was educated, did you? Eh?"

They made no reply. There was nothing to say.

A snuffling noise came from the small room. No one turned to check, but all had the same thought.

The commander stretched, reminiscent of a wild animal that had eaten its fill. "I feel good. I feel like some action. Tonight."

"*Tonight,* Commandant?" one of the bodyguards asked.

"You have objections?"

"No, Commandant . . . "

"You are thinking of the girl."

"Commandant, I . . . "

"No one gets her, for now. She wants to fight. She will have her wish. You can all have her later. I am finished with her. Go and find Serenic. Tell him she is assigned to his group."

"They have some of the most dangerous missions," the bodyguard who had stood by the door cautioned. "She won't last long."

"But if she does, all the better for you. There will be a fire in her for you to enjoy. Go, Dragan," the commander ordered another of the bodyguards. "Find Serenic."

The man left silently.

"When he returns, we shall leave."

"Where to, Commandant?" the bodyguard who had first spoken inquired.

"We're going hunting. Get your things ready. We may be gone for a while. I will leave Serenic in command until we return."

"What are we hunting?" the eavesdropping bodyguard asked quietly. He sounded as if he already knew.

"Not what. Whom. Nadia."

"But the Russians . . . "

"Fuck the Russians. This is not their colony. I want Nadia, whoever she is . . . for making a fool of me. There is no argument. Now get the BMP. We have work to do."

The BMP, an old armored personnel carrier that had once belonged to the commander of a former Soviet motor rifle battalion, was still in good working order. Like the Russians' APCs, it also possessed a turreted gun of the same caliber but with a forty-round load, plus an antitank missile launcher and a mounted machine gun that could be used against both ground and air targets. It could also hold eight troopers in addition to driver and commander. With just his bodyguards in tow, that meant more than ample space within the hull. As his personal vehicle, the militia commander ensured it was kept in perfect condition. His ego demanded it.

The second bodyguard went out. If he had any doubts, he kept them to himself.

The commander went back to the window to stare at the glow beyond the hills. Out there in the assaulted darkness, people would be cowering in the ruins of buildings. Some would already be dead, others in the process of dying. High above, the sound of jet engines added accompaniment.

"Son et lumière," he repeated softly.

5

November base, the Moray coast,
Grampians, Scotland

It was late morning the day after the Bosnian
commander had set out on his quest for the woman he
knew as Nadia. It was another bright day, and though
there was no wind, it was cold. McCann entered the officers' mess anteroom, a huge grin on his face. Selby and
Stockmann were there and looked up warily.

"Okay, guys," McCann said, repressed excitement in
his voice. "Come and see."

"Come and see what?" Stockmann demanded, showing no inclination to move.

"Why spoil the fun? You'll soon know."

"Do we have to?" Selby asked.

"Oh, yeah. You won't believe this."

"I believe you're capable of anything, Elmer Lee. So
I'll stay right here."

"Aw . . . c'mon, guys. Show some life."

"Don't you mean, Get a life, or whatever the phrase is these days?"

"That has other uses," McCann informed him, straight-faced.

Stockmann gave an exaggerated sigh. "Look at it this way," he said to Selby. "We don't go, he stands here all day . . . "

Selby stood up. "We go."

"Thought you'd say that," Stockmann remarked dryly, and followed.

"This had better be worth it," Selby warned McCann. "It's cold out there."

"It's worth it."

In the mess parking lot a short while later, they both stared, while McCann continued to grin.

"Oh . . . my . . . gawd," Stockmann exclaimed at last.

Selby stared at the bright-red vision. "It's . . . it's so . . . phallic."

"Sure it is," McCann said cheerfully. "Good old American iron. Meet the Viper. A sports car to kill for."

Selby and Stockmann continued to stare at the outrageous curves of the big open-top machine, with its fat wheels, its loud and proud stance.

"Oh . . . my . . . gawd," Stockmann said again.

"She's going to love it," McCann said.

They both knew he meant Karen Lomax.

"Jeez . . . " Stockmann began in surprise. "You're *giving* it to her? She'll die of . . . God knows."

"Not giving it to her, but she'll love riding in it. I decided no 'vette for me this year."

"Take a tip," Selby suggested. "Go back to your Corvette. The lovely Miss Lomax will . . . " Selby paused. "I'm lost for words. You have a go, Hank."

"Hey, I'm more lost than you."

"Well, thanks, guys," McCann said. "Thanks for your support."

"We're only thinking of you, Elmer Lee," Selby told him. "This looks like a fabulous car, but when you point that phallic thing at Karen Lomax, she might have other ideas."

"Oh, yeah? Well, we'll see." McCann entered the car and started it. The engine snarled defiantly into life, pounding out a beat full of power. "We'll see," he repeated, and roared away.

"I've got to say it sounds damn great," Stockmann remarked as they watched the car depart.

"He'd better not break the base speed limit," Selby said, "or the boss will have him—*and* that car."

"If you think I'm getting into that," Karen Lomax said, "you're out of your mind."

"What's wrong with it?"

"What's . . . it's . . . it's . . . "

McCann sighed. "I know. Phallic."

"Well, yes."

"Mark Selby and Hank Stockmann have already pointed that out. I know, I know what it looks like. That's the whole idea. . . . "

"Elmer Lee!"

"No, no. You're misunderstanding me. . . . "

"No, I'm not. You said you were getting your new Corvette."

"I saw this and thought . . . "

She looked at him fondly. "Elmer Lee."

"No, huh?"

She shook her head. "No."

He stroked the edge of the door.

"You like it that much?" she asked.

"Well, it is sort of cute. . . . "

"Cute!"

He sighed once more. "All right. It goes back."

While McCann was unsuccessfully trying to persuade Karen Lomax to like the Viper, Hohendorf and Morven were in London. He'd been given a couple of days leave, and they had decided to spend it in the capital, taking the air shuttle from Aberdeen.

Morven had declared she wanted to buy something she didn't want him to see until later, and had ordered him to wait for her in the coffee shop of a well-known department store. He'd been sitting there for about ten minutes when a striking dark-haired woman in her late twenties or early thirties entered, glanced around, and saw that every table was occupied. She looked toward him, saw two empty chairs, and approached.

"Do you mind?" she asked. "The other tables . . . " Her English carried an East European accent.

"Be my guest," he said. "You're welcome."

"Thank you," she said as she sat down. "You are not English? You sound American, but not quite. . . . Excuse me. I am not wanting to be rude."

He smiled at her. "It's okay."

"So. This is interesting. Not English, and not American."

"No. German."

"German." She looked as if she wanted to leave immediately. *"German."* The second use of the word made it sound like an insult.

Hohendorf looked at her with some resignation. "You are about to tell me how we Germans . . . "

"No. I am not about to tell you about the last war. You are too young, and so am I. I am Yugoslav, or what used to be a Yugoslav. Now I am Bosnian . . . Serb, Croat, Muslim . . . it does not matter. You Germans were *stupid.* You should not have recognized anybody. And as for the rest of Western Europe, they followed you like fools. Now look at what you have done."

"We have done?" Hohendorf felt a strange shiver go through him. After the negative feelings he'd so recently expressed at the base, it was unnerving to have this woman, a *Bosnian,* at his table.

"Of course. You gave all those madmen the very excuse they so badly wanted to do what they're doing right now to my country. The Germans are back to their old tricks, they said. And people believed. You are such, such *fools*. Will you never learn anything from history?"

Hohendorf stared at her.

"And now," she said, "you think me a very rude woman."

A waiter had come up. "Madame?"

"I will have a coffee. Strong. My friend looks as if he needs a cognac. . . . "

"It is too early to serve . . . "

She gave a sigh of resignation. "Of course, of course. I forget this is England. You will have another coffee?" she added to Hohendorf. "Yours is finished."

Intrigued, he nodded. The waiter went away.

"So," she continued, "you think I am rude."

"I didn't say that."

"It is in your eyes." She gave him a sideways look. "They have secrets, those eyes."

"They do?"

She nodded. "Yes. So. I am Zunica Paic. And you?"

"Max Wietze," Hohendorf replied, cautiously using only part of his family name, taken from the full-blown Axel Maximillian von Wietze-Hohendorf.

"That is your real name?"

"Yes."

"And Max is of course for Maximillian."

"Yes."

"Very German."

"I am German, as I have told you."

"And what are you doing here, German Max? Holiday?"

"You have many questions."

"I am a curious person. Where I come from, we are all curious these days. Life can be very short and there is so much to know."

She reached into her bag and took out a slim pack of cigarettes. It was white with green lettering. *Superleggera*, it said. They were the thinnest cigarettes he had ever seen. Elegant fingers extracted one and put it between her lips. She looked at him, and waited.

"I'm sorry," he said. "I do not smoke."

"Ahh. Do you mind? It is your table." She lit the cigarette, barely waiting for his reply. She took a deep draw upon it and gave a soft, bitter chuckle. "Where I come from, dying by cigarette is not a worry. So," she repeated, breathing smoke at him, "tell me, Max—you are holidaying in London?"

"Yes." That was true enough.

"And what do you think of what is happening in Bosnia?"

If only you knew, he thought.

"I think it is a 'tragedy,'" he said.

"A 'tragedy',' she mimicked. "A nice, safe word. Good for the conscience while you do nothing."

"The UN . . . "

She said something explosive in Serbo-Croatian that could not have been a pleasant description of the UN. Some people at the other tables turned to look their way. She seemed oblivious of them.

"Do you understand my language?" she asked.

"No."

"What I have just said would not be spoken in polite company where it could be understood. Even to translate it into English would not be very nice. That is what I think of the UN. They have been wringing their hands while my country is torn to pieces by . . . people who have become animals. When there is a need for action, they have *meetings!* Anything to delay taking action. Oh, sure, they have their convoys and their 'safe areas.'" She gave a short, contemptuous laugh. "'Safe areas'. To me, a safe area means only this—there are no guns, people eat, and people are not killed. If it is not so, it is not a safe area. You agree? Or am I misunderstanding the language?"

"You do not misunderstand."

The waiter came with the coffees.

"Thank you," she said to him, taking a swallow and then another draw on the cigarette almost before he'd gone away again.

"So," she went on to Hohendorf, "there are no safe areas. The UN could have saved my country but . . . they had no . . . guts to do what had to be done. Now, all their ridiculous 'safe areas,' 'safe havens', or what stupid name they wish to call them, will be taken . . . one by one. You should not have given us hope if you were not going to do anything about it. One little bomb dropped here, one there. It is all nonsense.

"There should have been one powerful blow right at the beginning, quick and complete. We have been saying this for two years. Instead, you will start losing your nice airplanes, and will lose more soldiers. Then after they have taken a 'haven,' a truce will be called for and you will be eager to agree, until the next 'haven.' And so it will go. And for what? It would be better if there had been no UN and no NATO—if you had not come.

"Every time I look at the news it is to see one Western politician after another trying to convince himself it is not in your interest." She used the Serbo-Croat expletive once more to illustrate her contempt. "Of course, they are being stupid. They have forgotten, or are trying to forget, how the Second World War started. Remember Spain? Of course you must. You are German. It will cost you all much, much more. You waited too long and now you are too late, whatever you do. No matter how it ends, we will never forgive you. Never."

She stopped suddenly, taking another swallow of her coffee and a quick pull on her cigarette. There was a frenetic urgency in her movements, but her dark eyes were oddly, remarkably still.

Listening to the passion in her voice, Hohendorf stared at her. "You are giving *me* the blame for all this?"

"You are German. Your country made the first recognition. You have the responsibility. I am not on holiday like you," she added. "I will be going back to hell."

Hohendorf said nothing.

She gave him another sideways look. "Your eyes . . . they interest me. They seem to know many things, I am thinking. What do you do for a living, German Max?" She glanced at his hands. "Those are not the hands of a manual worker. You are a professional."

As he sat there in his casual clothes, there was nothing that overtly betrayed Hohendorf's military background. His hair, though neatly cut, did not have the obvious brutality of Stockmann's marine crop. Even out of uniform, Stockmann looked the part. Hohendorf, on the other hand, could easily pass muster as belonging to any number of professional disciplines. He wondered what she would say if she knew the truth about him.

"This is becoming very personal," he said, trying not to sound too defensive. "A stranger sits at my table and asks me how I make my living."

"I will tell you my personal story."

"I did not ask . . . "

"I will tell you. My mother is half-Russian. My father was a Serb. When I was a child, they separated. Then I had a Croat stepfather. He died when I was twenty-one. My mother did not marry again, but now she has a Muslim partner, a lover. In my family, there has never been this ethnic stupidity. None of the men in my mother's life cared about this. I heard last year that my father had been killed, fighting for what he believed: that we are *all* Bosnians.

"*That* is your tragedy, German Max. Because if you continue to do nothing, this will poison the rest of Europe. Whatever your comfortable politicians think, it is also in *your* interest to stop what is happening in Bosnia. We are not a little country that is far away. We are on your doorstep. We are holding out our hands, saying Please help us. If you do not, you will suffer for it. You are condemning yourselves and will be cursed by this for generations."

"Hullo, darling." There was just a slight edge to the voice, a questioning tone that demanded an answer.

Hohendorf looked up at Morven and tried not to appear sheepish. In one of her hands was a full shopping bag, bearing the logo of the store's lingerie department.

Zunica Paic turned a languid eye upon her, glanced at the bag, then looked up once more.

"Ah," Zunica said. "Mrs. Max? Very beautiful, too. Please. Sit down. I have been amusing your husband. But you are English."

Morven looked from one to the other, unsure of how to react. "Yes," she said as she sat down. "And we're not married."

"Ahh. Not yet. But soon. I can tell."

"How very astute of you. Are you going to introduce me to your friend, darling?" Morven asked with emphasized sweetness.

But again, Zunica got in first. "You are angry, Mrs. Max. You think your Max has been . . . playing around. But no. I have borrowed his table for a cup of coffee. And now I am finished and must go. I am Zunica Paic. I am from Bosnia."

Morven's eyes darted toward Hohendorf at the mention of Bosnia. Zunica gave him one of her sideways glances, eyes narrowing briefly, but said nothing.

She stood up, searching in her purse for money to pay for the coffees.

"I'll do that," Hohendorf said as he too got to his feet. "I insist."

Zunica hesitated before saying, "Okay, Max. I let you pay. And look after Mrs. Max. She is very much in love with you. You are fortunate." She turned to Morven. "Good-bye."

"Bye," Morven said, bemused but still not quite trusting.

Hohendorf held out a hand. "It was . . . instructive . . . to have met you."

Zunica Paic took the hand lightly. "Instructive. A good word to use. Enjoy your holiday." Then suddenly she leaned forward to kiss him fleetingly near each corner of his mouth. She then stood back and looked into his eyes. "Perhaps you do understand," she said mysteriously, then turned and walked out of the coffee shop.

Hohendorf sat down again, slowly. His eyes followed her departure.

"And what was all that about?" Morven demanded.

"I have just received a history lesson," he replied quietly. He continued to watch until he could no longer see Zunica Paic among the crowd in the store. It was as if she had never been.

"She is very attractive," Morven remarked pointedly.

At last he turned to her, smiling and kissing her quickly on the mouth. "And she says you are very beautiful; but, of course, I already know that. Now, can I see what you have bought?"

"Hmm," Morven said, not quite mollified. "And no, you can't see what I've bought in here. So, who was your friend? 'I am Zunica Paic,'" she went on, copying the accent passably well. " 'I am from Bosnia.' Darlink."

"She didn't say 'darlink.'"

"I thought I'd add that to give it flavor."

"You are angry?"

"Should I be? Well, I'm not. Just curious."

"Another curious person. If you had not made me remain in here, I would not have met her. She would have had the table all to herself. It is as if it were meant to be."

"How very exciting for you both."

"Morven, Morven. You are not angry, but you are jealous?"

"Of course not."

"So forcibly spoken." He took her hand. "Come on," he said gently. "I'll pay for the coffees and we'll go to the flat. Let us forget about Zunica Paic. I want to see what is so special in that bag. I have waited very patiently in this place and now I must see what I've been waiting for." He stood up.

They had come straight from the airport to the store, bringing their overnight bags with them. The waiter appeared and Hohendorf paid for the coffees, then picked up the bags.

He looked at Morven. "Okay?"

Her smile held anticipation, and promise. "Okay."

• • •

But he did not forget about Zunica Paic. They had caught a taxi to the Maida Vale flat, and throughout the journey he was so lost in thought that Morven had to rouse him twice to receive answers to questions she had asked. She waited until they were inside the large and very comfortable apartment on the first floor before demanding some explanation.

The place belonged to a close friend and had a history. It was the very flat where Kim Mannon had first seduced Mark Selby. Morven had at first hesitated about taking Hohendorf there, then had decided it was appropriate for their first trip to London together and was looking forward to it. It was, after all, in this flat that everything had really begun, back before Mark had gone on to join the special unit where she'd met Axel at that very first Mess Ball. Now she was beginning to have renewed doubts about her decision.

But Hohendorf was enjoying his tour of the flat. "This is very beautiful," he said as they went from one room to another. "People should always have such friends."

"Have you really never seen that woman before, Axel?" she asked, unable to contain herself any longer.

He stopped and turned to face her. "Never. She is as much a stranger to me as she is to you."

"Then why have you been . . . "

"So thoughtful? Is that what you are about to ask?"

"Yes."

He took his time replying, then related the one-sided conversation he'd had with Zunica Paic. "The fact is," he added as he finished, "I agree with her. I have been thinking along those lines for some time. We should *do* something. We should have done so a long time ago."

She stared at him for a long moment, noting the strangely determined set of his expression. "Axel . . . I know you well now . . . I think . . . I *hope* I do. You look as if you have come to a decision of some kind. After what you've just told me, I hope . . . I really do hope you're not thinking . . . " She stopped, unable to give voice to the fear she was now experiencing.

Instead of replying, he continued his tour of the flat. She followed anxiously.

"Axel, I'm almost beginning to wish you *had* known her before. Please tell me you won't do anything. Apart from the obvious danger, you'll wreck your career. It will be a terrible waste. I don't want you to do that to yourself."

He said nothing.

"Axel? Tell me you won't. This is not like you."

"*Someone* has to do *something*."

This alarmed her. "It's the sort of crazy thing I'd expect of Elmer Lee, but not you. Do you know what the men in the ground crew call you? Captain Correctus."

He stopped once more, turning to face her. "They do? Who said?"

She hesitated, then said, "Elmer Lee. They mean it in a friendly way," she went on. "The ground crew all like looking after your plane because they say you always look after it. Everything done in the right way."

"Like a typical German . . . "

"That's not what they mean, Axel. They care about you . . . "

"Well, this typical German intends to do something atypical."

"Axel! What's got into you? I . . . I don't understand."

"To understand, you have to be . . . German." He did not look at her.

She recoiled as if struck. Her eyes filmed over. "Axel? What is this? I . . . "

It was as if the sound of her voice brought him back. He stared at her as if for the first time. His arms reached out for her and she came into them, hugging him tightly.

"I . . . I am so sorry," he told her softly. "It was a stupid thing to say. I have been thinking about the Bosnia problem for so long, I am allowing it to interfere with my life. I am sorry. I'm sorry."

"Oh, Axel. I love you so much. Please don't go and get yourself killed over there. And for what? Whatever you're planning, don't do it. If . . . if you won't think of yourself, or your career, think of Wolfie, who will be flying with you, and his wife and children. What if something happened to him? You'd never forgive yourself."

"I have thought of Wolfie," he said.

High above the Norwegian Sea

Selby and McCann's Tornado ASV was on a routine combat air patrol, with Bagni and Stockmann on their wing in trail formation.

"Yo, Mark," McCann said.

"Yes," came the resigned acknowledgment.

"You know the Cold War's supposed to be over." ·

"Yes. But the Bears still come out to play. That's why we're up here. I realize it must be all routine to you, Elmer Lee, but . . . "

"I reckon it isn't over."

"Direct line to the Kremlin, have you?"

"Take Bosnia."

"No, thanks. You take it."

"I mean," McCann continued as if Selby had not spoken, "the Russians are playing their own game over there."

"They probably think the West's doing the same."

"Exactly. Just like the Cold War."

Selby allowed a sigh to escape into his mask. "McCann." "Yo."

"Do you have these thoughts often?"

"Scoff if you must. You'll see," McCann finished ominously.

A silence descended between them, broken only by the sounds of their own breathing and the constant background noises of the aircraft at work. McCann kept up his routine, continually monitoring his displays and regularly surveying the air around them. Far to their starboard rear quarter, the barely distinguishable speck that was Bagni and Stockmann's ASV kept perfect station.

McCann let his eyes wander over to the inclined panel at the front of the left-hand console. The twin doll's eyes blinked at him rhythmically. The small indicators, marked with black-and-white diagonal stripes, were set in the panel. These monitored the flow of oxygen in both cockpits and blinked each time they took a breath. A similar pair, closer together, was in Selby's cockpit, but on the right-hand panel.

In both cockpits, the right hand doll's eye was McCann's. He'd always wondered what his first feelings would be if it stopped blinking as he breathed, and no oxygen came through. He looked at it, almost mesmerized, mentally playing a game of chicken and daring it to stop.

"Yo, Mark."

"What now?"

"You know you and Kim are getting hitched . . . " McCann let the words hang.

There was silence from the front.

"Mark . . . "

"What makes you think we are?"

"Aw, c'mon. Everybody knows she's not going to let you get away this time, and we all reckon you'd have to be really dumb to let her get away. . . . "

"I'm glad you're all making my private decisions for me."

"Now, every groom needs a best man . . . "

In the front cockpit, Selby grinned into his mask. He'd already decided on McCann, but had no intention of telling his backseater just yet. McCann would be insufferable right up to the wedding day if he knew too early. He was also going to be insufferable *not* knowing. It was a no-win situation.

"Plenty of things to sort out," Selby said. "We haven't really started to make any arrangements. You know how it is with her father."

"Yeah . . . but . . . "

Just then, the electronic tone that signified a change

of course in the combat air patrol pattern sounded in their helmets, and Selby rolled the ASV suddenly to pull hard onto the new course.

"God*dammit*, Mark!" came McCann's aggrieved tone. "You always do that! Warn me."

"You heard the tone," an unrepentant Selby told him as they settled on the new course. "You knew it was coming."

"Yeah, but that doesn't mean you've got to try and break my goddamn head."

"I should be so lucky."

"British sadist."

"Colonial ape," Selby retorted, an unseen grin again creasing his features.

They settled back into their routine high above the cares of the world below, Bosnia wiped from their immediate thoughts.

A lonely mountain road in Bosnia

The APC convoy had stopped and the Russian major had climbed out of the lead vehicle. Soon after, everyone had begun disembarking from their respective APCs. The major now walked a short distance away. He was joined by the commanders of the other vehicles, their soldiers remaining watchful of their immediate surroundings and ready for action. They mingled, but not so much that they would be in each other's way should a firefight erupt from the slopes. Some took the opportunity to grab a quick smoke.

"Still nothing from the guards," the major said to the commanders, meaning the specialist mountain troops. "Not even a sign of passage. She's good."

"Will we get to her before she's picked up, do you think?" one of the commanders, a young lieutenant, asked.

The major turned a baleful eye upon him. "If you want to make it in the new Russia, Lieutenant, you'd better sharpen your ideas."

The young lieutenant stood his ground. "I was not casting doubt, Comrade Major. I was asking a serious question."

The major continued to stare at him. "The possibility of failure has not crossed my mind." He glanced up at the sky. "If any NATO jets come sniffing around, you all know what to do."

They nodded. The antiaircraft systems on their vehicles were all armed and ready for use.

The major now studied the slopes on either side of the road. No one had fired at them since they had started out. He was certain none would dare. The news should have gotten around that their convoy was to be left strictly alone; but you never knew in a war. There were always hotheads and fools—which, when all was said and done, were the same things. Anyone stupid enough to take them on would be in for a very rude awakening.

He again glanced at the sky. Up there, way out in space, he knew the satellites would be monitoring. Let them. They were impotent.

"All right," he said to the commanders. "Back aboard. We've got work to do."

She watched as the lead APC started up and began to move. The others followed. She stayed where she was until she could no longer hear them. She knew that somewhere behind the armored carriers a screen of mountain troops would be moving toward her. She knew how these searches worked.

They'll be using the guard troopers, she thought to herself. For a hunt like this, she knew, they'd use the best trackers and specialists.

There was only one thing to do. She would find somewhere to go to ground and wait till the screen had passed; then she'd double back, moving in the opposite direction. The wildlife in the area she chose would tell her when the danger was past. If one knew how to read the signs, the change in wildlife patterns was practically a shout, telling the watcher when danger was approaching, and when it had passed.

The trackers would be able to read the signs, too, so she'd have to settle in long enough to allow the wildlife to its return to normal routine. She'd also have to ensure she left no signs of her passage on the flora. Going to ground also meant she would have to miss the next rendezvous.

The helicopter probably wouldn't be there anyway, she consoled herself.

She began to move away, making certain she left no tracks by avoiding any ground with patches of late spring snow.

Maida Vale, London

Morven carefully removed the lingerie from its wrapping and slowly laid it out on the bed. She stared at her purchase, not at all sure now that it had been such a good idea to buy it. There was very little material, and on grounds of cost for quantity, it was an absolute rip-off. However, the gossamer thinness of the clothing, its beauty, and the delicacy of its texture made it an understandably expensive buy.

Even so, it was an extravagance she would not normally have allowed herself. But she had wanted their first time together in London to be very special. The lingerie was meant to celebrate the occasion. She wanted to put it on for him, to make love while wearing it, and then to have him take it off her for more lovemaking. She had been looking forward to that.

She had asked him to wait in the living room while she put it on. But now she simply stared at the flimsy material, and made no move to do so. Zunica Paic had put a cloud over everything. Her presence at Axel's table had obviously helped crystallize whatever crazy scheme he'd been dreaming up about Bosnia.

Morven Selby had that magical combination: great sensibility, high intelligence, and great beauty. There was a hidden wildness in her luminous green eyes that she allowed only someone very special to see. And even though the lustrously thick dark hair that fell past her shoulders gave the overt impression of untamed passion, only a few ever got to see or experience the true intensity of what burned within her. Hohendorf was in a fortunate minority of one.

She was strongly built, yet possessed a soft, curvacious body that Hohendorf normally had great difficulty leaving alone. A heart-shaped face, a firm chin, and a high, curving forehead warned that this was no empty-headed, weak bimbo. A strong nose and thick dark eyebrows were countered by a mouth with soft, full lips that were strangely vulnerable; and when she smiled, a powerful radiance came from within her eyes.

That smile had captivated Hohendorf from the very first time he had seen her. He had discovered a great warmth about her that he loved far more than he'd originally thought he could. But he'd also come to realize that she was very strong willed, and was not given to folding easily when faced with a critical situation. He had seen her cope admirably with Anne-Marie, and anyone who could stand up to Anne-Marie the way she had was no weakling. Her reaction was thus a great surprise to him.

As he relaxed on a sofa in the living room, waiting for her to call out that she was ready to show him the mysterious purchase, he wondered at the way she had seemed so terrified by the mere thought of what she believed he intended to do. It was not like her at all, and it made him feel uncomfortable.

He had not actually said he was going to do anything, only that *someone* should. It was true he had thought up a plan. It didn't necessarily mean he was going to carry it out. There would have to be very careful preparation. . . .

Hohendorf stopped. Perhaps she was right. It was crazy. Yet . . .

He turned on the TV with the remote control and sat back to watch. The news came on. A safe haven in Bosnia had fallen. He wondered if Zunica Paic already knew, had known, even as she had spoken to him. The usual crop of experts came on, followed by a politician who said that the troops shouldn't be there in the first place, that they were not looking out for the country's interests.

Sickened by the doublespeak, Hohendorf turned off the TV and found Zunica Paic's words coming back at him with all the force of a returning boomerang.

Someone *had* to do something.

Wearing just bra and pants, Morven sat cross-legged on the bed and continued to regard the lingerie with uncertainty.

The fear within her seemed to be growing with each passing moment. True, Axel had not actually said he intended to carry out any plan he might have dreamed up; but deep within her, she felt a strange disquiet that was so palpable it was as if she'd eaten something that had upset her. Unconsciously, she rubbed her stomach.

"Hey, in there!" his voice called. "Do I get to see what you have bought? Or is it to be a mystery forever?"

"A little longer!" she called in return, forcing herself to reply cheerfully. Get hold of yourself, girl, she went on firmly to herself. Do you want to spoil this? After you've planned it for so long?

She began to slowly remove her bra and pants. When she was totally naked, she sat back on her heels on the bed and stared at the lingerie she had laid out.

Then she put it on.

"You can come and look!" Hohendorf heard her call out to him.

An expression of eager anticipation on his face, he went to the bedroom and opened the door. He entered, then stared.

Morven was spread-eagled on the bed, clothed in something so flimsy, it was almost as if she had nothing on.

"Well?" she said anxiously, frowning slightly as he approached. "What do you think?"

"What I think," he said softly after a while, "is oh, yes, yes, yes!" His eyes caressed her as she lay there.

"You like it? Really? You don't think I'm being . . . "

"Shh! Let me enjoy this."

He began to remove his clothes. He took his time, although what he really wanted to do was leap upon her. When he was finished, he climbed onto the bed and began to kiss her through the material. He did that for a deliberately long time, until she was almost clawing at him in her desire to receive him.

When at last he entered her, her body shuddered and seemed to leap at him. She gave a long, drawn-out sigh as her longing ended and she felt him moving deep inside her. Then abruptly, her body began to shake violently.

She was crying.

He stopped. "Morven! Have I . . . "

The strong legs gripped him. "No, no." Her arms held him tightly. "You've done nothing to hurt me. It's just that I love you so much. I don't want to lose you."

"What an idea! You're not going to lose me," he assured her.

"Is that a promise?"

"It's a promise."

"You won't do anything silly like going to Bosnia, will you?"

"I shall have to if they send me."

"But they won't, will they? Not your lot. That's not what you do."

It's what we should be doing, he thought. But he didn't tell her that.

6

The November base, two days later, 1100 hours

**The crews had been summoned to briefing room
Alpha.** Everyone knew that Alpha meant something very
special had come up, as that particular briefing room
was only used in such circumstances. Four crews were
involved: Selby and McCann, Hohendorf and Flacht,
Bagni and Stockmann, and Cottingham and Christiansen.
Morton was included, unexpectedly, without an assigned
backseater.

As they filed along the corridor in their flying overalls
toward the briefing room, Hohendorf found himself next
to McCann.

"Hey, buddy," McCann greeted. "How was the little
trip to the capital city?"

"It was good fun."

McCann gave an exaggerated leer, then glanced ahead
to ensure Selby was out of earshot. "*Just* good fun?"

"That is all you will get from me, Elmer Lee."

McCann shook his head slowly. "A clam. The man clams up on me."

"Captain Correctus clams up," Hohendorf said pointedly.

"Uh–oh," McCann said. "You know."

"Yes."

"She told you?"

"Yes."

"I asked her not to," McCann said reproachfully.

"There were special circumstances."

"Oh?"

"I would like to talk to you about them. And by the way, I am very sorry I nearly chewed off your head the other day."

McCann stopped walking. Hohendorf paused, too.

"Don't worry about it," McCann said. "I've already forgotten." He was looking at Hohendorf with great seriousness. "I detect something else lurking in that correct soul of yours."

"Bosnia," Hohendorf said.

"What about Bosnia?"

"I have an idea." Hohendorf glanced along the corridor. The others had turned a corner. "We had better get going or the boss will have to send someone to look, and he won't like that."

"You've got my attention," McCann said as they continued walking.

"I will tell you afterward. Let's see what this briefing is all about."

They were all very surprised to see who was waiting. Bowmaker and Thurson were there, in civilian clothes. Charles Buntline, immaculate as ever, was with them, and leaning heavily on his cane, in full uniform, was Jason. All four were standing.

The crews came to attention as they filed through the second of the two sets of secure doors.

"At ease, gentlemen," Jason told them. "Please take

your seats." He waited until they had done so before continuing. "I can see by the expressions on your faces this comes as a considerable surprise. And well it might."

Jason was standing next to the briefing dais. On the dais was a lectern, and behind it a large white screen had been lowered. Next to him was a small table holding a black telephone.

"We are about to show you a piece of film, gentlemen," Jason went on, "taken from a news broadcast." He picked up the phone. "Run it," he said into the instrument.

The lights dimmed and an obviously edited strip of film appeared on the screen. It began with a shot of an advancing tank, then cut to a group of people in a shattered town. The film ended, but the lights remained at a low intensity.

"You are all no doubt wondering what was so special about that small piece of film," Jason said. "Look again." Once more, he gave instructions into the phone.

Again, the film was shown.

"Anyone got any ideas?" Jason queried when it had ended for the second time.

Hohendorf had felt a tightening in his stomach, but said nothing. They all knew they had watched part of a broadcast about Bosnia.

"Bosnia?" McCann offered.

"Yes, Captain McCann, it is Bosnia. But that's not the answer. Look again."

For a third time, the film was run—and for a third time, they could see nothing special about it.

"No need to feel embarrassed, gentlemen," Jason told them. "The fact is, you're not meant to see anything special about this film. It means that one of the people you've just looked at has done the job perfectly. Even I was taken completely by surprise. And I had no idea until I was told." Jason gave further instructions by phone.

The film was run once more, except this time it was

frozen at a particular point. Then a bright blue square outline appeared on a section of the frozen frame, rapidly and repeatedly quartering off that section, continually enlarging it. Eventually it stopped, and the picture of someone with a black armband tied upside down filled the screen. The person was in the loose overalls of a combatant, face away from the camera.

"Anyone know who that is?" Jason asked.

There was no reply.

"Hold on to your seats, gentlemen. You are looking at Sergeant MacAllister."

There was an explosive chorus of, *"Mac?"*

Then McCann said, "You've got to be kidding . . . sir."

"Thank you, Mr. McCann."

"Sir."

"Major Morton?" Jason asked.

"I . . . I can't believe it, sir," Morton replied, confused. His heart was thumping. "It . . . doesn't look like her at all. Even from this angle, I should have recognized her. We worked together for a long time back in Washington."

"You're not supposed to recognize her—even someone like you who has worked with her in such proximity. That's what makes her so successful."

"I don't get it, sir. What's Mac doing in Bosnia?"

"I think I'd better let General Bowmaker explain."

The film was turned off and the screen raised. The lights returned to their normal brightness. Bowmaker climbed onto the dais and stood at the lectern.

"Gentlemen," he began, "you have been looking at the person you knew as Sergeant Mac. Her name is not Mac, and she is not a sergeant. Matter of fact, she outranks you all."

There was a collective gasp of astonishment.

"Yes," the general said dryly. "It took me by surprise, too. I am afraid I cannot tell you more about her, except that she is a very important and very brave person, indeed. That picture you just saw was a signal. It means she's in trouble, and needs to be pulled out. *Fast.* Or as fast as can be arranged."

"A helicopter?" someone suggested.

"It's not as easy as that," Bowmaker said. "In fact, the entire operation will be quite dangerous."

"Who the hell put her in such a position?" Stockmann asked, adding, " . . . General?"

"I know how you feel, Mr. Stockmann. I had those same feelings when I found out. Again, I'm afraid I am not at liberty to divulge any more than I shall be telling you. It's enough to say that getting her out is of the highest priority. The November unit has been selected as the best and only means by which to carry out this task. This will be a precise mission, running totally autonomously. We will not be engaged with any other NATO forces. We will be quick, and bring as little attention to ourselves as possible."

"And if that doesn't work?" Morton asked quietly.

"You can say good-bye to the person you once knew as Sergeant Mac," Bowmaker replied with candid brutality. "There are those who will do anything to capture her. We have intelligence reports that suggest she is already being hunted."

"Semper fi," Stockmann remarked softly.

"What?" McCann, who was next to him, whispered.

"You ignorant or something?" Stockmann hissed. *"Semper fidelis.* It's our motto, our code. Always faithful. Any marine knows that."

"I'm not a marine."

"Hey. What a surprise. I want in on this operation."

"Cut the whispers, gentlemen, and settle down," Bowmaker ordered. "This will be a ground-attack mission, with fighter cover. The attack will be precise, and *only* the designated targets are to be attacked. This is of vital importance. We do not want to stir up a hornet's nest out there. We're going to get Mac out, and whatever any of you may feel about the state of the UN's Bosnian operations, do *not* translate it into independent action. I give this warning because I know how individual crews in my own service feel. I have no doubt that some of you here share those same feelings."

Bowmaker's eyes raked them.

Hohendorf stared straight ahead, while McCann glanced surreptitiously at him.

"I do not have to explain to you," the general went on, "how quite unsympathetic both the wing commander and the air vice-marshal would be to such actions. Think hard about that when you're in Bosnian airspace. Forget the tank that looks like a fat target, or the aircraft that might be on a bombing run, or the artillery pieces, or troops advancing on some village or town. There are other forces to handle those problems. Your task is to get in, do the job, and get out. There will be those on the ground, as well as the rescue helicopter crew, who will be working in concert with you. Their lives, and Mac's, are at stake. Remember that above all else. She *must* be gotten out. Now, gentlemen, I shall hand you back to the wing commander. Take over, Wing Commander."

"Sir."

Jason removed his cap, wiping his forehead with the back of his hand as he did so. He put the cap back on.

"You will excuse me if I don't mount the dais," he told them. He tapped gently at his legs. "Gammy legs."

They laughed quietly with him.

"So, gentlemen, we've been assigned this problem. As the general has said, this is primarily a ground-attack mission, and I have already selected Mr. Hohendorf to carry it out." He paused. "Unless you'd rather not, Mr. Hohendorf. The selection is not set in stone. You all have the option of turning this down." He waited. No one spoke. "Thank you, gentlemen. To continue. The same aircraft that was used for the radar site attack—the updated Tornado IDS—is being readied, even as I speak. Yes, Mr. Hohendorf?"

Hohendorf had raised a hand slightly.

"Sir, may I speak with you after the briefing? Privately."

"Is that a vital requirement?"

"Yes, sir."

"Very well. I shall see you afterward."

"Thank you, sir." The other crews were giving him curious glances, but Hohendorf ignored them.

"Selby and McCann will be the first escort," Jason continued. "If—God forbid—there is trouble, Bagni and Stockmann will be backup, waiting on the airfield on quick reaction alert. Wingmen for this mission will be Cottingham and Christiansen in the second ASV."

There was a chorus of "sirs," some in protest.

Jason studied them. "I expected this might happen. My selections, while not set in stone as I've just indicated, are not liable to change without very good reason. Yes, Major Morton."

"Sir, Mac was with me from the beginning. I feel I ought to be there."

"Commendable, Major, but you're not yet ready. I don't send crews out for the privilege of getting killed. You have been invited to this briefing because of your past association, not to take part in the operation. I don't mean to sound harsh, but I assure you if I genuinely felt it was all right to have you aboard on this one, you'd be there. There will be other opportunities, I promise you. Pragmatism before emotions, Major."

"Yes, sir," Morton said, understanding Jason's decision, though clearly unhappy and disappointed.

"Your turn, Captain Stockmann," Jason said to the marine. "What's your reason?"

"Sir, Mac . . . whatever she is, she's still a marine. I'd kind of like to be up top giving her cover."

"Your job, Captain, is to be on the QRA backup. Again, I understand the sentiments, but they do not come into this. Mac deserves the best we can give her. It gives me a secure feeling to know you'll be there as backup, should the need arise."

Stockmann nodded. "Sir."

"Very good, Captain. Anyone else have anything to

say? No? Very well. You all know Mr. Buntline. He has some news that should focus your minds. If you'd be so kind, Mr. Buntline," Jason added.

"Thank you, Wing Commander."

Looking sleek, Buntline stepped forward and climbed the dais to stand at the lectern.

"I shan't cover old ground," he began, "but get straight to the point. As you've heard, Mac . . . let us continue to call her Mac . . . is on the run. The reasons do not concern you at this point. We have received intelligence reports that indicate she is being pursued by a formidable force. A convoy of six heavily armed APCs has been spotted . . . "

"Jeezus!" someone said. "*Six?*"

Buntline looked hard at McCann, but made no comment.

"These APCs," Buntline continued, "do not seem to be part of any massed assault by any of the Bosnian forces on specific objectives. It is therefore to be assumed that they're on a quite different mission. I should point out that this armored column is equipped with antiaircraft weaponry."

No one said anything.

Buntline glanced at Jason, who spoke into the phone. The lights were again dimmed and the screen lowered once more. A computer-generated map of Bosnia appeared on it, then a series of small red disks appeared on the map itself.

"If you look at the position of the disks," Buntline said, "you'll note that they form a recognizable pattern of the constellation we call the Big Dipper, upside down. Each disk represents a rendezvous point. At one of those, a helicopter is supposed to collect Mac. If she's working to schedule, she should already have reached the first. Because of our . . . er . . . difficulties, there was of course no helicopter waiting. She will then have headed for the second. If she has made it, again there won't be anyone waiting. She will thus try for the third, and so on.

"She will not be heading for any of these rendezvous points in linear order. That is to avoid anyone knowing the chronological position of the pickup points, should they by some mishap get to know of the pattern. It also allows her to approach from any direction. For example, if number one was here at the tail, the second would not be the next in line, but possibly this one here in the middle. The third is somewhere else, out of sequence. This was meant to work on the assumption that she would not be chased so comprehensively. We had allowed for a possible pursuit by Bosnian forces. This hunt, we are virtually certain, is being directed by elements in Moscow."

Buntline paused to allow that to sink in.

"We're assuming that the troops engaged in this task are specialists, from one of the Intelligence Services' own regiments. Like so many things that did not happen during all the wishful thinking about the 'new world order,' old habits did not vanish overnight but instead are returning with a vengeance. We have been monitoring the progress of the APC column. In the past few days, it has traveled this distance. Look at the screen."

On the screen, a bright-yellow line traced its way along a mountain road and stopped. Its path seemed perilously close to the Big Dipper pattern of the pickup points.

"Each of the APCs has a complement of ten—including the commander and gunner. However, despite the proximity of the track to the rendezvous points, it is actually some distance away and there's plenty of high ground in between. As long as those troopers remain with their vehicles, Mac is reasonably safe . . . so far. They have no specific idea where she is, nor where she's actually headed, or they would have concentrated on a single point. However, they have decided on a general area, based upon where she was last seen. Her real problem, unfortunately, is something else entirely. That."

"That" was a wide spread of orange dots that had

appeared like measles in a sweeping line, heading toward the APCs. The dots would eventually cross into the Big Dipper.

"Those dots, gentlemen, are more troops, experts in mountain warfare. They're conducting a wide sweep and will eventually make contact with the APCs. Mac is somewhere in the middle."

"Sweet Jesus." This time it was Morton who had spoken.

"I agree with you," Buntline remarked surprisingly.

"With respect, sir," Morton said, "who the hell was dumb enough to get her into this fix?"

Buntline glanced at Jason.

"Major," Jason said quietly.

"Sir." Morton shut up.

"We're here," Buntline went on coolly, "to get her *out* of her predicament. An awful lot of effort is being made to ensure it. The attack aircraft's task will be to stop both those troopers and the armored column."

Hohendorf cleared his throat. "Just the one aircraft?"

"Just the one aircraft, Mr. Hohendorf. You'll have to make every piece of ordnance count. Your aircraft will be loaded with the right stores for the job. The escort aircraft," Buntline continued smoothly, "will be there to ensure no . . . sympathetic pilots turn up unexpectedly in MIG-29s, or worse. We have reason to believe that such mercenaries may well be around, not necessarily with the knowledge or authority of the elected government in Moscow.

"If we carry out the job with the element of total surprise, we should be able to get in and out before they're able to call up any fighter cover they may have in the wings. So far, we have no reports that state precisely that they do have these fighters; but neither can we say unequivocally that they haven't. Despite this, all is not as desperate as it might seem for Mac."

"That's what he says," McCann muttered to Stockmann.

Buntline appeared not to hear. "She is a highly skilled

operative, and I suspect she may well not have bothered to try for the next rendezvous and has gone to ground somewhere, waiting for the mountain troops to roll over her position. She will then double back to make for the next point. The whole thing was contructed to allow for this eventuality."

"That was for Bosnian troops, sir," Stockmann reminded him. "Not these . . . specialists."

"She can cope. One last point." Buntline waited while new symbology appeared on the screen. "We have discovered that a Bosnian command center has been positioned here." An arrow appeared in the same area, marking a spot that was in a direct line, west to east, to the APC column. "It belongs to the people who have been doing all the attacking in this nasty little war. It's along your route, Mr. Hohendorf. You are to leave it strictly alone, no matter how tempting. As General Bowmaker has said, there are other forces to deal with it if necessary, and you will not engage . . . I repeat . . . *will not engage* the Bosnian Serb forces. Save your weapons for the job at hand. Got that?"

"Yes, Mr. Buntline," Hohendorf said dutifully, face deadpan. "Thanks for pointing it out. I might have made a mistake otherwise. What do I do if they fire at us?"

Buntline looked at him suspiciously, then looked toward Jason, as if expecting to find some kind of answer. Jason was stony-faced, as were the other aircrew except McCann, who was trying hard not to smile.

"Try to avoid areas where there is a concentration of antiaircraft defenses. You will be furnished with the positions of known sites."

"Known sites, sir? Some of these things are mobile. By the time we've got the information, they may not be there anymore."

Buntline gave Hohendorf another suspicious look. "We shall endeavor to make it as up-to-date as possible, Mr. Hohendorf. Does that make you happy?"

"Not a word I would have used, sir."

"Well, yes. Thank you, Mr. Hohendorf. I'll now return you to the wing commander."

He stepped down after a brief nod to Jason.

The screen went back up and the lights were again brought back to normal.

"Would you like to say anything, sir?" Jason asked of Thurson.

"You carry on, Christopher."

"Sir. That's all for now, gentlemen," Jason said to his crews. "Back here in two hours for a complete briefing on the route, timings, and expected weather. You will be deploying to Italy—the start point of the mission—in two days. Oh, yes . . . not surprisingly, you're all confined to base and are to make no calls discussing your coming departure. As far as your various loved ones are concerned, nothing out of the ordinary is happening. I'll see you now, Mr. Hohendorf."

"Yes, sir."

They all stood and waited for the senior officers to leave first.

As Jason stood by for him to pass, Buntline said, "A word with you, also in private, if I may, Wing Commander."

"I'll get Hohendorf to wait. . . . "

"No, no. See him first. I can wait."

"Very well, Mr. Buntline."

Jason led Hohendorf to a small office where they could talk privately.

"Well, Axel?" Jason began. "What's the problem?"

"Wolfie Flacht, sir," Hohendorf replied.

"What's wrong with him? He's one of our best back-seaters. Sometimes it's a toss-up who's best . . . he, or the turbulent McCann; though I consider McCann to be slightly ahead."

"Nothing's wrong with Wolfie. But I'd like to request a change of crew."

Jason, leaning against a desk to ease the pressure on

his wounded legs, looked keenly at him. "I'm waiting."

"I'd like to use Elmer Lee, sir, for this mission. He used to be on Phantoms, both in the air-to-air and air-to ground-roles. . . . "

"Flacht was on ground-attack and naval-attack Tornados on your old *Marineflieger* unit," Jason reminded him, "before he came here. He was picked because his performance convinced me he belonged with the November program. Perhaps you'd better tell me the real reason."

Hohendorf paused, searching for the right words. "Sir, for the attack on that radar site in the Sahara, we temporarily pulled my former *Marineflieger* backseater, Johann Ecker, from his squadron for the job. We had flown together on Interdictor Strike Tornados for a long time, which was why you sent for him."

"You've not got that track record with McCann."

"No, sir. . . . "

"Spill it, Axel. Say what you really mean. Even if I disagree, it will go no further."

"Wolfie has a wife and two small children," Hohendorf said quickly, as if afraid the words would not come out unless he did so. "On the mission before the desert strike, he was seriously injured and could have died. The nature of this mission makes me feel . . . "

"All right, Axel. I get the drift. Explain this to me: How do you think Selby would take my removal of his navigator to pass him on to you? He and McCann may appear to be like cat and dog, but splitting them would not be a very good idea operationally. Like Flacht and yourself, they think as one in combat."

"He could have Wolfie for the mission. As you've just said, sir, Wolfie is as good."

"Am I reading this correctly? You want Flacht to take the escort role, presumably to keep him from possible danger from the ground defenses."

"Yes, sir."

"Was he wounded by ground defenses that last time?"

Knowing that Jason was well aware of the circumstances, Hohendorf said, "No, sir. It was an air-to-air
near miss."

"Quite. And the subjects themselves? How would they
feel? Would Flacht thank you for mollycoddling him?
And would McCann enjoy being dragooned into your
backseat?"

Hohendorf found he could not give an answer,
although he felt certain McCann would go for the idea.
Wolfie was another matter altogether. Wolfie would feel
slighted. The only way it could work would be for it to
appear to be an operational change.

Hohendorf found he was being keenly studied by
Jason.

"Do you wish to opt out of the mission?" Jason asked.

"Absolutely not, sir! I want to do it."

"But you're anxious about Flacht."

"Yes, sir."

"And you're hoping I'll make an operational decision
to switch him."

Hohendorf said nothing.

"Mr. Hohendorf, I'm not sure I like being manipulated
by my officers."

Again, Hohendorf chose prudence and kept his peace.

"Mr. Flacht is well aware of the risks of his profession," Jason said in a mild but firm voice. "He would not
be here if he didn't, and I very much doubt he would
take kindly to your trying to protect him in this manner.
I understand your motives, but if I chose to translate my
own personal feelings into action, none of you would
ever go into combat. That would not make me much of a
military commander, would it?"

"No, sir."

"Thank you, Axel."

"Sir."

Hohendorf went out.

Jason did not move for some moments. He rubbed his
legs thoughtfully.

"Something's just occurred to me," McCann said as he walked away from Alpha with the others.

"Take cover!" Selby announced loudly. "Elmer Lee's having one of his turns. He's doing some thinking."

McCann ignored him. "Don't you guys reckon Buntline made a production of telling us about that communication, command and control center for a reason? I think he wants Axel to take it out as well."

"Another of your direct lines to the powers-that-be?"

"I'm serious, guys. Think about it."

"I have thought about it," Selby told him. "Now you tell me why you believe Axel was being set up."

"Not being set up exactly . . . more like encouraged to pick a target of opportunity."

"That's your big thought for the day, is it?"

McCann was unperturbed by Selby's pointed comment. "Wait and see, my man. Wait and see. Bet you we get the full coordinates of the triple-C target."

"So that Axel knows what to avoid."

"Oh, sure." McCann was skepticism itself. "Speaking of which . . . What do you think Axel wants to see the boss about?"

"I thought you had the direct line. You tell us."

McCann saw that they were smiling, as if at a secret joke.

"You guys are really funny. You know that?"

Hohendorf made his way slowly along the corridor. He found it quite ironic that they'd be going to Bosnia after all. He could have made his request to speak to Jason less publicly, but that would have felt even more awkward, giving a stronger impression of going behind Flacht's back. There was no easy way to get Wolfie transferred to Selby's aircraft, even though it would be a temporary arrangement.

As he walked, Hohendorf found he could not get Zunica Paic's words out of his mind. They were echoing repeatedly.

"When there is need for action, they have *meetings*." "Anything to delay . . . " "I am not on holiday. I am going back to hell." "When this is all over, no matter how it ends, we will never forgive you. Never."

Her words went around and around in his head.

Every day, the news that came out of the brutalized country shamed him: the lies of signed ceasefires; the open deceit; the sheer nastiness of it all.

"*I* will never forgive us," he said softly.

Jason had made his way painfully to where Thurson, Bowmaker, and Buntline were waiting for him in his office in the Alpha building. It was one of his many offices on the base. They were standing as he entered.

They remained standing, watching, as he seated himself behind his desk. He removed his cap, wiped at his forehead, then placed the cap on the desk.

"Those legs giving you hell, Wing Commander?" Bowmaker asked solicitously.

"Comes and goes, sir. At this moment, it's one of the comings."

"If you'd prefer . . . "

"If you'll pardon the interruption, General, I'm fine. Really. No need to worry. Can I organize some tea? Or would you prefer coffee?"

"I'll have the tea. I'm very particular about coffee. No offense meant."

Jason smiled tiredly. "Understood, sir. Mr. Buntline?"

"Tea will be fine, thank you."

"Sir?" Jason said to Thurson.

"I'll join you all."

Jason nodded and picked up a phone to order. He'd obviously had someone on standby, because almost immediately a female corporal entered with four mugs of tea.

The November logo was on each mug. She handed them around. They each nodded their thanks, and she went out again—after an anxiously caring glance at Jason.

"They all worried about you like that?" Bowmaker observed.

"They tend to overdo it, sir."

Bowmaker took a swallow of his tea and shook his head slowly. "I think not. I know you and your outfit pretty well by now, Wing Commander. Your officers and enlisted personnel hold you in high regard. All the more reason why we can't afford to lose you. I know all about your tussle with the minister." Bowmaker glanced at Buntline as he said that. Buntline's expression was neutral. "So how do you think your crews have taken the prospect of going into Bosnian airspace?" he finished.

"They're keen, especially as Mac's involved."

"And what do you feel about our keeping the knowledge of her true identity from them?"

"My crews are all highly responsible people, sir . . . even—contrary to outward appearances—McCann. However, I do appreciate the operational and intelligence reasons. I therefore have no problem with it."

"Good. I can further tell you that it is virtually certain that Mac *will* be executed if she is caught. There was no exaggeration at the briefing. If she's fit to travel, they'll undoubtedly take her back to Moscow. But the end result will be the same. There are too many scores to settle with her over there."

"We'll help you get her out, sir. We'll do our very best."

"I know you will."

"I only wish that we in the West had sorted the Bosnian problem out right at the very beginning. I think we'll still end up getting seriously involved, except it will cost more in casualties and could spread."

"It's a nightmare that keeps me awake nights. Decision-makers who can't make decisions, plus, in the States, a sort of ingrained national aversion to bodybags."

"I can understand, sir . . . but that won't sort out Bosnia."

"Tell me about it," Bowmaker agreed grimly.

"And what did Hohendorf want?" Thurson now asked as Bowmaker finished.

"A change of crew, sir."

They all stared at him.

"What?" Thurson said, voicing what the three were obviously thinking.

"There's a problem?" Bowmaker inquired.

"Not as such. Hohendorf wants to swap Flacht for McCann."

"Why? I thought your crews were so glued to each other they're like Siamese twins."

"Operationally, they are. But Hohendorf's reasons are not operational. He's worried about Flacht getting hurt and wants him with Selby on the escort duty, with McCann as replacement for the ground-attack mission. If you'll remember, sir, Flacht narrowly escaped death during that fight over the Mediterranean."

Bowmaker nodded. "I remember."

"Hohendorf appears to think that this mission is so dangerous, Flacht might get mortally wounded this time. He's worried about Flacht's wife and kids."

"What could happen to Flacht can happen to McCann," Thurson reasoned.

"Hohendorf obviously does not think so. I believe he thinks Flacht came too close for comfort."

"Flacht's a professional," Thurson remarked in a voice that was edged with a touch of impatience. "He knows the risks, as we all do. As does his wife. Did she make any attempt to try and stop his flying after that incident?"

"On the contrary, sir. She went out of her way to ensure I did not think that of her. I believe she told Hohendorf if her Wolfie couldn't fly, he would not be the same man she married."

"Damned good woman," Thurson said approvingly.

"So what are you going to do, Wing Commander?"

Buntline asked. His eyes seemed to be saying more as he looked at Jason.

"I told him his request was denied."

"But?"

"I have given it some more thought," Jason admitted, "but not for the same reasons. I need Hohendorf to have absolute concentration on that attack run. I can't have him wondering whether he's going to make his back-seater's wife a widow, and his children orphans. I'm quite certain that once this mission is over, Hohendorf will lose what I believe even *he* thinks is an unreasonable fear."

"But?" Buntline repeated.

"I'm remembering a young trainee pilot," Jason began, "who one day had an unreasonable fear. He was tasked with a solo cross-country navigation exercise and for some reason would not climb into the aircraft he'd been assigned. He'd checked and double-checked it, then pronounced it unserviceable. The crew chief insisted the aircraft was fully serviceable. But the pilot would not sign the 700—that's the form that a pilot signs to say he accepts the aircraft as fully cleared for flight—despite another complete check in the company of the crew chief."

Jason paused as the sounds of ASV engines, which had been whistling at taxi, suddenly exploded into a powerful roar as four aircraft hurled themselves down the main runway. Despite the double-glazing of the windows, the multiple thunder seemed to envelop the entire world. The noise faded quickly as the afterburners were cut and the aircraft rushed for the upper reaches of the sky.

"The pilot's instructor was called," he continued. "*He* pronounced the aircraft serviceable. The young pilot insisted it was u/s and, risking severe disciplinary action, refused as respectfully as he could to accept the aircraft. Fortunately for him, the instructor had faith in his instincts. The instructor took it upon himself to support the young pilot, found him another aircraft, and the exercise went off without a hitch. The rejected aircraft was virtually stripped down, but nothing was found wrong with it.

"When it next went up, it was flown by a pilot with operational experience. Halfway into its flight, it disappeared from the radar screens. There had been no transmission from the pilot to indicate that anything was going wrong. The wreckage was later found scattered across a large area of mountainside. The subsequent investigation eventually discovered that the controls had unaccountably seized."

In the hushed silence that followed, Thurson said, "I can vouch for that incident. Wing Commander Jason was the pilot in question, and I the instructor."

"I shall grant Hohendorf's wish," Jason told the startled Bowmaker and Buntline, "but not for the reasons he might think."

"As always, Christopher," Thurson said after a while, "I shall leave these operational decisions to you. The general and I are going over to the mess. Mr. Buntline?"

"I'll join you soon. I'd like a brief chat with the wing commander."

There were questions in Thurson's eyes, but he said, "Very well. See you there."

Jason looked at Buntline with curiosity as the two men left. "I'm intrigued, Mr. Buntline."

"Wing Commander," Buntline commenced, "when this whole November program began, you and I did not always see eye-to-eye. I have since . . . modified my stance, as you know. However, there are those who remain hostile to the entire project."

"I know of at least one," Jason said with grim memory, "and he's not on the outside."

"I believe we're thinking of the same person. Watch your step. He's after your head."

"A warning, Mr. Buntline?"

"Friendly caution from someone who is now firmly in

your corner, albeit with a certain degree of self-interest."
Buntline was quite shameless in his admission. "It was
suggested that I . . . er, find some way of smearing you,
to encourage your subsequent resignation."

Jason stared at him. "You what?"

Buntline told him about the minister's suggestion.

"He'd go that far?" Jason asked, astounded.

"He's an ambitious man. A wing commander like you
is an irritant that requires removal. Of course, if put on
the spot, he would deny everything. He didn't actually
say I should do anything, you see, and would almost certainly insist I had misinterpreted his words . . . assuming
he would even admit to having uttered them in the first
place."

Jason rested his arms on his legs, as if protecting
them from further injury.

"The people who caused this," he said to Buntline in a
voice made husky by pain, "are working against the
interests of the Alliance, and the West in general. You
know more about them than I do, since they are more
within your field of operations than mine. *They* want the
November program killed off. And despite the budget
ax-wielders, I did not expect to have to watch out for a
minister as well . . . in my own backyard, so to speak.
Now that wretched man wants to involve Antonia, and
the air vice-marshal."

"When people play for these stakes, they take no
prisoners."

"Thanks for the warning."

"We do need you, Wing Commander."

"Who's 'we'?"

"Ahh. . . . that would be telling. And say nothing about
this to the air vice-marshal. Leave the minister to me."

7

The Tornado IDS was already in an advanced state of preparation. The ground crews were all over it, making final adjustments to its airframe and systems. It was no longer in the desert pink colors that had been employed for the strike on the radar site in the Sahara, and was now sporting the mottled olive-green camouflage that was favored for flying over the European landscape. However, there were subtle additions to the color scheme which took into consideration the particular features of the Yugoslavian topographical background, and which would thus allow the aircraft to blend more successfully with its expected surroundings.

This particular IDS had already been substantially upgraded in preparation for that first desert strike, and was far removed from the standard version normally used by the squadrons of Germany, Italy, and the UK's Royal Air Force. Now that it had become a permanent addition to the November fleet, ongoing upgrades had become a feature of its service life.

Its engines were now more powerful, though not up to the standard of the Tornado ASVs, which were virtually redesigned aircraft. However, it now carried some of the more advanced systems used by the November aircraft, and its weapon-carrying hard points had been modified to enable it to go into battle with a greater, more varied load than was possible with the standard IDS. It had also been modified to carry four of the lighter and smaller, but highly advanced, Krait short-range air-to-air missiles for self defense, in place of the standard fit of two AIM-9 Sidewinders.

Its passive defensive aids had also been augmented. Conformal blisters on its lower fuselage not only allowed it the greater weapon load, but also incorporated a tube on either side that contained twenty-four each of the ASV's radar and infrared decoys. These were in addition to the normal chaff and flares. The radar decoys were extremely small, bomblike canisters. When ejected, stabilizing fins would spring outward and a small parachute would billow. The decoy would then proceed to broadcast powerful radar pulses which blinded a radar-homing missile to the presence of the intended target aircraft.

The infrared decoy sacrificed itself in much the same way, except its method was to turn itself into a superhot fireball to tempt an IR missile. With a full war load and brimming with fuel, the heavily modified November IDS still outperformed even the most up-to-date of its sister aircraft in normal squadron service. The November version of the IDS was now designated the IDS(E), the E for "enhanced."

Two further IDS's had now been acquired to cover any attrition suffered, and were being converted to the same level.

Hohendorf had decided to visit the aircraft shelter where the IDS for the mission was being worked on and had been inspecting it when McCann turned up. McCann stepped carefully over a fat power cable that snaked its way along the concrete floor. He stopped by the cockpit ladder. Hohendorf peered down at him from the front cockpit.

"Been looking for you," McCann called above the hum and whir of machinery as the ground crew labored.

"You've found me," Hohendorf said. "Come up, if the crew chief will let you."

The senior noncommissioned officer commanding the engineering team at work was approaching.

"Okay if I go up, Chief?" McCann asked.

"Quite okay, sir. They've finished in the back pocket."

"Thanks." McCann climbed the ladder, then eased himself into the backseat. He settled in, making himself comfortable as he looked about him. "This is sure bigger than the old rhino pit, but it brings back memories of my mudslinging days. You know, I wouldn't mind going on this joyride with you. Think Wolfie would let me?"

"What about Mark?" Hohendorf inquired calmly, as if this were the first time he'd considered the possibility. "He might have something to say about that."

"Oh, yeah, sure. But I can handle him. What about you? Would you let me?"

Hohendorf continued to speak calmly. "The boss would have to sanction it."

"Yeah," McCann agreed unenthusiastically. "He'd never okay that."

"You never know. . . . "

The public address system interrupted them. "Mr. Hohendorf, Mr. Flacht," it announced in a female voice, "Mr. Selby, Mr. McCann, Mr. Bagni, Mr. Stockmann, Mr. Cottingham, and Mr. Christiansen, to Alpha. I repeat . . . Mr. Hohendorf . . . "

"The two hours are not up yet, are they?" McCann said. He glanced at his watch as he began to climb out.

"No," Hohendorf answered, waiting for McCann to make it down the ladder before climbing out to follow.

"So what the hell's happened?" McCann queried as Hohendorf joined him.

"We'll soon know. Thanks, Chief," Hohendorf said to the ground crew NCO as they hurried away.

"Sir."

The crew chief returned his attention to the exacting supervision of the work being done on the IDS.

Jason was on his own, waiting for them as they filed in expectantly. He did not waste time.

"I have decided to make a slight operational change of crews," he began as soon as they sat down. "Every now and then, it's judicious to rotate crews to give you the experience of working with another pilot or navigator under combat conditions. As you have all flown with altered crews during routine flights, this won't be such a shock. Mr. Flacht, you were with Mr. Cottingham when you both flew escort for the desert strike. As you know, despite being bedridden at the time because of my . . . er, misadventure, I was very pleased with your performances."

"Thank you, sir."

"Nothing to thank me for. It's what I expect of my crews. How would you feel about doing the escort again? This time with Mark Selby."

Hohendorf made sure he showed no reaction. Jason was not looking at him, but was switching attention between Flacht and Selby. However, Hohendorf could sense McCann glancing surreptitiously at him.

Flacht said, "I'm happy if Mark is, sir." Then Flacht glanced at Hohendorf to see how he was taking it.

"Mark?" Jason asked Selby.

"As you know, sir, Wolfie and I have flown practice sessions before. We work well together. I'm happy to do the escort with him."

Jason turned to Hohendorf and McCann, his expression giving nothing away. "Axel? Elmer Lee? How do you two feel about doing the ground attack together?"

"Well, sir," they both began.

Hohendorf paused, motioning to McCann to go first.

"Be interesting, sir," McCann said, unusually succint.

"Interesting," Jason murmured, as if testing the word. "I see. And you, Mr. Hohendorf? Do you also find the prospect interesting?"

"I have every confidence in Elmer Lee, sir."

Jason nodded, eyes fixed upon Hohendorf. "Good. Intensive simulator sessions for you both, then at least one flight in the IDS before you leave for Italy. Detailed briefing on the mission begins in half an hour. You had all better remain in the building. That is all, gentlemen."

They stood up as he left; then there was a pause as everyone came to terms with the changes.

"I'll be damned," McCann eventually remarked. He was looking at Hohendorf. "I'll be damned," he repeated.

"Say that often enough," Selby told him, "and you will be."

"Man, it's weird."

"What do you mean?"

"Don't get mad. Okay?"

"What are you talking about, McCann?"

"Are you two guys going to talk to each other in questions all day?" Cottingham asked dryly. "Or do we get to know what's going on?"

"I was just in the shelter with Axel," McCann said to them, "checking out the IDS. No. *He* was checking out the IDS, and I just sort of turned up and said it would be neat to do the attack run with him."

"'Neat,'" Stockmann mimicked, his huge teeth grinning at McCann.

"Yeah. But we reckoned the boss wouldn't go for it. So what happens? He calls us here to tell us *he* made a change. Weird, huh? I must have wished it to him."

"Wished it," Selby scoffed. "What are you? Some kind of medicine man? No, no. Don't tell me. You're telepathic. Sometimes, Elmer Lee . . . " Selby, as he was driven to on such occasions, shook his head in defeat. "Sometimes."

"Hey. Laugh all you want. These things happen. When we're up there, we know what the other's thinking."

"That's because I know you too well, Elmer Lee." Selby gave a loud sigh. "Too bloody well."

Flacht, eyes searching, eased Hohendorf to one side. "And you?" he asked quietly. "Are you all right with this?"

Hohendorf nodded. "Yes. Just watch yourself up there."

"Okay."

They all made their way out. Hohendorf was last, and Selby hung back until the others were out of earshot.

"Did you put the boss up to it?" he asked Hohendorf.

Hohendorf fixed him with a level gaze. "Are you suggesting that *I* give the wing commander orders? Or that I can influence his decisions?"

"Of course not, but . . . "

"Just you look after Wolfie."

"Of course I will. I know he means a lot to you."

"And Elmer Lee? Does he mean a lot to you?"

Selby thought about it. "Bring that Kansas City ape back in one piece."

"I'll look after him. But it would help if once in a while you let him know you like having him as your back-seater. Don't be so stiff-upper-lip British all the time. There is nothing wrong in letting someone know you appreciate what he's doing."

Again, Selby seemed to give the idea some thought. "Actually, I've decided to have him as my best man," he said at last, surprising Hohendorf. "When Kim and I manage to fix a date, that is."

Hohendorf grinned. "That is one of the best ideas you've had. Have you told him yet?"

"You've got to be joking. And don't you tell him. He'd be impossible to live with."

"I think I agree with you."

They both laughed as they went out, the latent tensions between them forgotten for the time being.

Morton was sitting in the mess anteroom when he'd heard the call for the crews on the loudspeaker system.

He found himself wishing his name had been among the chosen.

He sensed, rather than saw, someone standing behind him. He turned his head to look, then leaped to attention.

"General. Sir!"

"Relax, Major," Bowmaker said. "May I join you?"

"Yes, sir." Morton did not relax.

"Relax, Chuck," Bowmaker repeated, "and sit down."

"Sir." Morton sat down again as Bowmaker took an armchair next to his.

"I guess you're wishing you were going with the others," Bowmaker remarked, studying Morton closely. "You feel because it's Mac out there, you ought to be doing something."

"Yes, sir, I do."

"Let me tell you something, Major. Wing Commander Jason is one of those rare officers—a commander who is also highly intelligent. If he says you're not ready . . . " Bowmaker paused for effect, " . . . then you're not ready. There's no argument."

"Yes, sir. Understood."

"Good." Bowmaker was still looking closely at Morton. "What are your feelings about Mac?"

The question was so unexpected, Morton floundered for some moments. "Well, sir . . . er . . . well . . . "

"That answers my question."

"We . . . we never fraternized, sir."

"I didn't think you had." Bowmaker touched him briefly on the shoulder. "We'll do our damned best to get her back." He stood up.

Morton stood with him. "Thank you, sir."

"You like it here?"

"Very much, sir."

"Then you'll be pleased to know the wing commander believes you're shaping up to be one of his top men. He reckons you'll be up there with Hohendorf, Selby, and the others."

"Well, sir, right now it doesn't feel like it."

"You'll make it. Just hang in there."

"Yes, sir."

"And don't worry about Mac."

"I'll try not to, sir."

"I'll see you around, Major."

"Sir." Morton saluted him.

The Bosnian mountains

She had made the burrow between two outcrops of rock among the trees. It had been so well constructed that only the closest of scrutiny would betray its presence. Her one anxiety had been the woodland animals. She'd hoped there would be enough time for them to acclimatize to her presence before the first of those hunting her came on the scene. She had remained within her hiding place until at last it seemed the wildlife had become accustomed to her presence, deciding she was just another animal that meant them no harm. She had also ensured she'd left no telltale evidence of recently disturbed vegetation.

She intended to remain in the burrow until the immediate danger had passed. That meant no hunting for food, so as not to leave tracks for the searching troops to spot. Among her remaining supplies were some hard biscuits, and her water bottle had been refilled in a mountain stream a good distance from her hiding place. She would live on biscuits and water until she could move on.

She had sufficient weaponry: the Dragunov rifle, currently taken apart; a Heckler and Koch submachine gun with a silencer; a big and powerful 9mm Stechkin APS automatic with a twenty-round magazine, also with its own silencer; and a large hunting knife that looked almost like a small sword. As if that were not enough, she also carried six high-explosive grenades. She had ammunition for all the weapons, certainly sufficient to make whoever had come after her pay very dearly for the privilege. They would not take her alive. She knew only too well what she could expect if that were to happen.

At least the burrow was not damp. She had lined it with dry earth, and had picked a spot that did not have water seepage. She could hear sounds outside the burrow. When they stopped, she would know something had changed and that alien presences were around. The woodland creatures were her alarm system.

The troopers had moved in a wide sweep that stretched for miles. Split into paired teams, they communicated only rarely with each search unit and the lead APC—and then only for the briefest of times, to minimize electronic eavesdropping. They gave no identifiable indications of their own positions, and contact was established only to communicate success or failure within the sector currently being searched. The sectors had been parceled off into grid squares, and were identified by letters and a number. So far, no one had reported a sighting.

They moved inexorably along the designated search route.

The sudden quiet of the wood alerted her. She had been dozing. Very carefully, she picked up the Heckler and Koch, easing it forward so that it pointed at the concealed entrance of her burrow.

They had arrived.

She knew she could not be attacked from any direction except straight ahead, dug as she was into the mountain slope. The entrance to the burrow itself was just wide enough for her to get through. She'd had to put her gear in first, and had then crawled backward into it. She knew this had left her without an effective escape route, but that had not been a requirement when she'd constructed the hide. She was confident that the entrance had been effectively concealed, and rain the previous night had helped make the general area seem as if no one had been there for months.

She heard a soft footfall, then quiet voices. She listened intently. Two of them, quite close, speaking Russian.

They stopped.

Unconsciously, she slowed her breathing until it was almost as if respiration had ceased.

They were utterly silent, and she began to wonder if she'd not been as careful as she'd thought, after all. Had she forgotten something obvious? A twig broken the wrong way? A boot imprint that had not been washed out by the rain? A crumbled biscuit?

The silence of the search troopers was unnerving. They were highly skilled trackers, she knew. They were behaving exactly as she would have. She knew that although they were not moving, their heads were turning, eyes tracking slowly, hunting out anomalies. Then she heard a familiar sound, and wanted to laugh with relief.

One of them was urinating.

It was strange, she thought, how something as simple as the call of nature could make even the most professional temporarily vulnerable. Mindful of this, she had ensured that her own calls of nature were timed to avoid putting herself at risk. She could effectively prolong the time for her own requirements.

As the man continued to urinate in what sounded like an unending stream, she remembered how she had once slipped past a sentry to disable an outlying signal relay station that had been so remote it had not been considered necessary to surround it with a fence. She had arrived during the early hours of the morning and had spent all day at a distance of half a kilometer, studying the sentry pattern and marking the changes of shift.

At nightfall she had gone close, and had again waited. One of the sentries had been caught short, and after shifty glances in the direction from which he'd expected the guard commander to approach on routine inspection, had left his post to answer the call. This had given her sufficient time to slip past, plant a timed explosive in the power supply junction box, and make good her escape. She had been at least a kilometer away by the time the explosion had come.

The sentry had literally been caught with his pants down.

The urination had stopped.

She listened intently. No movement, and no talking. What were they waiting for?

Then one of them spoke. "Good mother!" he exclaimed in disgust. "Your piss stinks. If she's within a kilometer of here, she'll smell you."

"You think your piss is perfume?"

They laughed coarsely.

The urinater was talking again, clearly to his radio. "Nothing," he was saying, and gave the sector identification. "Area clear. We're moving on."

A stench had begun to seep into the hide, and her nose began to twitch with the acridity of it. She forced herself to remain in control. They had still not moved.

Had it all been a trick? Were they trying to flush her out? And what of the radio call? Had that, too, been for her benefit?

She remained quite still as the stench became overpowering.

Then movement. They were definitely leaving.

She did not shift a muscle. The smell of the man's urine was almost choking her and tears welled in her eyes as she fought to control her reactions to the sharpness of it.

She waited until long after they would have gone a safe distance from her—if they'd really gone on. And still she waited. Then the sounds she'd wanted to hear returned.

The woodland noises were back. The troopers had definitely gone. She was free from any immediate danger.

Knightsbridge, London

Antonia Thurson was the type of young woman that men walked into lampposts for. At five feet six, her slender form seemed taller. It was the way in which she carried herself and the purposeful yet sensuous manner of her walk that were responsible. She was also someone of astounding beauty. Her eyes were a powerful violet and her dark hair, usually worn in a single plait down her back, was today hanging free about her almost translucent face.

A simple white blouse of pure silk was complemented by a two-piece outfit of jacket and short skirt in pale olive-green. Her tights were so sheer they gave the impression that her long legs were bare. Moderate-heeled matching shoes were on feet she sometimes considered too big, though in fact they were not. Her lightweight coat hung open. She walked firmly, her shoes hitting the ground in a way that announced her approach like a calling card. She knew she looked good and was comfortable with it.

Jason had known her when she was a child, and had watched her grow into a gawky teenager. During his time as a young pilot being coached by her father, she used to teasingly call him "uncle." Her metamorphosis into womanhood had induced a kind of shock. He'd first seen the new Antonia at the inauguration ball given in honor of the first November squadron to be declared operational. It had been a memorable evening.

Thurson had deliberately not warned him of her coming, and he'd been totally captivated by her. Afraid of becoming involved and of his own feelings, he had somehow managed to avoid her as much as possible afterward. The pressure of his duties had given him the safe excuse. They had thus seen each other only rarely and fleetingly ever since.

She had long since decided, however—even as a budding teenager—that Jason would be hers one day, no matter how long it took. She was musing upon this thought as she walked past the gleaming display windows of the expensive Knightsbridge stores.

Despite the time of year, it was a mild London day and she felt warm and cozy, happily preoccupied with her thoughts. It therefore came as a rude awakening when something flashed in her face. When her eyes eventually recovered from the assault, they focused on the snout of a camera, and the seedy-looking man behind it.

"Miss Thurson," the man began. "Is it true about you and Wing Commander Jason?"

The violet eyes seemed to grow round and catch fire. Twin spots of pink appeared on her cheeks. Her spine seemed to snap erect as she stopped before him. He should have read the warning signs.

"What did you say?" She had spoken so softly, he actually leaned forward to hear. Which put him well within reach.

"Wing Commander Jason. I believe he's doing some secret stuff and is having an affair . . . "

Her fist took him completely by surprise, landing with astonishing force upon his nose. He staggered back, hooting in pain. He dropped the camera. It fell, lens-first. Something tinkled alarmingly, and bright shards appeared on the pavement.

"You bitch!" he screamed at her, covering his face with his hands. "You broke my nose!" Then he saw the camera. "My camera! *You broke my camera!*"

"Which is it?" she asked sweetly. "Your camera? Or your nose?"

This enraged him further. The hands reached out for her. "You think it's funny, do you? You fucking little tart! I'll show you!"

He came at her, face now contorted with pain and fury.

She did not move. She watched him, then her right leg

flashed upward. It stopped when her shoe collided solidly with his crotch.

He gave a strangled howl. The hands were moving again, flying uselessly now toward this new source of excruciating pain. He fell to his knees, gasping for air, then rolled from side to side, drawing his legs up protectively, seeking urgent relief.

People were gathering, but they were looking at her with sympathy. Some were actually smiling.

"My father warned me about people like you," she said loudly. "Cramp in his brains," she added conversationally to the onlookers, then stepped over him and walked on.

"Bitch!" he gasped. "Bitch! Only doing my bloody job!"

They looked down at him and laughed, and wondered if she was someone famous.

Briefing room Alpha, November base

The very detailed briefing was almost over. McCann had been proved right. The precise coordinates of the communication, command, and control center had been clearly emphasized, though avoiding it at all costs was also stressed.

Apart from the various briefing officers, only Jason of the more senior ranks was in attendance. As for Bowmaker, Thurson, and Buntline, they were on their way back to London in the executive jet that had brought them.

The met officer had begun to wind down his weather briefing of the target area for the next seven days. "Of course, gentlemen, this general forecast does not include local variations. These will be given to you in Italy, on the day of the flight itself. Thank you." He stepped down from the dais.

"That's some kind of code," McCann announced in a stage whisper. "What he really means is that we can expect some shit stuff in those mountains."

"Zip it," Selby whispered back at him.

Jason cleared his throat warningly.

They both got the message, and said nothing further.

Just as before, Jason did not climb the dais. "You have it all, gentlemen. You each know what is expected of you. An ATARS aircraft will be on hand, though out of area, to give you secure datalink updates of the target situation. We shall also have it onscreen here at November One. You can, of course, go autonomous should tactical considerations demand it. In which case the attack aircraft and its escort will continue to communicate via secure datalink as and when needed."

The ATARS aircraft Jason had mentioned carried the advanced tactical air reconnaissance systems that could "see" what was happening on the ground from a distance that would put it well out of danger, from either fighters or antiaircraft weaponry. This enabled it to supply the necessary images to the IDS and ASVs. These would then be enhanced by the Tornados' own images and in some cases compared, to give a real-time assessment of the tactical situation. The same APC seen by both systems, if on the move even for the briefest of moments, would have its past, current, and several options of projected positions displayed onscreen. A choice of solutions would be presented to the IDS, even as the aircraft was on its attack run.

In the case of the ASVs, they would be presented with the positions of the most threatening antiaircraft batteries, and thus could seek to avoid them. For Hohendorf and McCann in the IDS, making their run on the target, that option would be decidedly limited.

"I shall repeat, Mr. Hohendorf," Jason was saying. "Tempting though it may be, the C^3 target must *not* be attacked. We don't want to upset the UN, do we?"

"The *UN?*" someone queried in a hushed voice. "What's that?"

There was a general rustle of subdued laughter.

"That will do, gentlemen," Jason told them firmly. "I

do understand your feelings, but let's keep them to ourselves, shall we? One of the simulators has been configured for IDS operations," he continued to Hohendorf. "You and McCann are booked for long sessions in it."

"When do we start, sir?" McCann asked.

"Immediately after this briefing. The systems are already on-line. You will suit up when you leave here and present yourselves for the first session. Tomorrow you will carry out a practice mission in the aircraft itself, in the area already designated. The day after, you will all head for Italy. The NATO base to which you have been assigned is already prepared to receive you. That is all, gentlemen. Thank you."

"I still think they want us to hit that target," McCann said as he pulled the zip down toward his right ankle, drawing the G-suit leg tight and snug. "This Kansas City kid's scalp is itching."

They were putting on full kit, as if the mission were actually being flown. The simulator would faithfully mimic the aircraft in every way, except takeoff; but once within the dome with the full visual and motion systems operating, they would believe they had done so, as the remarkably detailed artificial world came to life around them.

"Have you washed your hair lately?" Hohendorf asked with some amusement.

"I'm telling you, Axel," McCann insisted. "Bet you it comes up nice and fat in the simulator, and just like the real thing out there it's surrounded by surface to air missles, just waiting to cream us in the doughnut."

Hohendorf had completed his suiting up. He took his helmet off its shelf, checked it, then stood waiting for McCann. "Do you usually speak so graphically to Mark Selby?"

"Yep. All the time."

"I see." Hohendorf sounded like a man who was wondering whether he'd made a mistake. He watched as McCann pulled the last zip. "Ready?"

"Yep," McCann repeated, and picked up his own helmet. "Let's go give 'em hell."

Jason was preparing to leave his office for the simulator section to check on how Hohendorf and McCann were doing when the phone rang.

"Jason," he answered, picking it up.

"Call from outside, sir," the sergeant who was his secretary informed him. "Miss Thurson."

Very surprised, Jason said, "Put her through."

"Right away, sir."

"Chris?" She sounded strangely hesitant.

"Antonia! This is a pleasant surprise."

"It's easier to get blood from a stone than to get a call from you, so I thought I'd better take the initiative."

"I deserve that."

"Yes. You do."

"Chris?" She was definitely worried about something.

"Tell me what it is, Antonia."

There was a pause. "I . . . I kicked a man in the balls today."

This was so unexpected, Jason was not sure how to respond. The speed with which she'd finished the sentence, and the hesitant laughter in her voice, also made him want to laugh. He checked the impulse.

"Go on," he encouraged.

"He took my photograph. He's from the newspapers, I think. He asked me about you . . . about us."

Jason felt himself go cold.

"I'm afraid I got angry," she went on. "I hit him in the face, then kicked him. His camera broke."

Despite the implications of what she'd said, Jason found himself smiling. Good for her! At least that photograph was now ruined.

"Have you told your father?"

"Not yet. I thought I'd have a word with you first."

"Thank you for telling me." The conversation had gone on long enough on an open line. "Leave the rest to me. I'll handle it from this end."

"Will you be coming to town?"

"Probably."

"Oh, good," she said, and hung up. As an air vice-marshal's daughter, she was also very much aware of the need for circumspection on the phone.

He replaced his own phone thoughtfully, then picked up another with a scrambler button. He punched in a few numbers.

"Buntline," came the crisp reply.

"Jason. I wasn't certain you'd be back as yet."

"Just got in. If you're calling me on this line, it must be important."

"I'll leave you to judge. Antonia got her photo taken today. A man asked the usual scandal sheet question."

"And?"

"She hit him in the face, kicked him in the privates, and smashed his camera."

Buntline laughed out loud. "Woman after my own heart. We could use someone like that."

"No, you don't. Leave her alone."

"Just a little jest." Then Buntline returned to being serious. "I think we know where that came from. By his way of thinking, he obviously believes I may have sold out to you and doesn't trust me sufficiently. He has therefore decided to use other means. That was a grave error of judgment." Buntline was now sounding dangerous. "Concentrate on keeping a tight hold of your program. I'll handle this. Got that?"

"Yes. Thank you."

"We are on the same side."

"Sometimes," Jason said.

Buntline laughed again, ending the conversation.

8

McCann watched gravely as the world rolled above the cockpit, and Hohendorf took the IDS plunging into a valley at five hundred knots. The world rolled upright again for a few seconds before once more canting in the opposite direction. Trees hurtled past in a blur. The aquamarine of a large body of water streaked past on a wingtip. The sensation was so real, he found it hard to remind himself he was in the simulator. Even the G-suit squeezed at him as Hohendorf racked the Tornado clone into another tight turn.

McCann returned his attention to the displays. This rear cockpit was very different from the one he normally occupied in the ASV, but many of the upgraded systems possessed some similarities. The ground attack modes, however, differed widely. But he was coming to terms with them.

This was the third simulated mission they had so far carried out, and he was now feeling more at ease. The first mission had been a disaster. They had missed every target. Not Hohendorf's fault, but his. The second was better, if rated from a zero percentage hit. That time they'd gotten thirty percent. But that had been virtually worthless as almost immediately they'd taken a catastrophic SAM hit from the C^3 target they were supposed to avoid, and had been forced to carry out a simulated ejection.

According to the computers, they had survived— only to be subsequently taken prisoner. Very bad news, and hardly clandestine. In real life, such exposure of the November unit's activities would cause very serious embarrassment all around. The boss would not be pleased, as such an event would make him very vulnerable to those who wished to close him down. McCann was fiercely loyal both to his wing commander and to the November program.

Jason had been there to witness their chagrin and was still in the control section beyond the dome, observing their progress. They knew he was there because his firm voice had come on their headphones.

"Finger out, McCann. There's a good chap."

McCann was now determined to get a perfect score this time. He'd gotten the hang of it, and the magic was flowing.

"How are we doing, Elmer Lee?" Hohendorf asked as they shot past a mountainside, trees reaching for them.

"Your APCs are coming up," McCann replied calmly.

"Cluster bombs?"

"You got it."

McCann had selected the weapons that would saturate the target area with countless small munitions. The simulated APCs and their occupants would find themselves in an all-enveloping world of multiple explosions.

In real life, those that had managed to survive such a devastating attack would still not have been able to move. The entire vicinity, littered with delayed-action bomblets, would have made further progress suicidal until the area had been made safe—a consuming process that would have given the rescue chopper all the time it needed to collect Mac safely. He hoped they'd be able to pull it off when the time came.

"A straight pass along the road then," Hohendorf said.

"Yep."

"Okay." Hohendorf uncaged the master arm switch on the left of the base of the head-up display, then turned the key that was just a little further along on the left, on the cockpit rim. "Master arm *on*."

He banked the Tornado steeply and came around a mountain at less than a hundred feet, then rolled level in perfect alignment with the road.

"I have the target bars," he said. "Bomb fall line right in the middle. We're on target. Autorelease."

He had uncaged the release button on the stick and now depressed it with his thumb. The selected weapon load would be released when the systems had concluded the parameters were correct. This took fleeting fractions of a second. The aircraft vibrated briefly as the cluster bombs went on their way and Hohendorf rolled swiftly to rush upside down up the next slope and down into the next valley.

They were through. Nothing had come up at them.

"Well done, gentlemen!" came Jason's voice. "According to the results, you have obliterated the target. That's more like it. I want to see these same results for every subsequent attack run. Keep up the good work."

"Don't know about you, Axel," McCann said as they made their way back to the simulated airfield, "but I'm soaked. I feel like I've been in a shower."

"I have news for you. So do I. Three more runs, and we should be okay. Care for a break?"

"Yeah. I could do with a coffee."

McCann was looking at a folded brochure, about the size

of a standard business envelope. They were in one of the small crew rooms of the simulator section, reclining in standard issue utility chairs, their now-empty coffee cups on the low table before them. Jason had stopped briefly to check a few points with them, and had returned to his office.

"What's that?" Hohendorf asked, as McCann thumbed through the brochure.

"Got it from Karen. Her uncle took a holiday in Yugoslavia once, and brought some literature back with him. I thought it was funny. Listen to this. *'Yugoslavia,'*" McCann began to read. *"'Discover Bosnia and Herzegovina. Welcome to the country of inimitable beauty and hospitable, warmhearted people.'* Wonder if they recognize themselves today. *'You shall find the virginal beauty of nature,'*" he went on, *"'and discover customs and folklore perpetuated through the centuries.'* Yeah. Like butchering each other. It goes on and on, telling us about the beauty and wonder of the people. Hell, all the towns in the news are mentioned here . . . Bihac, Sarajevo, Mostar, Jajce . . . come and visit them all, it says."

McCann continued to read, *"'High up in the dense, vast forests, meet the good-hearted Bosnian peasants. This is the land to meet people who cherish friendship above all.'* Yeah. Croat, Muslim, and Serb grow up as friends, then kill each other."

He tossed the brochure away in disgust. "Shit. Do those people even remember what they were saying? Hell, that piece of crap's not even four years old. It was written in the nineties, for Pete's sake. They had a beautiful country, until they wrecked it. All those wonderful buildings they talk about, and those ancient bridges so full of history . . . they decide to shell the shit out of them. As for the warmhearted people . . . "

Hohendorf, remembering Zunica Paic, said, "Part of what's in that brochure is still there among some of the people."

"Yeah? But for how long?"

"Ahh. Now you have me. Come on, Kansas City warrior. Back to our labors. Let's have three perfect runs in a row."

"With me in the back, you got it."

"How could I possibly imagine differently."

"You can't," McCann told him shamelessly.

Princes Street, Edinburgh

Morven Selby brought her battered Citroën 2CV to a halt outside the imposing house. In keeping with her profession as a marine biologist, she was very eco-conscious. The little car was bright green, and tucked away in a corner of a side window was the sticker of a smiling whale.

She had long given up trying to reconcile her sense of ecological responsibility with the fact that the two men in her life flew—what some friends never seemed to tire of telling her—the most unecological of machines.

Kim Mannon had invited her to spend a couple of nights at the Edinburgh house, and having the time off, she had accepted. It was her first visit.

As she cut the engine, she looked out and saw Kim smiling and waving at her from the door. She returned the wave. It would be nice, she'd decided, to have Kim as a sister-in-law. They got on well with each other and frequently banded together to sort her brother out when he was having one of his bad days about her continued involvement with Axel.

Kim trotted down the steps to give her a welcoming hug as she got out of the car.

"I've got lots of food in," Kim said. "We can make pigs of ourselves, with no one to moan at us."

"That sounds like a great idea. I've brought the wine."

They grinned at each other.

"Good to see you," Kim said.

"Good to see you, too. Now show me this marvelous house of yours, then let's do some serious eating and drinking."

November base

In the simulator, Hohendorf and McCann had completed all three runs successfully, and had managed to evade the antiair defenses that the computers had placed within the scenario.

They were again heading back to the simulated airfied when Hohendorf said, "Patch me a readout of the SMS to confirm weapon state."

The November IDS—unlike the standard aircraft— had, in addition to the weapon control panel low down on the central console in front of the stick, a small display unit in the front cockpit. This gave a duplicate of the current weapon state detailed by the stores management system in a graphic presentation. It was the backseater's responsibility to program the attack package on his own control panel.

McCann patched the status over.

"We've got one bomb left," Hohendorf said. "There's a target of opportunity coming up."

"It wouldn't by any chance be that C^3, would it? The one we're supposed to ignore?"

"This is not the real thing, Elmer Lee. It will be good practice for you."

"Oh, yeah?"

"Set it up, please."

"I've already done so."

"What? But . . . "

"Knew you'd be going after it."

"Are you telepathic?"

"Funny you should say that. Okay. Target at ten miles, five degrees left offset. Do you want a pop-up? Or correct course for a straight pass?"

"A straight pass. Fast and low."

"You got it. Go two-six-two. That will give you target on the nose."

"Roger. Two-six-two." Hohendorf made the slight course correction and increased speed to six hundred knots.

"She's ready to go anytime you want," McCann said.

"Roger."

Hohendorf uncaged the release and held the button down. On the HUD, the target bars moved to the release point, then the bomb was gone. Ten miles was no distance at six hundred knots.

"And we're getting out of here," Hohendorf said, hauling the Tornado away in a tight, punishing turn that in the real aircraft would have had them straining against the onset of crushing G-forces.

But the scenario in the computer wasn't having any. All hell broke loose. The target was saturated with defenses, and each unit seemed determined to take out the attack aircraft.

"Holy shit!" McCann exclaimed. "We've got a hornet's nest there. I've got the decoys going."

As Hohendorf flung the aircraft into gyrating, evasive maneuvers, the decoys fed the SAMS. But antiaircraft guns had joined the fun, and though McCann was effectively jamming their guidance radars, some were still able to lay their fire uncomfortably close.

"Wow," McCann said. "This computer's a mean SOB. Let's hope the real guys are not so fierce."

Then they were out of the gauntlet and running free.

"Hey, Axel, that was some pretty good shit you did back there."

"I look after my backseaters," Hohendorf said.

"Keep doing that, and I'll love you forever."

"Such nice things you say, Elmer Lee."

"Yep."

●　●　●

Princes Street, Edinburgh

"If I say so myself," Kim Mannon began as she studied their empty plates, "that was not a bad meal. A very late lunch, or a very early dinner. Take your pick." She had worked magic with a chicken, and now raised her full glass. "To us. It will be good having you as a sister."

At the other end of the table, Morven raised her own glass. "To us. Good having *you* as a sister." They took generous swallows. "The day is old, or the evening's young. Good thing I'm not driving anywhere after this," she added, as she carefully put the glass down. "Pacified your father yet?"

They had finished their second bottle of wine, were now starting the third, and were quite mellow.

Kim Mannon, only daughter of Sir Julius Mannon, city magnate, would look, even in rags, as expensive as her upbringing. Her small, neatly formed body had driven Mark Selby to wild peaks of desire. She wore her hair in a short black crop over thickish eyebrows and wide-spaced dark eyes that were permanently full of mischief, as if the world were hers to dare. A small, sharp nose and a mouth of appealing generosity gave her a presence that was always extremely difficult to ignore.

The items of clothing in which she normally chose to attire herself tended to be as scant as possible, and the skimpier the outfit, the higher the price. But today she had put on a simple cotton dress. It displayed a fair amount of bare leg, but was by her standards quite restrained.

The two women were a formidable pair to behold. Any male fortunate enough to find himself in the same room would have considered himself doubly blessed; but equally, he would have cursed the luck that would have forced him to choose between them.

"My filthy-rich father," Kim now said, "is still sulking and hoping I'll come to my senses. Some hope! He really does believe that his pet financial rottweiler, one Reggie Barham-Deane, whom *he* calls his barracuda, is a more suitable match. Of course, he's absolutely furious he can't punish me by threatening to cut me off. Mummy had her own cash, you see, and when she died, I got the lot. No one else to give it to."

"Nice to have *both* parents rich. Everyone should have at least two."

They laughed, slightly uncontrollably. The Selby parents had both died when she was still in her teens. Mark had been just a bit older. There had not been a lot of money, but Mark had looked after her. It was one reason why he was so protective—sometimes overly so.

"Do you think we're getting drunk?" Kim asked lazily.

"On two bottles of good plonk? I'll have you know, Miss Mannon, we Selbys, good Yorkshire folk, can hold stonger stuff."

"And I'll have you know, Miss Yorkshire Folk, we Mannons can go the distance with the best lager-quaffer. Before my sainted grandfather became a tycoon and showed my sainted father how to make his own fortune, he worked in Dockland—when there were still docks to work in. The Mannons were river folk then."

"I'll drink to that."

"And me. Hey. Miraculously, my glass is empty."

"Then fill it, Miss Mannon, and mine while you're at it."

When Kim had done so, Morven said, "Do you know . . . do you know, Miss Mannon, that my brother the fighter pilot and god of the skies, flies with your red knickers in one of the pockets of his flying suit?"

"You know about that?"

"Course I do. After all, I did find those very knickers in the Maida Vale flat, the first time you two . . . " Morven began to giggle.

"Let's drink to red knickers."

"To red knickers!" they said together.

"And all who fly in them!" Morven added for good measure. "Oops!"

Fits of wild laughter from both of them exploded into the room. Kim's body shook with uninhibited abandon.

After a while she said, between deep sobs of breath, "Come on. Let's leave this stuff on the table and find somewhere more comfortable. Hey! Don't leave the wine. We need that."

They staggered into the living room and collapsed onto a huge sofa.

"See?" Morven said, putting the bottle down on a long, low table that looked as if it had cost as much as a small flat. "Didn't spill a drop. Not . . . not drunk yet."

"Plenty of time, plenty of booze. Blokes do it all the time. Why not us?"

"Exactly. By the way, have you two set a date yet?"

Kim shook her head. "Nope. I think we'll just spring it. That will prevent Daddy from planning sabotage. I don't need a fancy wedding. You'll never guess who'll be best man."

"It won't be Axel."

"Oh, I don't know. I think Mark would have asked him, if it weren't for someone else he had in mind. Mark likes Axel more than he lets on. It's just this thing with you and your baronial pal that he can't seem to get past, because Axel's still married. I know, I know. It's a nonexistent marriage and was dead in the water long before you came along. Believe me, I've had rows with Mark about it often enough."

Morven shrugged. "Doesn't worry me. Mark knows he won't change my mind. Now give. Who's going to be the best man?"

"Who else but Elmer Lee?"

"*Elmer Lee? The* Elmer Lee?"

"The same. Our very own Kansas City pixie."

"He'll be over the moon. Does he know?"

"God, no. Can you imagine the state he'd be in?"

"Yes," Morven said, understanding only too well. "I can."

"We'll tell him in just enough time. Less wear and tear on everybody that way."

"I'm really glad it's Elmer Lee," Morven said with a fond smile, imagining the look on McCann's face when he eventually did find out. "Mark cares about him a lot, but you'd only get an admission from my dear brother by strapping him to a dentist's chair and threatening to pull all his teeth without anesthetic."

Kim brightened suddenly. "Tell you what. Let's call them."

"With a date? *Now?*"

"Why not? I like sudden decisions."

"Mark might feel . . . "

"Don't worry about him," Kim said lightly. "'ee's putty in my 'ands," she finished in a comic French accent.

"Not *really* putty, I hope," Morven, emboldened by the grape, said with bawdy meaning.

Kim stared at her for a moment, then began to giggle as she made kneading motions with her free hand. Morven's shoulders began to heave as she watched. The giggles grew stronger until they both burst into another round of raucous laughter.

Their peals again rang through the house.

Eventually Kim, wiping her eyes, said, "We are drunk."

"Speak for yourself."

"Don't care what you say, Miss Yorkshire. You're drunk, too." She began to get up, fell back on the sofa, then tried again. Her drink was still firmly in her hand. "Phone call to make."

"Where're you going? Don't you know where your own phones are? There's one right here."

Swaying perceptibly, Kim looked about her. "Where? Oh. There you are," she said to the portable phone near the base of a lamp on a small table. She drained her glass. "Need more wine, though."

Morven, none too steady herself, got up. "I'll get another bottle. Have we really drunk *three*?"

"Wimping out on me, Miss Yorkshire?"

"On my way. Number four coming up."

As she went out, Kim picked up the phone, then

folded gratefully back onto the sofa. She dialed the open line to the November officers' mess.

"Flight . . . Flight Lieutenant Selby, please." She'd said that quite well, she thought. No hint of drunkenness. "Where's that wine, Miss Yorkshire?" she called to Morven.

"Coming up, Miss River Folk!"

Morven returned with an opened bottle just as Selby came on the line.

"Flight Lieutenant Selby."

"Hullo, Flight Lieutenant Selby, sir," Kim greeted expansively. "There are two randy women at the other end of this line, waiting for you and Baron Hohendorf to come out and play."

Morven put down the bottle, collapsed again onto the sofa, and succumbed to another fit of the giggles.

"Good grief," came Selby's hushed voice. "Kim!"

"Why are you whispering?"

"What if someone's listening?"

"Serves them right."

"Morven really with you?"

"She is, and we're ready and waiting."

"Kim! For God's sake . . . Are you drunk?"

She could tell by his voice he wasn't sure whether to laugh or remain serious and officerlike.

She looked at Morven, mimed the kneading routine. "Putty."

They both started to giggle loudly.

Selby heard. "What's going on down there? Am I missing a joke?"

"Come out to play and you'll find out."

"Can't, I'm afraid."

She paused, the jollity fading. "And Axel?"

"Same thing."

She knew from experience not to ask more. "Mark?"

"Yes?"

"I love you."

"Love you, too."

The line hummed as neither needed to say more, nor wanted to be the first to hang up.

At last he said, "I'll call you," and hung up.

She put the phone down slowly. Suddenly, she was no longer drunk.

Watching her, Morven felt her giggles subside until she, too, grew serious. "What's up?"

"They're off somewhere," Kim said, voice now remarkably steady. "I know it. It's . . . it's the way he spoke. Is this what I'm going to marry, Morven? Suddenly everything's beginning to feel very different. It's not as if I don't know what he does. I'm going into this with my eyes wide open. I mean . . . I've known these moments were bound to come, and I'll always wonder and worry . . . "

"Second thoughts?"

Kim shook her head. "None at all. But this is the other side of the coin, isn't it? The reality. I've worried about him before, but the thought of actually being married . . . I never thought I'd feel like . . . I have a fear about this one, Morven. Don't ask me why. Ah," she went on dismissively, "must be the drink." She made no move to refill her glass.

"Don't scare me, Kim," Morven said, looking anxious. She was thinking of Bosnia, and remembering what Hohendorf had said about Zunica Paic.

"I'm not trying to," Kim said. "I know it can't be easy for you . . . having the two men you really care for doing that kind of job. Perhaps it's because we *are* going to get married that suddenly I'm afraid of losing Mark. Oh . . . I give up. I don't know what I really think. Do you mind?" she added, pushing her glass away. "I . . . I don't feel like drinking anymore."

"It's all right. I don't feel like it, either."

"And I didn't even mention the date," Kim remarked softly.

● ● ●

Moscow, same day, same time

Before the momentous changes had taken place in the old
Soviet Union, Feliks Alexandrovitch Kurinin had been a
full colonel in the KGB, and young for the rank. He was
now a general, doing his old job in the renamed organization. But there were other important things about Kurinin.
He was one of the prime movers in a drive toward re-
creating the Union in a better, more efficient form.

It rankled him very strongly that the motherland had
seemingly capitulated to the West. He saw the chaos
that followed as the fault of both the traditional enemies
and those within. He was thus dedicated to removing the
sources of his country's humiliation, including those
who now believed they were in charge.

What made Kurinin extremely dangerous was that
he was not the average fanatical nationalist. He had
nothing overtly to do with such forces, though his hand
was deep in the ferment. He was not seen on the world's
media threatening to take back lost territory. He was not
in a hurry, and allowed events to take their course, posi-
tive they would eventually lead to a situation that would
give him all the leverage he needed to put his long-term
strategy into action. He was like a predator waiting in
the shadows, knowing his prey would eventually, and
inevitably, pass his way. It was simply a matter of biding
time. Meanwhile, he carried on with his planned skir-
mishes, one of which was the eventual destruction of
the November program.

"Come in!" he now ordered in answer to a respectful
knock on the door to his office.

A woman in captain's uniform entered with a loose-
leaf folder. "The last hour's messages, Comrade General."

"Thank you. Put them there, Captain." He indicated
a spot on the large, highly polished desk. "Anything from
Yugoslavia?"

"Routine signals, Comrade General. No results yet
from the search."

"All right. Thank you," he repeated, nodding to her that she could leave.

As she went out, he opened the folder and began to read through all the electronically eavesdropped communication from the West, particularly transmissions between NATO and the UN.

He smiled with genuine humor as he read. It was a picture of abject confusion. Decisions and counterdecisions; statements of intent and counterstatements, and so it went. As always, he found it extremely hard to accept that the mighty Soviet Union had succumbed to such a bunch of incompetents. The mess they were making of their Yugoslavian adventures was there in the glare of the world's media, for all to see. They were so vulnerable, had so clearly lost their way, it was pathetic.

"And yet," he said to himself, "they bested us."

He was not one to pretend otherwise. Serious mistakes had been made. The West's boots had been licked by those upon whom the Union had laid its trust. But all that would change. A new Union, like the legendary phoenix, would arise from the ashes of its discredited predecessor—one that the West would trifle with at its peril.

For the time being, however, tactical moves—no matter how seemingly small—would continue. The thinnest of tendrils all led to the core of his purpose and would be ruthlessly pursued to an ultimate conclusion.

As he read through the papers, he saw nothing that mentioned the person his people were hunting in the mountains of Bosnia. Hardly surprising. He was certain, if the western agents had done their job properly, there was a pattern of pickup points to follow. There had to be. It was how he himself would have arranged it. The question was, what sort of pattern? How many points? And in what order?

The hunters would not find it easy. She was good, Kurinin thought with unreserved admiration. But she was also dangerous; too dangerous to be allowed to live.

They had to find her. That was why he had sent in his special troops. That was why he had also arranged fighter cover, should the West attempt a rescue.

If they had decided not to abandon her and were planning anything, they were in for a shock. So far, however, nothing had come from the mole he'd installed at the Pentagon. Perhaps she was, after all, on her own—a sacrifice worth making.

It had been a remarkable stroke of luck, the sort of thing that could so often transform an intelligence operation. Who would have thought she would have been recognized by a member of the old KGB who had infiltrated a peacekeeping force? He was grateful for the major's keenness and ambition. One to look out for when things changed. A man who would be useful.

Kurinin shut the folder. He wondered with clinical interest where she was, what she was doing, and what physical state she was now in.

The Bosnian mountains

She had left the burrow after she'd satisfied herself that the danger was well past. She'd also obliterated all traces of her presence there, in case they chose to backtrack. Now she was moving in a direction opposite to the one her pursuers had taken.

She was hungry, and she stank. When she thought it safe to do so, she would have a quick wash in a mountain stream; for the time being, distance from her pursuers and a replenishment of energy were the immediate requirements. She'd had it with hard biscuits. She needed meat.

With her knife, she had fashioned a weapon that within its own range was silent and lethal. She could not use any firearm. The echo of a single shot in this part of the mountains, despite the ongoing war, would still command interest. She would use her guns only if it was a matter of her own survival. In such an event, the need for silence would be immaterial.

She'd constructed the catapult from a fork made from a supple yet strong cutting she had taken off a tree. She'd been careful about the way she had obtained the small branch before cutting the forked twig off it. First she'd made an incision at its base, and instead of cutting it all the way through, had ripped it off so that it would look as if it had come away naturally. To age the wound in the tree trunk, she had then roughened the incision with a stone, and had followed that by scouring the whole rip with handfuls of earth until the white of the new tear had become soiled and stained.

She had then searched for and found some soil that was home to a mixed population of earth-dwelling beetles and small centipedes. She had slapped some of that in place on the now-dirtied tree wound, letting the excess fall off. Thus disturbed, the centipedes and beetles moved about frantically. One centipede caught a beetle, immediately beginning an *alfresco* meal. After a while, the tree looked as if it had been like that for some considerable time. She had then buried the remainder of the small branch.

Knowing there was a possibility that she might one day have to make a run for it, she had prepared herself. Long before, during one of her visits to the small town, she had cut two strips of rubber from the inner tube of a bicycle tire. She had also cut two pouches from the tire itself. There was a surfeit of discarded and war-destroyed cycles throughout Bosnia, and no one in the little town had taken the slightest notice of her scavenging. Scavenging had become a way of life. The second strip and pouch were spares.

She had cut slits into the ends of the small rectangle of tire, and threaded the rubber strip through them. Each end of the strip was then secured to a prong of the fork. She had tested the catapult by holding it in one hand and hooking the pouch with two fingers of the other, then pulling back to see how the elasticity of the rubber strip performed. The fork was nice and springy, and the rubber had a powerful resistance. Her weapon was ready. Now to find game.

The rock dove, with its white rump and black wing stripes, perched contentedly on the outcrop near the top of a tree that grew close to the sheer face of a low cliff. Now and then, it shifted position slightly, but was not agitated. It felt secure.

It therefore had no warning when the small stone collided forcibly with its head. It was dead before it hit the ground.

She picked up her game and checked it. It had fattened up nicely since the onset of spring. In this part of the mountains, the snows were well in retreat. It had clearly found plenty to eat.

She would have to build a fire to cook it, but this had to be carefully done to avoid being observed, even from a distance. The smell of roasting meat would also have to be limited.

She decided that a good hour's strenuous walk would give her the safe distance she needed. In the cool of the mountain air, the bird would keep.

Having reached terrain where there was no snow, the two troopers had removed their mottled white outer garments, which they now carried in their packs, to reveal the more standard camouflage battle dress beneath. One of them stopped suddenly.

"Something's been nagging at me," he said to his companion.

The other had also stopped and was looking at him. "What?"

"Remember that place where I had the piss?"

"Yes," came the unenthusiastic reply. "It smelled like a whore's behind."

"Been sniffing whores, have we? Something about that place wasn't quite right."

"We had a good look. There was nothing."

"But if you remember, I felt . . . as if there *were* something I should look for. I even stopped when we were leaving and turned around for another check."

"Don't remind me, and don't even say it."

"We should go back."

"Oh, *no, no, no!* That's several kilometers back there! The major . . . "

"The major wants results."

The second trooper looked up at the sky in despair. *"Shit!"* he yelled. He turned again to his companion. "I can't *stand* it when you get into that let's-look-under-every-stone mood."

The first trooper had his radio out. "Do *you* want to tell the major you think it's a bad idea?"

The second trooper sat down on the ground in disgust, without comment, while his comrade made his report suggesting that the particular sector in question might be worth a second look. The major gave permission to go back.

"Come, Viktor," the trooper said, putting the radio away. "On your feet. And stop behaving like someone's bad-tempered babushka. You're meant to be one of the elite."

The other got up reluctantly. "We'll have to spend another night up there," he grumbled.

A sharp laugh greeted this. "What's the matter? Afraid of the dark? Look at it this way . . . the Romans, wearing skirts and sometimes carrying more equipment than you've got, used to march twenty-five miles before nightfall, *then* build a fully autonomous fortified camp before going to bed. You can do a few kilometers."

"I've already done a few kilometers," the other

retorted testily. "And anyway, fuck the Romans. If we do find that woman, she'd better not give me any trouble. I'll have her . . . "

"You'll have nothing. The major wants her in one piece."

"He does, does he? What do you think she's going to do? Hold out her hands and say Take me? I'm not getting myself killed just because he wants to be a colonel."

"If we have to defend ourselves, that's a different matter. I'm not getting killed for him, either."

"So we understand each other."

"We still do everything possible to take her alive. The general himself would not like it if he thought we had been incompetent. In which case, you'll wish it were only the major you had to deal with."

"You didn't have to tell him about that sector. You could have left it for some other bastard to check out."

"It's our sector, Viktor. *We* have to check it out."

"Shit!" Viktor said with feeling. He was now in a foul temper.

They began to retrace their steps.

9

The militia commander's BMP had been trailing the APC convoy for some time now. One of the search teams had spotted it, and had radioed ahead to warn the Russian major. The major had allowed this to continue for most of the day. He now decided it was time to take action and ordered his deputy, a captain, to take the lead. Pulling to the side of the mountain road, he waited as the other APCs negotiated their way past.

The tearing sound of high-flying fast jets made him glance upward. If any of the Western aircraft came his way, his men were already under orders to shoot them down. Nevertheless, it wouldn't do to be caught here like this.

"Move it!" he barked into his radio as the APCs bunched alarmingly, making themselves a fat target.

As a precaution, he had made a decision to deliberately space members of the the convoy a kilometer apart. This would make the success of a single pass attack more difficult to achieve, but the gap could still be closed quickly enough to allow for mutual support.

This section of road, however, while wide enough to make passing reasonably easy, was also on a bend.

"Come on, come on," he urged. "We haven't got all day."

At last all the vehicles were through, and once more rapidly began to increase the distance between members. The major then turned his own APC around and started back down the road. A while later, he came to another bend and called a halt, ordering his driver to turn the armored personnel carrier across the road, blocking it completely.

"Dismount!" he barked.

The troopers climbed out and fanned out, weapons held ready. The major and his driver remained aboard, with the major standing through the hatch. The APC's cannon was pointed down the road, waiting for anything that might come.

The BMP came around the bend and went into a panic stop. It just made it. The militia commander's upper body was also out of his own hatch. He'd been given a severe fright.

"What the hell's the idea?" he yelled in his execrable Russian at the major. "You could have killed us all!"

"Why are you following me?" the Russian asked coldly.

"This is *my* country. I go where I like. We were not one of your colonies before, and we're not going to be one now."

The major looked at him contemptuously. "Do you make these speeches up? Or has someone taught you how?"

"Are you going to let me pass?"

The cannon seemed to be pointing directly at the commander's head.

"No. This is Russian business. I don't need interference from you. I warned you before we left. You should have taken the advice. I suggest you turn back before something we'll both regret occurs. And keep your men inside your vehicle. My soldiers will shoot if they climb out."

The commander stared at the gaping snout of the cannon. He tried looking away from it, but it kept drawing his eyes back, mesmerizing him like some malevolent creature. He hated the thought of backing down yet again in front of his bodyguards, especially after the macho way in which he'd begun the pursuit.

Damn this arrogant Russian major! he thought viciously.

"You had better let me move," he blustered, "or your government will hear of this!"

The major laughed softly. "My government? What government?"

The commander's eyes widened perceptibly. "You are doing this on your own?"

"Don't act more stupid than you already look. This is something bigger than you could ever hope to understand. Now that's the end of any explanations. And don't even imagine you can shoot your way through. I will remind you we are not like the West. We will not make a polite protest. We will simply shoot . . . to kill. Go back to your little town and lord it over your miserable people, if that feeds your ego. Or . . . you can stay here and die."

The Russian major's emotionless delivery carried a deadly message that was not lost on even someone like the militia commander.

The commander stared at the cannon, at the major, at the ready, eagerly alert troopers, and knew he had no chance of coming out of this confrontation alive. That cannon, he was certain, would take his head off with the first shot to be fired by either side; then his men would be roasted inside the BMP.

His attitude changed. He tried to seem reasonable, pretending he didn't mind losing face yet again.

"Look," he began. "Why do we have to fight each other? We are brothers. That woman killed *my* people . . .

not Russian soldiers. I should be with you. If any of those jets up there come your way, you could do with the extra guns."

But the major was not having any. "No. I will not repeat this. My men will shoot if you do not turn around."

They stared at each other for long moments. The commander's eyes were filled with naked hatred for the major, for this second humiliation. The Russian stared back at him coolly.

"Turn around!" the commander snarled at his driver in his own language.

In fits and starts, the BMP turned around, making a production of it. Throughout, the commander kept his hate-filled eyes upon the Russian, turning his head as the vehicle maneuvered so that he could maintain eye contact. He kept looking until his BMP eventually moved out of sight of the Russian APC.

A kilometer down the road, he called a halt. He was not taking orders from any jumped-up Russian. The Russian didn't want his company? Fine. He could carry out his own search independently. He knew these mountains. The Russians didn't. His BMP was lighter, and could maneuver better across inhospitable terrain. He would go off-road.

"Get out, everybody," he ordered. "Stretch your legs."

As they disembarked, he pulled a map out of a pocket and spread it across one of the track guards of the BMP.

"Come here, all of you."

They gathered around, and he began indicating with a jabbing index finger.

"This is our road, and this is the direction that bastard Russian is taking." He drew a wide imaginary curve. "The mountain troops will be spread across this line, moving toward the Russian APCs. This means that somewhere in the middle they expect to find Nadia. But Nadia is smart. We'll go off here, to the left and behind the troops."

"You think she's *behind* them?" one of the men asked.

"I told you she's smart. She has to be, to have fooled everybody for so long. In her place, in these mountains, I would lie low and let them pass, then double back."

"But where is she going?"

The commander shrugged. "Only she knows. But it would be good to intercept her before that shithead of a Russian with all his APCs and his fancy troops find her. She won't be expecting anyone to be coming up from behind. Wouldn't that make him look like a fart?"

They grinned, nodding in solidarity against what to them was inexcusable foreign arrogance.

The commander folded the map and put it away. "We'll capture her ourselves. So, are you with me?"

"We're with you, chief."

"All right. Soon the light will be gone. We'll go off the road and continue until just before dark, then stop for the night. Tomorrow we'll begin bright and early. Let's go."

The recent unpleasantness with the major thrust out of their minds, they climbed back aboard. It never occurred to the commander that his lone armored vehicle would be dangerously exposed.

The major had rejoined his convoy and was once more in the lead. The incident with the militiaman caused him little worry. The stupid, vain, and unpleasant creature was a mere irritant. He would simply have blown the BMP off the road and down the mountainside. His mind was more seriously occupied with the hunt and its lack of success so far.

He had spread the net well, he thought, based upon the information he'd been given. But the mountains were vast, and good as his men were, they could not work miracles. Still, he did not expect to fail. The net was closing. Sooner or later, she would be found.

He again considered the request from the omega pair to return to an area they had already searched.

True, it would cost time; but if they found something, *anything*, it would have been worth it. He did not regret giving them permission to go back. It demonstrated the sort of dedication to the task that would be very much needed in the new order to come. Meanwhile, he had ordered the other teams to spread out to compensate for the temporary gap in their lines.

"Nearly there, Viktor."

"I should damn well hope so," Viktor remarked, taking long, deep breaths. "Not even the instructor sergeant put me on a march like this."

"Do you good," came the cheerful rejoinder. "You were getting fat in your old age."

"Balls." Viktor was twenty-two and very fit. "I think *you* want to be a sergeant."

"Nothing wrong with ambition. Isn't that what they tell us these days?"

"The major wants to be a colonel, you want to be a sergeant, and you both want me to help you get there." Viktor thought about that. "As long as you bastards don't get me killed."

"You worry too much."

Two kilometers later and the light nearly gone, they arrived at their destination.

"Can't see much in this light," the senior trooper said, "but something's wrong." He used his low-light torch for a better look, but saw no obvious sign.

Viktor had begun to remove his pack in preparation for making camp for the night.

"Keep your pack on. We're going on."

"*What?* You're crazy! We've just done a forced march . . . "

"We're going on," the senior man repeated.

"Why?" Viktor was determined to know.

"Something's wrong."

"You've already said that."

"She was here. *Damn!*"

Viktor paused. "You're pulling my leg."

"You think I'd joke about this?"

"How do you know she was here?"

The other sighed. "Where's your sense of smell?"

"Right where it's always been. I can't smell anything in particular."

"Exactly. You said my piss stank."

"That's not news. It *always* stinks . . . " Viktor paused. "No smell," he went on softly. "No damn smell. But would it last this long? A lot of time has passed. . . . "

"Not long enough, if it hadn't been disturbed. It hasn't rained, or snowed. Nothing to wash it away. Normal piss stinks for a long time, and according to you, mine pastes itself to anything it touches. This place has been recently disturbed. She was here. Definitely." The senior man looked about him, torch sweeping in a slow arc. "She made a hide and waited for us to turn up. She must even have heard us talking. When she was certain we'd gone, she left. Damn!" he repeated. He turned off the torch and clipped it back into place by his left armpit.

"Which direction?"

"The opposite one. Which do you think? I'd have done that in her place. She's doubling back. So we move on."

"Are you going to report to the major?"

"Not yet. We have no real proof. An animal could have deliberately wiped out my scent by roughing up the area, or spraying its own scent; but my instincts tell me *she* did it when she erased evidence of the hide. If I hadn't pissed, she'd have succeeded. She's good." There was genuine respect in the voice. "This isn't going to be easy at all, Viktor."

"Then we should call the others for backup."

The senior man shook his head. "We can't risk the line on just this. If I'm wrong . . . "

"But you said . . . "

"I know what I said! It's still down to us. Let's go."

"Shit!" Viktor said.

She had built a snake-hole fire to cook the bird. First she had dug a horizontal hole in a bank of earth and had pierced its top with a small stick to create a ventilator shaft. This had the advantage of allowing only small wisps of smoke to escape, while the hole itself hid the fire completely. She had lighted it using the small magnesium block with a flint edge that she carried. For fuel, animal droppings and dry hardwood gave a hot, long-lasting flame with little smoke.

Using a forked stick as support at the mouth of the hole, she had pierced the cleaned bird with another, jabbing the free end into the earth at the far end of the hole for secondary support. She had then rotated the stick as the dove roasted. Its fat basted it, as well as continuing to fuel the fire. She had also put all unusable parts of the bird into the flames. Keeping the fat might have been a good idea, but she hoped she would not reach a stage so dire that she had to keep everything for possible future use. She hoped she would be picked up long before such need arose.

The dove made a good meal. When finished, she killed the fire, put everything into the hole, plugged it and the ventilator shaft, then covered the lot with forest detritus. It was nearly dark by the time her work was completed. There was nothing to show that any cooking had been done recently. Even the smells of cooking were gone. She hoped that any that had escaped on the light wind would dissipate long before anyone got the scent.

Satisfied with her efforts, she was about to move on when the sound of an engine came faintly to her. The sound wavered on the wind. She was a long way from where she had first seen the APCs and could not believe one of them was so close. Whatever made that sound, it could not be one of the vehicles she had seen. Had they put a second wave into the hunt?

She decided she would have to take the risk to find out. No point running from something you couldn't assess. She'd also have to watch out for more troops.

She made her way carefully toward the sound. It took her the best part of an hour before she heard low voices. She went flat and inched forward until she found she was looking over the edge of a steep, rocky incline. She lay flattened upon the high ground and looked down two hundred feet or so upon the BMP, visible in the light of a small fire. Suicidally stupid, she thought, but that was their problem. Four men were grouped around the vehicle. She knew that BMP.

The local commander had joined the hunt.

Princes Street, Edinburgh

The phone rang and Kim Mannon answered it. She appeared remarkably sober, and neither she nor Morven had drunk any more wine. In the interim, they'd been drinking coffee and trying to figure out where Selby and Hohendorf were off to. Morven was certain she had a fair idea, but had stuck by her decision not to say anything about the incident with Zunica Paic.

"Axel!" Kim was saying, turning to look meaningfully at Morven. "Yes. She's here. Are you all right? Good. Right. I'll put her on." She covered the mouthpiece with a hand as she passed the phone over. "You won't get any more out of him," she whispered. "He's as bad as Mark."

Morven nodded her thanks as she took the instrument. "Hullo, Axel. Mark's obviously talked to you."

"Yes. Are you okay?"

She knew there were hidden questions behind the words. "I'm fine. Spending the night here with Kim."

"Mark says you are having fun. Sorry we can't come down to see you tonight."

"That's the way it is."

"Yes."

Bosnia was a huge, almost tangible presence between them. Each knew the other was thinking about it, but neither brought it into the conversation.

"Be careful," she said quietly.

"You know me. Always careful."

"Axel?"

"Yes?"

"Just that."

"Okay."

They hung up together. The love they felt for each other was so palpable, there had been no need to say more.

The Bosnian mountains

It had taken her twenty careful minutes to find a safe and secure way down to the level where the men were. Her route had taken her some distance from the BMP, but its position was clearly marked by the glow from the fire. She could still not believe their stupidity.

Originally she had considered leaving them to it, but she'd decided it was not a good idea tactically. It was one thing being hunted by true professionals. You could plan, because there were certain ways you already knew they would operate. It was all a matter of making sure you kept well away from them.

In the case of the militia commander and his men, driven as they were by the need to prove their *machismo*, all sorts of imponderables had entered the equation. Because of their lack of discipline, they were the most dangerous and thus had to be eliminated. They had already blundered across her path, and could easily bring unwelcome attention to the area. The last thing she needed was another group of people on her trail. She cursed the commander for forcing this upon her. By positioning himself behind the sweep line, he had strayed into the relatively safe territory she had made for herself.

The BMP had come as far as it could in this terrain. That meant they would have to leave it, perhaps with just the driver remaining, and continue the chase on foot. Not good at all.

She found a secure place to hide her pack, then taking the Heckler and Koch, the Stechkin, and the knife, made her way back to where the BMP had stopped. She had equipped each firearm with its silencer.

She didn't really want to use the submachine gun, preferring instead, in this particular instance, the automatic. But you never could tell how some things might turn out. The middle of a firefight was not the best place to find out you were short of weaponry. She wanted this to be quick, if at all possible.

When she got back to the spot she had picked as the best position for what she intended to do, she lay in cover, watching carefully, studying the scene before her.

The BMP was almost at the base of the virtually perpendicular incline, nose-on to where she lay. The small fire was just in front of it; the men loosely gathered around. Two squatted on their heels, one was doing some cooking, while the fourth, AK-47 at the ready, stood close to the vehicle. There was no sign of the large bulk of the commander.

Where was he? she wondered. She doubted very much that the men would have been given permission to use the BMP without him. He was inordinately proud of the vehicle and treated it as his personal limousine.

Perhaps he was inside. She would take out the bodyguards, then when he came scrambling out, she'd have him nicely silhouetted against the fire, and that would be that.

She couldn't hang around much longer. It was time.

From where she lay on her stomach, protected by deep shadow, she braced herself on her forearms, the

Stechkin held two-handedly, lower hand resting on the ground. She had a clear field of fire and was well within range. She'd have to be quick.

The big automatic coughed suddenly and rapidly. First to go was the man with the AK. He slammed back against the BMP while his companions, momentarily stunned by the unexpectedness of it all, began to move like startled minnows. They were already much too late, and even as they moved, they were felled by her accurate shooting. The man who was cooking fell across his fire and began to burn. He screamed loudly just once, and retaining the barest instincts of self-preservation, rolled off it as he died.

She did not move. She watched the silent bodies. *Where was the commander?*

If the slam of the first bodyguard against the BMP had not roused him, the screaming man should have. So where was he? Had they killed him, after all, and then deserted? She doubted that. They were as steeped in blood as he was, and there were many who wanted revenge—even among their own group. The bodyguards and the commander needed each other for mutual protection—he needed them for their boneheaded muscle, and they needed him for the power he wielded in the area, giving them a semblance of immunity. No use to them now.

Where was the commander?

"Looking for me?" a voice asked in Serbo-Croat with gleeful softness from behind and above her.

She did not move. *Damn it, damn it, damn it!*

"Well, Nadia," he continued. "You are very good, but not good enough, eh? You have killed my men. Very good shooting. I was going to get rid of them, anyway. They had become too big for their boots and were acting like commanders themselves when they were on their own." His voice hardened. "I have a gun pointing right at your head. You will move only when I tell you, and how I tell you. Otherwise, you are dead. I cannot see you prop-

erly, but enough to know I am close enough not to miss.
Now, first throw the pistol to one side. Make no other
movement."

She did so, gauging how far it had gone.

"Now that fancy German gun."

One-handedly, she removed the Heckler and Koch
and threw that to her left, again gauging the distance of
its fall.

She waited for him to call for the knife. But he did
not. Then she remembered he had never seen her with
it. *He did not know she also carried a knife.*

"*Don't* turn around!"

"I wasn't going to," she protested in the same language, into the scrub where she lay.

"Shut up! I see you speak our language well. You
think you're so smart," he went on. "Smarter than me, a
peasant from the mountains, eh?"

"I . . . "

"*Shut up!* You and that fucking Russian major. You
people think you are so much smarter than us. But I
caught you. I thought you might double back. And where
is he? Farting around out there with his fancy troops.
Before I kill you, Nadia, I am going to teach you a lesson
you won't forget until the moment you die."

She said nothing.

"Do you remember your little friend from the café?"
He was enjoying himself. "I told her you were a traitor
and that if she wasn't nice to me I'd have her shot for
associating with you. Well, guess what . . . she was very,
very nice to me—for hours. I had her in all sorts of ways.
She has a nice, generous backside and great tits. Bigger
than yours, but no matter. I will enjoy you, too."

He gave a strange chuckle.

"Wondering how I caught you? I had gone for a shit.
Great joke, eh? I didn't even know you were there until I
heard the silencer. I picked up my gun and came to look.
My trousers are still back there. Lucky for you. I am
ready for action. Now stay on your stomach, and take

off your clothes. Do it very carefully. I am close enough to kill you, but too far for you to reach."

She felt her heart lift. It was the opportunity she'd hoped for. While making a production of removing the outer jacket of her camouflaged battle dress, she unhooked the knife from her belt and slipped it beneath her stomach.

"And the rest of it," the commander ordered harshly. "That one-piece thing you usually wear. Get it off."

She took her time about it, shivering a little as her flesh was exposed to the cold mountain air.

"Hurry up!"

"I'm doing my best. It's not easy, you know, lying here like this."

He gave another of his grotesque chuckles. "You stink," he said cheerfully. "But that is all right. I like the strong smell of woman. Very exciting. The great Nadia," he went on with contempt. "Not so great now, eh? You didn't think I was good enough for you. Come on, come on! Hurry it up. My balls need warming. Take *everything* off. Your tits are just not big enough, but they'll have to do."

She had removed all her clothing, but the knife, now out of its sheath, was still safely hidden beneath her stomach. She heard him move closer.

"Raise your backside," he commanded. His breathing had grown perceptibly quicker. Once or twice, he made an odd sound. He was licking his lips. "I'm going to give you what I gave your little friend, only much more of it. She was nice and plump, not like you . . . but you're stronger. You will have a real man inside you. I will enjoy this. You will, too."

She complied, propping herself on her elbows. The knife was now gripped in one hand.

He came closer still. "If you try anything, this gun will go off, and your head with it." He got down on his knees.

She felt him hard and aroused against her inner

thigh, and he trembled with excitement at the touch of the smooth skin. He was breathing openmouthed, the rate increasing by the second, betraying the extent of his eagerness. He made another of his strange sounds, gave a shudder of anticipation, and was in such a hurry to enter her, he stumbled briefly. He tried to compensate, but it was all she needed.

She whirled suddenly, knife coming up and plunging into the large, exposed belly with a savage force that wrenched the startled breath from him. He gave an agonized wheeze, and hot, unpleasant air fanned at her as he vainly tried to scream.

The knife came out and went in deeply again, with brutal swiftness. It was expertly done.

"And *this*, is for my 'little friend,' you piece of dung," she snarled at him in a low, tight voice.

She felt the warmth of his blood spill over the hilt and onto her hand, to trickle down her forearm. She withdrew the knife a second time and rolled quickly away from him. She knew her blows had been fatal, as she'd intended them to be.

Incredibly, he staggered to his feet, the AK still clutched in his hand. His dying body fired the entire magazine into the air, the shots echoing into the night.

The whole world must have heard that she thought, as she lay naked in cover. She wondered whether enough of his senses had remained so that in his dying moments he'd still had his revenge—firing off deliberate warning shots.

She thrust the knife into the earth to wipe it clean, then rubbed some over her hand and forearm. She would have to get away from here swiftly. God knew who might turn up to check.

The commander, his gun now empty, was still staggering about in the half-light from the fire, making noises like a dying pig. Then, abruptly, he stopped. He stood perfectly still for long moments, then simply toppled backward. He never moved again.

She collected her clothes and dressed quickly. She strapped the knife back on, then searched for the weapons she had thrown, finding them easily.

She did not go near the BMP, but headed swiftly to where she'd left her pack.

Both troopers had heard the faint but unmistakable noise of the echoing stream of shots.

"Could be from anywhere," Viktor said as they paused to listen. "In this wretched country, every damned village is a battleground as neighbors kill each other."

"This is not a firefight," the senior trooper said. "No answering shots."

"So what was it?"

"A warning, perhaps."

"Oh, come on. A warning? From whom? And to whom?"

"We should check."

"Now I wonder why I thought you were going to say that."

"We've come this far. Might as well."

"'We've come this far . . . might as well,'" Viktor mimicked. "Don't know when to stop, do you? I don't know why I stick with you. You're promotion happy and every soldier in the world knows that's almost as bad as volunteering for anything."

"You stick with me because we're friends."

"Balls," Viktor said good-naturedly as they walked on.

An hour later, they saw the glow of the fire. It took them a further twenty minutes of careful approach to arrive at a point where they could see the BMP, and the bodies lying nearby. They did not go closer but remained in cover, surveying the grisly scene.

"Good mother," Viktor said in a hushed voice. "What the hell happened here? Those shots we heard killed them?"

"I doubt it. That was one burst, not carefully spaced as if someone were taking them out. One of them must have fired as he died."

"You think *she* did it?"

"Possibly."

"But how? How could she take them all out without firing herself? And how would she have gotten close enough?"

"Who knows? They were a bit stupid lighting that fire. . . . Wait a minute. That BMP . . . isn't that the same one we saw in that town? The one with that idiot who had the argument with the major?"

Viktor was uncertain. "It could be. So what's it doing here?"

"One guess. He was after her himself. Probably thinking he'd show us Russians how to do it. That's the sort of thing to expect from a moron like that. Can't see the big bastard, though."

"Dead?"

"Either that or he ran away. If he didn't, he must be lying out there somewhere. Well, we're not going to get any answers staying here."

"We're going to check," Viktor suggested dryly.

"You're beginning to read my mind, Viktor."

"Balls."

They took every precaution as they approached the vehicle and its dead companions. They need not have worried. They made a thorough check of the BMP, using their low-light torches. Then they checked the bodies.

"Well, we know how they died," Viktor said grimly. He was looking at the one who had been doing the cooking. "This poor bastard fell on the fire but managed to roll off. Didn't help him though."

"Shot from cover," the senior trooper said. "If she did it, she stayed out there and never came in close."

"But we didn't hear any other shots."

"Use your head, Viktor. Assuming she did do the shooting, she'd have used a silencer for the purpose. It makes sense. That still does not explain the commander. Let's have a look around."

Weapons at the ready, they began a careful search. It was Viktor who found him.

"Shit," he said loudly. "Take a look at *this*!"

The other came hurrying up and shone his torch next to Viktor's, upon the large body.

"Knife," he said. "Bled like a pig, too."

Viktor moved his torch so that it shone upon the lower half. "He raped her?"

The other shifted the light of his own torch to look. "I doubt he got the chance. Not with all that stuff down his leg. He didn't get it in. Looks like he came while he was dying."

"So they caught her, and then he brought her out here to try and rape her? Greedy. Wanted her all to himself."

The senior trooper shook his head. "I don't think that's what happened. While I was searching, I nearly stepped in some shit. I think he already had his pants down when she shot his men . . . "

"And he surprised her?"

"Something like that. Then the stupid bastard, instead of shooting her on the spot, tried to have a quick one first. For centuries, men who can't resist raping women in war have always risked their necks for a quick bang. A lot of those arseholes have died trying that game. I'd personally shoot one of my own comrades," the senior trooper went on, "if I found him raping . . . "

"Including me?"

"I wouldn't expect you to rape anyone, Viktor . . . but if I caught you . . . yes."

"Well, thank you! You're not only promotion crazy, but you're a homicidal moralist as well."

"I haven't got an overdose of morals, and if I'm homicidal, so are you. Remember, I've seen you kill. My reasons are entirely practical. If a man gets himself blown away while trying to stick it into some woman he's caught, it's the waste of an extra gun you might need in a tight spot later. Without that extra gun *you* might get killed, and all for someone else's quick fuck— or worse, one that he tried to get and failed. Look at this fat bastard. Not much good to his militia now, is he?"

"I salute the practical mind," Viktor said. "But we can't be certain she was here," he continued doubtfully. "You could be wrong, you know."

"Unless you think he came out here to play with himself while he was having a crap, then stuck a knife in his own gut for sexual pleasure . . . "

"All right, all right. You can leave out the sarcasm."

"Besides, there's no knife around here."

Viktor remained silent.

"Time to tell the major," the senior man said. "This woman is something else."

10

November One, the next day, 0800 hours

" . . . nosewheel steering to low . . . " McCann was
coming to the end of the pre-takeoff checks.

"Nosewheel to low," Hohendorf confirmed.

"Wings at twenty-five . . . "

"Wings twenty-five."

Hohendorf checked that both the wingsweep lever
and the position indicator on the instrument panel confirmed the wings were at full spread. The IDS, unlike
both the standard Tornado F.3 ADV and the November
units' Super Tornado F.3S ASV, did not have auto
wingsweep.

" . . . flaps to mid . . . "

"Flaps mid . . . " Hohendorf again checked for confirmation, this time reaching for the flap lever and
swiftly double-checking the instrument panel. "Call for
permission."

"Roger," McCann said and spoke to the air traffic

control tower. "November tower. Condor Zero-One permission to takeoff."

"Roger, Condor. Clear to takeoff. Wind three-three-zero, five knots."

As soon as he heard the confirmation, Hohendorf pushed the throttles into combat burner and released the brakes simultaneously. The IDS leaped forward, its uprated engines powering it along the runway. It was not the familiar unleashed fury of the ASV's normal takeoff run, but even with its full practice war load, it did not hang about. Soon he was easing it off the tarmac, pulling gently on the stick.

He brought the wheels up quickly, then moved the flap lever forward to the up position to avoid damage to them as speed increased. He'd known people who had forgotten, only to discover their error when the warning light for flap malfunction came on.

"Gear traveling," McCann intoned.

Hohendorf let the speed build, leveling out at two hundred feet as the aircraft crossed the coast, heading out over the Moray Firth. To simulate crossing the Adriatic, they would travel some distance out to sea before turning back toward land, this time making for a range that was normally used by ground-attack aircraft. For the practice mission, it had been reserved exclusively for them.

On the range itself, a mixed convoy of stripped scout cars, tanks, and personnel carriers seeing out their days as static practice targets had been positioned on a rough track in a valley. The IDS carried special practice ordnance that would emulate with remarkable accuracy the effect of a cluster bomb attack. The submunitions within the bombs contained nothing more destructive than white paint. When released, a small charge would detonate, leaving a sunburst of white at the point of impact. This would enable the range marshals to judge whether the attack had indeed been accurate.

The IDS also carried an instrumentation pod that simulated an air-to-air defensive load of four Kraits. At some point during the mission, they would be attacked by two USAF F-15Es. The formidable two-seat Eagles, though designed as multirole aircraft, were no less capable than the single-seat versions and were meant to simulate Su-27s and MIG-29s. No times or directions of attack had been given. It would be up to them to fight their way out of the ambush whenever it came, from whatever quarter.

"Keep an eye out for those Eagles, Elmer Lee," Hohendorf said. "I don't want to be bounced."

The F-15 pilots might well have decided to wait out to sea, hoping to catch them unaware and force them into a fight. Hohendorf would then be compelled to jettison all the attack stores in order to lighten the aircraft for air combat, which would be bad news. Getting tangled with fighters *before* unloading over the target effectively meant the mission was a failure, even if you avoided getting shot down. They had prevented you from making it to target—which was what it was all about.

"Nobody bounces old Elmer Lee," McCann announced firmly.

"I am relieved to hear it." In his mask, Hohendorf's face creased into a brief smile.

"Waypoint coming up," McCann said. "Two-one-eight . . . *now*."

"Roger . . . two-one-eight."

Hohendorf reefed the IDS into a tight left turn, banking steeply as he changed onto the new course. At a hundred fifty feet, they headed landward. As yet, no Eagles had put in an appearance to spoil their day.

Bosnia

The major had made a fundamental error.

In his eagerness to get his APCs to the sector that the lead omega team had called in, he had decided to travel through the night on roads with which he was not familiar. It was a mistake that was to cost him dearly.

The sector was itself in an area that would take him along a different route. Also, when he did get there, the road was well away from where the team had reported finding the militia commander's vehicle and the dead bodies. It would thus take considerable time for the troopers aboard the APCs to reach the spot. As for the specialist search teams already in the mountains, they were now so widely spread out they would be of little use to the first omega team if it got into trouble. Hence his hurry.

In their headlong dash through the night, the APCs had turned onto a narrower road with many more bends than previously. The major's deputy had been given the lead, to scout ahead, and his APC had hit a mine. It was the first they'd encountered, and its effect was devastating.

The explosion had flung the APC onto its back and spun it, so that it lay like a roadblock across the road. The captain and three soldiers had been killed instantly. Of the remainder in the vehicle, one had escaped totally unscathed and the others were, severely wounded. Dawn had found the rest of the column still bunched at the scene of the explosion.

They had removed the bodies and the wounded; then the armored carrier, still on its back, was shoved off the road and down the steep mountainside. It rolled ponderously, taking an avalanche of rock and trees with it, down into the waiting gorge below.

The major watched it emotionlessly, but inside he was seething.

The woman was becoming expensive.

Zunica Paic had made it back to hell. She'd taken a roundabout route by air via Germany and Greece. She'd then continued by road and finally on foot, hiking across the mountains with a small guerrilla team which had escorted her to the little town where she had once been a teacher.

The school had long since been shelled into a gaping

skeleton of its former self. Many of her former pupils were dead. The war had taken her from teaching and turned her into a highly competent nurse. She had, in her time, treated the wounded from all sides, civilians and soldiers alike.

Her trip to Western Europe had been to attend meetings, where others like herself had been lobbying for firm action to try and save what was left of her decimated country. She had been brought out to describe in graphic detail the horrors she had herself witnessed.

While McCann and Hohendorf were heading toward their practice attack run, she was in a cramped room in a makeshift hospital that was minus a large chunk of its outside wall. In the woefully underequipped room, she was attending to three seriously wounded combatants: Muslim, Serb, and Croat. Two were comrades-in-arms, the third their current enemy. All were swathed in dirty, blood-soaked bandages, and were far too ill to care about whom they were lying next to on the dust-strewn floor. Their appalling injuries had given them a kind of mutual solidarity. They might even have spoken to each other, had they been able to.

None of the four people in the room heard the shell that blew them to oblivion. The room, the three casualties of an insane conflict, and Zunica Paic simply ceased to exist.

Two hundred feet above the Grampians, Scotland

Hohendorf felt a shiver go through him and found himself thinking of Zunica Paic.

"Strange," he muttered.

"You say something?" McCann called, head moving continuously as he searched the sky for sign of a possible ambush by the Eagles. Nothing had alarmed the warning systems, but he found himself wishing for the long radar and optical reach of the more familiar advanced systems of the ASV.

"No," Hohendorf said.

"Must clean out my ears when we get back. Next waypoint," McCann went on before Hohendorf could make comment. "Right, right . . . two-seven-six."

"Right, two-seven-six."

"Going to full auto?" McCann suggested as Hohendorf banked the aircraft onto the new course.

"Yes. Let her take us ten miles to target."

Hohendorf programmed the autopilot and flight director system just aft of the flap lever, and let the Tornado IDS fly itself across the landscape at two hundred feet, making its own changes of course as and when required.

Like McCann, he too scanned the sky, and again like McCann, he missed certain aspects of the ASV. Like the helmet sight, for one. He knew that somewhere out there, the Eagles were already waiting to pounce.

Moscow, about the same time

Kurinin was scanning the early sheaf of eavesdropped transcripts. So far, he'd found nothing that gave a single clue to any rescue mission that was being planned. Yet it was inconceivable that one was not even now in the process of being put into action.

There was no evidence, either, to show that she had communicated with anyone. Clearly, it had long been decided that she would not do so, in order to avoid a possible eavesdrop and subsequent pinpointing of her signal. While this ostensibly left her isolated, it also gave her considerable freedom to do as she pleased.

But there had to be some form of contact.

Kurinin was convinced she was working toward a pickup point that had been set up well in advance. He did not believe for a second that she had been abandoned, no matter what it looked like on the surface. She was far too valuable—to both sides.

The major had better come up with results, and soon.

Two hundred feet above a valley floor

The IDS stood on a wingtip and appeared to skim past a hungry-looking cliff face. McCann looked at it with clinical detachment. No point worrying about hitting it. If they did, he wouldn't know much about it. At this speed, he'd be toast in fractions of a second.

As the world tipped the other way, he checked his attack display.

"Target fifteen point five miles . . . " he advised Hohendorf, who waited for him to continue. " . . . fourteen . . . twelve point five . . . ten miles."

"Roger," Hohendorf confirmed. The wings were now level. "Reverting to manual." He briefly squeezed the switch on the front of the stick at the base of the handgrip, disengaging the autopilot.

"Still no sign of the Eagles."

"They're out there," Hohendorf remarked with certainty. "They will do their best not to warn us."

McCann checked their tail. Nothing. He glanced up through the canopy.

"Clear as a teenager's face without zits," he announced. "Five miles to target. Looks like we've got this one locked up. Ready when you are."

"Okay. Master arm on."

"Confirmed. We're hot and ready. Target four miles."

"Okay. Speed five-fifty. We're going in fast. I've got the fall line. Burners in."

Hohendorf moved the throttles to combat thrust. The engine nozzles flowered open as twin tongues of flame torched their way out of the tail. The Tornado surged forward. On the HUD, the glowing numerals of green began to count up the airspeed. Soon it was at six hundred knots, nearly seven hundred miles an hour.

He uncaged the release.

"Pickle-pickle now!" McCann called.

Hohendorf held his thumb on the button. The computers checked all was well with the release parameters. The aircraft gave the barest of vibrations. The bombs were gone.

The Tornado swept over the target area at nearly seven hundred knots—just over eight hundred miles an hour—flashing over the derelict armored vehicles and temporarily breaking the sound barrier at that altitude, until Hohendorf came out of burners as they made their exit.

The bombs showered their submunitions and bursts of white began to pepper the area. Soon, every vehicle was sporting a dalmatian color scheme. With live ammunition, they would have obliterated the entire target.

The range marshal's voice came on their headphones as they fled the area. "Well done, Condor! A perfect straddle!"

They did not acknowledge, in order to keep the F-15s guessing, and for security reasons. The range marshal would understand. With the exception of their own secure intercockpit communication, they would not converse with anyone during flight—until the approach to November One, which would also be secure. For the real mission itself, not even takeoff and landing communication with the tower at the designated base in Italy would be made.

"Looks like we foxed the Eagles with our waypoint pattern," McCann now said.

They had deliberately taken an unpredictable route to target, with Hohendorf sometimes flying manually as low as fifty feet. At other times, he'd left it to the autopilot, which was a permanently set up program on the IDS and would not go lower than two hundred feet. So far, they appeared to have eluded the Eagles. The best result would be to get back to base without ever making contact.

"Let's make sure we beat them all the way," Hohendorf now said cautiously as they hurtled at a hundred feet through a tight valley, "and make it back to November One without a single contact."

McCann was looking up through the canopy during

one of the rare moments when Hohendorf had the wings level.

"Uh—oh," he muttered warningly.

"What? What?"

"Forget about not making contact. I just saw a flash up top. Someone's canopy, maybe. Something's prowling up there, waiting. He probably hasn't seen us yet, so I'm leaving the radar on standby."

"Okay. But don't worry about him. His friend might be down in the dirt with us. That's the one who'll be the first danger."

McCann took a quick look behind. "Zilch. They're not using their radars, either, in case our warning receivers go beserk. They're hoping to sneak up on us."

"Make sure they don't."

"Count on it." McCann took another swift look behind. "We've got a tail!" he exclaimed sharply. "You were right, Axel. One of the bozos is down with us, although not so low. Maybe he's scared of bending his nice new airplane."

"Then let us use that weakness." It was significant that Hohendorf did not waste valuable time by questioning McCann's sighting. "Is he still there?"

"He's dipped behind a mountain way back, but he's there all right."

It had been the smallest of fleeting specks, skimming a distant ridge. Someone less sharp-eyed would have completely missed the shape that, despite the Eagle's great size, had been made minute by distance.

Hohendorf had activated the instrumentation pod, and the simulated Kraits were now armed. He brought the Tornado up to two hundred feet and tipped it onto a wing; then he banked more steeply until they were streaking along a mountain flank with the ground above the canopy, heading for the crest.

"Uh, yeah," McCann was saying as nonchalantly as he could. "I've heard about this upside down stuff from Wolfie. Do that often, do you?"

"Only when I need to."

"That figures."

They breasted the summit, then dropped into a parallel valley. Hohendorf reversed bank, bringing the canopy the right way up as they continued along the opposite side of the mountain.

McCann again checked all around. Nothing.

Then Hohendorf was throttling back, bringing the speed down to four hundred knots. The IDS was now at its most agile for the speed and this low down could turn surprisingly well, actually having a turn radius that was better than the F-14 Tomcat, though not the mighty Eagle. The medium to lower levels were its arenas, and Hohendorf intended to use that.

No other aircraft, including the Eagle, could keep up with it for long in a high-speed dash in the dense lower air without shaking its crew and possibly itself out of the contest. The IDS could take nearly a hundred twenty minutes nonstop at any given time, whereas the Eagle E, with its beautiful big wing, would have to give up by forty minutes. Before upgrading to IDS(E), only the Sukhoi Su-24 could have matched it.

Many other opponent aircraft would also be confounded by its turning and burning ability so close to mother earth, while their pilots desperately attempted to keep a wary eye on the hungry ground, as well as trying to stay in the fight. An Eagle was about to find out.

"Hey," McCann said, "why are we killing speed?"

"We're going to have to fight, so we're now rigged for air combat." Hohendorf spoke rapidly. "The high boy is the stopper in the bottle. The one you saw behind us is in another valley, waiting to slip onto our tail. His buddy up top is spotting for him, when he can see us. As they're not using the radar, they've got to go visual. That will make it very difficult for them, and good for us."

"How do you know he's in the next valley? Or the next?"

"Simple. We look until we find him."

"Now why didn't I think of that?"

"Also, by going slowly I might force him to slip ahead without his realizing it."

"Fiendish. I *like* it."

"Keep those eyes working, Elmer Lee."

"You got it."

They had flipped into the third valley when dead ahead and trapped by the valley walls was a fat Eagle, forced to follow the route or flee skyward. Either option left it easy meat for a Krait shot.

Hohendorf was on to it with alacrity as soon as he got the sighting. On the HUD, the symbology showed it was well within Krait range. He got the tone and the locked diamond. He squeezed the trigger.

Both the acquisition tone and the launch tone on the Eagle's warners must have startled its pilot. It leaped for the sky like a game bird flushed by beaters.

But it was already too late.

"Shit!" they heard on the airwaves.

"There goes one pissed Eagle jock," McCann crowed. He kept the Eagles' frequency open so he could eavesdrop.

A voice said something else, very crossly.

"Well, ah do declare," McCann said, exaggerating a southern accent. "Someone just said 'fuck' for everyone to hear. You just can't tell with kids these days. Do we go to radar?" he added.

"No. If his friend wants to play as well, let him come looking for us. We'll stay passive. Keep monitoring their transmissions. We might hear what he's planning."

At Hohendorf's words, McCann had looked upward.

"Oooh boy," he said.

"Company?"

"And how! The top Eagle's madder than a hornet and is coming down for revenge. Any ideas?"

"We'll *wait* for him. I want him down here."

"No mud-moving Tornado's going to make a weak tit out of me," a hard voice said.

"We wait? Didn't you just hear that guy? Axel, ol' buddy, I've seen you work. I know you're an ace. But up there and coming like an express train is one ferocious Eagle. We're not in our all-singing, all-dancing ASV. Right now, we're flying a mudslinger *not* a gunslinger, and upgrade or no upgrade, this baby is not a *real* turner and burner . . . especially . . . " McCann twisted around for another look at their nemesis. " . . . especially when the other guy jockeying that Eagle is feeling meaner than a cottonmouth."

"We wait for him," Hohendorf insisted. "If he's getting angry, that's good. Angry means mistakes."

"Reckon he knows that? Oh, hell."

"What, Elmer Lee?"

"They must have figured we're listening. They've either switched to a secure channel, or they're not talking to each other anymore."

"No matter. We've still got plenty up our sleeve."

"I sure hope so."

McCann, trying to keep the Eagle in sight as Hohendorf flung the IDS past the granite face of a sheer cliff, wondered whether his pilot had bitten off more than he could chew this time. In the ASV, Axel was magic; but this was not the ASV, no matter how good the upgrades incorporated for the specialist November missions. The enhanced IDS, though vastly improved, was still no dogfighter; not, as he'd just told Hohendorf, in a real sense, and most certainly not against this latest model of the Eagle. True, they'd just got the first one, but that had been because of good tactics. It had not been a turning fight.

On the other hand, Hohendorf was cunning as well as extremely daring, so perhaps . . .

The sudden blaring of a lock-on tone jarred McCann out of his reverie. Almost immediately he sighted the Eagle, still high, but coming down now on their right rear quarter.

Hohendorf, having carefully noted the position of the Eagle on his threat warner, had already worked out his tactic. He rolled the aircraft onto its back, and pulled gently.

Looking up through the canopy at the ground, McCann felt certain it was reaching for them. But they were quickly the right way up again, and even lower down. The warning tone died.

McCann looked for the Eagle. It was nowhere to be seen.

"When we were upside down back there," he said, "a stone waved at me."

"I thought it was just getting out of the way."

"You ever thought that perhaps if God wanted us to skate on our heads, He'd have put wheels on them?"

"Better have a word with Him about that."

McCann grinned. "And I thought *I* was crazy."

In the Eagle, the backseater was anxious. "Joey, that guy up ahead's a nut. Watch it, will you? He's going to drag the fight very low and keep us there."

"I know what he's trying to do."

"Yeah. Well, just watch it."

"You play with your displays and leave the jockeying to me," the pilot growled. "I'm going to ream that god-damned Tornado."

The backseater said nothing. When Joey Gialpini got into a mind-set, there was no changing him. Gialpini was a good pilot, one of the best, but he had a flaw. He some-times didn't seem to know when to temper aggression with common sense.

The backseater watched as they entered a valley at five hundred feet. The Tornado had been skimming the ground, it seemed, and *upside down*. A real crazy. He hoped Gialpini would not attempt to pull that stunt, or go lower. Five hundred feet was low enough in these mountains.

● ● ●

Three times, the Eagle had achieved a lock-on, and each time, Hohendorf had broken it. Never once did he leave the mountains.

To be successful in air combat, a smart pilot would use anything to his advantage, while making those very things a disadvantage to his opponent. Hohendorf was employing a substantial armory.

He kept forcing the Eagle to come low, maneuvering in an environment where its fuel consumption and turning ability would not be at its best. By keeping the opposing aircraft where it did not really want to be, he was loading the tactical dice in his favor, while also increasing the tension of its crew. The Eagle pilot would certainly not enjoy being dragged into the mountains when life would be so much easier if he could zap the smaller fleeing target with a shot from up top.

But Hohendorf was not about to give him that opportunity.

The Eagle pilot, he reasoned, should be getting increasingly impatient by now—which was precisely the state of mind he was aiming for.

McCann was doing a periodic check of the airspace behind the tail when he said, "Looks like he's blown his cool, Axel. He's heading down like he means it."

They were flying between two mountain peaks at five hundred feet, which for them was a high altitude. The Eagle had gone skyward for better missile acquisition, but the target Tornado, darting across and between the peaks, was making life impossible. The Eagle decided to come down for another try.

Hohendorf was now baiting the trap.

McCann studied the threat display. "I've got him at twelve miles, and going through three-zero." He meant three thousand feet. "Still heading down. This guy's after blood," he added.

Ahead of the Tornado was a narrow chasm that seemed to disappear into darkness. The lighting conditions made it look as if the depression continued for a great distance, but in fact, high ground blocked it not much further ahead. From their current distance, however, the high ground was invisible. McCann knew of pilots who had plowed straight into a mountainside after having been caught out by such visual phenomena under similar lighting conditions. He knew Hohendorf was going to make that mountain work for them.

"Arming the Kraits," Hohendorf said. "Keep an eye on him."

"He's still there, and closing. He wants to make sure."

"A man who likes a precise kill. Good."

"For him? Or for us?"

"For us, of course."

"Just checking."

Hohendorf began to lose height imperceptibly. By the time they'd reached the relative gloom, they were at a hundred feet and still descending.

McCann glanced back. The Eagle, still in bright sunlight, continued on its way down. The invisible mountain was closer.

"He's still there," McCann said, noting that their own altitude was approaching fifty feet. He decided not to comment. "We should be getting his lock-on tone soon," he advised in a voice he hoped was as calm as he thought it sounded.

Almost at the moment he'd spoken, the tone gave its urgent warning. At the same instant, Hohendorf took the Tornado into a high and wide barrel roll. But he intended to complete only the top half of the maneuver.

The IDS(E) seemed to rise swiftly, like a strange fish leaping out of the deep, to displace itself sideways in a great sweeping arc, and clearing the peak, to dive into the valley on the other side.

The pursuing Eagle had suddenly found itself with no target, and a great wall of earth blocking its way.

"*Jesus Christ!*" the pilot shouted. He slammed the throttles as far forward as they would go and hauled fiercely on the stick, all thoughts of nailing the Tornado forgotten. Survival had become the utmost priority.

In the backseat, the weapons systems officer stared at the looming mass, convinced he was about to die. His heart beat furiously. He held his breath and made no sound.

But the Eagle was free. It leaped for the sky, seeming to claw its way upward on twin tongues of flame.

The backseater let out his breath slowly. He was still alive. Then to add insult to injury, he heard the long continuous tone that told him they had just been shot down.

"Fucking shit!" Joey Gialpini snarled. "That son of a bitch suckered me. The guy's a maniac. He nearly put us into that fucking mountain!"

The backseater, heart rate slowly returning to normal, said quietly, "Wrong, Joey. *We* nearly put ourselves into that mountain. The guy played hard, and in a real fight, we'd have died. We may think he's crazy, but he plays for keeps."

"Hey, you listen. Don't tell me how to fly this bird. Okay? You backseat drivers are all the goddamned same. Frustrated goddamn pilots." Gialpini used to fly single-seat Eagles and sometimes tended to wish he'd never been posted to two-seaters.

The backseater said nothing.

Pilots, he thought with world-weary resignation. Always thinking they knew it all.

"Knock it off, knock it off," McCann heard on the original frequency. The Eagles had decided to call it a day.

"Hear that, Axel?"

"I heard."

"Yeeharr! Man . . . we just nailed *two* Eagles in this baby. Two! Count them! Axel, that was some hot pilot stuff. Pure, sweet magic. If we do meet any MIGs over there, I reckon we can take them on in this ship after all."

"I prefer to say wait and see."

But McCann was not listening. "Man," he repeated. "That was *nice*. Yeah."

Hohendorf had taken the Tornado to ten thousand feet. He rocked the wings once to let the Eagles know he acknowledged the end of the fight. Then he rolled the IDS onto its back and again plunged earthward.

It had been a good practice mission.

II

Moscow, late afternoon, same day

The long room was lined with computer terminals, at each of which sat a uniformed operator. Interfaced with each computer was a digital audiotape recorder and a printer. Every so often, a lieutenant would enter the room to pick up a sheaf of papers from one or more of the operators, then leave.

At one of the terminals, a young female sergeant with headphones was studying her screen intently. The onscreen graphics had been quartered into windows with different displays. On the bottom right was the generic icon of a tape recorder; top left showed a frequency display. At top right was a map with radial distances marked upon it, and bottom left was a document screen. The language on the document was English. All the operators were fluent linguists.

The sergeant reached with a forefinger to touch a button on the tape recorder display. The spools began to rewind. When they stopped, she touched the play button. The recorder began its playback. She put her hands to the headphones as she listened, then began to type at the keyboard. She went through this routine several times.

The next time the lieutenant turned up, she removed her headphones to speak to him.

"Comrade Lieutenant, I think the comrade general should see these." She handed him two sheets of paper.

He stared at her neutrally, then glanced at the papers. "Plain-language transmissions between NATO aircraft. What's so special about that?"

"I . . . made some notes." She handed him another sheet of paper, which he accepted reluctantly.

"You made some notes," he remarked coldly. "You would not by any chance, *Comrade* Sergeant Kaminova, be trying to further ingratiate yourself with the comrade general, would you? You would not be looking for advancement to lieutenant, perhaps? Is it possible you see yourself as my replacement?"

She fought to keep the contempt this display of stupidity triggered in her from reaching her voice. "No, Comrade."

The problem, as she well knew, was that she had once turned down the lieutenant's advances. She knew he considered her little more than a whore because she had once slept with a westerner who had been attempting to illegally sell weapons to one of the republics. The westerner had succumbed to pillow talk, and the evidence gathered had successfully terminated his activities. She had done a good job, but the lieutenant had deliberately chosen to mistake duty for lust.

The lieutenant stared at her for some moments. "I'll check this out," he said. "I'll see if it's worth taking to the general. You can continue with your work now, Kaminova."

He continued to stare at her until she returned to work at her computer. Then he collected more eavesdropped material from two more operators and went out.

■   ■   ■

The Bosnian mountains, early evening

She had watched them all day, and there was still enough light to see them clearly. She had decided to risk back-tracking toward the BMP—not to check on it, but to throw off any pursuers who would have expected her to continue in the opposite direction. She had known that there was always a chance that she'd run into them; she had therefore not been too surprised to spot the omega pair.

She was surprised to find, however, that they appeared to be the very two who had stopped by her hiding place. She was convinced of this because they were in the same area as the BMP, which meant *they* had doubled back and were indeed tracking her. Though they would not have found any evidence of the route she had taken, they'd certainly have come across the armored vehicle and the bodies. She'd therefore decided it was necessary to neutralize them. They were smarter than their colleagues, and that made them dangerous.

They would almost certainly have contacted the major, she reasoned as she watched them approach from her vantage point. She had positioned herself in good cover, and in such a way that they would be bound to come into her line of fire.

As they drew nearer, they talked to each other in a relaxed manner, clearly not expecting her to be so close.

Then they were where she wanted them.

"Stop!" she called out in Russian. "And don't even think of doing anything stupid. You won't make it."

The effect was profound. They were certainly startled, but like true professionals, neither made a move, choosing instead to remain perfectly still. They knew she would shoot, and would not miss. Having seen her work by the BMP, they weren't about to make mistakes.

She remained in cover.

"Smart work," she said to them. "I wondered whether you would double back. What made you?"

"A hunch," the taller one replied.

"Hunches sometimes pay off," she admitted grimly.

"What are you going to do with us?"

"I won't kill you unless you give me reason. You saw the bodies?"

"Yes. You did a job on the fat one."

"The pig raped my friend and boasted about it."

"Seems like he was trying for you, too," the second one remarked. "Did he make it? We'd like to know."

"Viktor can be a bit blunt sometimes," the taller one said conversationally.

"What do you think?" she asked. He was clearly weighing his chances, she thought. But it was a lost cause. He had none.

"We think not," the taller one replied dryly. "We think the fat commander was listening to his dick, and not his head."

"That's the trouble with men."

"Some men," he corrected. She thought he was smiling.

"Some men," she agreed. "You have warned the major, of course."

"What do you think?" from the shorter one.

"I think you have, and he's on his way right now."

"If you don't intend to kill us," the tall one said, "you have a problem."

"No, I haven't. Take off your equipment. *Now!* I said I would not kill you without reason. Try not to give me any."

They hesitated only slightly, then removed all their equipment. Neither made a move toward a weapon.

"Now step back. Further. Stop. Turn around. Backs to me. Now hands clasped behind your heads."

They obeyed every order.

She scrutinized them carefully.

"Now," she snapped. "The clothes. All of it."

"What?" Viktor was scandalized. "It will be a freezing night this far up the mountain. We'll freeze to death."

"I doubt it. You're specialists. You'll survive. Plenty of clothes by the BMP. By the time you get there, you'll be very warm. I think you're more worried about what your comrades will say when they hear what happened. Now get those clothes off. I haven't much time to waste. Don't force me to kill you. *Do it.*"

With great reluctance, they began to do as they'd been told.

"The major won't be so considerate when he catches up with you," the tall one said.

"He won't catch up with me. I won't be helping him to make colonel."

Viktor gave a sudden laugh. "You, too? We were saying the same thing . . . about us. We don't want to die just so he can make colonel. So you know our major?"

"I know him," she said, but did not elaborate.

"At least we've got something in common," Viktor went on. "We can't stand the bastard, either."

They were now both naked.

"Now off you go," she commanded. "Move it! And don't try to sneak back and be heroes. Not for the major. You'd be dead. And if either of you tries to track me again after you join up with him, you *will* be."

She waited long enough to make certain they had taken her advice and were not attempting to sneak back to ambush her; then, working swiftly, she grabbed what could be of use from their packs and piled the rest in a heap. She also took one of their radios. It would help to listen in on the major. She took all their weapons and the remaining radio, with the intention of dumping them into the first water she saw.

Then she moved on.

"Look at it this way . . . "

"Shut up!"

"Oh, come on," Viktor said. "She had us cold. She could have killed us at any time. Would we have done the same in her place? Would we have let her walk away?"

"Suddenly you're in her corner? She took our radios. She can hear every damn thing the major's planning."

"Not everything," Viktor countered unworriedly. "Only what comes on the radio. Besides, when the major realizes what's happened, he'll change frequency."

"And that's good, is it? What if he takes a long time to work that out? 'If she gives me any trouble . . . ' Do you remember saying that?" his companion sneered. "I'm walking back with my balls freezing, to put on dead men's clothes. You think this is a joke?"

"Look at it this way," Viktor repeated. "You could be dead. Like those militia bastards out there."

"Shut up!"

Moscow

The jealous lieutenant had a serious problem. His powerful sexual attraction to Sergeant Kaminova came up against an equally strong feeling of revulsion. The revulsion was due to the fact that she had, according to the tapes of the incident, indulged in quite uninhibited love-making with the western arms smuggler.

Every time he thought of the tapes, he had visions of the young sergeant being vigorously straddled by that sleek, unpleasant man. The cries she made on the tapes haunted his waking and sleeping hours. He kept seeing the man pumping away into her; pumping and grunting, pumping and grunting, shifting her into all sorts of positions while still inside her.

And all that had happened afterward was that the bastard had been deported. So what if his details were on file for future use at some unspecified time? The man had enjoyed the woman he fancied, the woman he had himself dreamed about doing all those things to. But *she* had enjoyed being screwed by that western criminal.

The lieutenant felt rage boil within him. She was just a stinking whore carrying the rank of sergeant, he persuaded himself. And as for that western thug, what he did to her was an insult to . . .

The lieutenant halted his thoughts. As a professional intelligence officer, he ought to know better.

Unfortunately for him, and Kurinin, he would not be the first nor the last professional to allow his emotions to cloud his judgment. His jealousy made him believe Sergeant Kaminova was trying to suck up to the general. She clearly believed they now had a special relationship which would bring rapid promotion to lieutenant in its wake. The entrapment of the arms smuggler had been the general's idea.

As a result of his bitterness toward the sergeant, the lieutenant decided that the transcripts, and the notes she had made, were not of sufficient interest to the general. After all, everyone knew that NATO aircraft transmissions were routine stuff that came in such quantities most were binned.

He graded Sergeant Kaminova's transcripts accordingly, and began to scrutinize the next batch.

The Bosnian mountains, midnight

Not wanting to hit another mine, the major had stopped his column of APCs for the night. He was still some distance from the sector that the first omega team had called in, and was somewhat agitated that he'd heard nothing further from them for quite a while now. There was no regular reporting schedule as such. Though he'd been working on the principle of the fewer transmissions the better to avoid eavesdrops, he was feeling uneasy. He therefore broke his own rule of never contacting the teams, but speaking to them only when they made their terse reports.

"Omega One," he called. "This is Alpha. Report."

There was no reply. Were they deliberately ignoring him? he wondered. The warning tone on their personal radios should have alerted them to open the channel.

The specialist troops were not like his own men. Though they were nominally under his command and duly gave his rank the necessary respect, he always got the impression they accepted him with sufferance and did not look upon him as a real soldier. Their *real* commander was the lieutenant in charge of them, one half of the Omega Nine pair. The lieutenant had an attitude that bordered on the contemptuous, which he barely disguised.

"Omega One," the major repeated. "This is Alpha. Report."

There was still no reply.

Hating to do so, the major contacted Omega Nine. "Omega Nine, this is Alpha. Report."

"Omega Nine," came the supercilious voice. There was an air of patient expectation that was palpable. It was as if the Guards lieutenant had been interrupted by a tiresome child.

"Omega One do not report."

"They must have their reasons."

The major considered that remark and kept a hold of his temper. *"Call them!"* he demanded firmly. "That's an order!"

"Omega Nine," the lieutenant acknowledged with infuriating calm. "Out."

"Omega One," the major heard the lieutenant call. "Omega Nine. Report."

There was a sense of familiarity in the voice that made the major feel as if he had eavesdropped on a private conversation. It served to annoy him and he took pleasure in the petty victory when Omega One still did not reply.

"Omega Nine to Alpha. Omega One do not . . . "

"I heard."

"Well?" The question hung on the airwaves insolently.

You're in command, Major. What are you going to do? The major could hear the unspoken words ringing in his ears. If the other omega teams were listening, they were propably sniggering at him.

Tightening his lips, the major made a decision. "To all omega teams. Kappa Four."

They should now all be retuning their radios to the new frequency. If Omega One had been compromised, at least no one should be able to find the new frequency without a very powerful static frequency hopper. The radios were prtected against mobile hoppers, and if the woman they were hunting had somehow managed to neutralize Omega One, the radio would now be useless to her.

It gave the major a malicious pleasure to think that the arrogant specialists might have been humbled by a woman on the run, despite the fact that this failure would eventually land in his lap. If Omega One had been killed, he could say that their grudging acceptance of his command had served to undermine his authority, and that he had not received the backup due him from their lieutenant.

"Omega teams," the major now called on the new frequency. "Report." If Omega One were still operational, they would be forced to call in.

The teams all reported in, except Omega One.

"All teams close in on that sector," the major ordered sharply. "Omega One is compromised. I'll be with you in the morning. Alpha out."

She'd heard everything . . . until the radio had suddenly gone dead, and she'd realized that the frequency had been changed. Until that moment, however, she'd heard the other teams making their last reports for the night and suspected they were heading toward the two men she had ambushed. Now that they knew the men they called Omega One were out of the game, they would move swiftly in the hope of trapping her.

But she had already altered her route and was a long way from there. She'd heard enough on the radio, and did not really need it anymore.

Some time before, she had come upon a deep lake

into which she had thrown all the unneeded weapons, and the other radio. But she did not now throw away the one she had retained. That would have left an obvious clue to where she'd been. Instead, she kept it in her pack.

She had also dumped the Dragunov and her grenades in the lake. She had not done so before because the right opportunity had not presented itself. The omega team, however, had given her the chance to get rid of the heavy gun, which was now of little use to her. The rifle carried no model or manufacturer's serial numbers on it. If the weapons she had dumped were ever found—which she doubted—it would look as if her rifle had come from the same source as the others. Those who would know it did not would be most unlikely to say anything.

She had, however, appropriated the tall trooper's own gun and ammunition. Remarkably, he'd been carrying an American M16A2 assault rifle—or a very good illegal copy—which was coupled with an M303 grenade launcher. There was a bandolier with spare 40mm grenades which she now wore across her chest. The rifle ammo came in four magazines, taped in pairs for rapid reloads.

Without the Dragunov, she was able to carry everything easily. The grenade launcher gave her a longer reach, and more accuracy. She wondered whether any of the other omega teams had similar rifle/grenade launcher combinations, or whether that had been the tall trooper's own personalized armament. Perhaps he'd gotten it off some soldier he'd killed somewhere on a clandestine mission, and had been allowed to keep it.

She decided to travel through the night, certain that was what the omega teams were doing.

November base, 0100 hours

Hohendorf pushed the throttles into combat burner and the Tornado IDS(E) began its run down the dark swath between the runway lights. Behind the aircraft, the twin plumes of flame seared at the night as it hurtled forward, as if being pushed by the thunder of its roar. He watched as the lights streamed past, then the merest of touches on the stick and the darkened landscape with its firmament of earthbound stars began to fall away. He brought the wheels up quickly.

"Gear traveling," McCann said from the backseat, "and locked. Well, this is the big one."

"The big one indeed," Hohendorf concurred. The world always seems so peaceful up here, he thought.

McCann glanced behind. Three other pairs of flame were rapidly climbing and following. "And here come the guys."

Hohendorf cut the afterburners and took the aircraft in a shallow climb to transit altitude. Dark shapes began to position themselves about the IDS.

"Escort in formation," McCann said.

The four aircraft continued to climb, on their way to Italy.

"There they go," Bowmaker said, looking up into the dark chill of the night. His eyes tracked the now invisible aircraft by their navigation lights.

"Yes, sir," Jason said quietly, head craned upward. "There they go."

"Wish you were with them?" Thurson asked.

"You know I do, sir," Jason replied, glancing briefly in the direction of the air vice-marshal.

They had dispensed with a driver, and with the station commander acting as chauffeur, had all four piled into the group captain's staff car and driven to a spot near the runway threshold to watch the take-off.

"The *Fregattenkapitän's* a good man."

"He is indeed, sir."

Dieter Helm had gone on ahead in the transport aircraft with the backup systems and personnel. By the time the Tornados arrived, everything would be ready at their temporary home on the NATO airfield near the Adriatic. Helm would also conduct the final briefing.

The night departure was deliberate. They would arrive within two hours. The aircraft could be tended to and stowed out of sight and their crews would get to bed with very few people knowing they had arrived. With the constant movement of standard NATO aircraft due to the Bosnian crisis, they would be effectively hidden in plain sight.

Listening to the sounds of the aircraft fading, Jason said, "It's going to be extremely difficult choosing pilots for the new single-seat Starfire when it eventually becomes available for squadron service. I'm hoping we get the first batch off the line, mad budget ax-wielders permitting.

"It's not going to be at all easy, considering it may be necessary to break up very successful crews in order to get the best pilots. I personally favor a two-seat version, although operational requirements may render that unnecessary."

Bowmaker turned toward him. "Starfire? Is that the name you've settled on?"

Jason smiled briefly in the gloom, the airfield lights making his expression ghostly.

"Actually, sir," he replied, "it was our resident maverick, McCann, who suggested it. The British among the crews naturally went for Spitfire. Given the emotional ties, not to mention the fact that it was arguably the most famous and charismatic of the World War Two fighters, such a preference was not entirely unexpected. The Eurofighter—as that aircraft's currently known—is seen as its natural heir."

Jason paused as a silence that was never quite total descended upon the base.

"McCann, however, came up with an ingenious suggestion," he continued. "The Starfighter, U.S.-designed and manufactured, has seen service with many NATO forces, some of whose personnel are now serving with this unit. The November program is multinational. The Eurofighter is a multinational effort. McCann felt this would be best represented in the new fighter by a name that is at once evocative and essentially 'new.' He also felt that as the new fighter is really a twenty-first century airplane with all manner of advanced electronic wizardry, Starfire perfectly encapsulates the spirit both of the endeavor and of the age."

"McCann said all that?" Bowmaker sounded surprised. "Kind of poetic for him, isn't it?"

"He didn't use those precise words, but he was most passionate about it—even excited. Took me rather by surprise, too. But the crews like the name and, I might add, so do I. We hope to get two Starfires for evaluation in the not-too-distant future . . . a two-seat and a single-seat. The competition for those particular cockpits is going to be rather fierce."

"And where is that eventually going to put your Tornado ASVs and IDS(E)s?"

"Oh, the Starfire's not meant to replace them, sir. It's going to *add* to the flexibility of the November program. I'm also considering giving Caroline Hamilton-Jones a try at the Starfire."

There was an odd little sound from Thurson, but the air vice-marshal kept his peace.

"The same young lady who put you down and gave you those crutches?"

"With respect, General, the would-be *assassin* put me down. Flight Lieutenant Hamilton-Jones's remarkable flying skills actually saved my life and possibly the November project as well. I'll make no concessions to her when it comes to joining us as a pilot. She can either hack it or she can't; but she deserves the chance, at the very least."

Bowmaker was silent for a while. "Wing Commander, I have to say you are one hell of an ambitious man, and stubborn when the occasion demands. But your detractors are going to use all of what you've just said—if you express those views to them as forcibly as you have to me—as more ammunition with which to try to blow your program to hell, and cry foul while they're doing it."

"Detractors always look for ammunition at the slightest excuse, sir, and cry foul as a matter of principle. No point pitching your sights low if you believe in something. An interlocking organization on the November principle would have sorted out that long-running, tragic farce in Bosnia by now."

Bowmaker turned to Thurson, who'd been listening to it all with great interest. "First he offers his resignation to the minister, then he makes a pitch for the next generation airplane, then he talks about including female fighter pilots, *and* slams the West's efforts in Bosnia for good measure. Do you ever think of reining in this officer, Air Vice-Marshal?"

"No," Thurson replied succinctly.

"Thank God," Bowmaker said.

London, 0200 hours

A brief shower of rain had left the deserted streets of the city looking shiny and clean. The lights gleamed off them, giving the impression of a vast airport constructed with crazy runways and taxiways by someone in the middle of a nightmare. Yet there was a sense of fearsome order and beauty, brought on by the silence of the night beyond whose shadows the real nightmare lived. Even the lone black cab passing by seemed to do so on silent wheels, and a solitary horn blaring unexpectedly in the distance left its discordant note imprinted upon the stillness like a sacrilege.

In a side street in Mayfair a small group of people were standing outside a private club, saying good-bye to each other. Presently they parted and went their separate ways in pairs. There were six of them: three men and three women. All were mellow, obviously having drunk freely. Three waiting taxis turned on their lights, and each couple each got into one.

Across the road, a shabby man sat in an equally shabby-looking car. He was not interested in the couples. His eyes were on the doors of the club, watching expectantly.

Jimmy Tyne was the kind of photo-journalist everyone loved to hate. Even those who employed him despised him. He was waiting for the sort of scoop he was infamous for: the sight of another couple, who definitely should not be together. Tyne always planned his "raids," as he liked to call them, at unexpected hours and moments. He'd heard that a certain TV personality was at the club that night with someone who was not her husband. The picture he intended to take would be worth plenty, especially syndicated.

He waited with an easy patience born of long hours of stalking. He always got his man—or woman.

A soft knock on his door made him sit up. An elegantly dressed man seemed to be smiling at him. He lowered his window.

"Hullo, Jimmy," the man greeted pleasantly.

"Do I know you?"

"That was a bit abrupt, Jimmy. Be nice."

"Piss off!" He began to raise the window.

The man sighed, grabbed the door, and yanked it open. "Jimmy, Jimmy."

Tyne grew indignant. "What the hell do you think you're doing?" He climbed out quickly, looking belligerent.

The man seemed to be still smiling. A car went past, lights briefly illuminating the face. Tyne had never seen him before.

"You've been naughty, haven't you, Jimmy?"

Tyne's attitude became slightly less belligerent. "All right. I'm beginning to get the message. What are you? Private detective trying to buy me off? Special Branch? Military Intelligence? Customs? Bloody Inland Revenue? Some slug chasing me for child support? If it's that drunken bitch I met at a news conference, I deny all paternity. She's had so many men . . ."

"My, my. We do have a guilty conscience. What have you done to upset all those august agencies? Calm yourself, rodent."

"So which of those bastards are you?"

"None of those. I'm infinitely worse. How are the balls, Jimmy?"

Tyne, suddenly feeling a phantom pain in the region of his crotch, paused to take stock before replying. "It's that fucking tart, isn't it? RAF, are you? One of the wing commander's heavies come to warn me off? Forget it, mate. I don't scare easy. You're wasting your time."

"None of those," Buntline repeated with distaste. "However, it is about the young lady. I'll ignore your rather crude description, but I do hope the balls still twinge now and then."

"Be careful, mate. I've got powerful friends. Now, if you'll let me get on with my work . . . "

"*Work?* Ha–ha. I've seen more elegant alley cats fighting for scraps in a rubbish bin. And as for powerful friends . . . you really would not like to know mine—or me, for that matter. But I'm suddenly very interested in you, and I want to discuss a few things. Bad, bad news, Jimmy."

"Piss off! This is a democracy. I can do what I fucking well like."

"Ha–ha." Buntline spoke the words. "An idealistic gutter rat." He grabbed Tyne by the upper arm. "Do let's have that chat. I've got a rather busy schedule, and as you've so kindly advised, I don't want to waste my time. I positively hate doing that. It's so . . . time-consuming."

"Let go! You're hurting me!"

"Oh, I can hurt you much more than that, Jimmy, old boy."

The NATO base, Italy, about the same time

Hohendorf taxied the Tornado IDS(E) past lines of F-16s and F-15s to the specially allocated area that had been reserved for the November crews and aircraft. As he did so, aircraft were taking off to carry out their regular, UN-sanctioned patrols in Bosnian airspace. The base was like a huge city, alive with both air and vehicular traffic.

McCann was looking about him. "Lot of airplanes, huh?"

"It does seem a little crowded," Hohendorf agreed.

The flight had gone without a hitch. Behind them, the other November aircraft taxied in single file.

"Reckon old Helm is going to let us get some shut-eye pretty soon?"

"He'll probably want to talk to us first."

"Figured he might," McCann said without much enthusiasm.

Helm did not keep them long. After the aircraft had been put under cover, Helm got all the crews together in one of the rooms of the building that had been set aside for them for the duration.

"We shall be guests here for only the rest of tonight," he began, "and part of tomorrow night. On completion of the mission, you will recover directly to November One. Refueling tankers will be on hand for the trip home. You will have from now until mission briefing as free time. Use it wisely, and make sure you are all properly rested."

Helm's eyes surveyed them with steely command as he continued, "No one—that means aircrew and ground crew—will fraternize with any of the personnel on this base. The only exceptions are the liaison team and myself, who will be dealing with the administrative requirements of our detachment. The reasons for our presence concern no one but those who need to know. In effect, we are totally self-contained. By the time I see you again, your aircraft will be armed, fueled, serviced, and mission-ready. Mission briefing will be at 0330 tomorrow. Thank you, gentlemen. Now get some sleep."

Sarajevo Airport, 0530 the following morning

The Hercules C130 plunged in its steep descent
toward the runway. Although the area was meant to be
antiaircraft artillery free, no pilot in his right mind who
had spent even minimal time in Bosnia would put much
faith in such an assurance. Taking potshots at aircraft
just for the sheer hell of it was a common pastime.

The Hercules went for the runway like a suicidal homing pigeon. It landed remarkably smoothly, a testament
to the fantastic skill of its pilot, and taxied to its allotted
space. Its engines then wound down to a halt.

Among the people who got out was a group of four
men and one woman. By the time they had collected
their kit, it was apparent that yet another TV team had
descended upon the unfortunate Bosnian capital. At
least that was how it would have seemed to a casual
observer.

In fact, the eager-looking group of newshounds,
despite having three lightweight TV cameras for all the
world to see, would have avoided the media like the

plague. Only one of those cameras actually worked. A more discerning observer would have noted that they managed to avoid curiosity without seeming effort. An armored long-wheel base Land Rover arrived to pick them up. It ferried them quickly to a far side of the airport where a big olive-green helicopter waited with rotors slowly turning, its sole mark of identity a small group of serial numbers on the tail boom.

If the discerning observer was of an even more curious nature and somehow managed the virtually impossible feat of inspecting their luggage, he or she might have been astonished to find an assortment of weapons and combat attire. Even the fake TV cameras had their part to play. They concealed items of advanced electronic signaling equipment for which any genuine TV crew would have sold their souls.

"When we were coming down to land in that Herc," one of the men said, "I felt sure those bastards out there had their triple-A zeroed in on us. My skin was crawling at the thought."

"Nah," another said. "It's your lice."

They all laughed as they got out of the Land Rover and swiftly climbed aboard the helicopter.

The UH-60 Blackhawk lifted off, heading for a destination only those aboard knew of. At the airport, no one gave it more than a cursory glance. Helicopter movements were part of the Bosnian madness.

When it was well out of sight, one of its crew swung a 20mm, six-barreled rotary cannon outboard. The gun was attached to a triangular bracket that allowed free movement for a wide field of fire. This was in turn fixed to a high-backed armored seat that slid and locked into place whenever the gun was moved to its firing position in the gaping space on the starboard side where a door used to be.

The flak-jacketed gunner, strapped into the seat by a full quick-release harness, was linked to his gun by an umbilical cord that came from the helmet he wore. The helmet, visor down, contained an infrared sighting system that locked on to any heat source within its targeting range, presenting the gunner with an image identification of the acquired target.

Within the helicopter, the bogus TV crew was changing into combat gear and sorting out equipment. When they were finished, the man leading them checked them over. He appeared satisfied.

"Watches," Buntline said over the noise of the helicopter. They each raised their wristwatches to check them in the early light. "I have 0607 . . . *now*." And when they were synchronized, he went on: "The chopper will drop each of us off at the prearranged points. Whoever finds her first will not use voice transmission but will instead activate their individual beacon and the rest of us will join you. She is following a prescribed pattern, but could be anywhere within our area of search.

"We *must* find her before the Tornado carries out its attack on the armored column, and hopefully before the mountain specialists get within firefight distance. As we have no idea of her current status, we must assume she could be in serious need of backup. She may well have already made contact on her run and could even now be wounded and holed up somewhere.

"An extremely capable operative, it's most likely she will find you before you find her, provided she is still mobile. For obvious reasons, she has been operating without communication. You must therefore all ensure you are wearing your identification armbands *at all times.*"

Buntline smiled thinly. "Wouldn't do to come all this way for the dubious privilege of getting shot by her, would it? She will almost certainly spot you long before you know she's there. Finally, and most seriously . . . I don't want casualties. If you see trouble coming, your first priority is to *avoid* it. As far as the outside world knows, we have never been here."

His eyes surveyed each of them steadily. "Our primary

objective is to get that lady out while making ourselves scarce. If you cannot avoid trouble, neutralize the opposition and make a fast exit. If you're unavoidably accosted, speak Serbo-Croat, but make sure you're using the correct inflections to the appropriate person.

"Don't sound like a Serb to a Croat and vice versa, or either of those two to a Muslim. You're on this mission because you're all capable of understanding the nuances of that particular language. Improper use of a single word could get you killed. Don't get bogged down in a holding fight while the opposition awaits reinforcements. That's risking capture, and we don't want any show trials, do we? Fast and furious, then out. And *lose* them. Are we all clear on that?"

They nodded.

"Good. We've got plenty of ground to cover, and just twenty-four hours in which to do it all. Whether we find her, or not, within this window, we all rendezvous with the helicopter at the specified time, and place. If any of you do not make it within the prescribed time it will be assumed you are either dead or, God forbid, captured. Chilling as it may sound, I'd rather you were not captured. The chopper will *not* wait. If you're going down, hit your panic button so we know where the trouble is."

"I wish you'd let me go, sir," the woman said when Buntline had finished.

"No. We need you on the chopper. I'm not refusing because I think you're the 'little woman' who should stay out of harm's way and that sort of nonsense. Frankly, you're a genius with all the marvelous electronics we've got aboard. You're our link with the ATARS aircraft, and our homing beacon. I'm simply maximizing the capabilities of my force. Besides, you could be facing antiaircraft fire, as well as a possible attack by fighter aircraft. Believe me, this may well not be the safest place to be when the stuff hits the fan."

Buntline glanced at his watch, then looked at one of

the men. "Your drop zone's coming up in six minutes."

The man, eyes neutral, nodded.

At about the time that Buntline was preparing to drop his first searcher, the Omega One team watched from cover as the team they recognized as Omega Seven cautiously approached the BMP. Two of the bodies were now naked, their clothes appropriated, as had been their weapons. Omega One had lost so much time returning that after they had clothed and rearmed themselves it had been pointless trying to go after the woman. It made more sense to await one of the teams they knew would have been sent out once they had not reported.

Viktor watched as the soldiers checked out the area. "Took them long enough to get here," he remarked sourly. "Better late than never, I suppose. The major must have overworked his brain cells trying to figure out what had happened. If she had wanted to kill us, all they'd be looking at now would have been our dead bodies, like those cadavers out there."

His companion scratched. "Those bastards didn't wash. I've got an army of things living in these clothes. We'd better make our presence known." He did not sound enthusiastic. "This is going to take some explaining. They might not recognize us in time in these clothes, so let's do this carefully. I don't particularly want to get blown away by that Siberian."

"Hey, you down there!" Viktor called. "Enjoying yourselves?"

He watched with dry amusement as the soldiers immediately dived for cover at the sound of his voice.

"And don't shoot, you trigger-happy gangsters," Viktor went on. He always called his colleagues gangsters, and he hoped they would pick up on that. "This is Omega One. We took the clothes off those stiffs."

There was a long silence as Omega Seven digested this amazing piece of news.

"Viktor?" one called up after a while, uncertainty mixed with astonishment. "Viktor Ilyitch? Only one person calls us gangsters."

"Viktor Ilyitch Pakov at your service. Who else, you Siberian ape?"

"Code word."

"Why do you need the code word? Who else could call you a Siberian ape and get away with it?"

"Code word."

"Stop farting around and give it to him, Viktor," the taller trooper said.

"I was only having some fun."

"You won't feel so funny if that idiot starts firing, or when the major gets here. Give it!"

"You take life too seriously." But Viktor gave the required code word.

One of the Omega Seven came out cautiously while the other remained hidden, giving him cover.

"All right, Viktor," he called. "Your turn, if it's really you. You're supposed to be dead."

"Of course it's me, you vodka-swilling pig," Viktor retorted, moving out of cover.

The Omega Seven team member was wide-eyed as they came down the slope toward him. His colleague, now satisfied they were indeed Omega One, joined him.

"What the hell happend to you?" the Siberian asked, walking around them with the sort of stare normally reserved for circus animals. "What are you doing in those clothes? And where's your kit and weapons?"

"If you'll ease up on the questions," Viktor told him, "I'll tell you."

He did . . . and Omega Seven laughed their heads off.

"Having fun?" Viktor's companion snarled at them.

"You'll never make sergeant now," the Siberian said, the tears of his laughter marking his cheeks. "The major's going to love you."

"I always told him he was too worried about rank," Viktor remarked cheerfully.

The Siberian kept laughing. It got on the tall trooper's nerves.

He lunged for the Siberian. "Listen, you shit . . ."

The Siberian's laughter had stopped abruptly, his knife out and at the trooper's throat, eyes as cold as the wasteland he came from. "I'll finish off what she started right here, if that's what you want."

"Stop it, you two!" Viktor commanded, forcing his way between them. "Save it for when we catch up with that woman. Right now, we have the major to deal with. Listen."

They all listened. The sound of laboring engines came clearly to them.

"The APCs," Viktor said. "The bastard will be here soon, and he's not going to be happy."

"The lieutenant will sort him out," the Siberian said.

"The lieutenant and the others are out in the mountains," Viktor reminded them. "It's we four against his troops if we try anything. If that craphead tries to arrest the two of us for failure, we let him do it. I don't want you getting into trouble on our behalf. I'll try to persuade him to let us continue the hunt on the grounds that since we're the only ones to have made contact, we have an idea of how she operates. But you never know with that KGB shit. The lieutenant can sort him out later if he screws up."

"Your call, Viktor," the Siberian said.

Viktor glanced at the tall trooper who, keeping his temper in check, nodded.

"All right," Viktor said. "Leave the bastard to me."

The bastard was furious and immediately ordered the arrest of Omega One. Omega Seven looked on, ready to take action, but responded to the warning look in Viktor's eyes as they were virtually frog-marched a kilometer down to the road where the APCs were waiting, to be bundled unceremoniously into the back of one.

The major strode up to Omega Seven and stood before them, legs planted apart, hands on hips.

"You wouldn't be thinking of going to your comrades' aid, would you?"

"No, sir," the Siberian replied quietly. "We await your orders."

"Good. Good. I'm glad to hear it. Continue the search. Now that one of your much-vaunted Guards teams has failed, perhaps you can do better. I'll leave some of my men to accompany you. Who knows? They may succeed where you have so far failed. My APCs will continue along the road, dropping troopers off at intervals. Now that we have identified the area, it should only be a matter of time before we get her. The net is closing."

If the Siberian thought the major was displaying a mean-spiritedness in refusing to acknowledge that it was Omega One who'd found the woman in the first place, he kept his thoughts to himself. He didn't think the major would find the woman so easy to trap, either, but kept that thought to himself as well.

As his team moved off, they maintained a fast pace, deliberately moving ahead of the major's less capable troopers.

The major remained where he was, watching them until they had moved out of sight. He then began walking back to the APCs, in the company of four of his own men who had stayed with him quite obviously, as bodyguards.

"I hope she fucking blows his fucking head off," the Siberian said with vicious feeling to his teammate when they were out of earshot of the troops the major had detailed to accompany them. He had the strong feeling they were also there to watch them and eventually report to their wretched commander.

"We can take out those pretend soldiers he left with us," the other suggested.

"No. That would only get the lieutenant in trouble."

"All this for just one woman. Who the hell is she, anyway?"

"Someone the major needs very badly. Did you watch his face? He's really scared of failing and is prepared to get us all killed, his troops included, in order to succeed."

"So what's new? There are officers like that all over the fucking world."

"Not the lieutenant," the Siberian said.

"For every one like the lieutenant, there are ten like that craphead of a major."

"True. Very true."

They continued at their fast pace and soon had left the major's men far behind.

As they walked, the distant *crump* of shells came to them intermittently, seeming to echo faintly through the mountains.

"I wonder which side is shelling which."

"Who fucking cares?" the Siberian remarked callously. "You realize," he went on conversationally, "she'll probably keep Maliev's combination gun . . . the M16 with the grenade launcher he took off the western mercenary he killed in Azerbaijan. If I remember correctly, those grenade rounds are not standard. The mercenary was using some kind of special ammo that was very nasty. What if she uses that fucking thing on us?"

His companion made no comment.

Moscow, same time

The discreetly respectful knock on the door to Kurinin's office was followed by the entry of a lieutenant colonel with cropped iron-gray hair, wearing an extremely smart uniform. He carried a file beneath an arm.

Kurinin looked up from his desk as the man approached. It was clear from his demeanor that their relationship was less formal than would be expected between their individual ranks.

"We have an odd problem," the lieutenant colonel began.

"A problem is a problem, Gregor."

The lieutenant colonel, Gregor Levchuk, seemed unsure of how to phrase his next words.

"There's . . . a sergeant from the monitoring section who insists on seeing you. Personally."

Kurinin stared at him. "Where is this bold person?"

"At the moment, waiting in my lieutenant's office. She has a folder with her, which she insists she will hand over . . . only to you."

As Kurinin continued to stare at him, Levchuk went on, "The lieutenant ordered a sergeant to take it off her. I'm afraid the sergeant . . . failed. He came off somewhat the worse for wear."

"Two sergeants, one male, one female, brawling in your offices?"

"Not . . . exactly. The sergeant tried to pull the folder away when she disobeyed the lieutenant's order to give it up, saying this should be done through proper channels. She virtually told him to hell with channels, and if he didn't attend to her request, *you* might . . . er, make the lieutenant's life difficult. She tripped the sergeant and not expecting her reaction, he fell heavily. Twisted his ankle."

"Let's hear the rest," Kurinin said evenly.

"The lieutenant then tried, first politely, then as a command. She still refused to hand it over, even under the threat of disciplinary action. He reported it, and I ordered him to bring her to me. She then actually refused a direct order . . . from *me*." Levchuk sounded amazed. "You are the only person she will hand the folder to. She appears to be quite unafraid of a mere lieutenant colonel."

"So you have no idea what's so important about that folder?"

"None. I could have it forcibly taken from her, of course. A couple of burly . . ."

"One female noncommissioned officer has my staff officers in a mess. Incredible. What is the name of this bold sergeant?"

"Kaminova."

"The name's familiar. Any specific reason why I should know her personally? Or why she appears to think I should?"

Levchuk laid the file on the desk. "I looked her up. You might find this interesting."

Kurinin opened the file, glanced quickly through some pages. "Ahh. *That* Kaminova. All right. Give me a few minutes with this to refresh my memory, then have her sent in. Despite what's in her file, her reasons had better be good. Thank you, Gregor."

"General."

Levchuk went out.

When Sergeant Kaminova, in full, smart uniform, was eventually summoned into the general's presence, she was ushered in by the lieutenant colonel. With her left hand, she clutched the folder to her well-endowed chest. Her right hand went smartly up in a salute that would have brought tears of joy to the eyes of any drill instructor.

"At ease, Sergeant Kaminova," Kurinin said, "and thank you, Colonel," he added to Levchuk. "I'll take it from here."

With a knowing look from behind Kaminova's back, Levchuk said, "General," and left the room, closing the heavy, polished door softly behind him.

Kaminova remained at attention, though she was no longer saluting.

"I said, at ease, Sergeant," Kurinin reminded her.

"Yes, Comrade General!" She relaxed only slightly, eyes staring ahead.

"Sergeant."

"Comrade General?"

"If we're going to have any sort of conversation, you're going to have to stop saying Comrade General every time you open your mouth. From now on, and for the duration of your stay in this office, when appropriate, you may address me simply as 'sir.'"

"Yes, Com . . . Yes, sir."

"Very well. And now, perhaps you can tell me why you have gone over the heads of your superior officers, why you were insubordinate to my staff officers, *and* gave the orderly sergeant a twisted ankle, in order to come directly to me. Your reasons will have to be very good." There was a cold warning in Kurinin's voice.

Kaminova swallowed, permitted herself to look upon the splendor of the general's uniform, and was for a moment intimidated by all that rank. Then she mentally took a deep breath. She'd come this far and in any case, her head was already very much on the block.

"There is a good reason . . . sir."

"Good enough to risk landing you in trouble?"

"Yes, sir."

Kurinin fell silent once more. He kept looking at her.

"It's . . . it's in this folder." She quickly opened it and took out two sheets of paper. "If the general permits, may I come forward?"

Kurinin nodded. She approached the huge desk, handed him the sheets of paper, then stood back to wait as he read their contents.

The first one was of transmissions between NATO and UN aircraft over Bosnia and the Adriatic, and their various controllers in the air, on the ground, and on aircraft carriers. The second one was different, but seemed no more interesting at first glance.

"That's it, Sergeant?" Kurinin again looked up at her, eyes emotionless. But lurking within them was something very dangerous indeed. Sergeants who demanded to see generals without using proper channels could pay for their presumption. "NATO aircraft transmissions over Bosnia? I see those every day."

Waste my time, and you're in the deepest of trouble, the eyes were saying.

She stood her ground. "With respect, sir, only those considered important, and not this one . . ."

"I have highly trained officers who know what to look for."

"Yes, sir. But . . . but this one came in yesterday. If the general would please read the second paper again. Read it aloud, General."

Kurinin stared at her once more. "Is this a joke?"

"General, I've come this far. If I'm in trouble, I'm already in so deep it doesn't matter."

He continued to stare at her, then said, "Very well. *'Well done, Condor!'*" he began to read in unaccented English. "*'A perfect straddle!'*" He looked up at her, switching back to Russian. "More?"

She nodded wordlessly, astonished by her own temerity.

"*'No mud-moving Tornado's going to make a weak tit out of me,'*" he read on. Then the last line: "*'Knock it off, knock it off.'*" He stopped, staring at the paper. He reread the whole page silently.

Emboldened by his silence, she said, "I made some notes, sir." She went forward again. "On this."

He took the final sheet, still without saying anything. After each line of transmission, she had written, "No response from receiving aircraft!"

Kurinin put down the sheets of paper slowly. "What are you suggesting, Sergeant?"

"Those three lines of transmission were spoken by different voices, but within a small time frame, in the same area . . ."

"Which was?"

"Scotland, General."

Kurinin could feel a tingling up his spine. "Continue."

"It occurs to me, sir, that the recipient aircraft did not

want to be identified in any way. We cannot be certain that the one addressed as Condor was the same referred to in the second line . . . but if it was, then I would suggest that it may be preparing for a special mission."

"You've come to this conclusion from three simple lines of transmission?"

"The general will note how there is always answering chatter on the first sheet. Unsecure messages which prove they don't care who's listening. No frequency-hopping datalinks for us to try to break through. If the ones on the second sheet are also meant to be unsecure transmissions, why no reply from the other aircraft? There may be a very simple answer, but I felt you ought to know, sir. Perhaps it would make sense to you."

"It does indeed," Kurinin told her softly. "This is excellent work, Sergeant Kaminova. You are to be commended on your vigilance. But why did you not bring this to the attention of your watch commander?"

She hesitated.

"I'm waiting," Kurinin said, his eyes drilling into her.

"I did, General."

"And?"

"He . . . he disregarded my suggestions. I made copies and decided to bring them to you personally. I also taped the conversation, in case what I have just said is denied."

"You are thorough. I like that. You have done good work before, Sergeant. That affair with the westerner, for example."

She actually blushed.

"General, I . . ."

"There's no need to say anything. As a result of your activities, we now have another very useful pawn in the West, to be exploited when the moment is right. All things taken into account, I believe, Sergeant, the time has come to advance you to lieutenant. I shall advise the colonel and you should receive confirmation within a few days. As for your watch commander, he will soon find himself the subject of a new posting. Somewhere to keep him busy. One of the republics in the East should be suitable. Thank you, Lieutenant Kaminova."

"Thank you, General!" she said, blushing once more.

"Oh . . . and Lieutenant . . ."

"Yes, sir?"

"From now on, I want you to come to me directly when there's *anything* you believe I should see immediately."

"Yes, General!" She saluted him smartly, and then walked out with a smile on her face.

Levchuk entered soon after. "She looked happy."

"We've got a new lieutenant."

"So, she did bring in some dynamite, after all."

"A very sharp young woman, Gregor. If she's right, what she brought in are a few tons of high explosive. That MIG-29 detachment we've got on standby . . . how soon can they be ready to move to the forward base?"

Levchuk's eyebrows did a quick dance. "You're prepared to use them? On the strength of what she bought in?"

Kurinin pointed to the papers. "Read those. How soon?" he repeated.

"They can deploy and be on patrol by tomorrow morning." Levchuk read through Kaminova's notes quickly. "You obviously think they're after the APCs."

Kurinin stood up and began to pace. "It's a rescue mission, and those November people are involved. *Damn!*"

He had stopped and had raised a tight fist, but instead of slamming it on the desk, he brought it down sharply, halting just before it hit.

The gesture conveyed more power, Levchuk thought, than if he had actually slammed the fist on the desk.

"Because of an idiotic watch commander," Kurinin went on, fingers slowly uncoiling, "we have lost twenty-four valuable hours. Those APCs could be so much twisted metal by the time the MIGs are in the air." He resumed his slow pacing.

"We don't want to drag American aircraft into this. The Yanks are itching for some air combat and feel constrained by the UN."

Kurinin stopped pacing once more and stood before Levchuk. "The MIGs are to go into action *only* if our people are attacked. If the November aircraft are indeed involved, you won't hear a peep out of the West. The Americans will ensure that their fire-breathing pilots are kept out of the area. Clandestine missions in Bosnia?" He gave a short, sour laugh. "We could seriously embarrass them with this one."

"And they could embarrass *us*. We are not immune, Feliks."

"Perhaps not . . . for now. But one day we shall be, Gregor. We shall be. Order the MIG detachment to deploy immediately. Let's hope they're in position in time to give cover to the APCs. *We must get to that woman before she's rescued.* And as for the watch commander, I want his balls for his display of stupidity." A hard chill had entered Kurinin's voice. "Break him to sergeant, then post him to one of those infernal eastern republics. Find him an isolated outpost near the Chinese border."

The Bosnian mountains, 1000 hours

Things had begun to go very seriously wrong for the major. Before he'd had time to deploy any more of his troops, he ran into the worst kind of traffic jam. Three tanks were blocking his way on the narrow mountain road, and the bad news was that the commander of the small column was no indisciplined militiaman, but a battle-hardened soldier—a captain who appeared quite happy to blow the Russian APCs out of his way.

The major had off-loaded his troopers who had

fanned out, ready to back their argument up with high explosive. Antitank teams had taken up positions on the wooded slopes on both sides of the road.

The three Russian built and supplied T-34s, though tanks of Second World War vintage, were still considered to be some of the best medium tanks around. The examples on the road were in excellent condition and were well-armored, packing a massive punch with their 85mm guns. Grouped together in a tight triangle so that all three main guns had a clear field of fire along the road, they would make light work of the APCs at what was virtually point-blank range. It was all down to who delivered the first blow and the tank commander seemed quite happy to oblige. The problem was, his tanks were also vulnerable to the antitank teams. It was a standoff that looked as if it would take all day, at the very least, to sort out.

"You cannot go further!" the tank commander was shouting in quite good Russian. "This is a sensitive area."

"I have authority to be here!" the major shouted back. "All your forces are meant to cooperate."

They were only feet from each other, having walked away from their respective vehicles to meet in no-man's-land while their men looked on, ready to fire upon each other should matters deteriorate even further.

"You have no authority to be in *this* area," the captain insisted.

"This is insane!" the major retorted furiously. "If you do not let my APCs through, you'll be in serious trouble. Your superiors . . ."

"My *immediate* superiors," the captain interrupted, stressing the difference, "would have my guts for breakfast if I let you through. I don't care what deal you've got, and with whom. *No* one comes up here."

The major was exasperated. Time was ticking inexorably on. The embargoed region covered an area of over fourteen hundred square kilometers and *she* was in there somewhere, getting further away from him and closer to her pickup point with each passing second, while this man flaunted his ego like a flag. It never occurred to the major to take his problems with his own ego into consideration. He said nothing about the omega teams, the soldiers he'd already put in, and the woman, who were all prowling within the so-called sensitive area, even as they argued about rights of entry.

"We're *Russian*," he said with as much patience as he could muster and making a bad job of it. "We're . . ."

But the captain was not playing. "I don't care what kind of arseholes you are. NATO, UN, or Russian. No one comes up here."

"I see you like our tanks," the major barked snidely.

"We have some old American Pattons, too," the captain retorted. Two could play *that* game.

"All your *new* tanks are Russian. T-72s, T-74s . . ."

"Want them back, do you?" The captain was smiling thinly.

"Don't be ridiculous!"

"Tell you what," the captain said. "Instead of standing here trading insults, let me suggest this. Your men and my men remain here. You and I, Major, will go and see my superiors, and *if* they say you can pass, then I shall of course obey their orders. I doubt they will agree to let you through . . . but you never know. Perhaps . . ."

"And how long is this supposed to take?"

"I shall request a vehicle be sent for us . . ."

"How *long* is this supposed to take?" the major repeated crossly.

"As long as it takes. My unit HQ is some kilometers . . ."

The major lost his cool. "Are you *insane*? I haven't the time to go to your headquarters to while away the hours with some half-baked Yugoslav who thinks he's the greatest soldier since Julius Caesar! I have urgent matters to attend to."

"You really should be more polite, Major. As a guest in our country . . ."

"Your country? *What country*? Just listen out there. Everywhere you turn in this pisshole, there's the sound of guns, and up in the air, NATO is farting all over you."

Very faintly, the sporadic sound of machine-gun fire could be heard. Distance made it impossible to judge precisely where the shots were coming from. High above, as if to confirm his words, the sound of a NATO aircraft tearing across the sky rasped at them. The major wanted to glance up anxiously, in case the aircraft decided to come for a closer look, but he had no intention of giving the captain such satisfaction. The captain had himself not deigned to check.

"I got the same shit from another of your moronic countrymen, now deceased," the major continued with relish, warming to his theme and not bothering to explain how the militiaman had met his death. "You're wrecking your so-called country, you idiots. My business has nothing to do with your stupid war. Kill each other, if you must. Cleanse as many villages and towns as you like. Shell each other senseless into the Stone Age. I don't give a shit. Just don't get in my way . . . unless you want new enemies, with enough firepower to turn this pisshole into a wasteland. Am I talking slowly enough for you?"

The major paused, eyes boring into the captain with undisguised contempt. The captain stared right back at him, in silence.

"We're not Americans, NATO, or the UN," the major went on with a cold savagery, "who will wring our hands abjectly while we do nothing. We'll pound your stupid heads into the dirt, *then* talk to those of you still left. So don't make the mistake of firing on my APCs. You won't like what would follow."

The captain had been listening to all this with seeming interest, an insolent look upon his face. His was the air of someone who was facing up to an unwelcome guest he wished had possessed the wisdom to stay away. He was about to make a reply when his personal radio squawked. He unclipped it from his belt.

"Yes," he said into it in Serbo-Croat. He kept his eyes on the major.

"Headquarters wants to know what's going on," the voice of the radioman in the lead tank said in his ear.

"Tell them . . ." The faintest of smiles came and went as he continued to look at the major as he spoke. "Tell them I've got a bunch of Russians who want to enter Area Two of District Seven. I've blocked the road. They think because they've given us some tanks, that makes them colonists and they can go where they like.

"Tell HQ I've offered to bring the major to make his case, but he's refused. He seems to think any area in our military districts is open to him. We've got a kind of standoff and our men are facing each other with weapons. I can get their APCs, but they've got antitank weapons deployed. That's the situation. Oh, yes . . . the major thinks our country is a pisshole and promises to pound our stupid heads into the dirt. He means the whole country. Got all of that?"

"Got it all, Captain." The man sounded as if he, too, were smiling.

"Come back to me immediately with the reply."

"Yes, Captain."

The captain replaced his radio. He had no idea whether the Russian major understood the language, and didn't particularly care one way or the other.

"I know your language," the major said coldly.

"Oh. That's very good. Now I don't have to translate."

"I suppose you think you're very funny."

"No, Major. I don't think that at all. All I know, until I'm told differently, is that this area's closed to *everyone* except those with authority to be here."

The major still said nothing about the omega teams, or the fugitive woman. If the captain didn't know, all the better. So much for "everyone" being forbidden entry. So much for "sensitive" areas. The major took a certain pleasure in knowing that the zealous captain didn't have everything as tightly sewn up as he thought, after all.

"That's over fourteen hundred square kilometers you're blocking me from!" he objected, refusing to back down. "I've told you. I have urgent business, and the arrangements have long been made. You have absolutely no right to stop me."

The captain shrugged.

"You're playing a very dangerous and foolish . . ." the major began, his rage boiling over; but he was interrupted by the captain's radio squawking for a second time.

"Yes," the captain said into it.

"HQ, Captain. They're sending a vehicle. You and the major are to go up. They'll talk to him there."

"Thank you. Out. Seems as if HQ does want to see you, after all," he went on to the major, who glared with undiluted fury at him. He was completely unmoved. "It's either that," he went on with the insufferable insolence which, as far as the major was concerned, was so annoying, "or we spend the rest of the day here. Or . . . we fight it out. The choice is yours, Major."

The major looked about ready to explode. He was stuck, and knew it.

"*This is a criminal waste of time, you lousy, stupid people!*" he snarled. "You'll hear more of this!"

The captain just shrugged.

13

November base, 1100 hours

The Super Tornado ASV was at the threshold, lined up for takeoff. It was a bright, cold day and a stiff head wind came off the Moray Firth to slice along the wide runway, as if challenging the aircraft to a test of strength. But the sleek nose pierced the wind, unmoved.

Morton held the stick with a light touch. His feet rocked forward on the rudder pedals, holding the ASV on the brakes as he pushed the throttles into max dry, remaining just short of afterburning thrust. He felt the power surge through the aircraft, threading itself into his body, making him at one with it. Over the hard months of training, the invisible umbilical had consolidated its attachment to him, giving him the instinctive feel of the aircraft without which no fast-jet pilot could seriously feel at ease with his mount.

For the day's training mission, he had been allocated one of the newest aircraft on the unit's strength, a measure of the level at which his growing capabilities were now held. In addition to all the advanced specifications of the other ASVs, Morton's aircraft also possessed the fully automatic deployment of flaps, slats, and maneuver devices though with a manual reversion capability, which all crews insisted on retaining. The other ASVs were also equipped with the auto maneuvers, but flaps were manual only.

Morton checked both the graphics on one of his multi-function displays and the standby cluster of analog instruments on the lower left of the panel. All readings and dislays showed the flaps moving to takeoff position. He pushed the throttles firmly into combat burner, releasing the brakes simultaneously.

The Tornado seemed to hurl itself forward with glee, its awesome power building so rapidly that for one nearly panic-stricken moment, he thought it was running away from him. But the moment passed as quickly as it had come even as the nose was lifting skyward, and he raised the gear and pulled the aircraft into a steep climb. It surged for the upper reaches.

"Very impressive," Carlizzi congratulated from the backseat. "You're beginning to think with the bird. It's not the two of you anymore. You are now one with your machine. Good stuff, Major. I think we've got a November pilot on our hands."

Morton felt very pleased. He'd always found it difficult to dispel the feeling that he was very much the new boy, even though technically he outranked many of the other pilots. However, he'd long realized that though a major, his true position at November One was equivalent to a captain's. People like Carlizzi were the *real* majors. This caused him no worry, so pleased was he to be even considered for the unit.

Now that he was beginning to feel secure in his own ability to fly *and* fight the ASV, he was able to devote more thinking time to Mac. He tried not to let himself become too distracted by his anxiety for her, but he could not always prevent worrying thoughts from surfacing. There was so much he wanted to tell her. He'd wanted to take part in her rescue, feeling he owed it to her for old times' sake, at least. But General Bowmaker had been right. It was never smart to act solely upon emotional responses. If the boss had thought it operationally appropriate, he knew he would have been selected to go on the detachment.

In his room, he'd placed the one card she'd sent him on his bedside table. He reread it every day. "Missing me?" Just the two words, but they held a wealth of meaning for him.

Ironic, he thought. When they were together at JOSIS, he had observed the nonfrat rules and had kept his growing interest in her a secret even from himself. Now that she had at least acknowledged some interest in him, *she* was *his* superior.

"Hell of a life," he muttered to himself.

"What was that?" Carlizzi asked.

"Uh . . . nothing, Carlo. Thinking out loud."

"Stop talking to yourself and put this bird through her paces. Surprise me."

"You got it," Morton said, and immediately rolled the ASV, pulled firmly on the stick, and plunged diagonally toward the earth, forty thousand feet below.

"Hey!" Carlizzi exclaimed. "Let's have some warning here."

"You asked for surprise," Morton told him unsympathetically, promptly racking the Tornado into a tight, descending spiral. "Surprise is what you get."

For the next half hour, he treated Carlizzi to a dazzling display of airmanship, making the aircraft dance with abandon across the vast arena of the sky. He enjoyed his mastery of his uncertainties; of his aircraft; of the very air. The fledgling had at last become a hawk.

I am now one of the gods, he thought with exhilaration.

At the end of it all, he said, "Good enough, Carlo?"

Carlizzi was breathing hard, having himself worked overtime to counter the varied and seemingly multidirectional demands of the punishing G-forces generated by Morton's flying.

"Point made," he said at last. "I will recommend to the boss that as far as I am concerned, you have truly made it as a November pilot. I am certain the deputy bosses will agree."

"Even Helm?"

"Especially Helm."

"Thanks, Carlo."

"You do not have to thank me. You worked hard for it."

"You put your life in my hands, taking that seat back there and sticking with me. I owe you that."

"I like people with generous feelings. You can buy me some good wine in the mess."

The Bosnian mountains

She found herself suddenly thinking of Chuck Morton and wondered what he was doing, and whether he was thinking of her.

From within the hide she had made, she was waiting out the day. She had positioned herself within easy reach of the next rendezvous, which she expected to get to during the early hours of the next day. She hoped the helicopter would be waiting this time. Her options were fast running out.

She was reasonably secure in her hiding place, provided none of the searchers blundered upon it. There was no need for her to go foraging for food as she'd amply replenished her stocks with the rations she had taken from the troopers. Their combined packs had yielded more than enough for her to go for several days without once having to hunt. In addition to the cold rations, there were even self-heating tins of food, eliminating the need for a fire.

Pleased with the weaponry she'd also chosen to keep,

she had given the rifle/launcher combination a detailed examination and had discovered that while the 40mm launcher rounds outwardly appeared to be standard issue, there was something about their individual weight that gave them a different feel. They were clearly specialized rounds, but displayed no markings to denote type. Whoever had first owned the weapon had clearly not wanted the true nature of the ammunition to be openly known. It would be interesting, she thought, to see their effect if she were forced to use them.

To the south of her position and rather closer to her than he would have dared hope, the Russian major was having a very bad time. He glanced at his watch irritably. It was one-thirty, and already he'd been kept waiting for over an hour. The waiting continued. A foul day was progressively turning worse.

The entire morning had been squandered. He was a good thirty kilometers from his APCs, still bunched at the spot they'd been forcibly halted, and thus a nice target for any wandering NATO jet. The only satisfaction he derived from that particular nightmare was the thought that the insolent captain's tanks would be equally endangered, should an attack occur. But it didn't make him feel much better.

"Is there something special about that watch, Major?" the general asked mildly in Serbo-Croat. He did not look up from the map he was poring over. Those were the first words he'd spoken to the major since the Russian's arrival at the headquarters unit. "You keep checking it over."

"I am checking the time, General," the major said with as much calm as he could muster. What he wanted to do was kick the general where it would hurt most, so great was his frustration. "My men will be wondering where I've got to."

"Ah, yes. Your men."

The general, poised on his solid, tree-trunklike limbs, continued to lean over the large open map on the standard-issue field table. There was just one other officer in the small and sparsely furnished room: the tank captain. Another silence descended.

"You believe I'm a half-baked Yugoslav with a Julius Caesar complex who thinks he's a soldier," the general remarked abruptly, several minutes later. "Hmm? You also threatened my captain with enough firepower to turn this . . . 'pisshole,' I think you said, into a wasteland. Hmm?" the general repeated for good measure.

The general, in combat camouflage, straightened from his labors with the map and turned to face the major. He was a big man with a bullet head and small eyes that tried to hide in the folds of skin at the sockets, from which they peeped out malevolently. Unexpectedly, the corners of his mouth were upturned, as if he tended to smile readily. It was a chilling incongruity.

The major drew himself to full height and standing at attention, said, "With respect, General . . ."

"Respect! Ha!"

"With respect, General," the major repeated determinedly, "I do have authority to go about my business. It was agreed by . . ."

"And *I have my own authority!*" the general countered with a sudden raising of his voice. "Do you see this map?" He jabbed a thick finger toward it without bothering to look. "It is of this area—*a very sensitive area.* There are reasons, our reasons, why it is sensitive. *My* authority is to ensure that no one without very good reason is permitted to be within it. Whatever authority you may have is overridden by mine."

The major was not impressed. "You may find such a position difficult to sustain, General . . ."

"Ha!" the general barked once more. "Do you hear that, Captain?" he added to his subordinate. "All the foreigners in our country . . . including those who claim sympathy with us, think they can also tell us what to do. We are . . .

half-baked, you see. Because of that, a mere major thinks he can tell a general his position is . . . what was it? . . . 'difficult to sustain.' Tell me, Major," the general continued to the Russian, "do you believe that one of your majors is equivalent to one of our generals? Do you sometimes make jokes like that among yourselves? You know . . . when you're having a good laugh at our expense."

The malevolent eyes demanded a reply.

The major said nothing.

"*Well?*" the general roared. "Do you?"

"Our purpose is not served . . ."

"Don't talk like a politician to me! Soldier to soldier, Major. Does that happen? You'd better give me an answer. I can keep you here for days until you do. I can even shoot you, if I choose to. I have my authority. Of course there would be protests, but you, Major, would be dead. Hmm? Not much use to you then, those protests. So, Major, do you laugh at us?"

Anything to get out of here, the major thought grimly.

"Sometimes when the troopers are fed up . . ." he began.

"Only the troopers? What about the officers? I'm certain *you* think we are the idiots. Your whole manner screams it."

The general seemed determined to pick a fight, and for the first time, the major began to think that perhaps he might well be in danger from what was beginning to look increasingly like a raving megalomaniac. With his troops a good thirty kilometers away, he now felt horribly isolated. He'd gone with the captain, totally confident that his nationality virtually made him invulnerable to the sort of petty caprices that were suffered by members of the other foreign military forces in the country. This general did not seem particularly disposed to observe those unspoken rules.

"Some officers, perhaps . . ."

"*Some* officers? Perhaps? Not you, perhaps? After all, you said I had a Caesar complex."

"General, I am under orders to carry out a particular mission. I have very little time left in which to complete it . . ."

The general smiled. It was ugly. "I will assume that you have made those jokes." Then he made a dismissive gesture. "Let us forget it. I make jokes about Russians all the time, some of them not very polite. Everyone makes jokes about everyone else. It is the way of the world. Hmm? Let us talk about other things. Perhaps you can tell me about your mission. I might be able to be of assistance to . . . friends like yourselves."

"I am sorry, General. I cannot."

"How unfortunate. In that case, I'm afraid you will have to remain as my guest until I know why you have decided to enter my area, when you were clearly warned not to . . ."

The major was horrified. "General! With great respect . . ."

"*Great* respect! I have been promoted, Captain."

"Yes, sir," the tank captain agreed.

The major tried again. "General, you cannot . . ."

"*I can do whatever I like, Russian!*" the general snarled insultingly. "Captain, make arrangements to see that the major is comfortable until he chooses to speak to us."

"Yes, sir. Major . . . come with me, please." The captain motioned with the cut down AK-47 assault rifle he was carrying.

"There will be a very severe protest about this, General," the major snapped with baleful dignity. "And some kind of punitive action might well be undertaken."

"I'm trembling," the general said, smiling. "See?" He spread his hands, palms outward, and shrugged. "Trembling. Let us hope you will not be . . . 'undertaken.' Hmm?" He laughed at his own grim joke. "You should not use all these long words, Major."

The major said nothing as he went out with the

captain, who gave the general a smart salute, which
was returned.

The major did not salute.

She had been studying their approach all afternoon
through her powerful binoculars. They were passing
along a narrow valley, well below the current snow line,
which in the past days had retreated to the peaks. As a
result, they all wore combat greens. Well in the lead
were two of them, clearly an omega team, and far
behind came a small group of soldiers whose movements and general postures showed they were not specialist troopers.

It was now five o'clock, and the light was still strong.
The men had made no attempt to climb the slopes. She
had made the hide quite high up, and even if they'd suspected she was somewhere up there, they would still
have found it difficult to spot—even through binoculars.
Her own, with coated lenses to prevent reflection, were
concealed by a natural foliage screen. She had done this
deliberately. Broken branches used to screen a vantage
point could be detected by a good spotter.

She tracked the binoculars away, searching for others. There were none. She widened the area of search.
Nothing.

Then she stopped. She had seen movement. She
remained focused on the spot where she thought she'd
caught the barest shift of something. But nothing more
happened.

An insect on the lens?

She didn't move, instincts telling her to keep zeroed in
on the target area. Then she saw it. A man was rising
from cover.

Her heart lifted. He was wearing the armband. *They
had come for her.* The rescue was on!

The man was still some considerable distance away,
but she felt elated. All she had to do was wait until the

right time to make contact. At last. She was really getting out. Were there more of them, she wondered? There would be a search, so there would be others. She knew how the patterns worked.

The problem now was to avoid contact with the omega teams and make it to the helicopter without a firefight, if at all possible.

She tracked the binoculars back toward where the omega team should be by now . . . and froze.

They had disappeared.

She backtracked. The other troopers were still plodding along. She swung back to the man with the armband. He was still there. Everything was as it should be . . . except for the omega team's sudden disappearance. She felt a strong sense of foreboding. They had spotted the man with the armband. She was certain of it.

It was inconceivable that they were on their way back toward the troopers, when they had spent most of the day outstripping them. She knew they could not have spotted the hide so far up the mountain. That left the man with the armband. Somehow, during the time she'd been studying his progress, he'd been spotted by the omega team. Now they were hunting him. They would not be certain of what they were hunting and would not do anything unless they were sure; but if they caught him, it would not take long.

She felt impotent. She couldn't help him under the current circumstances without betraying her own position. She kept the binoculars on him, willing him to get back under cover. He must have seen the troopers. Was that why he had been in cover in the first place? But how had he missed the omega team?

It took nearly an hour for them to spring their trap. One came toward him openly, holding his attention, while the other came up silently from behind.

They did not kill him immediately. First they talked, clearly questioning him and establishing an identity, almost as if they were all on a ramble together and had met at a rendezvous point. At first, no overt hostile move was made toward him. It was almost as if they were themselves uncertain. Whatever he was saying to them was causing them to ponder their options. He'd be speaking Serbo-Croat to them, she knew, and they'd be wondering about that. Then it all seemed to be okay. They waved at each other, and he began to move away.

The omega team stood and watched for a while. Then the bigger of the two threw something.

The man with the armband suddenly arched and vainly tried to pull something from his back before collapsing. The big one ran up, pulled the knife out, then plunged it in again, finishing the job. Unknown to her, the victim was the first searcher Buntline had dropped off.

She felt her eyes grow hot. "Bastards!" she whispered. "Bastards!"

She made a decision. It carried some risk, but she was determined they were not going to get away with it. It was not the same omega team whose lives she'd spared, but she still felt outraged by what they had done. Their victim had clearly not intended to engage. What they had done was cowardly.

She began to make preparations to temporarily leave the hide. The light would be poor by the time she got to them. Exactly the conditions she wanted.

"You didn't have to kill him, you Siberian psycho."

The Siberian looked at his colleague. "Why not?"

"He was a Croat, you big ape!"

"Don't call me an ape, or a psycho. Only Viktor gets away with that."

"All right, all right!" the other said irritably. "Keep your shirt on. Since when did we start taking sides?" he went on. "That's for others. Not us. We've got a job to do, and that's it. That's what the lieutenant made a point of saying. Remember that. To hell with the major, but the lieutenant's one of us."

The Siberian had wiped the knife and placed it back in its sheath. "Let me ask you something," he said calmly as they walked on. "What was he doing here?"

"What do you mean?"

"He was a Croat. Right?"

"Yes. You heard him! Couldn't speak Russian properly, and my Serbo-Croat is crap."

"I can speak it."

"*You!* I never thought . . ."

"Perhaps you should a little more. So he's a Croat. So what was he doing here? All by himself? This place is not exactly where I'd choose to be if I were a Croat. He didn't think we'd know the difference, being ignorant Russians. And how about that small armband?"

"What the hell are you on about? As for the armband, they've got so many groups in this damned country, they wear something so they know what not to shoot at, or maybe what to shoot at. The hell I should care."

The Siberian grinned and showed his companion something that looked like a pocket telephone, but with no digits.

"Everything on him was genuine Croat . . . except this piece of technology. It was under his body. It's some kind of field communicator. We haven't got anything to compare. How come a Croat's got it? I can't even open the fucking thing."

"What are you saying?"

"I think our man was here for a very special purpose. He was doing exactly what we are, and he's probably got a team he keeps in touch with. He was looking for the woman." The Siberian paused, then sniffed at the cooling air. "Could snow up here tonight. His team will be looking for him."

"Then it was stupid to kill him. We don't need that kind of attention."

The Siberian grinned once more. "I smell a fight coming on."

He didn't sound at all unhappy.

The Blackhawk helicopter was well hidden, waiting for the signal for the liftoff. At the bank of avionics and signaling equipment, the female operative Buntline had left on board stiffened as a red light came on.

"Shit," she exclaimed in a tense whisper.

"What?" the gunner demanded.

"We have one down."

"Shit," he echoed. "I'll tell my boss, you tell yours."

She nodded and sent a single pulse to Buntline, while the gunner spoke into his mike to the pilot.

Leaving the copilot up in the cockpit, the pilot came into the cabin. "How bad?" he asked her.

She touched her headphones briefly and glanced up at him. "Very. I got the panic signal, then nothing. He's dead."

"Shit," the pilot said. "I've been instructed to take the liftoff order from you. Just tell me when you're ready."

"We wait," she said.

He nodded, and went back to the cockpit.

"Chocolate?" the gunner offered, breaking off a piece from a bar he'd taken from a pocket in his flak jacket. "It's fruit and nut."

"Thanks," she said, taking it. She popped the lot into her mouth and began to eat.

A cool one, that, the gunner thought as he watched her.

She had come down off the mountain and had positioned herself perfectly for what she intended to do. It would have to be very quick. She wanted to be out of there by the time the struggling soldiers, who were still vainly trying to keep up with the omega team, came within fighting distance. The light was now at the sort of level that made all the difference between a clear sighting and an imagined one.

Beyond the mountains, the sky flashed intermittently in the twilight. Now and then, a faint rumble could be heard. Somewhere, another village or town was living through its own particular nightmare.

She wanted the big one first, the one who seemed to relish using his knife. She had traveled light, weapons only. The rifle/launcher would be used if things got really sticky; but for the kill, she intended to employ the silenced automatic pistol.

She watched as they approached. They were taking it slowly now, as if sensing that someone was waiting out there for them. Then the big one stopped, putting out a restraining arm to his colleague, who was some feet to one side.

The big one seemed to be listening.

"What is it?" she heard in whispered Russian.

The big one said nothing. In the fading light, a finger went to his lips.

She remained perfectly still, willing him to move. He was not yet in the right position for a good, killing pistol shot. The rifle would do it, but there'd be the noise, too. She'd have to wait it out.

The big one took a couple of cautious steps, then stopped again. He seemed to be fidgeting with something on his belt. The other was staring in his direction.

"What are you doing?" came another whisper.

Again, the big one did not reply. Again, a finger went to the lips. He was no longer holding his rifle across his chest with one hand. It was now hanging by its sling, while both hands seemed occupied.

Then she knew. *Grenade.*

He was not sure of what was up ahead, but he was taking no chances and was clearing out the immediate area. He did not have to worry about noise.

Even as the realzation hit, she was moving swiftly,

getting out of range. The noise of the explosion would cover any sounds she made getting to a new position. She changed her strategy on the run, deciding to work around them instead, in order to take out the less alert companion first.

She actually heard the grenade going through the bushes as the big soldier threw it. She flung herself into a hollow, flattening hard against the earth. She had traveled a good distance by that time. The depression in the ground was like a shallow foxhole.

When the explosion came, it was well to her left. But she felt a chill go through her. The big soldier's instincts had been right on. Had she remained in her old position, she would have caught the full blast.

Even as she thought this, she was moving again and was coming up on them from behind; then she was close enough to the second soldier. She wasted no time. Propping herself briefly against a tree, she fired. She didn't miss. The cough of the pistol and the choking cry of the man as he flung his arms upward seemed to come as one.

As he began to fall, the big Siberian—who must have been very surprised by the turn of events—still managed to dive for cover with astonishing speed for one of such size.

A silence fell upon the woods, punctuated by the fading gasps of the dying soldier. It went on for some time, then he too was silent. The big man never risked his neck by leaving cover to go to the aid of his fallen comrade.

"Are you the woman?" the big Siberian suddenly called in Russian. "Or another of those Croats?" He giggled. "Did you like the way I killed him? Did you watch?"

She said nothing, listening. He was moving. He had gauged where the shot must have come from and was working his way toward her.

"Let us forget the guns," he was saying. Definitely closer. "Let us use our sweethearts. Cold steel. If you are the woman, I saw how you did a nice piece of gutting back there, so I know you have a knife. If you are not the woman, you must have a knife. Yes?"

She did not move. Let him come.

"Come on," he said. "Don't be shy. Just the two of us—before the others get here. They will have heard the grenade. How about it?"

She didn't think for a moment that was what he had in mind. All that talking was a ploy. Every time he fell silent, he would be working his way around. The extraneous noises she heard were part of it. He was probably throwing bits of old wood and anything else that came to hand to give the impression he was somewhere else. Then he'd move in for a quick kill, or a disabling shot or knife thrust, in order to capture her.

She was not about to fall for that.

Fifteen minutes later, she stood up in the fading light and said, "I'm here."

She was behind him, out of knife range she hoped, and holding the rifle/launcher. A 40mm round was ready to go. After his grenade, the noise wouldn't matter.

Astonished, he whirled. He was indeed holding his knife. She could just make it out.

"The woman! Ah," he went on admonishingly, arm swinging even as he spoke. "You tricked me."

She fired and ducked almost at the same time. She actually felt the knife go past her cheek. God, he was fast—and accurate. He'd have gotten her if she hadn't moved. But the grenade struck home. What then happened shocked her.

The blast was far greater than anything she'd expected, and she was thrown to the ground. Things like angry wasps buzzed past as a hellish inferno erupted where the big man had been. Something flaming arced its way toward her. She rolled to one side and it landed with a soft thump, scatttering blobs of whitish light. The flaming thing was a cooking hand.

She rolled further away, putting some distance

between herself and the grisly result of her actions. The noise echoed in her head, and the stench of cooked flesh and explosive assaulted her nostrils.

She shakily got to her feet, hearing quickly returning to normal. There was nothing where the big man had been except an intense fire that was rapidly burning itself out. At least, nothing she could see. She thought of the hand and hurried away from there.

Whatever those 40mm rounds were, they were devastating. The one she had used had been like a napalm, phosphorus, and very high explosive fragmentation round all in the one package. Whatever the mixture that had been packed into it, it had certainly done the job. She didn't feel so worried now about having to fight her way out, if the need arose. No wonder that other trooper had kept the weapon. Even if it couldn't stop a tank, it would certainly stop an APC.

She began to swiftly make her way back up to the hide. By the time the other soldiers arrived at the scene, darkness was complete, and she was already safely under cover.

"Look at that, Sergeant!"

The major's infantry troopers were searching the area with their torches. The one who had spoken had found a half-roasted foot. He sounded as if he wanted to vomit.

The sergeant, a hardened veteran of street fights in his not-so-distant youth, came up and shone his torch on the find. "Never seen a foot before?"

"But it's . . ."

"Get a grip on yourself!" His eyes tracked slowly upon them. In a gloom relieved by the weak light of the torches, their faces were ghostly. "All of you! If you don't want to end up like this, behave like soldiers. Come here, Makirov." The soldier with the radio came forward, and the sergeant picked up the handset to call the APCs. "The rest of you fan out and see what else is around. Be *careful*. Whoever did this is long gone, but you never know. He, she, or they could have left nasty surprises." He began to speak urgently into the handset.

His conversation was brief. "I don't believe it," he said with exasperation as he replaced the handset with such force it caused Makirov to stagger slightly.

"What's wrong?" the radioman asked, wrinkling his nose against the smell from the dismembered foot.

"The APCs are still blocked by those tanks, and the major's missing."

"*What?*"

"He has not returned since he went off with that tank captain," the sergeant told him grimly. "This thing is turning into something worse than a night in Baku. Whoever that whore's daughter is, her price keeps climbing." He stared at the foot and spat at it. "So much for specialists. You rushed ahead of us to prove you were supermen. What did it get you? Cremation."

"Sergeant!" came a voice out of the dark.

"That's right," the sergeant growled to himself. "Tell the whole stinking world. Come on, Makirov."

They went to where the others were waiting, clustered around another body. It was the man the big Siberian had knifed.

"Think he did it before they got him?" someone asked as the sergeant crouched to inspect the body.

"That's a feat," the sergeant replied sarcastically as he straightened. "First he shot one, blew the other into mincemeat, then they got up and slit his guts. *Wake up!* They killed him, but someone else got *them*."

"How do you know . . ."

"Because, Chernyev, you head of piss, his pistol has not been fired. He didn't even get it out. His AK is still around his neck. And do you see a grenade launcher anywhere? He's not even carrying ordinary grenades." The sergeant shook his head slowly and sighed. "This army has gone down the drain since all this crap about democracy. Come on! Move it!"

"We're not stopping for the night?"

The sergeant turned to glare at the one who had spoken. In the light of the torches, he looked fearsome. "Hoping your mother will tuck you in for the night, Lavrenin?"

"No. No, Sergeant."

"Thank you, Lavrenin. Now listen, all of you. She's in this area. She must be. It's only an hour and a half since the explosion. We'll move on tonight and stop for a break just before dawn. Then we search."

"Shouldn't we call up the omega teams?" Makirov the radioman suggested tentatively.

The sergeant was dismissive. "The omegas? She stripped two of them naked and killed these two here. Then there're the locals she left by their BMP. That's a lot of scores down to her. Let's show those so-called specialists what real soldiering's all about."

The men gave each other surreptitious glances, but none went against the sergeant.

"Put those lights out and let's go!" he barked, and strode on ahead.

The dead Siberian had been wrong about the snow.

14

The major had been listening in the dark to the sounds for over an hour.

Even though he couldn't see from his vantage point at the window of the small room they'd put him in as their "guest," he did not need a visual confirmation. Tanks were massing in the small village that had been commandeered to serve as the district HQ. This was indeed a high-value area. A nice fat target for NATO jets, too, if the westerners got itchy trigger fingers.

He wondered what the general's men had done with the original inhabitants.

A knock sounded on the door—remarkably discreet, all things considered.

"Are you awake, Major?" the tank captain called through the door, in Russian.

"Why shouldn't I be awake at two o'clock in the morning?" the major retorted with cold sarcasm. He switched on the weak light of the naked bulb that hung from the ceiling. It was more like a glow, but still gave enough to enable him to see by.

The captain entered. "I apologize for the noise." He shut the door behind him with unnecessary care, given the continuous rumble of the tanks. "It will be over soon. The last ones are just arriving. Are you comfortable? It's a better room than the one I've got."

The major came away from the window. "I'd rather have my weapons back and be with my men, or at least be able to communicate with them."

The captain shook his head. "I'm sorry, but you know the general would not allow it."

The major jerked a thumb at the window. "Planning a big push? It sounds like a lot of tanks."

"You know I can't answer that."

"Then answer me this, Captain. . . . What are you going to do with me? You've kept me here all day, all night . . ." The major paused. "And tomorrow . . . ?" He left the question hanging.

"That's up to the general."

The major turned away and returned to the window. "The general. By virtually keeping me hostage . . ."

"Hostage? Who said you were . . ."

"By keeping me hostage," the major repeated with emphasis, staring out at the dark, "your general will have upset the very people he's going to need when your mad little war is finally over. He's going to need friends—strong friends."

The major remained stiffly at the window. "However," he continued, "after this little episode, he might well find them few and far between, *if* he does not allow me to return to my men. He might also find that those who could have been friends have become enemies, more of which he hardly needs right now."

"There you go again, Major," the captain said regretfully. "Making threats. It's not the best way . . ."

"Those were not threats, Captain," the major snapped, whirling to glare at the tank commander. "Those were promises."

"I . . ."

A loud knocking on the door interrupted whatever the captain had been about to say.

"Captain! Captain!" a voice called urgently in Serbo-Croat.

"Yes?"

"It's the general, sir. He wants you. Immediately."

"On my way."

"Yes, sir." The man hurried away.

The captain looked at the Russian. "Perhaps we're about to get the answer to your question," he said in his own language. He saluted in a casual manner. "If you'll excuse me. Mustn't keep the general waiting."

The major did not return the salute as the captain went out. He switched off the light and went back to the window.

The noise of the tanks had stopped.

The captain hurried along the darkened village street to the school that now served as the general's staff and planning headquarters. Tanks were squeezed everywhere. The smell and heat of their now-quiet engines exhilarated him as he threaded his way past them. He walked past the guards at the former school and was immediately shown in.

The general was alone.

The captain wondered why the general didn't seem to need any sleep.

"Ahh, Captain," the general began as he entered. "I have a little job for you. Think you can handle it?"

"I won't know until you tell me what it is, General."

The general gave one of his contradictory smiles. "Good answer. Come here and look at the map." When the captain had approached the map table, the general stabbed at a low mountain peak with a meaty finger. "We've got a small fixed-site signal monitoring unit on that mountain. Two soldiers are manning it. They picked up something earlier today and again earlier this evening which they relayed to my signals headquarters down here. Until you brought in the major, those relays did not make any sense."

The general straightened, spread his legs, and arms locked behind his back, gave the captain the full attention of his small, deep-set eyes.

"The first signals," the general went on, "were pulses. Very brief. Too brief to decode even if we had the time, or knew where to begin. Then this evening there was a longer signal. Not a pulse this time, but voice communication, scrambled. The voice communications were two-way. All of it, Captain, came from within this sector." The general freed one of his hands long enough to draw a rough circle around the peak where the monitoring unit was positioned. "In the *middle* of our restricted area. I am not blaming you for this, Captain, so don't look so worried.

"It is clear that our Russian has placed troops in there. I want to know what he's playing at. I'll give you eight men. They're all I can spare. Go up to the signals unit. Those two up there may need help. You are to take command and defend it, against *anyone*. Russians included."

The captain, hoping he'd be returning to his beloved tanks, could not hide his disappointment.

"With great respect, General, I'm a tank man . . ."

"And very good you are, too. But before you were transferred to tanks, you were also an excellent infantryman. You have a very good record, Captain. Don't spoil it. So, you will accept my little job?"

"Yes, sir."

"Good. Your men are waiting. You should be there by early morning if you start now and don't waste any time."

"The major . . ."

"Leave that Russian to me," the general said ominously. "I'll get him to tell me what the hell he is doing in my patch. One way or the other."

"Yes, sir," the captain said. He saluted smartly.

The general waved vaguely in his direction, mind already on other things.

The captain went out, cursing the moment he'd first set eyes upon the major. Infantry indeed.

At about the same time, Buntline was listening to his own set of sounds. Like the Russian major, he found that those also needed no visual confirmation. He waited until he judged the moment right, then rising from cover, rushed swiftly across the short open space to halt within the darker shadow of the small signals outpost. Not totally lightproof, its internal illumination marked it out clearly at such range.

The sounds continued unabated, louder now that he was closer to the source. The small cabinlike structure, its aerials barely distinguishable in the dark, had obviously been carried in sections up the mountain, and then erected onsite. The sounds from within were growing in intensity.

Buntline reached cautiously forward to try the door. The handle turned easily. He grinned. They had not even bothered to lock themselves in.

In a way, he preferred the option this presented to him. Blowing up the entire structure from outside had the considerable disadvantage of noise and a flash that would be seen for miles in the darkness. Besides, he did not want to kill indiscriminately. Better to destroy the unit from within.

In a controlled economy of movement, he flung the door open. Light flooded out. He remained where he was in shadow, allowing his eyes to become accustomed. The sight that greeted him would have been hilarious in other circumstances.

"Stay exactly as you are!" he commanded sharply in Serbo-Croat, with the correct regional accent.

Their sounds halted in midgasp as they froze.

The soldiers manning the signals unit were male and

female, and it was clear that their other activities frequently helped pass the time. The woman's combat trousers and her knickers had been drawn clear of one leg. Both the bared smooth leg and the clothed one were locked across her male companion's back. She still had her boots on. Her top clothing had been pushed up so that the man could get at the full endowment of her ample breasts. His eager hands were now trapped there. Her hair, spilling darkly, looked damp. She stared out at their as yet unseen unwelcome visitor in shock and fear.

The man had dropped his own trousers to his knees. Caught in midthrust, he was locked deep into her. He was desperately trying to look around.

They were a long way from their weapons, Buntline noted.

"Don't move!" he barked.

The man stopped.

Buntline entered the little building, making it seem crowded. The woman stared up at him. There was plenty of fear in her eyes, but a strange defiance, too.

To those who only knew Buntline as the elegant animal at embassy parties, his appearance would have come as a distinct shock. In full combat gear and face marked with camouflage paint, he was an altogether different and menacing creature. It was little wonder that the woman, despite her look of defiance, was also very frightened.

"I've nothing against fraternization between comrades," he told them conversationally. "Just carry on. Don't mind me."

In one hand was an automatic pistol which he trained upon them. The other held a cut down, silenced AK-47 with which he proceeded to wreck all the equipment. The two on the floor shrank into each other as the weapon stuttered its rounds into the consoles, sending pieces flying and showering sparks all over the place. When it was all over, he looked down at them benignly.

The man's fear appeared to have created an involuntary arousal, for he suddenly began to thrust at the woman.

She looked at her companion in horror. "*What . . . what are you doing? Stop. Stop!*" She beat at his back with her fists, legs jerking involuntarily to the urgency of his movements. "*Stop! Stop!*" she repeated with frantic despair. "*No! Nooo!*" Her voice faded gradually and a faint whimper was forced out of her, punctuating the soldier's grunts of exertion.

"A man's got to come," Buntline said mildly.

The grunting soldier, driven by his own fear and temporarily uncontrollable excitement, ignored them both and kept at it, pounding dementedly at her. Perhaps he thought he was about to die. The woman eventually stopped beating vainly at him and began to weep in anger, and in shame.

"I'm sorry," Buntline said clinically and not sounding sorry at all, "but now I'm going to have to tie you both as you are."

"No!" the woman objected, her voice quavering as the soldier kept up his pounding, the fear seemingly replaced by the humiliation she now felt.

"Yes."

"You . . . you filthy *Ustash!*" she spat out, keeping the last syllable silent in order to make the word sound more savagely expletive. "Do you like watching? Do you like this?"

"I've seen better," Buntline said, deliberately planting the wrong idea into her mind. "Look at it this way. I could have killed you both."

The man gave three loud and drawn-out groans of release.

"Your friend's finished," Buntline said.

"Bastard!" she screamed. She could have meant both the soldier and Buntline, but the tear-filled eyes were looking at Buntline.

"What a way to talk to someone who just gave you your life. You didn't really expect me to stop him, did you? This keeps him occupied while I get on with what I've got to do. Besides, you were already enjoying yourselves before I got here."

He'd spotted coils of flex which were clearly meant for landline relays. There were cutters next to them. Keeping his prisoners covered with the pistol, he quickly set about cutting four lengths one-handedly.

"Don't try to rush at me," he warned. "You'd never make it. Even with my left hand, I'm a very good shot. Anyway, your friend would take some moving. He's a bit wiped out."

"Bastard!" she said again.

"I can live with that."

He put the pistol down within easy reach and swiftly made four loops with the pieces of flex he'd cut, then picking up the gun, he went back to them.

"Keep your arms and legs locked as they are," he told her.

She glared at him, but obeyed. The tears of shame marked her cheeks.

"Thank you."

He secured her by the wrists and ankles, then linked both so that she could not pull them apart. That way she'd be unable to bring her arms back over her companion's head and perhaps manage to free herself by getting him to work at the knot with his teeth.

"Bastard!" she said a third time.

"If you keep saying that, I'll think you're beginning to like me."

A look that was at once embarrassed and outraged greeted his words, but she kept her mouth firmly shut. Her eyes continued to glare at him.

He tied the man's ankles together.

"Now, my friend," he said, "hands behind your back."

The man complied silently, and Buntline tied his wrists to the woman's.

"Very cozy," he said when he'd finished. "Sorry I can't wait till any of your comrades get here, as they're bound to when you don't call in. But they should be amused. Have fun." He studied the woman, head a little to one side. "You know, you're quite attractive—especially with that flush on your cheeks. Uh-uh," he cautioned. "Don't say it."

He went out, shutting the door quietly behind him.

He'd been traveling for about forty-five minutes when he heard subdued voices—Russian voices. He made his way slowly forward until he could see whom the voices belonged to. They had made camp for the night, and he could just make out two of them, standing, conversing quietly.

Specialist troops would not have been so lax, he thought. So where were they?

Then one of the soldiers moved a little distance away, to lie down. The other began to pace slowly.

Change of guard.

Buntline, following his own orders to avoid contact, gave them a wide berth and continued on his way. The monitoring unit had been a different matter. It had been too close to the intended pickup point. Rendering it useless had avoided the possibility of a chance pinpointing of the landing zone, especially as there might well be increased signal activity during the pickup itself.

He wondered whether the encamped soldiers had been the ones who had taken out his operative. Then he found himself doubting the possibility. It was far likelier, he decided, that the man had come up against a team of the specialists. The soldiers he had just passed had appeared too indisciplined. They had behaved as if they expected no one to come out of the darkness at them— the same mistake made by the crew of the monitoring unit he'd recently put out of action.

He moved on, getting ever closer to the area where Mac should be hiding.

• • •

The NATO base on the Adriatic, Italy, 0430 hours

Fregattenkapitän Helm came straight to the point. "Gentlemen," he began in the small briefing room they had been allocated, "you may be wondering at the change of timing for this briefing. Quite simply, events have dictated it. Things are moving faster, so the mission has been brought forward."

All the November crews, including the standby team of Bagni and Stockmann, were present. A screen had been erected and an image of the target area was on it. Superimposed upon the image was the bright track, showing where the ATARS aircraft had indicated was the current position of the APCs.

"You will see by the new position of the APCs," Helm continued, the hard eyes settling on each in turn, "that they are now practically within the pickup area. Worse, there are now also tanks there, some of which are with the APC's. But even that is not all, gentlemen. We have intelligence reports that confirm that several tanks, perhaps in battalion strength, are massing just where we would not like them to be . . . close to the target. We have clearly stumbled onto some kind of big push.

"You will remember, Mr. Hohendorf and Mr. McCann, that mention was made of a C^3 high-value target. The greatest concentration of the armor is within its vicinity. Needless to say, the C^3 will be heavily protected. Though your target is now close to it, you are still strongly forbidden to attack it."

"What if *it* attacks us?" McCann asked, adding, "Sir?" almost as an afterthought.

Helm gave McCann the full benefit of a steel-like stare. "You get out of the way. Your first priority *must* be the APCs. If the tanks with them are too close, then so be it. The C^3, however, will be left absolutely alone. This is not our war."

McCann thought about that, and didn't like it at all. Looking at the target area, it seemed to him they'd be overflying the C^3. That was now the only route to the priority target. If they had triple-A and SAMs down there and started popping off . . .

"Your revised waypoints," Helm was saying, "now means a longer ingress to target, and therefore you will need to refuel earlier on the way out. Distance to target is now four hundred fifty nautical miles. The mission is lo-lo-lo . . . low in, low over target, and low out. You will go for altitude only when you're back over the Adriatic. Your tanker will now be waiting in the specially designated air-to-air refueling area—Papa One-Zero—at thirty thousand feet, closer to your egress point than originally. You should therefore have no fuel problems if you come out clean."

"You mean no battle damage, sir," McCann remarked.

Helm's eyes zeroed in on him. "That is precisely what I mean, Captain."

"Yes, sir."

Helm looked at Hohendorf. "You will have autonomy to modify your waypoints in-flight, should circumstances demand it. However, the current route is recommended as the best to avoid the ground defenses, while still giving you plenty of cover for terrain masking. For the actual run in to target, if you can devise a better ingress, then of course you are free to do so.

"Recovery will not be back to this base, but directly to November One. This means *all* November aircraft. However, the support aircraft will remain here until after the mission, should battle damage repairs be necessary.

"The escort aircraft will position themselves at medium level. This is a fluid requirement and again, you have full autonomy to alter this according to the tactical situation at any given time. The standby aircraft will remain on the ground on full alert, in case a requirement to launch becomes necessary."

Helm paused, as if waiting for comments; when none were forthcoming, he continued the briefing.

"Call signs," he went on. "The mission call sign is Stormbird. Hohendorf and McCann—you are Stormbird One. Selby and Flacht, Two; Cottingham and Christiansen, Three; Bagni and Stockmann, Four. The helicopter pickup is Kestrel. The ATARS aircraft is Avatar. Your tanker is Jellyfish . . ."

"Jellyfish?" someone asked, trying not to laugh.

"Yes, Jellyfish. Don't ask me why. All communication will be by secure datalink. And finally, gentlemen, whatever happens, *don't* get shot down over there. We could all do without the heat that would generate. Questions?" Helm looked at each in turn.

They looked back at him solemnly. Even McCann seemed at a loss for words.

"Very well," Helm said. "Thank you, gentlemen. I'll leave you in the capable hands of the met officer."

The meteorological officer for the trip was a tall U.S. Navy lieutenant from San Diego, California, named Fogerty, whom—inevitably—everyone called Foggy. A very clearly defined topographical map had appeared on the screen. Using a light pen, he directed an arrow upon it as he spoke.

"There will be a light fog in the valleys here . . ." he began.

A loud, collective groan of disgust greeted this. He smiled, and continued with his forecast.

Buntline came upon the burned out swath left by the grenade launcher just as the darkness was beginning to pale. The sickly mixed smell of cooked flesh and napalm was still strong; it had practically guided him to the spot. There was now just enough light to make out the prone shape of the dead omega soldier and the few pieces of what used to be his comrade, the big Siberian.

He looked about him, surveying the carnage. Whose

hand had been responsible? A Russian versus Russian fight? He doubted it. Those careless soldiers he'd passed earlier would not have been capable of taking on even the outnumbered specialists. That called for someone who could beat them at their own game and was even more ferocious in action. It could only have been Mac, he decided. This was the area where she should now be—if she'd made it this far.

A short while later, he found his own dead colleague. He crouched down to inspect the body and saw the gaping knife wound. It was the second one that had been made by the big Siberian, completing the kill. He turned the man over, hiding the ugly gash. The body couldn't be left lying there to be found, and would have to be taken to the helicopter when it came in for the pickup.

Remaining in a crouch, Buntline studied the landscape about him in the still-hesitant light of the new day. She had to be around here somewhere, he thought, perhaps even now studying him through her night-compatible binoculars. Deliberately, he fingered the armband. If she were indeed watching, she would take note of that and know help had at last arrived.

She *had* to be there. Time was running out.

The sergeant had broken camp before dawn and had urged his troopers to begin an extensive search, getting them to fan out to a distance of a hundred meters between each other. As daylight began to weakly filter through a thin mountain mist, one of them spotted the monitoring unit and alerted him. He called them together and they all trudged up the mountain toward it.

Motioning them to remain outside and again spread out around the small structure, he opened the door. At first, he refused to believe his eyes. He stared at the woman, looked around at the destroyed equipment, then back to the woman soldier, who stared up at him, fear returning to her eyes. Her male companion tried to turn to look but could not get his head around far enough.

"Well, well, well," he remarked softly in Russian. "Been like that all night, have you? You must have enjoyed yourselves. You! Do you speak Russian?"

"A . . . a little," she replied haltingly.

Someone said from outside the door, "Sergeant . . ." The voice stopped abruptly as the speaker took in the scene. Then, "Hey! Come and see this!"

There was the sound of hurrying feet, then they were crowding at the door. They all tried to speak together.

"Oh–oh–oh!" one of them said. "I could use some of that! Look at that leg. Is he really in?"

"Of course he's in. Can't you see? You've been doing it with yourself too much. You're going blind."

"Speak for yourself . . ."

"Give her to us, Sarge . . ."

"*Shut up, all of you!*" the sergeant roared. "*Get back to your posts or I'll have you all court-martialed!*"

The doorway was cleared.

The sergeant again turned to the woman. "What happened here?"

"Sergeant!" came from outside.

"Shut *up!*" the sergeant yelled.

Whoever it was shut up as ordered.

"Now," the sergeant went on to the woman, "what happened?" He made no move to untie them.

Then the sergeant heard a click that he knew could mean only one thing.

"Put your weapon down," a new voice ordered in Russian. "Very slowly, and don't turn around until that weapon is down."

The sergeant complied.

The tank captain had made much better time than even he or the general had expected. The men he had been given were fit and at ease in the mountains, and had maintained without much difficulty the punishing pace he had set. They had therefore been in time to spot the Russians making for the monitoring unit, and had been able to set up an ambush for them.

The captain now entered the small cabin; he, too, stared at the couple on the floor. Then, like the sergeant before him, he took in the wreckage of the monitoring equipment.

He turned to the Russian. "Is this your idea of appropriate behavior when in my country?" he demanded in a harsh voice.

"Not guilty, my Yugoslavian friend," the sergeant said. "Since you obviously had time to set up an ambush, you must have seen us arrive. There wasn't time for us to do this. And if you look really closely, you will see he is deep inside of her. We Russians are good at many things, but I don't think even we could have done this in such a short time.

"Although it is anyone's guess how long they have been like that, they do not seem to have tried to free themselves; but to be fair, whoever did this knew what he was doing. Direct your questions at her. She has obviously got the thrust of things." He grinned at the captain.

"Dragovic!" the captain shouted in Serbo-Croat.

"Yes, Captain!"

"Take this man and put him with the others."

"Yes, Captain."

The soldier called Dragovic came to the door—and gaped.

"What the hell are you gawking at?" the captain snapped. "Do as I say!"

"Ye-yes, Captain. Come on, you!" Dragovic ordered the Russian sergeant, the words needing no interpretation. He took another surreptitious look as the sergeant, smiling thinly at him, came out.

"And shut the door!" the captain barked. "Keep your eyes on those Ivans. If one escapes, you're in serious trouble."

"Yes, Captain!" Dragovic acknowledged. "All right, all

right!" he shouted at the Russian sergeant. "Move it!" He shut the door.

The captain looked down at the woman soldier, eyes hard. "Were you made to do this? Or were you caught like that? I want the truth!"

Tears of shame, for the second time since her torment began, coursed down her cheeks. "We . . . we were caught, Captain."

"Are you telling me, soldier," the captain began softly, "that you deserted your posts and were *fucking each other, enabling a saboteur to get in here to do this?*" The sweep of an angry arm indicated the ruined consoles.

She mumbled something.

"Is that a yes or a no?"

"Yes! Yes, yes, yes, Captain!"

The captain regarded her silently, without emotion. "You do realize what the both of you are facing? The general may well order that you be executed."

She paled.

"What did you expect?" he demanded savagely. "That he would kiss you?"

"Please, Captain," she begged. "Set us free."

"I have a mind not to. I have a mind to let the entire army witness your stupidity, and your failure to carry out your duties. However . . ." He drew his knife and began to cut at their bonds. " . . . if you tell me the complete truth about what took place here, I may be able to save your lives, if given enough information about the person or persons who came in here. I will not be able to save you from any other punishment the general might consider fitting. Is that clear?"

"Yes, Captain," they both said.

"Names!" he commanded.

"Private Olga Sevic, sir," the woman said.

"Corporal Milan Milanovic, sir."

"You won't be a corporal for much longer. Now make yourselves decent," the captain ordered with contempt, "then we shall have a long chat. Your lives depend upon what you tell me."

He listened to their report of the events of the night.

"Are you quite certain," he began when they had finished, "that he was Croat?"

"Yes, Captain," she answered. "His accent was from the northwest. I . . . I recognized it. Before . . . before the war . . . I . . . used to have a friend from there who had the same accent."

"Didn't you find it strange that he was as polite as you have said?" the captain suggested. "Would a genuine Croat saboteur not have killed you both? Instead, he makes you compound your folly while having a good laugh. He even left you your weapons. He has an interesting sense of humor . . . warped, but definitely interesting.

"But at least he treated you relatively gently—which is more than the general will. As he was not wearing a mask, you saw his face. You've told me that before this war, you had Croatian friends. *I* had Croatian friends. Was he not afraid your description of him might eventually make someone recognize him?"

"He didn't seem to care about that. He was just . . . amused."

"Polite, and amused." The captain considered the saboteur's unorthodox behavior, then went to the door and opened it. "Dragovic!" he bawled.

"Yes, Captain!"

"Bring in that Russian sergeant."

"Yes, Captain."

When the Russian was back inside the cabin and the door again shut, the captain switched languages once more.

"Tell me, Sergeant . . . why are you Russians in this area? And don't play dumb with me. We've got your major sitting on his high horse down at HQ. He's not talking, but my general is not a patient man. In fact, he'll be wondering why there haven't been even routine transmissions from this place, and will expect me to make contact soon. For all I know, your major may be singing right now, Russian or no Russian. Your people are in an area that is barred to everyone."

The sergeant allowed himself a studied glance at the electronic ruins. He did not seem worried. "Not to the person who did this."

"You're telling me it wasn't your lot?"

"It's the truth. We have no interest in your stupid war."

"Ah, yes. Our stupid war. Then why are you here?"

The sergeant remained silent.

"Sergeant," the captain said patiently, "it is one thing to invite a Russian officer to our HQ to explain himself to the general. It's another thing entirely to find *foreign* troopers, not even belonging to the UN, in an area where they have no authority to be. I don't care what arrangements your major has made, and with whom. *I* have direct orders from my commanding general to defend this unit against anyone—and I quote him—*including Russians.* We could shoot you right here, and be within our rights. Think about it."

"I'm thinking," the sergeant said.

"Don't take too long."

15

The NATO base on the Adriatic, Italy, the same moment in time

The Tornado IDS(E), fully loaded with fuel, four air-to-air Kraits, two air-launched antiradar missiles—ALARMS—and a war load of cluster bombs, roared down the runway as the dawn tentatively felt its way out of the night. It was still dark enough for the afterburners to sear the gloom like blowtorches.

The antiradar missiles, because of the small size and light weight of the air-to-air weapons, were carried in a triple pack of two Kraits and one ALARM per outer wing pylon. If their route brought them across a SAM or triple-A radar, they would be able to eliminate it, hopefully before the surface-to-air weapon that needed it for guidance could be fired.

Hohendorf eased the Tornado into the air and brought the wheels up quickly, letting the speed build. He climbed to one thousand feet, set the height ride for a terrain referencing two hundred feet, and engaged the autopilot to follow the waypoint track. The aircraft headed toward the sea and leveled out at two hundred feet as it sped eastward at six hundred knots. The ASV escorts had already taken off and were at patrol altitude, watching over them.

"It's show time!" McCann said from the backseat as he checked the track display. "At current speed, our time to target is forty-five minutes. Time to first waypoint, ten minutes. And time over target, if nobody gets in the way, will be 0600 hours . . . which is exactly when the chopper should be landing to pick up Mac . . . if they've found her. Our little diversion should keep unwanted interest from them."

"We must hope they will have found her by then," Hohendorf said. "When we strike, all hell will break loose."

McCann glanced to his left at the twin doll's eyes at the top of the weapons control panel. The small, oblong oxygen flow indicators with their attention-getting stripes—duplicated in the front cockpit—were blinking regularly, confirming that each occupant was still breathing. He expected to see them still blinking merrily on the way back from target. . . .

Neither mentioned the hot C^3 area, but each knew the other was thinking about it.

In Stormbird Two at escort altitude, Selby was thinking about an unexpected incident prior to takeoff. Just as he was about to climb up the ladder to his cockpit, Helm had grabbed his arm, causing him to pause briefly in surprise.

"There may be instructions on Guard channel Alpha. Follow them! Say nothing to Flacht unless you receive those instructions." That was all Helm had said before turning to walk quickly away.

On November aircraft, the Guard channel was reserved for highly secret and secure communications only, during extreme emergency situations. Among these was all-out nuclear war, or the escort of the head of state over hostile territory. Guard channel comms was also to individual aircraft only, which meant none of the other Stormbird aircraft had been informed.

Helm had deliberately singled him out. Why?

As he scanned the air about him, Selby felt distinctly uneasy. From time to time, his gaze would unwillingly and warily be drawn toward the console that housed the Guard channel equipment, as if eyeing a dangerous snake.

On the mountain top, the tank captain was still waiting for answers from the Russian sergeant. The sergeant appeared to be in no particular hurry. The signals corporal and his female assistant stood to one side surveying the captain warily, wondering about their fate.

"Sergeant . . ." the captain began in Russian, his exasperation out in the open.

There was a knock on the door.

"*What?*" he barked, switching back to Serbo-Croat.

"It's the general, Captain," came a voice urgently.

He gave the sergeant a hard stare, then turned to his compatriots. "Watch him. Your lives depend upon it."

"Yes, sir," they said together as they picked up their weapons and pointed them at the sergeant.

The Russian smiled superciliously.

The captain opened the door and climbed out, shutting it after him. He took the handset from the radioman with a nod of thanks.

"I'm here, sir," he said into it.

"You made good time, Captain. What's going on up there? There have been no transmissions, and we can't raise them."

"I have bad news, sir."

"It's been attacked?" the general asked sharply.

"Yes, sir. Sabotage. Everything's wrecked."

"And those two?" the general yelled in the captain's ear. "What were they doing? *Helping?*"

You could say that, the captain thought.

"They were . . . overpowered, General," he said.

"*Overpowered?*" the general shouted. "*Why aren't they dead? Why didn't they defend it?*"

"They were taken by surprise, sir."

"Taken by surprise?" the general repeated, outraged. "Were they sleeping?"

That's another way of looking at it, the captain thought dryly.

"It happened very quickly, sir."

"How many saboteurs?"

The captain gave an embarrassed cough. "One, sir."

There was a sudden silence at the other end, and the radio link hummed with the general's anger. The captain almost expected to see the handset begin to melt.

"One?" the general said at last in a hushed voice. "*One?*" he bellowed.

The captain had to move the receiver away from his ear.

"*Captain!*"

"Sir?"

"I want those two arrested! *Do you hear me?*"

"Yessir."

"And I want a full report. Everything. Do you hear?"

"Yes, General."

"Who carried out this attack?"

"They think he was Croat, sir."

"They *think?*"

"I have my doubts, General."

"Why?"

The tank captain explained, without mentioning the situation in which the signals crew had been found.

The general gave it some thought.

While he was doing so, the captain said, "There's more, General."

"What do you mean 'more'?"

"We've also detained a squad of Russian soldiers . . ."

"*What?* Ivans? Up there? What the hell are they doing . . ." The general stopped, then went on, "Are they that arrogant major's men?"

"Yes, sir. They're not wearing any national insignia, and only the sergeant has his rank up, but I recognize the combat gear as the same as that worn by the ones my tanks are blocking."

"Are they responsible for the sabotage?"

"No, sir."

"Then who?"

"That's what I'm trying to get out of the sergeant. They're on some kind of mission, but he's not talking any more than the major has."

"Tell him I'll shoot his major if he doesn't open his trap."

"Will you, General?" the captain asked uncertainly.

"Do you think I don't mean what I say?"

"No, General. But . . . but he *is* Russian. . . ."

"No one asked them to go into a sensitive area. If they get caught in a cross fire, that's their funeral. Are there more of these Ivans strolling about in our mountains?"

"I think there may well be, General, although I am not totally sure."

The general swore eloquently. "Stay where you are," he eventually ordered, "in case they turn up. Do you need reinforcements?"

A while ago he could spare only a few; now he could offer reinforcements. The captain experienced a sense of resignation rather than bitterness. He'd hoped the general would order him back down the mountain so that he could return to his tanks.

"I'm okay, General. Somehow, I don't think they'll be coming this way."

"All right, Captain. You work on that sergeant, and I'll get that major to talk. Out."

"Yes, General," the captain said wearily to the dead radio.

He handed the receiver to the radioman, then went back inside the signals cabin.

"You can put away your weapons," he said to the crew. He turned to the Russian sergeant. "Can you speak my language?" he asked in the man's national tongue.

"No," the sergeant replied succinctly, as if that were beneath him.

The captain chose to ignore the intended slight. "My general's in a nasty mood," he continued in Russian, "and he'll take it out on your major. You'd better tell me all you know. It might help."

The sergeant kept his supercilious smile pasted upon his face.

The big Siberian had made a mistake about the snow.

To Buntline, however, the swirl of light mist that shrouded the slope was an asset. But it wouldn't last, for the coming day promised to be warm enough to disperse it. Thicker at lower levels, it would give sufficient cover for the landing—provided it remained that way long enough. He hoped the timings would hold. The dead soldiers would have friends, and it would not be a good idea to hang around waiting if the helicopter, or the Tornado attack, proved to be late.

He was slightly anxious that he'd seen nothing as yet of Mac. Surely she must have seen him by now—unless she hadn't succeeded in getting this far. But that would not explain the soldiers. If he'd been wrong and she hadn't got them . . . who had done the killing?

Standing in an area that was relatively mist-free, he glanced up at the sky.

There was no cloud, and thus no cover for aircraft.

Aberdeen, Scotland

At the time that Buntline was wondering about Mac's

whereabouts, Morven Selby came awake suddenly. Approaching the end of her night's sleep, she'd experienced an intensely detailed dream so vivid it was imprinted upon her consciousness like the flash of a camera that could still be seen long after the picture had been taken. She'd been reliving the first moment she'd set eyes upon Axel von Hohendorf.

The definition of the November Mess Ball had been so clear, every face was still sharply visible, even though she was now awake. She had seen the six-foot-tall man with the crop of fine blond hair and the palest of blue eyes talking to his commanding officer, Wing Commander Jason. In his *Marineflieger* mess kit, she had considered him the most handsome of all the pilots. The controlled stillness of his lean body had attracted her, and she'd found his shy correctness when she had asked him to dance during the Ladies Excuse Me an endearing trait.

In her dream, the young eyes, which normally appeared far older and wiser than his years, had come close to hers, until she'd found herself being swallowed by them. Then she had woken out of the dream.

She sat up in bed slowly and passed a shaky hand through her rich hair as she recalled it. Her heart, she realized, was beating quickly. For long moments, remaining as she was, staring across the bedroom, her eyes focused on a distance far beyond her immediate surroundings.

"Oh, Axel," she murmured softly. "Do be careful."

The Bosnian approaches

"First waypoint in three-zero seconds," McCann announced.

Precisely thirty seconds later, the Tornado banked hard left, hauling itself onto the new course of zero-nine-zero. This would take them eastward between the islands of Korčula and Lastovo, and on to the Yugoslavian coast.

Leaving the primary controls to their devices, Hohendorf monitored the instruments, constantly checking that the systems were functioning as they should. The stick moved around as if by magic as the aircraft righted itself and settled onto the new heading. It maintained its altitude of two hundred feet.

"Aerial cable ahead when we hit the coast," McCann said. "Fourteen-fifty feet above mean sea level, three hundred and five feet above the highest point. Do we go over or under?"

"Under."

"Figured you'd say that. Under it is. 'Former Yugoslavia,'" he went on. "Weird, huh? Saying that about a country. Like looking at a woman and saying 'former virgin.'"

"In a way, that's what Yugoslavia was."

"A virgin? Or former?"

"A virgin . . . until her people raped her. Now they've turned her into a harlot."

"Perhaps she was never a real virgin."

Remembering Zunica Paic, Hohendorf said, "Some people believed she was." He wondered where Zunica was now.

McCann was silent for some moments as they hurtled toward the coast. He glanced upward, searching out the specks that would signify the presence of Stormbirds Two and Three. He didn't really expect to see them. They'd be using the Chameleon and would have been invisible to his eyes at that height, even if they'd been in the patch of sky he had looked at.

He called up the tactical aerial display on one of the MFDs and there they were, keeping perfect station.

He switched to secondary track display and manipulated the waypoints. As this was not as yet programmed into the navigation systems, the aircraft would ignore it.

"Take a look at this," he said. "Patching over to you."

Hohendorf looked.

"This revised plan will save us fuel," McCann went on. "It will also give us more terrain masking." He had superimposed the new track diagram upon a bird's-eye view of a topographical image of the target area and its environs. "Although ops gave us what they think is the optimum route, we do have autonomy, as the deputy boss said."

"But?"

"Initial point to target is still the same. Because of where the APCs now are, we're forced to overfly the C^3. You know what that means."

"Hot SAMs and triple-A."

"Sounds like a menu, but yes. Give the man a hot dog. Now take a look at this." McCann had again altered the planned route, adding a second target point.

"*Two* targets."

"Yep. We need to take out some stuff so we have a clear run. Otherwise, we're going into wall-to-wall, surface-to-air shit. Don't know about you, but I'd rather not have my hair parted by a lump of thirty-mill, or a smoking singer."

"We were ordered not to hit the C^3."

"We're not hitting the damned thing. We're taking out some teeth to give us a clear run to target. Hey, if some tanks down there get in the way . . . tough. It's either that, or we abort. Which kind of leaves Mac deep in the stuff. There's no other route in. That's my tactical advice."

Hohendorf said nothing. It was exactly how he'd read the situation, even as Helm had been conducting the briefing. But he'd wanted McCann to arrive at the same conclusion and to recommend the action. He'd wanted McCann to be fully committed. He was also certain that Helm had been well aware of the choices, but had preferred to allow the crew to make their own decision. Helm had done to them what he'd done to McCann.

"I accept your advice, Elmer Lee."

"All right! Way to go. I'm selecting weapons for both targets, and inserting them into the system. I'm also patching the new route format to Stormbirds Two and

Three. Next waypoint will be on the revised route." McCann carried out a secure datalink transfer of the new pattern to the escorting ASVs.

"Roger," Hohendorf agreed.

"And here's the coast. Watch out for that cable, man."

"Disengaging autopilot," Hohendorf said. "And I'll watch out for that cable, man."

"Hey, Axel. You making fun of the way I speak?"

"Elmer Lee, Elmer Lee . . . not me, not me."

"Just so I know."

In his mask, Hohendorf felt the creasing of his face in a brief smile. There was only one Elmer Lee. On his MFD was a display that McCann had patched over, showing two glowing red bars beneath a representation of the cable. Bearing, altitude, distance, and ground clearance were also shown. Hohendorf's best path beneath the cable was between the red bars. There was plenty of room to spare.

From now on, he would be flying manually and going considerably lower than two hundred feet.

In Stormbird Two at fifteen thousand feet, Flacht studied the revised route format he'd received from McCann.

"They have altered their waypoints," he told Selby in his careful English. "Transferring to you."

Selby watched as the new waypoint plan appeared on one of his multifunction displays. "*Two* targets? What are they up to, Wolfie?"

"They must have revised the tactical situation. I am amending our escort pattern and transferring to Stormbird Three."

"Okay. This is taking us closer to hostile territory. When you've got confirmation of receipt, I'll talk to them."

"Roger. I have confirmation . . . now."

Selby selected a secure channel and contacted the ASV of Cottingham and Christiansen. "Stormbird Three."

" 'Bird Three," Cottingham answered.

"Revised positioning. Go high, twenty-five thousand."

"Roger that. Going high."

A brief flash to the right of their position marked the Double-C ship's fast climb to the new altitude.

"I hope they know what they're doing down there," Selby remarked, thinking of Hohendorf and McCann in the low-level IDS(E).

"I am sure they do," Flacht said loyally.

Selby, feeling guilty about keeping Flacht in the dark, continued to worry about Helm's mysterious command.

Operations center, November One

Down in the "hole," Jason, the air vice-marshal, and Bowmaker stared at the large tactical screen.

"They've changed the flight plan," the air vice-marshal said, watching as the screen showed Stormbird One's new track. "What the devil are they up to?"

"I did authorize autonomy, sir," Jason told him. "The new position of the APCs, so close to the pickup point, must have necessitated it. Those tanks aren't helping, either."

"We don't want them going down over there, Christopher."

"And *I* don't want to have to dodge anything coming off the fan in Washington," Bowmaker put in.

"We'll make certain that doesn't happen," Jason assured them both.

"Let's hope the guys behind those surface to air missiles think the same way," Bowmaker said in a way that sounded suspiciously like a prayer.

"That, sir," Jason said, "would be asking too much."

"Kind of thought it would."

Each seemed to glance at the other surreptitiously, as if concealing something unspoken between them. Jason's eyes seemed particularly haunted.

• • •

The Bosnian mountains

"Looking for me?" a voice asked softly.

Buntline turned quickly. About thirty feet away, a shape made ethereal by the mist was standing, carrying full pack and weapons.

"You made it," he said with relief. "Thank God! I was afraid you'd not seen me." He pressed the signal button to let the others know she'd been found.

She came toward him. "I watched you for a long time, until I was quite sure." She stopped a few feet from him. "After the less than friendly way in which we first met, I never expected you to come over." She moved closer and held out a hand.

"Ah, well," Buntline said as he shook it. "Neither of us really knew about each other's . . . activities." He studied her face carefully. "You're . . . leaner."

"Thin, you mean."

"No. I do mean leaner—and perhaps more dangerous."

"That's what being in the field does to you," she said calmly, putting no particular emphasis on the comment. "I saw your man get killed. I was too far away to intervene."

"The other two . . . you took them out?" Buntline was looking at the rifle/grenade launcher.

She nodded.

He pointed at the weapon. "Yours?"

"One of theirs. I got rid of the Dragunov. The soldiers who killed your man were the special troops. There are more of them around, plus the ordinary troopers with the APCs. By the way, just wait till you see what this launcher can do. You may want to run a check on the rounds when we get back. I'll try to save one if we do get into a fight." She went on to tell him about the others she had killed during her run, and how she'd come by the weaponry.

"And here I was thinking you needed help," he remarked dryly when she'd finished. "They must want you very badly indeed."

"That," she said, "is classic British understatement at its best."

He gave a fleeting smile. "I suppose it is. Well, let's make sure they don't succeed. We've got a couple of miles to go to the landing zone, so let's put the show on the road, shall we?"

As they moved off together, he continued, "By the time the chopper arrives, our little diversion to persuade them to keep their heads down should have started. They'll be more worried about remaining alive than about your whereabouts. But just in case, the helicopter's well-armed; and of course, two more of my men are in the area. They'll be joining up with us."

"Thanks for coming," she said.

"All part of the service. Between us, we've got enough of an armory plus that portable artillery of yours to make life extremely difficult should some of those troopers manage to reach us."

"As long as they don't hit the helicopter."

"That would not be good news," he said. "Incidentally," he went on, giving her a sideways look, "exactly what brought them into this?"

"I was recognized."

"Oh."

"By someone I never expected to see over here, even allowing for the unforeseen in our line of business. Although I'm certain there are many infiltrators posing as observers in this lunatic civil war, seeing him in the little town I visited only at rare intervals was a shock. The last time I saw him, it was back . . . home. He was a captain then, KGB, and very ambitious. He is now a major, with aspirations of becoming a colonel. A very hungry man."

"Oh, very bad news indeed," Buntline said in commiseration. "Awful stroke of luck. Still, not to worry. He's lost this round."

"Let's hope so," she said.

They walked on in the thinning mist.

In the helicopter, still waiting for the go-ahead and ensconced in her own flak jacket, the woman at the electronics console watched as the signal light came on.

"*Yes!*" she said.

The gunner looked at her expectantly.

"They've done it!" she told him with some excitement. "They've found her!"

"Well, bloody hell," he said, grinning. "I'll tell the boss." He spoke rapidly to the pilot, who again left the cockpit to come into the cabin.

"They've really done it?" he asked her.

She nodded. "And the diversion's on its way."

"So we're in business."

"We certainly are, but we're not out of the woods yet. We've still got to pick them up and get out in one piece."

The pilot peered past her and out at the surrounding trees, which masked the clearing in which they'd been hiding as they waited.

"I won't be sorry to leave this place. I'd hate to have any local marauding combatants spot us. That could ruin everything."

"Not much longer now to liftoff," she told him.

"Can't come soon enough for me."

The pilot went back to his cockpit.

The gunner looked at her with the suggestion of a smirk. "He doesn't like to get his nice airplane scratched."

"I don't like to get *me* scratched," she said.

The gunner smirked, stroking the minigun in heightened anticipation.

"One minute to next waypoint," McCann said.

"One minute," Hohendorf confirmed.

The minute passed and he tilted the aircraft steeply

into the right turn, grunting as the accelerometer briefly
hit 7G, seven times his own weight. Whirlpools of super-
heated air streamed from the wingtips. He leveled out on
the new course which took them low along a river in a
deep valley at six hundred knots. The Tornado seemed
to be almost touching the water.

McCann looked calmly out of his cockpit and up at
the high slopes on either side.

"Gone fishing," he crooned.

"I have moved you to song, have I?" Hohendorf asked.

"Just exercising the cords. Pretty good terrain masking there, Axel, ol' buddy."

"I am glad you think so."

"Just along for the ride." McCann glanced down at one
of his displays. "Bridge up ahead. Five miles . . . two
miles. Bridge, *bridge!*"

The Tornado, wings swept, hurtled beneath the
sweeping arc of the bridge.

"I saw it," Hohendorf said mildly as he banked the aircraft to follow a bend in the river.

"Jeez!" McCann uttered, momentarily shaken. "That
was a *low* bridge. This place is lousy with them."

"You okay back there?"

"Me? I'm fine. Like I said . . . just along for the ride.
Okay, Axel," McCann went on, composure quickly
regained. "The next waypoint is one of the new ones. It's
going to take us to the initial point diagonally across this
mountain there. I'll superimpose it on your MFD. There.
Got it?"

Hohendorf took a quick glance. "Got it."

"Once we're across that mountain, the show begins.
From then on, anything that's alert is going to try to
paint us with their radar. We hit them with the ALARMS
from distance to kill their tracking, then we should be
on them. A load of clusters should keep them occupied,
leaving us a nice corridor to target. How's that sound?"

"Sounds good to me, Elmer Lee."

"Okay, buddy. Then we're cooking."

Suddenly, Hohendorf heard music on his headphones.

"Elmer Lee! What's that?"

"Uh . . . 'The Book of Days.' It's by Enya. I'll turn it off . . ."

"No, no. Leave it. As long as it does not interfere, and off it goes when the fun begins."

"You got it."

They flew along to the strains of the music for some minutes.

"Axel?"

"Yes."

"Hey, thanks."

"No problem."

"You know, Mark hates me doing that. The music."

"I'm sure 'hate' is too strong a word."

"I guess."

Some time later, Enya's music stopped and McCann reverted to being the supreme professional he really was.

"Waypoint to IP," he began, "one minute."

The Tornado arrived bang on time and Hohendorf rolled it tightly into the turn, then continued the roll until the canopy pointed earthward as they rushed up the mountain. Pulling over the peak would minimize exposure as they crested, before plunging down the opposite slope.

Looking up at the trees whizzing by, McCann said, "Now why did I think you were going to do that? Show him a mountain and he goes skidding on the canopy. This ain't the heather-strewn slopes of Scotland, my man. Those are damned *big* trees!"

"They're happy," Hohendorf said. "I'm happy."

"He's happy," McCann murmured. "He's happy. Hey, I should have thought of that, too."

In Stormbird Two the sudden, electronic screech of Guard channel Alpha being activated made Selby jump involontarily. One of the multifunction displays in his cockpit automatically switched itself to a message page:

GUARD ALPHA INSTRUCTION: FOR STORMBIRD TWO ONLY. STORMBIRD ONE IS ON COURSE TO C^3 TARGET. INTERCEPT AND DISCOURAGE. USE ALL MEANS. REPEAT. USE ALL MEANS. MESSAGE ENDS.

"*What?*" Selby shouted in his mask, feeling dread descend upon him and his guts tighten. "Are they crazy? Wolfie! Have you got that onscreen?"

There was no reply.

"*Wolfie!*"

At last, Flacht said in a flat voice, "I have it. Did you know of this? Was that what *Fregattenkapitän* Helm had to say?"

"You saw?"

"Yes."

"Your head was down in the cockpit, checking your systems. I thought . . ."

"I saw," Flacht said.

"They can't mean this . . ."

"It is perfectly clear. They want us to stop them . . . by any means."

"Shoot them down if need be."

"Yes."

"This is crazy! They're already on their target run!"

"We have a long reach . . ."

"How can you be so calm? Axel's your pilot! And I can't shoot down Elmer Lee, for God's sake!"

"I do not want to do this," Flacht said. "But you are the pilot, and we have a Guard channel instruction."

"Obeying orders?" The word were out before Selby could stop them.

An eloquent silence came from the backseat.

"Christ, Wolfie . . . I'm, I'm sorry . . . I didn't mean . . ."

"What it is to be German," Flacht remarked softly.

"Wolfie . . ."

"It does not matter. What are we going to do?"

"We contact Stormbird Two," Selby replied heavily. "Datalink."

"Roger."

But events were about to decree otherwise.

Guard channel Alpha screeched for a second time:

FOR STORMBIRD TWO ONLY: CANCEL ALPHA INSTRUCTION.
REPEAT. CANCEL ALPHA INSTRUCTION. ENDS.

"I should bloody well think so, too!" Selby exclaimed with huge relief. He had been about to arm a Skyray. "Something must have happened to change their minds. Wolfie? Got that?"

"I have. Would we have done it?"

"We'll never know. We'll never know," Selby repeated. "Thank God."

"This must be our secret," Flacht told him shakily.

"Yes," Selby agreed, certain there was a slight tremor in his own voice. "Yes. And Wolfie . . ."

"Yes?"

"I'm really sorry about what I said . . ."

"It never happened."

"Thanks, Wolfie."

"It would not have been easy to take Axel, even in the IDS(E). He would have fought back as soon as we had launched. *If* we had launched."

"I know."

"He might have won."

"I know that, too."

Above them on high patrol Stormbird Three, and below, the ground-skimming Stormbird One, were quite unaware of the tragedy that had nearly occurred.

On the mountain top, the tank captain's patience was at last wearing thin. He glared at the Russian sergeant.

"Sergeant, I've treated you more correctly than you

have a right to expect. If my compatriots had done the same thing in your homeland, I believe we would have received much harsher treatment. You have . . ." He stopped, listening. "What the hell is that?"

He went to the door and opened it. Outside, all the soldiers, including the Russians, had stopped to listen. The captain went out quickly. The Russian sergeant followed. The captain was so preoccupied by the growing sound, he did not appear to notice. The signals crew followed them.

A swelling thunder was charging toward the very spot where they all stood. Then a great shape, mere feet above their heads it seemed, filled their world with its roar; then it was streaking past and heading down the relatively treeless slope, appearing to hug the ground as it went. The smell and heat of its engines seemed to envelop them. They watched openmouthed, as it rolled upright and disappeared. They could still hear its fading thunder.

"My God!" someone said. "It was upside down!"

"Tornado," another remarked.

Then it was the Russian sergeant, speaking rapidly, who pointed out something that no one else seemed to have noticed. Perhaps it was because the aircraft had come upon them so suddenly, and upside down, that they'd missed it.

"Since Iraq," the Russian began in a hard, dry voice, "everyone can recognize a Tornado." He didn't say "even you," but that was implicit in his tone. "And this Tornado is *armed!*" he yelled. "*The APCs!*"

The tank captain worked it out immediately. "*My tanks!*" He pulled out his pistol and grabbed the Russian sergeant. "All right, you bastard!" he shouted. "You tell me what the hell's going on, or I'll blow your brains out!" He put the pistol against the sergeant's forehead.

The unarmed Russians moved forward, but were halted by the guns of the captain's men pointing at them.

"Talk, damn you!" the captain snarled. "What's that plane got to do with your APCs? If it drops any bombs, my tanks are going to get it, too, and my men. *Talk, you shit!*"

"Shoot me and you'll have an international incident on your hands."

The captain laughed, a little madly. "We've already got an international incident! That plane is off to hit a target. Unless you think it flies like that because the pilot wants to show off! Desic!" the captain shouted in Serbo-Croat.

"Yes, Captain!"

"Get the general. *Hurry!*"

"Immediately, Captain."

"Now, you!" the captain snarled at the sergeant. "I want you singing by the time my general comes on the line. You *will* tell us what the hell you've been doing in our mountains." He glanced anxiously in the direction the aircraft had taken, as if already expecting to see distant columns of smoke rising skyward. "Or your head turns into a squashed tomato."

The captain brought back the hammer of the automatic. It made a click that seemed as powerful as the rushing thunder of the aircraft that had just passed.

The sergeant began to talk.

16

"I saw a bunch of soldiers back there," McCann said, "by that cabin thing. I looked up through the canopy and I swear I could have touched them! I wonder what they were up to."

"If they're sharp," Hohendorf said as they breasted a low rise to plunge down the other side, "they'll be warning someone we're on the way. But we may be lucky. We might get there before any message gets through, even if they do guess where we're going."

They banked sharply between two low hills.

"Initial point coming up," McCann said. "Now we're about to see the color of their money. Time to IP, one minute forty. Well, will you look at that. We got ourselves a village."

Hohendorf brought the wings level. "Selecting ALARMS, in case they've got SAMs hidden out there."

"Alarms hot," McCann confirmed.

The symbology for firing the ALARMS was on the head-up display, but as yet there was no acquisition. The radar warning receivers were all quiet.

"They didn't get through, after all," McCann said. "All quiet on the . . ."

Then the pulsing tone went berserk and two symbols that told them they were being painted by SAM radars appeared on their threat warners. At the same instant, the first ALARM acquired and the target cross appeared a little to the right of their heading. The ranging circle began to count down.

"You were saying?" Hohendorf remarked in the calmest of voices, it seemed.

He fired. The second ALARM immediately acquired the other SAM. He fired again. Both missiles were streaking inexorably away toward their respective targets, trailing fierce white plumes that marked their passage.

"The SAMs have shut down their radars." McCann announced. "Too late, bozos," he crowed. "You've already been acquired. No ducking and weaving on this one."

Hohendorf watched as the ranging circle ate itself in a counterclockwise disappearing act as the range closed.

"I've got you some clusters," McCann was saying as they tore toward the scattered village, so low he was certain they were well below the treetops. "Holy *shiiit.* Will you look at those tanks! My God, Axel. There's a whole goddamned army down there!"

"We leave them unless they start firing . . ."

The tanks began to fire at them.

"*Pickle, pickle now!*" McCann yelled as the world ahead turned into a curtain of fire. "I'm spoofing their acquisition radars, and giving them decoys."

Hohendorf needed no second bidding. He squeezed the release button. The symbology on the HUD had changed to bomb release. The fall line appeared, then vanished as the parameters were satisfied. The IDS(E) shuddered slightly as the selected bombs dropped, showering their deadly cargo over a wide area.

McCann had turned his head around to catch a

glimpse of what was happening as they sped away. Flashes of light seemed to be heading directly toward his eyes as the antiaircraft fire reached for him. But miraculously, the Tornado had threaded its way through without being hit.

A rash of explosions was erupting silently in their wake, flashing in a firework display of random and demented fury. Then a massive explosion that dwarfed it all ripped into the still visible cluster bomb eruptions.

"Boy, oh, boy," McCann said quietly. "Looks like we hit something big back there."

The general was on the line to the tank captain when the first of the ALARMS hit, startling him. Then he heard the tanks begin firing their antiaircraft weaponry.

"*The sergeant has said what?*" he shouted. "My tanks are . . ." He stopped as an overhead roar made him look up at the ceiling in astonishment.

The Russian major was with him, having still not given any replies to a barrage of questions. The major looked up, too, a strange expression on his face. It was of both resignation and despair.

Then the multiple explosions began, followed by a massive detonation that filled the world about them with a terrible fire. A force they could not withstand shredded their bodies instantly as the former school, close to an ammunition dump, took to the air as it was torn apart, before collapsing into the hole that had opened up to swallow it.

Up on the mountain, the captain held the handset away from himself, staring at it as if it had suddenly turned into a strange and deadly animal. After a while, he handed it back to Desic, the soldier with the manpack.

"Too late," he said in a dazed voice. "I heard the explosion on the phone. But you all heard it, even at this distance. The ammunition dump's gone. The general's gone. *And you!*" he yelled suddenly at the Russian sergeant. "*You fucking stupid Ivan! Your major's gone, too.* If you'd spoken earlier, we might have been able to do something." He pointed his pistol at the sergeant in an abrupt movement and shot him.

The sergeant barely had time to register surprise, and for the first time, a real fear, before falling to the ground, mortally wounded. He shuddered briefly, drawing his legs up as if to delay the inevitable, then relaxed and lay still.

Both sets of soldiers stared at the body numbly. The captain, his breathing shallow, stood to one side, his automatic pointing toward the ground.

He did not look at them.

They had picked up the faint sounds of firing. Then had come the rolling sound of the massive explosion, muffled by distance and the mountains, yet still seeming to echo about them.

"It's begun," Buntline said sharply. "The ATARS aircraft will have given the word to the chopper. It's on its way!"

Mac, carrying her rifle across her chest, ready for use, had been looking around constantly, alert for any presence that should not be there. The greatest danger was always when you thought you were home safe. Buntline's men had not yet shown up, and were probably heading for the landing site. She therefore felt certain that a slight movement to her right among the mist-shrouded trees was not one of them.

"We've got company," she said.

Buntline did not break his stride. "Far?"

"Still out of range, but will be close enough soon. To my right."

"Anything opposite?"

"I've seen nothing, but that doesn't mean nothing's there."

They were in somewhat of a clearing, but over to their left was a rich clump of tall shrubbery.

"That clump to our left," Buntline said.

"Seen it."

"We'll head toward it at our normal pace."

"Okay."

She hadn't changed her pattern of search and kept it up as if she'd seen nothing. On two separate occasions, she'd caught more fleeting shapes.

"Company's growing," she said.

"How many?"

"At least three. Maybe more."

"They must be gathering. We need the chopper. It's got a nasty gun. It must also be warned we've got company so it isn't caught by surprise."

She tapped the launcher briefly. "Your boys in the chopper won't miss this when it gets going."

They'd reached the shrubbery. The clump was several meters thick. They made their way through to the other side, remaining at the edge. Beyond it was another clearing, big enough to take a helicopter. There was no sign of Buntline's men.

Buntline peered through the screen of bushes. "That's our landing site."

Crouching in cover, she turned to look behind them. "Then we'd better do something about our company."

She removed her pack and, after taking the ammunition for her weapons, stowed it beneath some bushes. She marked the spot by simply twisting some foliage about itself, but in such a way that it would appear to have been a normal consequence of two plants growing in close proximity.

"I'm ready," she said.

He looked at her calmly. "You *are* going to get out. Don't take any chances."

"I seldom take chances. Those are omegas out there. Take chances with them and you're dead."

"What about the men you spared?"

"That was then. If they've come back . . . I warned them
there'd be no second chance. See you on the chopper."

Then she was gone, hunting out the omegas.

Flying nap-of-the-earth and even lower than Hohendorf
had taken the Tornado, the helicopter was on its way
toward the landing site, having received the "go" signal
from the ATARS aircraft.

The gunner, his rotary cannon shifting from side to
side in a slow arc like a hound sniffing out a quarry,
searched the flashing landscape for targets.

Buntline's female operative was still at the console,
but she now had a folding-stock Uzi across her chest. It
was ready for instant use.

"I love these trips," the gunner said.

High above them in one of the patrolling ASVs, Flacht
said, "It has started. If there are any fighters about, they
will appear soon."

"Arming Skyrays," Selby said. "Helmet sight on. Warn
Stormbird Three." He tried not to think of the aborted
Alpha.

"Done, and confirmed."

"Okay, Wolfie. Let's see if anyone comes out to play."

At November One, Jason watched as the computer-
generated position of Stormbird One left a flaring in its
wake.

"They've *hit* the C³!" he remarked sharply. "What the
devil? If Hohendorf's—"

"Done that," Bowmaker interrupted quietly, "he must
have had good reason."

"I do hope you're right, sir. This could turn very nasty
indeed." He said nothing about the canceled Alpha
instruction.

"No point worrying about that now. What do you say, Air Vice-Marshal?"

"I concur," Thurson replied.

At the monitoring unit in Moscow, newly promoted Lieutenant Kaminova was in the office recently and hastily vacated by her predecessor. A special telephone had been installed, giving her direct access to General Kurinin.

She left the office to do her periodic round of the workstations, to check the incoming material at each terminal. She stopped at one that showed a sudden flurry of activity.

"When did this come in?" she asked the female operator.

"A few seconds ago, Lieutenant. More's coming. Lots of coded pulses. Nothing much."

"Let me be the judge of that. I'll take them now, and if any more like these come in, I want to know *immediately*."

"Yes, Lieutenant."

Kaminova grabbed the sheets and hurried back to her office.

The operator watched as she entered and shut the door. "A sergeant one day," she muttered to a colleague, "and an officer the next. People change, don't they, with a little power?"

"Know any friendly generals?"

They watched as Kaminova made a phone call, put down the receiver, then picking up her cap, went out with the transcripts in a folder, leaving a senior sergeant in charge.

The two operators looked at each other with knowing smiles.

Kurinin stared at the sheets, which confirmed his worst fears.

"Thank you, Lieutenant. You did well to act so quickly.

These are indeed important. I'll handle it from here. I'm keeping my eye on you. Do well and you'll go far."

"Thank you, General." She saluted him a trifle self-consciously and went out.

As soon as she'd gone, he summoned Levchuk.

"Get those MIGs in the air!" he ordered.

"They already are, Feliks."

"Well, we got through that okay," McCann said. "Target now at ten miles. A single straight pass like at the range?"

"Yes," Hohendorf said. "Then it will be over and we'll be on the way home. The rest is up to the people who have gone to get Mac. We'll have done our part."

"Sure hope they find her and she's okay," McCann said. "Target eight miles. Remaining clusters selected."

"Okay. Master Arm on."

"Target five miles . . . three . . . pickle, pickle . . . *shit!*"

McCann's sudden expletive had been preceded by the sudden stream of tracer that was coming toward them.

But Hohendorf had ignored the antiaircraft fire and squeezed the release button. For the tiniest fraction of a second it appeared as if the entire cockpit were being covered in tracers as the bomb fall line came and went. The bombs hurtled toward their targets.

Again, nothing hit the rushing Tornado as it swept over the tanks and APCs at less than treetop height, it seemed. Then the bomblets began to erupt, carpeting the immediate area and well into the trees beyond the narrow road.

Both the tanks and the APCs destroyed themselves in secondary explosions as their fuel tanks ruptured and ammunition exploded sympathetically.

The soldiers from both groups had listened as the distant rumbling of the destroyed ammunition dump came to them. They had still been staring in the direction of the noise when a low speck had appeared out of nowhere. In fleeting seconds, it had turned into a rapidly approaching aircraft with things falling from it.

Some of those from the APCs recovered just long enough to make a desperate dash for the woods, only to run into the exploding submunitions. The tank crews had faster reactions and set up a ferocious barrage of antiaircraft fire. But there had been little time for proper acquisition, and the attacking aircraft was gone, leaving its lethal bomblets to explode all around them before they'd been able to aim properly.

She lay hidden within the bushes, watching as two of the omega soldiers made their cautious way into the clump of tall shrubs. They had clearly not realized they'd been spotted, for though they were moving with practiced and fluid control, she did not think they were being sufficiently careful.

One of them dropped suddenly to the ground. His partner froze in midstep. They appeared to have heard something and were waiting to hear it again so they could pinpoint the position. They were in perfect range for the launcher. She had no intention of letting them get any closer.

Even as she fired, she wondered whether Buntline had set them up, deliberately making a noise to ensnare them.

The grenade round landed squarely between the two men, exploding on impact in the same terrifying manner as before. Even though she'd previously seen it happen, she was still astonished by the effect. The men simply vanished in a vivid hell of flame and sound, an awesome sunburst that consumed all it touched. She heard weighty lumps being spattered through the undergrowth and didn't look to see whether they were pieces of equipment or of the men themselves.

She moved swiftly, changing to another ambush position.

Not too far away, Buntline stared at the charred gouge that had been taken from the scenery. Here and there, tiny flickers of whitish flame lingered, and an oily smoke spread out from the center toward him. He had purposefully made the noise that had distracted the soldiers, thus giving Mac the opportunity to fire upon them. The result astonished him.

"Good God," he uttered softly.

Then his sense of awe disappeared. He'd caught sight of movement to his left. It wasn't in the right direction for Mac. He inched his assault rifle toward where he'd seen a shifting of foliage and waited.

Presently, a soldier moved into view and paused, rifle held muzzle upward as he began to negotiate his way slowly past an obstruction Buntline could not see. Beyond the clump of shrubbery, the mist had all but dissipated, but within the clump itself it still hung around, giving the place an air of unnatural stillness and mystery. It was as if the world of his immediate surroundings had been placed in a state of suspended animation, in some primeval era. The only sounds he could hear were of the faint lickings of tiny pockets of flame left by the explosion.

Buntline did not hesitate. He fired a short burst of three.

The sound of the shots, muted by the denseness of the foliage, seemed puny by comparison with the powerful slamming noise of the grenade. The effect on the omega soldier, however, was terminal. His rifle went flying out of his grasp as with a choking cry he tumbled out of sight.

Then Buntline heard the helicopter.

The gunner had seen the burst of flame flare from the greenery.

"Firefight!" he said into his microphone.

"Roger," the pilot said. "I see it. Check for targets and sanitize the area. Don't hit our people."

"Do my best," the gunner responded lightly. He tracked his head slowly and picked up something on his sighting system. Two people coming toward the clearing, one staggering, being helped by the other. "Two of ours," he murmured, and tracked the gun beyond them.

Two others, pursuing. The gun acquired, then locked.

"How about a little surprise?" the gunner said, and fired.

The rotary cannon seemed to vomit its 20mm shells. They tracered their way from behind the approaching men toward their pursuers, who discovered far too late what was happening. The arrival of the helicopter had surprised them and they were caught in the act of turning to run for cover when the shells seemed to pick them up and chew them to pieces. When the gunner stopped, the omega soldiers were a tangled mess of blood, bone, and flesh.

The gunner patted the gun. A whirring sound was coming from it as it wound itself down.

"You did just fine," he said.

The woman at the console looked at him. "You talk to your gun?" she asked loudly over the noise of the helicopter. The cabin was full of the smell of the weapon.

"Yeah," he replied. "Why not?" He grinned at her as the helicopter tilted to fly a circular track around the clearing. "Must dash," he said. "Got to look for more trade."

The incoming men were the two Buntline had been waiting for. On their way to the landing site, they had surprised two of the omega troopers. They had killed one, but the other, though severely wounded at the time, had closed in on them and had struck home with an expertly wielded knife before dying, hand still on the weapon.

They had then carried on, the wounded one having received a savage stab beneath the ribs. Fortunately, no vital organs had been hit, and though a field dressing had been put on, the wound would require proper medical attention at the earliest opportunity.

From his cover, Buntline watched his men stagger across the clearing and was about to work his way around to them when the one helping his colleague suddenly let go, threw up his arms, and fell. He did not move again.

The wounded man, after tottering uncertainly for a few moments, dropped to his knees, breathing hard, desperately looking around to see where the shots had come from. He painfully tried to bring up his own weapon.

It had been a coldly calculated move. The wounded man was going nowhere.

Buntline had a dreadful premonition of what was about to happen and frantically tried to work out where the shooters were hiding. He knew he would not get to his man in time, and even if he did, would himself be walking into a hail of fire.

He wondered if the helicopter crew could see where the shooting had come from.

The gunner had seen what had happened.

"The bastards!" he snarled.

He had seen the shooters, nicely picked out in infrared on his sights. They were beautifully grouped for the gun. Unfortunately, he'd also seen another figure making its way toward them. If he fired, the gun would rake the area, almost certainly killing whoever was creeping up on them. He had to wait.

"*Shit!*" he said.

"What?" Buntline's operative asked.

"I've got a target, but I can't fire." Even as he watched, the wounded man on his knees seemed to collapse. "Bastards, bastards, bastards! They could see he couldn't do anything." The gunner thumped his gun in frustration.

"What's it look like down there?" the gunner heard in his headphones.

"Don't take her down yet," he told the pilot. "Hang on a bit. It's a bit tricky."

"We've got to get down!"

"Yes, yes! I know! Just wait!"

She had seen what had happened as she worked her way to a good firing position. Like an angry and giant frustrated wasp, the helicopter patrolled the clearing impatiently. She knew that any moment now, the omegas would start firing at it; but they didn't know she was behind them.

She propped herself against a half-buried boulder and fired the launcher.

They heard the sound and whirled . . . and caught the explosion full in the face. She ducked as splinters and flaming pieces of material and bodies fanned out from the blast; then she began hurrying to where she'd left her pack.

The gunner watched the violent flame billow upward.

"*Eat shit, bastards!*" he yelled. "Okay, okay!" he went on to the pilot. "Down! Down!"

The Blackhawk began to descend.

Buntline felt a mixture of sadness and elation. He was pleased that Mac had taken out the shooters, but deeply saddened by the loss of his men.

She joined him as he ran across the clearing toward

his dead colleagues. The helicopter swooped downward, landing gingerly.

"We can't leave them here," he said to her. "I've already left one behind."

"I'll dump my pack and come back to help you."

Watching her run toward them, the gunner said to the pilot, "Can't we get closer?"

"Not if you want us to take off again. We'll be too close to the trees for a fast liftoff in the event more of those other people turn up."

"Doctor Livingstone, I presume," the gunner said to Mac as she reached the aircraft.

She grinned at them both, dumping her pack. She kept the rifle/launcher. "You may presume."

The gunner stared at the launcher. "*You* used that thing just now?"

"Yes," she replied as she turned to run back toward Buntline.

"They're making some tough women these days," the gunner said.

"Believe it," Buntline's operative said.

He looked around at her. "I'd better give them a hand with those blokes."

"You'd better stay here," she countered. "They'll need you to give cover if anyone turns up. *We'll* need your gun to keep this chopper safe, or none of us will be going anywhere."

She was still sounding cool, but a tightness at the corners of her eyes betrayed the shock she felt at the deaths of her colleagues.

"You're right," he said. "Here. Have some chocolate."

"Don't mind if I do," she said, taking the offered piece.

"Tough women," he said.

She smiled fleetingly at him and watched from her seat as Mac helped Buntline pick up the first body. They began making their way back.

The gunner was watching, too, but looking beyond them to the trees and what might come out of there. The gun's multibarreled snout tracked incessantly, giving its customary impression of sniffing the air for prey.

They heaved the body as gently as they could into the Blackhawk, the woman getting out of her seat to help them. They ran back for the second.

"I've got an itch up my spine," the gunner said.

"What do you mean?"

"We've got to get off soon. Trouble's coming. Come on, come on!" he added softly to Buntline and Mac as he watched them pick up the second man.

They were on the return trip when the gunner shouted, "*Hurry!*" and sent a stream of fire into the trees.

The pilot, understanding the reason for the burst, increased power to prepare for liftoff. Buntline and Mac, crouching and staggering under the weight of the heavier body, hurried as fast as they could, seemingly right down the tracer stream from the gun as it rasped away.

A soldier came out of the trees, flung himself to the ground, and aimed his rifle at Mac. The tracer stream marched toward him and across his waist, chewing him in half. The noise of the gun, the yelling of the gunner, the whipping of the helicopter blades—all mixed into a hellish cacophony.

Then Mac and Buntline were heaving the second body into the aircraft, none too gently this time, and scrambling in themselves.

"*Go, go, go!*" Buntline shouted.

"*Go, go, go!*" the gunner yelled into his mike at the pilot, all the time maintaining the ferocious delivery of the 20mm shells, ravaging the foliage and anything hiding within it.

"Going!" the pilot acknowledged, lifting the Blackhawk off the deck as if rocket-propelled.

Several soldiers ran into the clearing as Buntline and Mac secured themselves to seats. The soldiers lifted their weapons at the helicopter and some tracer rounds began to arc toward it. A sound like hissing pebbles striking rattled through the helicopter. One made a sharp plopping sound. The only body hit was already dead.

The gunner, yelling obscenities, poured a stream of devastating fire into the soldiers. Many appeared to collapse, as if beneath a great weight. Then suddenly they were out of range, and the Blackhawk was diving into a valley, skimming fast on its way home.

The abrupt end to the firing brought a relative silence so palpable that, despite the noise of the helicopter itself, the whirring of the cannon as it wound to a stop sounded penetratingly loud.

"Send the signal to the ATARS aircraft," Buntline said to the young woman. "Mission successful."

She was looking at the bodies. "It could have been me." She looked at Mac, who had a faraway look in her own eyes.

"Send it," Buntline repeated gently.

"Yes, sir."

She turned back to the console and sent the signal.

The Tornado was fleeing along a deep, narrow valley at high speed. Hohendorf, flying manually, watched as the speed readout on the HUD touched six hundred fifty knots.

"Hey!" McCann exclaimed. "Good news, ol' buddy. From Kestrel via Avatar . . . mission successful. They've got Mac, Axel. We've done it! The November boys strike again. How about that?"

"We give good service."

"Thanks for the ride. It was kind of . . . interesting."

"Glad you enjoyed it."

"This calls for some Enya. Okay with you?"

"Okay with me. Let us fly through the valleys with her."

"You got it. Here goes . . . *Ooh*, shit." No music came on. Hohendorf, immediately on the alert, instinctively selected air-to-air weaponry. The HUD changed to the Krait acquisition symbology.

"Trouble?" he asked.

"Could be bad," McCann replied in the cool, laid-back manner that Hohendorf had come to recognize meant serious trouble was indeed brewing. "There's something down here with us."

"There's nothing on my threat display."

"It was very, very brief. He gave us a quick flash of his radar to check position. Not enough to activate the attention-getters. This guy's a neat player, Axel. Hell, the guys up top *and* the ATARS boys have missed him."

Hohendorf knew McCann was very good. He was reluctant to ask for confirmation. McCann saved him the trouble.

"Trust me, Axel. He's there."

"I've taken your word. I have armed the Kraits."

"Okay. Let's see what he does next. Uh, Axel?"

"Yes?"

"I've got this feeling he may not be alone."

"You mean they're waiting for us?"

"Something like that. Or they were meant to stop us but we beat them to it. Which means . . ."

"They'll be very angry."

"And after blood," McCann said. "I'm warning the guys."

"Do it."

"Stormbird One to Two and Three," McCann called on a secure channel.

"Stormbird Two."

"'Bird Three."

"Heads up, guys. We've got a bogey down here with us."

There was a clearly surprised silence.

"Nothing picked up," came Flacht's voice after a brief pause.

"Believe me, gentlemen. Where there's one, there may be more. They're doing some good masking and are low,

low down. But they won't be able to hack this for long. Stand by for when they come up for air."

"Roger," came both acknowledgments simultaneously.

"Now all we do is wait," McCann said to Hohendorf.

17

McCann was watching the threat display like a hawk. Something lived briefly within its dark surface.

"Got him again," he said to Hohendorf. "Seen him on yours?"

"Still nothing."

"Oh, he's a neat dude. He hits us with the radar just long enough to get an update, then he ducks behind high ground. Whoever he is, and whatever he's flying, he used to be a ground-attack jock."

"Like me?"

"Like you. He's doing pretty good right now. He's been down with us longer than I thought he would. Whatever he's flying can't take low-level punishment like a Tornado. But he's hanging in there. He's a stubborn dude, man, and he's going to be tough to beat."

The Tornado stood on a wingtip as Hohendorf hauled it around a bend in the valley.

"I've been trying to get enough of his radar to identify it," McCann said. "Maybe next time he tries."

A minute later, McCann got his sample. The pursuing aircraft gave them a long enough scan for the attention-getters in both cockpits to go briefly into panic mode.

"Got him!" McCann exulted. "I think he just made a mistake and scanned too long. Uh–oh."

"And?"

"Oh, boy, Axel. This is bad. The radar ID gives me a MIG-29, though how the hell he's staying down here this long beats me. He must be bouncing all over the place."

"MIG-29 is okay," Hohendorf said.

"You *kidding* me? We're not in the ASV, Axel. I know this ship is enhanced, but it's still no ASV. That's a MIG back there. Read my lips: Mike India Golf Two-Niner."

"I can't see your lips. You haven't forgotten the Eagles already, have you?"

"I haven't forgotten, but that guy's got real missiles and real shells, and he's madder'n a hornet in a bottle."

"We'll take him. Tell the others."

"We'll take him, the man says. Okay . . . you got it. Stormbird Two and Three."

"Two."

"Three."

"This'll wake you up. The bogey down here is a MIG-29. Repeat, Mike Two-Niner. Watch for his friends."

"Stormbird Three."

"Stormbird Two."

"I hope all these guys are not down here with us," McCann said to Hohendorf with feeling. "This valley comes to an end just before the next waypoint. We're going to have to break cover."

"Good."

"*Good?*"

"Yes. He'll break cover, too, to follow."

"Hey, that's nice. And then?"

"The fun begins."

"I hope he enjoys it."

"He won't," Hohendorf said calmly.

"Uh . . . yeah. Next waypoint five miles . . . two miles . . . *now*."

Hohendorf hauled the Tornado into a tight right-hand turn, continued the roll, and shot up the mountainside canopy down. Almost immediately, the attention-getters started their song.

"He's acquired!" McCann announced sharply. "No lock though. Yet."

Beep beep beep beep . . .

"Shit! The son of a bitch's got lock . . ."

Bmmmmmmmmmmm!

"Goddammit! He's launched! Spoofing." McCann set the electronic countermeasures going, launched a radar decoy, and ejected blooms of chaff into the wake of the Tornado.

Hohendorf rolled the aircraft upright as they plunged toward the next valley. But instead of following it, he brought the throttles back slightly, extended the air brakes for a rapid deceleration, put the wings at mid-sweep with maneuvers out, and quickly rolled left to haul into a punishing turn, grunting deeply as the G-forces pressed upon him.

The missile lost its lock and fed itself on the decoy. But they were now heading back toward the mountain they had just left.

McCann swiveled his head around to check the tail. The sudden change of speed and the tight turn had brought the MIG into visual range.

"Well, one thing's for sure," he said. "It's a 29, all right. We've got trouble."

The MIG was pulling into one of its famous tight turns to try to cut into their own turning circle, the mongoose nose coming around ominously.

But Hohendorf had other ideas. He kept taking the Tornado lower as they charged up the mountain, then he rolled inverted again and hauled back down the opposite side. This time, however, he continued the roll almost immediately so that the aircraft was on a wingtip and cutting to the right and diagonally across the slope and still going down.

McCann had vivid flashes of being consumed in a fireball among the trees.

But Hohendorf had again reversed bank and now the Tornado was turning left and heading, it seemed, straight for another slope.

McCann forced himself to look away and turned to check on the MIG. The MIG pilot had tried to follow but had not fancied going across the mountain canopy down. Instead, he had breasted the peak too high and was now on his back, pulling tightly to reacquire the IDS. He was coming too fast, and was pointing steeply down. Unless he did something very quickly, he would not pull out in time.

The thought must have flashed through his mind, for even as McCann watched, the MIG wobbled slightly, rolled upright, and began to pull out. The MIG pilot was now helpless, and Hohendorf had him.

Hohendorf had hauled off the mountain in an extension of the tight left-hand turn and was waiting as the MIG concentrated on pulling up to avoid impact with the ground. He knew he'd have just the one chance before the MIG pilot regained his composure. The Krait acquired and got a solid lock. The characteristic tone sounded and Hohendorf fired immediately.

The MIG pilot must have felt like a rabbit trapped in headlights on a dark, wet night. Nothing was going to stop the coming blow. Flares began to stream from his aircraft in a last-ditch attempt to spoof the incoming missile, but the Krait was not having any. Caught in a tight pull-up, he tried desperately to maneuver, but the small, highly agile Krait had him in firm lock and refused to let go. He had been robbed of all options.

The missile streaked toward the target aircraft and entered a tailpipe. The resultant explosion seemed to vaporize the MIG. It had simply ceased to exist—along with the highly intelligent and highly skilled man who had been in its cockpit.

Watching as the dying banner of the MIG plunged to the forests below in several pieces, McCann heard himself give a sigh of relief.

"Axel . . . are you some pilot, or what?"

"I'm okay."

"Just 'okay'?"

"It will do. How much time have we lost? We are still okay for fuel, but I would prefer not to have to worry."

"We can catch up if we alter the route to the next waypoint. Save fuel, too . . . if we don't have another fight." McCann transferred the revised plan to Hohendorf's display. "Take a look. That okay?"

"That's fine. Patch over to Two and Three."

"Doing it."

"Stormbird Two and Three." And when they had acknowledged, McCann said, "New waypoint plan coming up."

"Stormbird Two. Roger."

"'Bird Three. Roger." It was Cottingham who replied. "So you're still there."

"We're still here."

"And the MIG?"

"We're still here," McCann repeated smugly.

In Stormbird Three, Cottingham said to Christiansen, "Sometimes that guy gets right up my nostrils."

"You do not like him?"

"Listen, the guy's a good backseater . . . a great one, even. But he's got a flaw . . ."

"A flawed diamond? Is that how you say it?"

"Something like that. Look . . . let me explain. I like crayfish, but too much of it makes me sick to my stomach. Am I making sense here?"

"I . . . think so." Christiansen's voice suddenly became

brisk. "Message from Avatar . . . *three* hostiles coming our way."

"We're in business," Cottingham said, voice tense with anticipation of the coming battle. "Talk to me, Lars."

"Searching, searching . . . Ah! They're coming up for air, just as McCann said. One at thirty miles, nine thousand feet, bearing zero-six-three. He's priority."

"Helmet sight's on. Got him."

The targeting arrow on the helmet sight pointed like an accusing finger in the direction of the designated hostile aircraft. Cottingham turned his head until the targeting box appeared within the helmet sight. He selected a Krait and decided to close to twenty miles. He sent the Tornado ASV surging upward in a fast climb, then pulled hard into a high, G-intensive turn that brought the rapidly climbing MIG into a Krait lock.

But the MIG pilot read his mind and, half rolling, pulled out of the climb to head away from the direction of the ASV's turn.

"Reckon you're smart, huh?" Cottingham grunted.

He watched as the targeting box danced past the periphery of his vision, knowing that once the MIG had completed its extension, it would turn to come right back at him from a different quarter and altitude. He countered, pulling into another tight turn to follow. The ASV spread its wings to bite harder at the air as it wrenched itself around.

The MIG was back in the box, but the range had increased. Cottingham switched to Skyray A, the intermediate missile which, like the other missiles carried, was fully autonomous. He regained lock and got the tone.

"Launching!" he said, then fired.

The Skyray tore explosively away, searing into the distance on its mission of death.

Christiansen watched on his display as the MIG image went into a series of avoidance maneuvers. The readouts for altitude, speed, course, and rates of climb and descent all whirled constantly as they tried to keep up with the different changes being initiated by the target aircraft. The track of the missile went toward it inexorably until a flaring that quickly vanished told him they'd scored a hit.

"We have got him," Christiansen said evenly.

"Hey, Lars, don't you Danes even get excited?"

"Of course we get excited. I get very excited when I see a woman I like."

"We just got a kill," Cottingham pointed out, racking the ASV around in search of another MIG.

"We just killed a man."

"If you feel so strongly about that, what are you doing in the backseat of this killing machine?"

"I like flying. I like fast jets. I am good at my job."

"That supposed to make sense?"

"No. Put it down to the complexity of human nature."

"You've been to university. Right?"

"Right."

"What did you major in?"

"Philosophy."

"What a surprise."

"Just got a download from Avatar," McCann said. "There's a battle going on upstairs. Looks like three MIG's couldn't hack the low-level stuff any longer and made like homesick angels. Stormbird Three got one, and the other two are turning and burning with Mark and Wolfie and the Double-C."

"That should be over soon," Hohendorf commented as he banked hard to avoid a pylon that seemed to be growing in the middle of a valley.

"I wish they wouldn't put these things there," McCann complained in an aggrieved voice. "Gets in the way."

"We must remember to lodge a protest," Hohendorf remarked coolly. He brought the wings level. "So now we're home free."

McCann saw something that lived briefly on the threat display. "Reckon not."

"What?"

"Looks like one of those bozos decided to stay down." McCann glanced around, but could as yet see nothing following them. "No visual, but he's there all right. Keep those Kraits armed."

"I haven't disarmed."

"Okay. Keep on to the next waypoint. Let's see what this one's up to."

They were heading northeast along a river upon whose banks multiple pylons supporting aerial cables seemed to sprout like a dark forest of metal. McCann watched them flashing past. On some aircraft, the radiant power from those cables could cause system malfunction. On the Tornado IDS(E)—like the ASVs— the systems were hardened against such interference.

He was more worried about being fried, should Hohendorf misjudge the clearance as the aircraft hurtled past. He half expected to see the seemingly fragile space frames marching along the valley floor, like some monstrous army.

But Hohendorf flew with all the skill of a surgeon cutting his way through delicate tissue.

"Waypoint coming up," McCann advised calmly. "When we turn, the valley ends in twenty-five miles. Beyond the high ground at the end is a dam. The guy on our tail should make his move before then."

"Okay. Let's encourage him."

"Ten miles to waypoint. Six . . . three . . . *now.*"

They had come to a fork in the river, with the tail of the Y pointing to the northwest. Hohendorf banked into a left turn to take them along the tail.

"Ah ha!" McCann exclaimed, eyes on the threat display. "He's just popped up on the threat warner. Yep. Another MIG Two-Niner. And he's . . ."

The attention-getters went into their routine.

"And he's . . . very keen," McCann finished.

Beep beep beep beep . . .

"And here comes acquisition. We going to move out of here, Axel?"

"Soon."

McCann glaced around to look beyond the tail. *"Soon?"*

"He knows what happened to his buddy. He'll be more careful. Our advantage."

"I sure hope he knows that."

Beep beep beep beep . . .

"Notice," Hohendorf said, "he is not going for a lock as yet. He's flashing us with his radar to unnerve us . . . he thinks. He will not fire a radar homer. He will use infrared and his helmet sight."

"You *know* this?"

"It is what I would do. Get ready with *infrared* decoys. He will be hoping we use radar spoofing, which would allow his missile to get through. However, I have a little surprise for him. He may not get the chance to fire a missile."

McCann watched the pylons flashing past, wondering if the MIG's systems were being affected. It would be a bonus.

He glanced at the airspeed indicator. They were doing five hundred knots. "Two minutes to valley end," he informed Hohendorf.

"Okay. Stand by."

Hohendorf suddenly broke hard left, away from the valley's end and toward a deep rising cleft in the mountainside. He leveled the wings and pulled into a climb, seemingly to clear the mountain.

The pursuing MIG's radar acquisition was broken.

McCann took another look behind. "I have a visual!" He tracked his head upward, following the darting MIG. "He's accelerated and is trying to cut into our turn. He's gone up for a high reverse."

Hohendorf had the wings again at mid-sweep, with the maneuvers out to aid agility, and had continued to roll into the turn. The Gs mounted as the aircraft pulled itself tightly around. They seemed to scrape past the mountain, to head back the way they had come. The MIG, left hanging on top, was forced to avoid the high ground and plunged toward the parallel valley.

"He's down the other side," McCann said.

For answer, Hohendorf throttled back momentarily, popped the air brakes, and did a fast high and wide barrel roll that took them over the mountain and into the next valley. They were now behind the MIG.

"Hey," McCann said. "You pulled that stunt on the Eagle back at the range. And we've got our turkey up ahead. Neat, Axel. Boy . . . he knows he's in trouble. Look at him twist and turn!"

Hohendorf accelerated, drawing closer to the MIG. He knew the pilot would not dare use afterburners, in case the resultant large heat signature proved too juicy a meal for an infrared missile shot. The MIG pilot also could not leap out of the valley with his pursuer so close, without leaving himself equally open to a missile shot. His one hope was to maneuver close to the ground and keep out of target range until his pursuer either ran low on fuel or lost the nerve to continue.

Unfortunately for him, he was being pursued by a man to whom low-level fighting was instinctive, in an aircraft that could outlast his.

The MIG pilot was good. He flung his aircraft tightly around obstructions within the confines of the valley. Never once did he make the mistake of rushing for the higher levels. However, as Hohendorf fully expected, he was becoming more and more agitated by the continuous low-level flying. His aircraft was also reaching its limit.

To add to the pressure, Hohendorf kept radar and infrared acquisition on. The incessant noise of the warning systems would add to the psychological pressure.

"One of those bridges coming up," McCann warned. "Bridge, bridge, *bridge!*"

Like the last time, they flew beneath it.

"Bridge?" McCann said to himself. "What bridge?"

The MIG pilot had gone over, and as if suddenly realizing he was nicely silhouetted against the sky, headed back down rapidly. The chase continued.

"The poor guy must be a wreck by now," McCann said.

"He's getting there."

There was a precision in Hohendorf's words that caused McCann to shiver momentarily. Unaccountably, he felt a twinge of sympathy for the man in the frantically maneuvering aircraft, and was very glad *he* was not the hapless pilot in the MIG who was so desperately trying to avoid them.

Then it all happened with startling suddenness. One moment the MIG was rolling into another turn and the next it had plowed into a pylon, exploding in a great sheet of flame and debris. It brought down the pylon and its immediate neighbors. The cables began to snap and lash across the valley. Hohendorf hauled the Tornado up and out of the way as one of the cables, shooting sparks, sliced the air past them.

"Woo!" McCann said. "He lost it in a big way back there." He glanced back at the rising pall of smoke. "I feel kind of sorry for the guy. He must have been scared out of his head. Hell of a way to go."

"There's never a good way to go."

"I guess." McCann returned his attention to the cockpit as Hohendorf took the Tornado low once more. "We can still make it to the next waypoint without too much time and fuel use, if I amend the next leg to take us across there. A speed of five hundred fifty knots should do it." He inserted the course and watched as the new track joined the selected waypoint. "No threats indicated in that area. We should have a clear run."

"Let's do it."

McCann programmed the new course information

into the navigation systems. "Done. And I've just got more info from Avatar. The boys upstairs have cleaned up so it's on to Jellyfish for a drink, and home to November."

They were halfway along the new track when a stream of tracer suddenly rose from the forest they were passing over and curved its way toward them. A pebbly shower struck the aircraft, but it flew on steadily.

"Shit!" McCann exclaimed. "Where the hell did that come from? There are not supposed to be any threats around here."

"Any damage?"

"Zilch. Master caution's taking a nap. No lights. We're okay back here. You?"

"My warning panel is clean. We seem to have no system malfunction. Must have been some soldiers taking potshots at us. They like doing that to low-flying aircraft. Remember what they do to the C-130s landing at Sarajevo."

"Yeah. Their way of having fun."

The tank captain and his men had been marching the Russians down the mountain and were two kilometers from the disabled monitoring unit when they had seen the aircraft returning, flying close to the ground. More in anger and frustration than anything else, he had let off a stream of fire toward it.

Nothing had happened. He had not expected it to.

"Jellyfish at twenty miles and thirty thousand feet," McCann said. "Let's climb for our drink."

"Roger," Hohendorf said, and eased the Tornado into a gentle climb. They were back in friendly airspace.

When they were passing through twenty thousand feet, McCann said, "And here come the boys."

On either side of them Stormbirds Two and Three were joining up for close formation. Over to the right and coming up fast was Stormbird Four, having taken off from the NATO base on the Adriatic for the journey home.

"Thanks for the escort, gentlemen," Hohendorf said, "and for making a clean sweep on top."

"Glad to oblige," Selby told him.

"So," came Bagni's voice as he tucked in close, "you were *all* greedy. You left nothing for us."

"Next time, Nico," McCann said. "Yo, Wolfie. How do you like my seat?"

Flacht, in Stormbird Two, which was holding formation to his left, turned the helmeted, visored face in his direction.

"I like it fine."

"Remember you've got a temporary tenancy."

"And you," Flacht retorted.

They laughed.

McCann felt a sharp, fleeting twinge in his side and put it down to cramp. He thought nothing more about it.

They made their rendezvous with the tanker, and all four aircraft took on fuel for the flight home.

As they rejoined formation with the IDS(E) in the lead, McCann said to Hohendorf, "Yo, Axel. Remember how our musical interlude was interrupted by those nasty bogeys?"

"I seem to remember."

"I guess we can go back to Enya now?"

"Okay, Elmer Lee. We didn't do the valley, so let's do the clouds with her."

"I've got an idea."

"Will I like this idea?"

"Let's pipe it out to the guys."

Hohendorf gave that some thought. "That should excite their interest."

McCann chose a channel that would link them all and ran the tape.

"What the . . . !" came Selby's voice. Then to Flacht, he added on the cockpit channel, "That man haunts me, even when he's in another airplane."

"Perhaps he wants to be a disc jockey." Flacht was smiling as he said it.

In Stormbird Three, Cottingham shook his head slowly. "That McCann."

"Do you want to turn it off?" Christiansen inquired.

"Nah. Leave it. Kinda nice up here."

Half an hour later, McCann felt a ferocious pain that stabbed at him so severely that when he opened his mouth to scream nothing came out of it. His body arched in his seat against the harness as the pain ravaged him, tearing at his entire being. Vaguely and not understanding, he moved a hand to where the pain was coming from. The place seemed very warm to him, and somehow fluid.

Then he relaxed in his seat. The music played on.

Hohendorf was doing his periodic check of his instruments when he noticed the doll's eye for the backseater's oxygen flow was not moving. The music was still on.

"*Elmer Lee!*" he called urgently. "*Oxygen! Check oxygen!*"

There was no reply.

"*Elmer Lee!*" Hohendorf repeated. "*McCann! Oxygen, oxygen! Check, check, check!*"

While he'd been calling, Hohendorf rolled the aircraft onto its back and broke formation by pulling hard into a dive on a reciprocal course. He rolled level and continued to descend.

"Oxygen!" he called to the other aircraft, whose crews had been startled by his sudden maneuver.

They understood immediately, knowing he was heading for an altitude below eight thousand feet where the cockpit atmosphere would be breathable without oxygen. One by one they rolled onto their backs and followed him.

He made a rapid check of the environmental control panel on the right-hand console. The oxygen contents indicator told the horror story. The backseater's oxygen was not being used. No oxygen was being drawn.

McCann was not breathing. McCann could be dead.

Oh, God, no! Hohendorf thought in anguish. No, no, no!

"Elmer Lee!" he called once more, hoping it was not a futile effort. Perhaps the lower altitude would revive him.

Hohendorf passed through eight thousand feet and kept going. The other aircraft had caught up and were in formation again, though spread a little wider. The music kept playing.

What could possibly have happened? It seemed most unlikely that the supply had suddenly gotten contaminated. If that had been the case, his would also have been. But he was still breathing.

Damage to McCann's supply line? But Elmer Lee would have been gasping for air. He would have heard, and besides, McCann would have given some indication and they would have made a quick descent to lower altitudes.

"Elmer Lee!" Hohendorf called once more. *"Elmer Lee!"*

"What's the problem?" came Selby's voice.

"Elmer Lee's not breathing. I'm returning to the airfield."

They all heard, and their shocked silence was eloquent as he called the airfield.

"Stormbird One to Goddess."

"Goddess."

"Oxygen failure in backseat. Request immediate landing clearance."

"Roger, Stormbird One. You have clearance. Runway Two-Seven. Wind six knots, One-Seven-Eight."

"Stormbird."

A light crosswind was no problem. He'd make a straight approach to get down as quickly as possible.

He could not understand what had happened. Up until a short while before, McCann had been laughing and joking. What could possibly have happened since then?

Hohendorf cast his mind back, going over every detail. They had gone through the attacks, fought two air combats, without being hit. So what . . . He stopped. Wrong. They *had* taken hits. That single stream of tracer on the way back. The pebbly sounds on the aircraft. But that could not have damaged the oxygen equipment, surely. The oxygen caption on the central warning panel had not lighted. That would mean the system was okay.

Had Elmer Lee been hit?

But he'd not acted as if he'd been hurt. There had been nothing to indicate it.

Selby's aircraft was again close. "Do you know you've taken hits?"

"Yes. But there's no system damage. The lights are all out. Check him out. How is he doing?" Hohendorf had glanced around several times, but the back of the system display structure in the rear cockpit made it difficult to check out the rear crew member properly.

Selby's aircraft maintained station as both he and Flacht turned their heads to study McCann.

"His head's down," Selby said. "He's not doing anything."

Feeling a growing sense of despair and sorrow, Hohendorf brought the Tornado down for a gentle landing. The music stopped as he touched down. A medical team was waiting, and almost before the aircraft had stopped properly, well away from prying eyes, they were scrambling up the ladder to get at McCann in the backseat.

"*Be gentle with him!*" Hohendorf shouted at them.

"This is our job, sir," someone said. "Please get down and leave us to it."

Hohendorf climbed down and found Helm standing close by.

"What happened?" Helm asked.

Hohendorf turned to stare up at the medical people attending to McCann. "I don't know. A short while ago he was laughing . . . then . . . nothing. He just stopped breathing."

The other aircraft had also landed and were taxiing back.

One of the medical people by the cockpit straightened and looked around and down at Hohendorf.

"I'm sorry to tell you he's dead. . . ."

"But that's impossible!" Hohendorf said in a numbed voice. He found himself thinking of all the things he liked about Elmer Lee McCann. The Kansas City Dude couldn't be dead. "He was alive . . ."

"He's been shot. The bullet entered the aircraft, went into his side, and traveled upward toward the heart."

Hohendorf was stunned. "But I don't see how . . ."

The doctor came down the ladder and approached. He guided Hohendorf a short distance from the aircraft. Helm followed.

"I've seen this happen before," the doctor, a Yorkshireman, said kindly. "Your navigator was shot with a small caliber round . . ."

"A *rifle?*"

"Yes."

"But we were well out of the combat area, and it was only a single burst . . ."

"These things *do* happen. He kept going because of the shock to his system, and as I've said, the adrenaline was still strong in him, even for all that time afterward. I'm willing to bet he never even knew he'd been hit. That . . . is also more common than you'd think. We are all capable of sustaining quite painful blows without realizing it, if our mind's on something else."

Hohendorf nodded slowly. His cousin Erika sometimes walked into things. Days later, she'd wonder where she'd got the bruise. As a child she'd once run straight into a wall while playing. Everybody heard the sickening blow, but she'd continued to play without the slightest slackening of pace. It was a whole week before the swelling on the side of her face had started to go down. He assumed something like that had occurred with McCann.

"I also believe," the doctor was saying, "that the force of the bullet was virtually spent by the time it entered his body. It is quite possible that it continued to travel over a comparatively long period. . . ."

Hohendorf was staring at him. "Are you saying that he could have been saved?"

"If he'd been aware at the moment it happened . . . quite possibly, provided you'd made it back here in time."

Hohendorf shut his eyes and put a hand to his face. "Damn it!" he uttered softly. "*Aah scheisse!*" he added in German.

He took his hand away and looked up at the aircraft. They were beginning to take McCann's body out of the cockpit.

"*No!*" he said, hurrying back to the Tornado. "Leave him!"

They stopped, staring down at him as if he'd taken leave of his senses. The doctor and Helm caught up with him.

He turned to face them. "We flew out together. We're going back together."

"Are you quite mad?" The doctor remarked sharply, peering at him as if seriously considering restraints. "The man's dead!"

"He's not just *a* man. He's Elmer Lee McCann . . . and he's coming back with us. *We'll* attend to him. He's ours." Hohendorf looked at Helm. "It's what he'd want, sir."

Helm studied Hohendorf for long moments, his expression giving nothing away. Then he turned to the doctor, "The body has to be flown back anyway. This will be faster."

"It must be examined . . ."

"You don't cut him open," Hohendorf said firmly.

The crews from the other aircraft began arriving. Selby came up to Hohendorf. The others gathered around. There was no need to explain the situation.

Selby stared long and hard at the anguish upon Hohendorf's face, hiding his own sense of guilt. Suppose he'd fired that Skyray. . . ." I'm not going to blame you, Axel," he said at last.

"Thank you, Mark," Hohendorf said quietly. "I wish I had taken that bullet instead." He meant it.

"Then who would have got him down? He might still have died."

Hohendorf nodded slowly. "I suppose. He's flying back with me," he added.

Selby's eyes showed approval. "It's what he'd want. We'll get back to our aircraft and escort you. I want to say good-bye to Elmer Lee properly . . . back at November One." He nodded at Helm and the doctor, then returned to his aircraft, followed silently by the others.

"Tell them to do up his gear," Hohendorf said to the doctor. "Put his helmet back on and strap him in. We're leaving."

The doctor looked to Helm for guidance.

"Is there a lot of blood?" Helm inquired.

"All the damage is inside. There's not a lot . . ."

"All right, Mr. Hohendorf. Prepare for takeoff. Mr. McCann will have programmed the flight back, so you'll be okay."

"I do not approve . . ." the doctor began as Hohendorf headed for the aircraft.

"You may register your protest, Doctor," Helm interrupted. "I shall see that it is attended to. This mission ends when the aircraft are back at base."

The doctor did not give up easily. "Procedures, sir . . ."

"Will be attended to," Helm repeated in a voice that brooked no argument.

"Do him up," the doctor called reluctantly to his team. "Put his helmet back on and strap him in. This is most irregular," he added to Helm, looking furious.

"We are an irregular unit," Helm told him. "We get things done when others can't."

Hohendorf held the Tornado on the brakes as he opened the throttles, then slammed into combat burner and released the brakes simultaneously.

"Let's go, Elmer Lee," he said.

To the left, right, and behind him, the ASVs kept station as they hurtled down the runway. Once airborne, they lifted their wheels in unison and rose in perfect formation to head for altitude in a shallow climb.

Holding position on Hohendorf's left wing, Selby in Stormbird Two thought again of the Alpha instruction and its sudden cancellation. It seemed so unreal that McCann was dead. Yet had he carried out the order to its ultimate conclusion, he might well have been the instrument of Elmer Lee's death.

He glanced out at the Tornado IDS(E). In the backseat, McCann's helmeted head seemed turned toward him.

Before entering the front cockpit, Hohendorf had taken McCann's tape from the slot in the back, and had put it into his own. He now ran the tape, and broadcast it to the other three.

They climbed through a cloud layer. Once high above it, they turned for November One.

The music seemed to fill the sky as McCann was taken home.

CLOSING SHOTS

Whitehall, London

Buntline was in to see the minister.

"Well, Charles," the minister was saying. "You do realize questions will be asked about that little escapade in Bosnia. There are protests flying around about our deliberately attacking unauthorized targets. Taking sides."

"No one's taking sides, Minister," Buntline retorted, keeping the real anger he felt in check. The minister had expressed no regret about McCann and the personnel he himself had lost. After all that had happened. Buntline felt sick.

"That may be, but I've got to give some kind of reply."

Always "I," Buntline thought with contempt. The minister's only priority was always himself. Buntline's thoughts became positively insubordinate. He strongly felt he'd like to hit the man.

"If you'll excuse me, Minister. Things to do."

"Of course, Charles. I know you're a busy man. By the way, that little discussion we had some time ago . . ."

Buntline paused, relishing what he was about to say. "Glad you brought that up, Minister. Had a friendly chat with a worm of a photographer. You know the type. Sleazy—poking lenses into people's faces for the latest scandal. You'll be pleased to know he won't be any more trouble. Let myself out, shall I?"

Buntline strode out, leaving the minister to mouth silent words at the closing door.

The Pentagon, Washington

Bowmaker sat at his desk, feeling upset about McCann.

Damn it, he thought. I'm a general. I don't get upset about personnel losses. It's part of the job of being a commander.

But he knew that was not strictly true. He had seen Jason's expression when they'd lifted McCann's body out of the backseat. Jason, he knew, had been crying silently. By mutual and equally silent consent, they had not brought up the subject of the instruction that had gone out on Guard channel Alpha.

He cleared his throat. "Well, we got Mac out."

Morton had been taken to her at a safe house, and disregarding protocol, she had run to him to hug him tightly, reluctant to let go.

They had been granted leave to spend some time together. What Morton didn't know was that she'd be going away again. Mac was a valuable asset whose services were too vital to allow her to become some kind of housewife.

Moscow

General Kurinin stared at the reports, and if eyes could spit fire, they would have turned the sheets of paper to ashes.

Levchuk stood to one side, watching him cautiously.

"It is not ended, Gregor," Kurinin said in a remarkably calm voice. "I *will* destroy that program. That unit, and others that may spring from it, must *not* be allowed to flourish. They are inimical to our long-term strategy. However, other opportunities will exist. I am interested in the current fashion for cooperation with NATO. Get some of our people in there."

Levchuk nodded. "I'll see to it, Feliks."

"And our new lieutenant . . . Kaminova. She has assets that should not be wasted in the monitoring section. Prepare her for work in the West."

"She'll enjoy that."

"I'm sure she will."

They smiled knowingly at each other.

The Bosnian mountains

There was no telling for how long her body had lain there, grotesquely askew, all alone. If anyone had been around to examine her, they would have discovered that she had been gang-raped before being shot many times, at close range.

Mac, known as Nadia, would not have recognized the girl from the café.

Born in Dominica, **Julian Jay Savarin** was educated in Britain and took a degree in history before serving in the Royal Air Force. Mr. Savarin lives in England and is the author of *Lynx, Hammerhead, Warhawk, Trophy, Target Down!, Wolf Run, Windshear, Naja, The Quiraing List, Villiger, Water Hole,* and *Pale Flyer.*

☗ HarperPaperbacks *By Mail*

CAMPBELL ARMSTRONG

Agents of Darkness

Suspended from the LAPD, Charlie Galloway decides his life has no meaning. But when his Filipino housekeeper is murdered, Charlie finds a new purpose in tracking the killer. He never expects, though, to be drawn into a conspiracy that reaches from the Filipino jungles to the White House.

Mazurka

For Frank Pagan of Scotland Yard, it begins with the murder of a Russian at crowded Waverly Station, Edinburgh. From that moment on, Pagan's life becomes an ever-darkening nightmare as he finds himself trapped in a complex web of intrigue, treachery, and murder.

Mambo

Super-terrorist Gunther Ruhr has been captured. Scotland Yard's Frank Pagan must escort him to a maximum security prison, but with blinding swiftness and brutality, Ruhr escapes. Once again, Pagan must stalk Ruhr, this time into an earth-shattering secret conspiracy.

Brainfire

American John Rayner is a man on fire with grief and anger over the death of his powerful brother. Some say it was suicide, but Rayner suspects something more sinister. His suspicions prove correct as he becomes trapped in a Soviet-made maze of betrayal and terror.

Asterisk Destiny

Asterisk is America's most fragile and chilling secret. It waits somewhere in the Arizona desert to pave the way to world domination...or damnation. Two men, White House aide John Thorne and CIA agent Ted Hollander, race to crack the wall of silence surrounding Asterisk and tell the world of their terrifying discovery.

MORE THAN FRIENDS
Barbara Delinsky
The Maxwells and the Popes are two families whose lives are interwoven like the threads of a beautiful, yet ultimately delicate, tapestry. When their idyllic lives are unexpectedly shattered by one event, their faith in each other — and in themselves — is put to the supreme test.

"Intriguing women's fiction." — *Publishers Weekly*

CITY OF GOLD
Len Deighton
Amid the turmoil of World War II, Rommel's forces in Egypt relentlessly advance across the Sahara aided by ready access to Allied intelligence. Sent to Cairo on special assignment, Captain Bert Cutler's mission is formidable: whatever the risk, whatever the cost, he must catch Rommel's spy.

"Wonderful." — *Seattle Times/Post-Intelligencer*

DEATH PENALTY
William J. Coughlin
Former hot-shot attorney Charley Sloan gets a chance to resurrect his career with the case of a lifetime — an extortion scam that implicates his life-long mentor, a respected judge. Battling against inner demons and corrupt associates, Sloan's quest for the truth climaxes in one dramatic showdown of justice.

"Superb!"
— *The Detroit News*